The New Life

ORHAN PAMUK

Translated by Güneli Gün

The New Life

ARRAR, STRAUS AND GIROUX / NEW YORK

Farrar, Straus and Giroux
19 Union Square West, New York 10003

Copyright © 1997 by Orhan Pamuk
Translation copyright © 1997 by Güneli Gün
All rights reserved
Published simultaneously in Canada by HarperCollinsCanadaLtd
Printed in the United States of America
Designed by Fritz Metsch
First published in 1994 by Ilepşim Yayınları, as Yeni Hayat
First American edition, 1997

LIBRARY OF CONGRESS CATALOGING-IN-PUBLICATION DATA
Pamuk, Orhan, date
[Yeni hayat. English]
The new life / Orhan Pamuk ; translated by Güneli Gün.
p.   cm.
ISBN 0-374-22129-4 (hard : alk. paper)
I. Gün, Güneli. II. Title.
PL248.P34Y9313   1997
894'.3533—dc20   96-45722

The translations of passages from Dante's *La Vita Nuova* in Chapter 15 are by Barbara Reynolds (Penguin Classics, 1969) and that from Rainer Maria Rilke's *Duino Elegies* is by David Young (Norton, 1978). The other translations are my own, by way of the Turkish version. Neşati Akkalen and his book are Orhan Pamuk's invention.

FOR ŞEKÜRE

The New Life

The others experienced nothing like it
even though they heard the same tales.

—Novalis

1 I READ A BOOK ONE DAY AND MY WHOLE LIFE WAS changed. Even on the first page I was so affected by the book's intensity I felt my body sever itself and pull away from the chair where I sat reading the book that lay before me on the table. But even though I felt my body dissociating, my entire being remained so concertedly at the table that the book worked its influence not only on my soul but on every aspect of my identity. It was such a powerful influence that the light surging from the pages illumined my face; its incandescence dazzled my intellect but also endowed it with brilliant lucidity. This was the kind of light within which I could recast myself; I could lose my way in this light; I already sensed in the light the shadows of an existence I had yet to know and embrace. I sat at the table, turning the pages, my mind barely aware that I was reading, and my whole life was changing as I read the new words on each new page. I felt so unprepared for everything that was to befall me, and so helpless, that after a while I moved my face away instinctively as if to protect myself from the power that surged from the pages. It was with dread that I became aware of the complete transformation of the world around me, and I was overtaken by a feeling of loneliness I had never before experienced—as if I had been

stranded in a country where I knew neither the lay of the land
nor the language and the customs.

I fastened onto the book even more intensely in the face of the
helplessness brought on by that feeling of isolation. Nothing besides the book could reveal to me what was my necessary course
of action, what it was that I might believe in, or observe, and
what path my life was to take in the new country in which I found
myself. I read on, turning the pages now as if I were reading a
guidebook which would lead me through a strange and savage
land. Help me, I felt like saying, help me find the new life, safe
and unscathed by any mishap. Yet I knew the new life was built
on words in the guidebook. I read it word for word, trying to find
my path, but at the same time I was also imagining, to my own
amazement, wonders upon wonders which would surely lead me
astray.

The book lay on my table reflecting its light on my face, yet it
seemed similar to the other familiar objects in the room. While
I accepted with joy and wonder the possibility of a new life in the
new world that lay before me, I was aware that the book which
had changed my life so intensely was in fact something quite
ordinary. My mind gradually opened its doors and windows to the
wonders of the new world the words promised me, and yet I
seemed to recall a chance encounter that had led me to the book.
But the memory was no more than a superficial image, one that
hadn't completely impressed itself on my consciousness. As I read
on, a certain dread prompted me to reflect on the image: the new
world the book revealed was so alien, so odd and astonishing that,
in order to escape being totally immersed in this universe, I was
anxious to sense anything related to the present.

What if I raised my eyes from the book and looked around at
my room, my wardrobe, my bed, or glanced out the window, but
did not find the world as I knew it? I was inhabited with this fear.

Minutes and pages followed one another, trains went by in the

distance, I heard my mother leave and then return; I listened to
the everyday roar of the city, the tinkle of the yogurt vendor's bell
in the street, car engines, all the sounds familiar to me, as if I
were hearing outlandish sounds. At first I thought there was a
downpour outside, but it turned out to be the sound of some girls
jumping rope. I thought it was beginning to clear up, but then
there was the patter of raindrops on my window. I read the following page, the next one, and the ones after that; I saw light
seeping through the threshold of the other life; I saw what I knew
and what I didn't know; I saw my life, the path I assumed my
own life would take . . .

The more I turned the pages, the more a world that I could
have never imagined, or perceived, pervaded my being and took
hold of my soul. All the things I had known or considered previously had now become trivial details, but things I had not been
aware of before now emerged from their hiding places and sent
me signals. Had I been asked to say what these were, it seemed
I couldn't have given an answer while I still read on; I knew I was
slowly making progress on a road that had no return, aware that
my former interest in and curiosity for things were now closing
behind me, but I was so excited and exhilarated by the new life
that opened before me that all creation seemed worthy of my
attention. I was shuddering and swinging my legs with the excitement of this insight when the wealth, the multiplicity, and
the complexity of possibilities turned into a kind of terror.

In the light that surged from the book into my face, I was
terrified to see shabby rooms, frenetic buses, bedraggled people,
faint letters, lost towns, lost lives, phantoms. A journey was involved; it was always about a journey. I beheld a gaze that followed me on the journey, one that seemed to appear in the least
expected places only to disappear, making itself sought all the
more because it was so elusive, a tender gaze that had long been
free of guilt and blame . . . I longed to become that gaze. I longed

to exist in a world beheld by that gaze. I wanted it so much that I almost believed in my existence in that world. There was no necessity even to convince myself: I did in fact live there. Given that I lived there, the book must, of course, be about me. Someone had already imagined my ideas and put them down.

This led me to understand that the words and their meanings were, of necessity, dissimilar. From the beginning I had known the book had been written expressly for my benefit; it was not because these were portentous phrases and brilliant words that every word and every figure of speech pervaded my being, it was because I was under the impression that the book was about me. I could not fathom how I became subject to this feeling, but perhaps I did figure it out only to lose it trying to see my way through the murders, accidents, death, and missing signs with which the book was filled.

So it was that as I read my point of view was transformed by the book, and the book was transformed by my point of view. My dazzled eyes could no longer distinguish the world that existed within the book from the book that existed within the world. It was as if a singular world, a complete creation with all its colors and objects, were contained in the words that existed in the book; thus I could read into it with joy and wonder all the possibilities in my own mind. I began to understand that everything the book had initially whispered to me, then pounded into me, and eventually forced on me relentlessly had always been present, there, lying deep in my soul. The book had found the lost treasury that had been lying below the surface for ages and brought it up, and I felt I could appropriate for myself what I read in between the lines and the words. Somewhere in the final pages, I wanted to say I too had come up with the same ideas. It was much later, after I had been totally overtaken by the world the book described, that I actually saw death appear in the half-light before dawn, radiant as an angel. My own death.

I suddenly understood that my life had been enriched beyond my ken. Losing sight of the book was the only thing that frightened me then, but I was no longer as afraid of being unable to recognize what the book had told me of in the mundane objects around me in my room or in the street. I held the book between my hands and sniffed the smell of paper and ink that rose from the pages, just as I would do in my childhood when I'd finished reading a comic book from cover to cover. The smell was the same.

I rose from the table and pressed my forehead on the cool windowpane, as I used to do when I was a child, and I looked down into the street. Five hours ago, shortly after midday when I had placed the book on the table and begun reading, there had been a truck parked across the street which was now gone; wardrobes with mirrors, heavy tables, stands, boxes, pedestal lamps, et cetera, had been unloaded from the vehicle and a new family had moved into the vacant flat across the street. Since the curtains hadn't yet been put up, in the light of the bare bulb that lit the scene I could see the middle-aged parents, the son who was about my age, and their daughter; they were eating their evening meal in front of the TV. The girl's hair was light brown, the TV screen green.

I watched my new neighbors for a while; I liked watching them, perhaps because they were new or perhaps because watching them kept me safe. I didn't yet want to face the entire transformation of a familiar world now changed from top to bottom, but I was well aware that my room was no longer the same old room, nor the streets the same streets, my friends the same friends, my mother the same mother. They all implied a certain hostility, something dreadful and menacing that I could not quite name. I took a few steps away from the window but could not return to the book beckoning me back to the table. The object that had taken my life off its course was there on the table behind me, waiting. No matter how much I turned my back on it, the inception of everything was there in the pages of the book, and I could no longer put off embarking on that road.

Being cut off from my former life must have felt so horrifying for the moment that I too, like other people whose lives have been irretrievably altered by some disaster, wanted to comfort myself by assuming my life would resume its former course, that it was not something terrible that had befallen me, some accident or catastrophe. But the presence of the book standing open behind me was so palpable to my senses that I could not even imagine how my life could ever return to its old track.

It was in this state that I left my room when my mother called me to supper; I sat down like a novice unaccustomed to a new place, and tried making conversation. The TV was on; before us were platters with a stew of potato and chopped meat, cold braised leeks, a green salad, and apples. My mother brought up the new neighbors who were moving in across the street, my having sat down and, bravo, worked all afternoon, her shopping trip, the downpour, the evening news on TV, and the newscaster. I loved my mother; she was a good-looking woman who was gentle, temperate, and sympathetic; I felt guilty of having read a book that had estranged me from her world.

Had the book been written for everybody, I reasoned, life in the world could not continue to flow on this slowly and this carelessly. On the other hand, it wouldn't do for this rational student of engineering to think the book had been written specifically for *him*. Yet, if it hadn't been addressed to me, and to me alone, how could the world outside possibly go on being just what it was before? I was afraid even to think the book might be a mystery constructed for my sake alone. Later when my mother washed the dishes, I wanted to help her: her touch might restore me back to the present from the world into which I had projected myself.

"Don't bother, dear," she said, "I'll do them."

I watched TV for a while. Maybe I could get involved in that world, or else kick in the screen. But this was our TV set, the one we watched, a lamp of sorts, a kind of household deity. I put on my jacket and my street shoes.

"I'm going out," I said.

"What time will you get back?" my mother said. "Shall I wait up?"

"Don't, or you'll fall asleep in front of the TV again."

"Have you turned off the light in your room?"

So I ventured out into the precincts of my childhood where I had lived for twenty-two years, walking in the streets as if I were in the danger zone in some strange realm. Damp December air touched my face like a light breeze, making me think a few things had possibly penetrated through from the old world into this new world that I had entered, things which I should soon come across in the streets that constituted my life. I felt like running.

I walked briskly along unlighted sidewalks, avoiding hulking garbage cans and craters of mud, watching a new world materialize with each step I took. The plane and poplar trees that I'd known since my childhood still seemed the same planes and poplars, but they were bereft of their powers of association and memory. I observed the haggard trees, the familiar two-story houses, the grimy apartment buildings I had watched being built from the stage when they were mere mortar pits to the time when the roofs were raised and tiled, and where I played later as new playmates moved in; yet these images did not seem to be inalienable pieces of my life but photographs that I couldn't remember being taken: I recognized the shadows, the lighted windows, the trees in the yard, the lettering at the entrances, but the objects I recognized exerted no pull on my sensibilities. My old world was all around me, in the street across from me, here, there, everywhere, in the form of familiar grocery-store windows, streetlights at the Erenköy Station Square, bakery ovens still baking *çörek*, fruit crates

that belonged to the greengrocer, pushcarts, the pastry shop called
Life, dilapidated trucks, tarpaulins, tired and obscure faces. Part
of my heart, where I carried the book surreptitiously as if it were
a sin, had frozen itself against all the forms that were softly
shimmering in the city lights. I wanted to run away from these
well-known streets, away from the sadness of rain-drenched trees,
the grocer's and the butcher's brightly lit signs, neon letters reflected on the asphalt and in the rain puddles. A light wind rose,
droplets fell off the trees, and there was a roaring in my ears that
made me decide the book must be a mystery that had been bestowed upon me. I was gripped with fear. I wanted to talk to other
people.

At the Station Square, I made for the Youth Café, where some
of my neighborhood friends still met in the evenings, playing
cards, watching the soccer game, or just hanging out. Someone I
knew from the university who put in time at his father's shoe
store and another from the neighborhood who played amateur-
league soccer were at the table in the back, chatting in the black-
and-white light reflected off the TV screen. In front of them were
newspapers that had fallen to pieces from being read too much,
two tea glasses, cigarettes, and a bottle of beer bought at the
grocery and concealed on the seat of a chair. I needed to have a
long conversation, maybe one that went on for hours and hours,
but I soon realized I couldn't talk to these two. I was gripped with
a sorrow that brought tears into my eyes for a moment, but I
pulled myself together arrogantly: I could only bare my soul to
persons chosen from among those who already existed in the
world implied by the book.

That was how I almost came to believe I had total possession
of my future, but I also knew what possessed me at present was
the book. Not only had the book permeated my being like a secret
or a sin, it had dragged me into the kind of speechlessness one
experiences in dreams. Where were the kindred spirits with whom

I could talk? Where was the country in which I'd find the dream that spoke to my heart? Where were those who had also read the book? Where?

I walked across the train tracks, took back streets, trampled on yellow autumn leaves stuck to the pavement. A deep feeling of optimism surged up inside me. If only I could always walk like this, walking fast, without stopping, if only I could go on journeys, it seemed I'd reach the universe in the book. The glow of the new life I felt inside me existed in a faraway place, even in a land that was unattainable, but I sensed that as long as I was in motion, I was getting closer. I could at least leave my old life behind me.

When I got to the shore, I was astonished that the sea looked pitch-black. Why hadn't I ever noticed before that the Sea of Marmara was so dark, so stern, and so cruel at night? It was as if objects spoke a language which I was beginning to hear, even if just barely, in the temporal silence into which the book had lured me. For a moment I felt the weight of the gently swaying sea like the flash of my own intractable death that I'd felt inside me while reading the book, but it was not a sensation of "the end has come" brought on by actual death; it was more the curiosity and excitement of someone beginning a new life that animated me.

I walked up and down the beach. I used to come here with the kids in the neighborhood to look through the piles of stuff the sea deposited along the shore—the tin cans, plastic balls, bottles, plastic flip-flops, clothes pins, light bulbs, plastic dolls—searching for something, a magic talisman from some treasury, a shiny new article the use of which we couldn't begin to fathom. For a moment I sensed that if any old object from my old world were to be discovered and scrutinized now, from my new viewpoint enlightened by the book, it could be transformed into that magical piece children are always looking for. At the same time I was so besieged by the feeling that the book had isolated me from the world, I thought the dark sea would suddenly swell, pull me into itself, and swallow me. I was beset with anxiety and started walking briskly, not for the sake of observing the new world actualize with every step I took, but to be alone with the book in my room as soon as possible. I almost ran, already envisioning myself as someone who was created out of the light that emanated from the book. This tended to soothe me.

My father had had a good friend about his own age who had also worked for the State Railroads for many years and had even risen to the rank of inspector; he wrote articles in *Rail* magazine for railroad buffs. Besides that, he wrote and illustrated children's comics which were published in the series called Weekly Adventures for Children. There were many times when I ran home to lose myself in one of the comics like *Peter and Pertev* or *Kamer Visits America* that Uncle Railman Rıfkı presented to me, but those children's books always came to an end. The last page said "The End" just like in the movies and, reading those six letters, not only did I come to the exit point of the country where I'd wanted to remain, I was once again painfully aware that the magic realm was just a place made up by Uncle Railman Rıfkı.

In contrast, everything in the book I wanted to read again was true; and that's why I carried the book inside me and why the wet streets I tore through did not appear real but seemed like part of a boring homework assignment I'd been given as punishment. After all, the book revealed, so it seemed to me, the meaning of my existence.

I'd gone across the railroad tracks and was coming around the mosque when, just as I was about to step in a mud puddle, I leapt away, my foot slipped, and I stumbled and fell to one knee on the muddy pavement. I pulled myself up immediately and was about to go my way.

"Oh, my, you almost had a bad fall, my boy!" said a bearded old man who'd seen me take the spill. "You hurt?"

"Yes," I said. "My father died yesterday. We buried him today. He was a shitty guy; he drank, beat my mother, didn't want us around. I lived in Viran Bağ all those years."

Viran Bağ yet! Where in the world did I come up with this town called Viran Bağ? Perhaps the old guy was on to my lies, but momentarily I convinced myself that I was too clever by half. I couldn't tell if it was the lies I made up, or the book, or simply the old man's stupefied face that prompted me, but I kept telling myself: "Never fear, never fear! The world in the book is real!" But I was afraid.

Why?

I had heard of others who had read a book only to have their lives disintegrate. I'd read the account of someone who had read a book called *Fundamental Principles of Philosophy*; in total agreement with the book, which he read in one night, he joined the Revolutionary Proletarian Advance Guard the very next day, only to be nabbed three days later robbing a bank and end up doing time for the next ten years. I also knew about those who had stayed awake the whole night reading books such as *Islam and the New Ethos* or *The Betrayal of Westernization*, then immediately abandoned the tavern for the mosque, sat themselves on those ice-cold rugs doused with rosewater, and began preparing patiently for the next life which was not due for another fifty years. I had even met some who got carried away by books with titles like *Love Sets You Free* or *Know Yourself*, and although these people were the sort who were capable of believing in astrology, they too could say in all sincerity, "This book changed my life overnight!"

Actually, the frightening thing on my mind was not even the bathos of these scenarios: I was afraid of isolation. I was afraid of the sorts of things a fool like me might very well end up doing,

such as misunderstanding the book, being shallow or, as the case
may be, not shallow, being different, drowning in love, being privy
to the mysteries of the universe but looking ridiculous all my life
explaining the mystery to those who are not in the least interested, going to jail, being considered a crackpot, comprehending
at last that the world is even crueler than I'd imagined, being
unable to get pretty girls to love me. If the contents of the book
were true, if life was indeed like what I read in the book, if such
a world was possible, then it was impossible to understand why
people needed to go to prayer, why they yakked their lives away
at coffeehouses, why they had to sit in front of the TV set in the
evening so as not to die of boredom, unwilling to close even their
curtains all the way, just in case something halfway interesting in
the street might also be watched, like a car speeding by, a horse
neighing, or a drunk cutting loose.

I can't figure out how long it was before I realized I was standing in front of Uncle Railman Rıfkı's building and staring up into
his second-floor flat through the half-open curtains. I had perhaps
realized it without realizing it, and I was instinctively sending him
my regards on the eve of my new life. There was an odd wish on
my mind. I wanted to take a close look at the objects I'd seen in
his house when my father and I had last paid him a visit. The
canaries in the cage, the barometer on the wall, the meticulously
framed pictures of railroad trains, the breakfront in which cordial
sets, miniature railway cars, a silver candy dish, a conductor's
punch, the railroad service medals were placed in one half of the
showcase and maybe forty or fifty books in the other half, the
unused samovar standing on top of it, the playing cards on the
table . . . Through the half-open curtains, I could see the light
emanating from the TV but not the set itself.

A surge of determination suddenly hit me out of nowhere,
prompting me to get on top of the wall around the front yard and
see not only the TV set Uncle Railman Rıfkı's widow Aunt

Ratibe was watching but also her head. She was seated in her dead husband's easy chair at a forty-five-degree angle to the TV and had hunched her head between her shoulders, just the way my mother does when watching TV, but instead of knitting, this one was smoking up a storm.

Uncle Railman Rıfkı had died a year ahead of my father, who went of a heart attack last year, but Uncle Rıfkı's death was not due to natural causes. He was on his way to the coffeehouse one evening, it seems, when he was fired on and killed; the killer was never caught; there was some talk of sexual jealousy, which my father never believed a word of during the last year of his life. The couple had never had any children.

Past midnight, long after my mother had gone to sleep, I sat bolt upright at the table staring at the book between my elbows and, gradually, zealously, and wholeheartedly, I put out of my mind everything that identified this neighborhood as my own—the lights that went out all over the neighborhood and the city, the sadness of the wet and empty streets, the cry of the *boza* vendor going around the block one last time, the premature cawing of a couple of crows, the patient clatter of the freight train on the tracks long after the last commuter train had gone by—and I gave myself over totally to the light that emanated from the book. So everything that constituted my life and expectations—lunches, movies, classmates, daily papers, soda pop, soccer games, desks, ferryboats, pretty girls, dreams of happiness, my future sweetheart, wife, office desk, mornings, breakfast, bus tickets, petty concerns, the statistics assignment that didn't get done, my old trousers, face, pajamas, night, magazines I masturbated to, my cigarettes, even my faithful bed which awaited me for that most reliable oblivion—all slipped my mind completely. And I found myself wandering in a land of light.

2 THE NEXT DAY I FELL IN LOVE. LOVE WAS EVERY BIT AS devastating as the light that surged from the book into my face, proving to me how substantially my life had already gone off the track.

As soon as I woke up in the morning, I reviewed all that had happened to me on the previous day and knew at once that the new realm which had opened before me was not just a momentary reverie but as real as my own torso and my limbs. Finding others who were in the same predicament as myself was of the utmost necessity to save myself from the feeling of unbearable loneliness that beset me in the new world into which I was projected.

It had snowed in the night, and snow had accumulated on the windowsills, the sidewalks, and the rooftops. In the chilly white light from outside, the open book on the table appeared sparer and more innocent than it was, which gave it a more ominous character.

Even so, I succeeded in having breakfast with my mother as usual, savoring the smell of toast, thumbing through the morning edition of *Milliyet*, glancing at Jelal Salik's column. As if nothing were out of the ordinary, I had some of the cheese and smiled into my mother's good-natured face. The clatter of cups, spoons, and the teakettle, the noise of the citrus truck in the street were telling me to trust in the normal flow of life, but I wasn't deceived. When I stepped outside, I was so sure the world had been utterly transformed that I was not embarrassed to be wearing my dead father's worn and cumbersome overcoat.

I walked to the station and got on the train; I got off the train and boarded the ferry; at Karaköy I leapt out on the landing; I elbowed my way up the stairs, got on the bus and arrived at Taksim Square; on my way to the university, I stopped briefly and watched some gypsies hawking flowers on the sidewalk. How could I trust life to continue as in the past? Or forget I had ever read the book? For a moment the prospect before me seemed so terrifying that I felt like running away.

At the lecture session on stress mechanics, I solemnly copied down the schemata, the figures and formulas on the blackboard. When the bald-headed professor was not writing something on the board, I folded my arms on my chest and listened to his mellow voice. Was I really listening? Or just pretending to listen like anybody else, playing the part of a student in the department of civil engineering at the Technical University? I couldn't say. But a while later, when I sensed that the familiar old world was intolerably hopeless, my heart began to beat fast, my head began to swim as if a drug were coursing through my veins, and I was thrilled with the power that surged from the book, spreading gradually from its locus in my neck throughout my entire body. The new world had already annulled all existence and transformed the present into the past. Things I saw, things I touched were all pathetically old.

Two days before, when I first laid eyes on the book, it was in the hands of a girl from architecture. She was getting something at the canteen in the lower level and needed to find her wallet, but because she was carrying something else in her other hand, she was unable to rummage through her bag. The object in her

hand was a book and, in an effort to free her hand, she was forced
to put the book down just for a moment on the table where I
was sitting; and I had, just for a moment, stared at the book
placed on my table. That was all there was to the coincidence
that had changed my life. On my way home that afternoon, when
I saw another copy of it among the old tomes, pamphlets, volumes
of poetry and divination, love stories and political thrillers being
sold in a sidewalk stall, I had bought the book.

The moment the noon bell buzzed, most of the other students
hurried up the stairs to get in the cafeteria line, but I just sat
there at my desk. Then I wandered through the halls, went down
to the canteen, passed through courtyards, strolled down colon-
naded galleries, went into empty classrooms; I looked through
windows to see snow-laden trees in the park across the way, and
had some water in the bathroom. I walked and walked, up and
down all over Taşkışla Hall. The girl was nowhere to be seen, but
I was not worried.

After the noon hour, the hallways got even more crowded. I
walked the corridors all through the school of architecture, I went
into the drafting rooms, I watched coin games being played on
the tables; I sat in a corner and, putting together a newspaper
that had fallen apart, I read it. I took to the corridors once more,
went up and down staircases, listened to conversations about soccer, politics, and what was on TV last night. I joined a group
making light of some movie star's decision to have a child, I offered around my lighter and cigarettes; someone was telling a joke,
I listened to it and, what's more, while I did all this, I provided
good-natured replies to whoever stopped and asked me if I had
seen so-and-so. The times I didn't manage to find a couple of
friends to josh around with, or windows to look out of, or a destination to walk to, I walked briskly with great determination in
some direction or other, as if I had something very important on
my mind and was in an awful hurry. But since I had no par-

ticular goal, should I find myself at the library entrance, or up the staircase, or run into someone who asked for a cigarette, I changed direction, blended into the throng, or stopped to light up. I was just about to look at a newly posted announcement on a bulletin board when my heart began to pound, then my heart took off and left me helpless. There she was, the girl in whose hand I had seen the book; moving away from me in the crowd, but walking away ever so slowly as in a dream, she seemed, for some reason, to beckon me to her. I lost my head, I was no longer myself, I just knew it, I let myself follow her.

She was wearing a dress that was pale but not white, it was the lightest of shades to which I could assign no color. I caught up with her before she reached the staircase, and when I caught a glimpse of her up close, the radiance of her face was quite as powerful as the light that the book emanated, but ever so gentle. I was in this world, breathing at the threshold of the new life. The longer I beheld her radiance, the more I understood my heart would no longer heed me.

I told her I had read the book. I told her I'd read the book after seeing it in her hand. I had my own world before reading the book, I said, but after reading the book, I now had another world. We had to talk, I said, for I was left entirely on my own.

"I have a class now," she said.

My heart missed a couple of beats. Perhaps the girl had guessed my bewilderment; she thought it over for a moment.

"All right," she said, making up her mind. "Let's find a free classroom and talk."

We found a classroom on the second floor that was not in use. My legs trembled as I walked in. I couldn't figure out how to tell her I was aware of the world that the book promised me, considering that the book had spoken to me in whispers, opening up as if yielding a secret. The girl said her name was Janan, and I told her mine.

"Why are you so drawn to the book?" she asked.

I had a notion to say, Angel, because you have read it. But how did I come up with this angel business anyway? My mind was in confusion. My mind is always getting confused, Angel, but could it be that someone will help me?

"My whole life was changed after reading the book," I said. "The room, the house, the world where I live ceased to be mine, making me feel I have no domicile. I first saw the book in your hand; so you too must have read it. Tell me about the world you traveled to and back. Tell me what I must do to set foot in that world. Give me an explanation as to why we are still here. Tell me how the new world can be as familiar as my home and yet my home as strange as the new world."

Who knows how much longer I would have gone on in this vein, chapter and verse, but my eyes seemed to be momentarily dazzled. The snowy light of the winter afternoon was so consistent and clear outside that the windows of the little chalk-laden class-room seemed to be made of ice. I looked at her, afraid to look in her face.

"What would you be willing to do to reach the world in the book?" she asked.

Her face was pale, her hair light brown, her gaze gentle; if she was of this world, she seemed to have been drawn from memory; if she was from the future, then she was the harbinger of dread and sorrow. I gazed at her without being aware of gazing, as if I were fearful that if I looked at her too intently the situation would become real.

"I would do anything," I said.

She gazed at me sweetly, a hint of a smile on her lips. How must you act when a phenomenally beautiful and charming girl gazes at you like that? How to hold the matches, light a cigarette, look out the window, talk to her, confront her, take a breath?

They never teach these things in the classroom. People like me writhe in pain fecklessly, trying to conceal the pounding of their hearts.

"What do you mean by anything?" she asked me.

"Everything," I said and fell silent, listening to my heartbeats.

I don't know why but I suddenly had an image of long journeys that seemed endless, the deluges of myth and legend, labyrinthine streets that vanish, sad trees, muddy rivers, gardens, countries. If I were to embrace her one day, I must venture forth to these places.

"Would you be willing to face death, for example?"

"I would."

"Even if you knew that some people would kill you for reading the book?"

I tried to smile, listening to the engineering student inside me say: It's only a book, after all! But Janan was watching me with rapt attention. I thought with misgiving that I'd never get anywhere near her, nor the world in the book, if I were careless and said something wrong.

"I don't think anyone's going to kill me or anything," I said, acting the part of some character I couldn't name. "But even if that were the case, I would truly not be afraid of death."

Her honey-colored eyes flashed for a split second in the chalky light that filtered into the room. "Do you think that world really exists? Or is it a mere fantasy dreamed up and written in a book?"

"That world has to exist!" I said. "You are so beautiful that I know you come from there."

She took a couple of swift steps toward me. She held my head between her hands, reached up, and kissed me on the lips. Her tongue lingered briefly on my mouth. She stepped back, allowing me to hold her lithe body at arm's length.

"You are so brave!" she said.

I picked up some kind of a fragrance, the smell of cologne. I
stepped toward her as if intoxicated. A couple of boisterous students went past the classroom door.

"Wait a minute and listen to me, please," she said. "You must
tell Mehmet everything you've told me. He did go to the world
in the book and managed to come back. He came back from
there, he knows, you understand? Yet he doesn't believe others
can also get there. He's lived through terrible things and lost his
faith. Will you talk to him?"

"Who's this Mehmet?"

"Be in front of Room 201 in ten minutes, before class starts,"
she said and went out the door suddenly; she vanished.

The room felt totally empty, as if I weren't there either. I stood
there astounded. No one had ever kissed me like that before, no
one had ever looked at me like that. And now I was left alone. I
was afraid, thinking I would never see her again, nor ever again
be able to plant my feet squarely on the ground. I wanted to run
after her, but my heart was beating so fast that I was afraid to
breathe. The bright white light had dazed not only my eyes but
also my mind. It's all because of the book, I said to myself and
instantly knew that I loved the book and wanted to exist in its
universe—so much that I thought for a moment tears would
stream down my eyes. It was the book's existence that kept me
going, and I somehow knew the girl would surely embrace me
once more. But right now I felt the whole world had pulled up
and left me.

I heard a racket below, and looking down, I saw a bunch of
construction engineering students noisily throwing snowballs at
each other near the edge of the park. I watched them without
really registering what I was seeing. There was nothing left of the
child in me. I had slipped away.

It has happened to all of us: one day, one ordinary day when
we imagine we're making our routine rounds in the world with

ticket stubs and tobacco shreds in our pockets, our heads full of
news items, traffic noise, troublesome monologues, we suddenly realize we are already someplace else, that we are not actually where
our feet have taken us. I had long slipped away; I had melted into a
color paler than pale where I stood behind the windowpane made
of ice. If you are to come down to earth, or any kind of reality, you
must then hold a girl, *that* girl, hold on to her and win her love.
How quickly had my racing heart learned all this claptrap! I was in
love. I yielded myself to the immeasurable measure of my heart. I
looked at my watch. Eight minutes to go.

I walked like a ghost through the high-ceilinged hallways, oddly
aware of my body, my life, my face, my story. Would I encounter
her in the crowd? If I did chance upon her, what would I say?
How was my face? I cannot remember. I went into the washroom
next to the staircase, put my mouth on the water spout, and
drank. I looked in the mirror to see my mouth that had so recently
been kissed. Mom, I am in love. I am slipping away, Mom. Mom,
I am afraid, but I will do anything for her. I will ask Janan, who
is this Mehmet anyway? Why is he scared? Who are these people
who want to kill those who've read the book? I fear nothing. If
one has understood the book and believed in it, as I myself have,
one would naturally have no fear.

Back among the crowd, I again found myself walking briskly as
if I had important business. I went up to the second floor and
walked along the tall windows that look down on the fountain
courtyard, walked and walked, leaving myself behind, thinking of
Janan with every step. I went by classmates congregated for our
next class. Guess what! Only a little while ago a very attractive
girl kissed me, and how! My legs were taking me swiftly to my
destiny, a destiny that contained dark woods, hotel rooms, mauve
and azure phantoms, life, peace, and death.

When I reached Room 201 three minutes before class, I picked
Mehmet out of the crowd in the hall even before I saw Janan

standing near him. He was pale, tall and thin as myself, pensive, preoccupied, wan. I had a vague memory of having seen him before in Janan's company. He knows more than I do, I speculated; he has done more living; he's even a couple of years older than me. How he knew who I was, I cannot say, but he took me aside, behind the lockers.

"I hear you've read the book," he said. "What's in it for you?"

"A new life."

"Do you buy it?"

"I do."

His complexion looked so wan it made me dread the things he must have gone through.

"Look, listen to me," he said. "I too went for it. I thought I could find that world. I was always on some bus to some place or other, going from town to town, thinking I would find that land, those people, the very streets. Believe me, at the end there is nothing but death. They kill without mercy. They could be watching us even now."

"Don't scare him now," Janan said.

There was a silence. Mehmet looked at me for a moment as if he had known me for years. I felt I had let him down.

"I am not scared," I said, looking at Janan. "I am capable of pursuing it to the very end," I added with the air of a strong type in the movies.

Janan's incredible body was just a few steps from me, between the two of us, but closer to him.

"There is nothing to pursue to the end," said Mehmet. "Just a book. Someone sat down and wrote it. A dream. There is nothing else for you to do, aside from reading and rereading it."

"Tell him what you told me," Janan said to me.

"That world exists," I said. I wished to take hold of Janan by her long graceful arm and draw her to myself. I paused. "I will find that world."

"World shmorld!" Mehmet said. "It doesn't exist. Think of it as tomfoolery perpetrated on children by an old sap. The old man thought he'd write a book to entertain adults the same way he did children. It's doubtful he even knew what it meant. It's entertaining reading, but if you believe it, your life is lost."

"There's a whole world in there," I said, as strong but stupid men do in the movies. "And I know I will find a way to reach it."

"In that case, happy trails . . ." He turned away, gave Janan an I-told-you-so look, and he was about to leave when he stopped and asked, "What makes you so sure of the existence of that life?"

"Because I have the impression the book is telling the story of my life."

He smiled amiably and walked away.

"Don't leave," I said to Janan. "Is he your lover?"

"He actually liked you," she said. "Not for himself, but for me. He fears for people like you."

"Is he your lover? Don't leave without telling me everything."

"He needs me," she said.

I had heard those words so many times in the movies that I supplied the fervent response with spontaneity and conviction: "I will die if you leave me."

She smiled and joined the students crowding into Room 201. For a moment I had an impulse to follow her and sit in. Looking in the classroom's wide windows from the hallway, I saw them both at a desk they had found to sit at together among the other students all dressed alike in khakis, faded clothes, and blue jeans. They were waiting for class without talking when Janan pushed her light brown hair gently behind her ears, making another piece of my heart dissolve. Contrary to how love is portrayed in the movies, I felt more miserable than just miserable following my feet wherever they took me.

What did she think of me? What color are the walls in her

home? What did she and her father talk about? Was their
bathroom sparkling clean? Did she have siblings? What did she
have for breakfast? Were they lovers? In that case, why did she
kiss me?

The tiny classroom where she kissed me was free. I retreated
in there like a defeated army which was nonetheless staunchly
expecting new battles. My footsteps echoing in the empty classroom, my miserable, reprehensible hands opening a pack of cigarettes, the smell of chalk, the white light made of ice—I pressed
my forehead against the windowpane. Was this the new life I
beheld myself in at the threshold of this morning? I was exhausted
by all that had taken place in my mind, but still, the rational
student of engineering in me was busy in one corner doing his
calculations: I was in no condition to go to my own class, so I'd
wait for theirs to end in two hours. Two hours!

My forehead was pressed against the cold windowpane, I don't
know for how long, but I was full of self-pity; I liked wallowing in
self-pity; I thought tears were about to well in my eyes when
snowflakes began drifting on light gusts of wind. Beyond the steep
street that leads to Dolmabahçe, I could see the plane and chestnut trees. How still they were! Trees did not know they were trees,
I reflected. Blackbirds took wing out of the snowy branches. I
watched them with admiration.

I watched the snowflakes, which fell in gentle flurries, lingering
indecisively at some point in pursuit of their fellow flakes, unable
to make up their minds, when a light wind bore down and
whisked them away. And at times a single flake swayed in the air
for a moment and stood still, then acting as if it had changed its
mind, it turned around and began to rise slowly up toward the
sky. I observed many a snowflake revert to the sky before it could
land in the mud, the park, on the pavement or the trees. Did
anyone know this? Had anyone noticed?

Had anyone ever noticed that the acute point of the triangle which was formed at the intersection and which seemed to be part of the park pointed to the Tower of Leander? Had anyone noticed the pine trees which, under the influence of the east wind all these years, had leaned over the sidewalk in perfect symmetry, forming an octagon over the minibus stop? Watching the man with a pink plastic bag in his hand stand on the sidewalk, I wondered if anyone had realized that half the population of Istanbul goes around carrying plastic bags. Utterly unaware of your identity, I wondered if anyone had seen your footprints, Angel, in the tracks left by starving dogs and ragpickers in the snow and ash that cover dead city parks? Was this how I was to witness the new world, revealed to me like a secret in the book I bought at the sidewalk stall two days ago?

It was my heart and not my eyes that first became aware of Janan's shape in the graying light and the deepening snow on the same sidewalk. She was wearing a purple coat; my heart must have impressed the coat upon itself without my knowledge. Beside her was Mehmet, wearing a gray jacket and walking in the snow like an evil spirit that leaves no tracks. I had an impulse to run after them.

They stopped to talk at the same spot where the bookstall had been two days ago. Janan's hurt and withdrawn stance, accompanied by their wide gestures, indicated that, more than talking, they were having an argument, like a pair of old lovers all too accustomed to fights.

Then they started to walk again only to stop once more. I was at a great distance, but still I could coolly infer from their body language, and the looks they got from the sidewalk traffic, that they were arguing even more violently now.

This didn't last very long either. Janan turned around and began walking back to the building where I was, while Mehmet followed her with his eyes before continuing on his way toward Taksim. My heart kept missing a beat.

That is when I saw the man who stood at the Sarıyer minibus stop cross the street, carrying the pink plastic bag. Focused as my eyes were on the grace of the purple-clad figure, they were in no state to notice someone crossing the street, but there was something like a false note in the man's behavior. A few steps from the curb, the man pulled something—a gun—out of the pink bag. He aimed it at Mehmet, who also saw the gun.

I first witnessed Mehmet take the hit and shudder, then I registered the report; after that, I heard the second gunshot, expecting to hear yet a third. Mehmet stumbled and fell. The man dropped his plastic bag and made for the park.

Janan was still approaching, her steps wounded and dainty like a little bird's. She hadn't heard the gunshots. A truck full of snow-covered oranges rattled rambunctiously into the intersection. It was as if the world had gone back into motion.

I noticed some commotion at the minibus stop. Mehmet was getting up. In the distance the man was running without his plastic bag down the hill toward İnönü Stadium, skipping and hopping across the snow in the park like a clown bent on entertaining the kids, with a couple of playful dogs on his trail.

I should have run downstairs to meet Janan halfway and tell her what had happened, but I was riveted to the sight of Mehmet wobbling and looking around in a daze. For how long? For a while, a long while, until Janan turned the Taşkışla corner and disappeared from my angle of vision.

I ran down the stairs and hurtled past a group of plainclothes police, students, and janitors standing around. When I reached the main entrance, there was no sign of Janan anywhere. I quickly went upstairs but didn't see her there either. Then I ran to the intersection and still didn't see anything or anybody related to the scene I had just witnessed. Neither Mehmet nor the plastic bag that the man with the gun had disposed of were anywhere.

The snow on the spot where Mehmet fell had melted into mud. A two-year-old kid wearing a beanie went by with his stylish and attractive mother.

"Mom, where did the rabbit go?" the kid said. "Where, Mom?"

I ran in a frenzy across the street toward the Sarıyer minibus stop. The world was once more wearing the silence of snow and the indifference of trees. Two minibus drivers who looked exactly alike were much astonished by my queries. They had no idea what I was talking about. What's more, the tough-looking fellow who brought them their tea had not heard any gunshots either; besides, he had no intention of being astonished by anything. The attendant at the minibus stop held on to his whistle, staring at me as if I were the criminal who had pulled the trigger. Blackbirds congregated in the pine tree over my head. I stuck my head in the minibus at the last moment before it left and anxiously asked my questions.

"A young man and woman hailed a taxi over there and took off," an elderly woman said, "just a little while ago."

Her finger pointed to Taksim Square. I knew what I was doing was not sensible but I still ran in that direction. I thought I was all alone in the world among all the vendors, vehicles, and stores around the square. I was about to make my way to Beyoğlu when, remembering the Emergency Care Hospital, I tore off down Sıraselviler Avenue and went through the emergency entrance into the smell of ether and iodine as if I were a trauma case myself.

I saw gentlemen lying in pools of blood, their trousers ripped, their cuffs rolled up. I saw the blue faces of victims of poison and gastroenteritis whose stomachs had been pumped, and who were now stretched out on gurneys and left in the snow behind the potted cyclamens for a breath of fresh air. I showed the way to

the tubby but nice elderly man who was searching door to door
for the doctor on duty, all the while holding tight to the clothes-
line he had made into a tourniquet for his arm to avoid bleeding
to death. I saw the pair of old cronies who, after knifing each
other with the same knife, were now politely giving their state-
ments and apologizing to the arresting officer for failing to remember to bring along the offending knife. I waited my turn and
was informed by the nurses first, and later by the police, that no,
no student had showed up that day who was suffering from a
gunshot wound, accompanied by a girl with light brown hair.

Then I stopped at Beyoğlu Municipal Hospital too, where I had
the impression that I was seeing the same cronies who had knifed
each other, the same suicidal girls who had resorted to drinking
iodine, the same apprentices who had had their arms caught in
the machinery or their fingers under the needle, the same passengers who had been crushed between the bus and the bus stop,
or between the ferry and the ferry platform. I examined the police
reports carefully; I made an off-the-record statement for the benefit of a policeman who became suspicious of my suspicions; and
upstairs on the obstetrics floor, I was afraid I was going to burst
into tears smelling the cologne a delighted new father doused
liberally into our hands.

It was getting dark when I returned to the scene of the incident.
I wove in between the minibuses and made my way into the
minipark where blackbirds darted angrily over my head at first
and then kept watch skulking in the branches. I might have been
in the thick of city life, but I heard a deafening silence in my ears
as if I were a murderer who had knifed someone and was keeping
out of sight. In the distance I saw the dim yellow light in the
little classroom where Janan kissed me and surmised a class must
now be in progress there. The same trees whose distress had baf-
fled me that very morning had now turned into clumsy and pitiless stacks of bark. I walked on the snow in my shoes, tracking

the footprints of the man with the missing plastic bag, who four hours ago had hopped and skipped his way through the snow like a carefree clown. To make certain that the tracks were indeed there, I kept on his trail all the way down to the highway, then turned back, and as I backtracked I noticed that my footprints and the footprints of the man with the missing plastic bag had been inextricably intertwined. Presently, two dark dogs appeared from the bushes looking like just such a guilty party as I was, only to take fright and flee. I stopped for a moment and stared at the sky, which was as dark as the dogs.

My mother and I ate our supper watching TV. The news broadcast, the faces flashing on the screen, accounts of murders, accidents, fires, and assassinations seemed as distant to me as the stormy waves on a tiny section of an ocean visible in between mountains. Even so, the desire to be "there," to be part of that leaden ocean in the distance kept stirring inside me. Pictures kept flickering on the black-and-white TV for which the antenna was not properly set, but no mention was made of a student who had been shot.

I shut myself in my room after supper. The book stood open just as I had left it on the table, just so . . . I was afraid of it. There was brute force in the book's summons for me to return and wholeheartedly abandon myself to it. Thinking I would not be able to resist the call, I took to the streets once more and walked in the snow and mire all the way, again, to the sea. The darkness of the water gave me heart.

I sat down at the table thus heartened and, as if submitting my body to a sacred task, I held my face to the light that surged from the book. The light was not so powerful at first, but as I turned the pages it reached into me so deeply that I felt my entire being dissolve. An unbearable urge to live and run, aching with impatience and excitement in the pit of my stomach, I read until daybreak.

3 I SPENT THE NEXT FEW DAYS LOOKING FOR JANAN. SHE was not at school the following day, nor the next day, or the day after that. At first, her absence seemed explicable, I thought she would soon be there, but just the same, the old world under my feet was gradually retracting. I was tired of seeking, watching, hoping; I was head over heels in love and, what's more, under the influence of the book I kept reading throughout the night, I felt I was utterly alone. I was all too painfully aware that this world was contingent on a string of misinterpreted signals and an ingrained miscellany of indiscriminate habits, and that real life was located somewhere either outside or inside, yet definitely somewhere within those parameters. I had come to realize my guiding spirit could be none other than Janan.

I sifted through all the daily newspapers, local supplements, and weekly magazines where political assassinations, commonplace murders committed under the influence, lurid accidents, and fires were reported down to the last detail, but I didn't come across a single clue. After reading the book all night, I would arrive at Taşkışla around noon, hoping to run into her in case she had surfaced. I pounded the hallways, periodically looking in at the canteen, going up and down the stairs, reviewing the courtyard, pacing the library, passing through the colonnades, pausing in front of the classroom where she kissed me. I distracted myself by going to class whenever I could muster the patience, only to repeat the same pattern afterwards, again and again. Searching, waiting, and then reading the book all night was all that I could do.

After a week of this, I tried to infiltrate Janan's circle, although I didn't suppose either she or Mehmet had too many friends. A couple of their classmates knew that Mehmet lived at a hotel near Taksim where he did clerical work besides doubling as the night watchman, but no one had any idea why he hadn't been showing up at school. An aggressive girl, who had gone to high school with Janan but hadn't made friends with her, divulged that Janan lived somewhere in Nişantaşı. Another one, who said they'd once been up all night drawing plans together to meet a project deadline, informed me that Janan had a suave and handsome brother who worked at their father's place of business; she seemed to have taken more interest in the brother than in Janan. I didn't get the address through her but by telling the registrar's office that I intended to send New Year's greetings to all my classmates.

I read the book all through the night, until daybreak when my eyes were in pain and my stamina was depleted by the lack of sleep. While I read sometimes the light that reflected on my face seemed so intense and so incandescent I thought not only my soul but also my body was melting away and my identity being annihilated in the light that surged from the pages. I then imagined the light slowly dilating with me inside it, initially like a light seeping from a fissure in the ground, then getting more and more intense and spreading to enclose the whole world where I also had a place. For a moment I dreamed of that brave new world, a realm with immortal trees and lost cities I could barely visualize, where I would meet Janan in the street and she would embrace me.

One evening toward the end of December, I finally went to Janan's neighborhood in Nişantaşı. For a long time, I walked aimlessly along the main street where smartly dressed women with children were doing their shopping at stores decorated with lights for the New Year season; I studied the windows of trendy sandwich shops, newsstands, patisseries, and clothing stores.

It was when the crowds had thinned out and the stores were being closed that I rang the doorbell in one of the apartment buildings back behind the main street. A housemaid opened the door; I told her I was one of Janan's classmates; she went inside; the TV was tuned to a political speech; I heard some whispering. Her father came to the door, a tall man who wore a white shirt and carried a bright white napkin in his hand. He invited me in. The mother, whose made-up face was inquisitive, and the brother, who was good-looking, were sitting at a dinner table where the fourth place had not been set. The news was what was on TV.

I told them I was a classmate of Janan's from the school of architecture; she hadn't been coming to school and all her friends were worried; some of us who had called had not received satisfactory answers; besides, she had my half-done statistics assignment which I needed and I apologized for having to ask to get it back.

My dead father's discolored coat slung over my left arm, I must have looked like an ill-tempered wolf wrapped in a pallid sheepskin.

"You look like a nice kid," Janan's father began. He told me he was going to be candid. He wanted me to please answer his questions in return. Did I have any political sympathies, be it left or right, fundamentalist or socialist? No! Well, did I have any affiliation with any political organization outside the university? No, I had no such affiliations.

There was a silence. The mother's eyebrows went up with approval and empathy. The father's eyes, which were honey-colored like Janan's, drifted to the TV screen, wandered off momentarily to the never-never land, and then turned back to me with resolve.

Janan had left home, vanished. Well, maybe vanished wasn't quite the right word. She called home every day or so from some place far away, if the static on the line was any indication, telling them not to worry, she was fine; and disregarding her father's insistent interrogations and her mother's pleading, she would refuse to say anything more and hang up. Given the situation, they were justified in suspecting their daughter was being exploited to do the dirty work for some political organization. They had considered going to the police, but they had desisted because they had full trust in Janan's intelligence and were convinced she could always pull her wits together to get herself out of any fix. And the mother, who had taken complete inventory of my appearance from my hair down to my shoes, even my father's keepsake which I had draped over the back of the empty chair, tearfully voiced her one request of me, that I speak up if I had any knowledge or insight which might shed light on the situation.

I put on an astonished face and said I had no idea, ma'am; no idea at all. For a moment we all were occupied with staring at the platter of *börek* and the shredded carrot salad on the table. The good-looking brother who had been traveling in and out of the room apologized, explaining that he had been unable to find my incomplete assignment anywhere. I hinted I might be able to locate it in her room myself, but instead of granting me access to their missing daughter's bedroom, they motioned me halfheartedly to her vacant place at the dining table. I was a proud lover, I refused. But seeing her framed photograph on the piano just as I took my leave, I regretted my decision. It was a picture of a nine-year-old Janan in pigtails, wearing a sweet angel's costume, which I assumed was for a school play, whose every detail down

to the tiny wings was appropriated from the West, standing between her parents and smiling slightly through the melancholy
countenance of childhood.

How antagonistic and bitter was the night outside! How merciless the dismal streets! I realized why bands of stray dogs cram
themselves against each other so assiduously in the streets. It was
with tenderness that I woke up my mother, who had fallen asleep
in front of the TV, touching her on her pallid neck, smelling her,
wishing she would hug me. But once I retired into my room, I
felt all the more strongly that my real life was about to commence.

That night I read the book once more, submitting to it, pleading to be swept away. I read it with reverence. New realms, new
beings, new images appeared before me. I envisioned clouds of
fire, oceans of darkness, purple trees, crimson breakers. Then, as
on some spring mornings when the sun comes out immediately
after a shower and suddenly I see before my optimistic and confident approach the retreat of the foul apartment buildings, accursed alleys, and moribund casements, the chaotic images in my
mind's eye cleared up, and Love became manifest in a halo of
brilliant white, carrying a child in its arms. The child was the girl
whose picture I had seen framed on the piano.

The girl looked at me, smiling; she was perhaps about to say
something, or perhaps she had spoken but I had been unable to
hear. I felt futile. I was in painful agreement with an inner voice
telling me that I would never be part of this beautiful picture;
and I was overcome with regret. Then I observed to my deep
consternation the two of them rise and, ascending in a curious
fashion, vanish.

The fantasy awakened such terror in my being that, just as I
had done the first day when I read the book, I fearfully moved
my face away as if to escape the light that surged from the pages.
I was agonized to see my body here, in this other life, left dumb-
struck in the silence in my room, the peace provided by my table,

the stillness of my arms and hands, my belongings, my pack of
cigarettes, my scissors, textbooks, curtains, my bed.

I wished that my body, which was sensible to me through its
warmth and pulse, might relinquish this world; yet at the same
time I was aware that hearing the noises in the building, the
distant cry of the *boza* vendor, and burning the midnight oil reading a book were tolerable aspects of being present inside this moment. I hearkened only to the sounds of very distant car horns,
dogs barking, slight breezes, a couple of people talking in the
street (one said, It's already tomorrow), and the tumult of one of
those long freight trains that suddenly overwhelms the noises in
the night. A long while later, when everything seemed to dissolve
into absolute silence, a specter appeared before my eyes, and I
apprehended how deeply the book had permeated my soul. When
I again exposed my face to the light that emanated from the book
lying open on the table before me, it was as if my soul were the
pristine page of a notebook. That must have been how the book's
contents were infused into my soul.

I reached into a drawer and pulled out an actual notebook, one
with quadrille pages for graphs and maps, which I had bought for
my statistics course a few weeks before I came across the book
but had not yet used. I turned to the first page and inhaled its
clean white smell, and taking out my ballpoint pen I began writing
all the book imparted to me, sentence by sentence, into the notebook. After writing down each sentence from the book, I went on
to the next sentence, and then to the next. When the book
started a new paragraph, I too indented a new paragraph, realizing
after a while that I had written exactly the same paragraph as in
the book. This was how I re-animated everything that the book
imparted to me, paragraph by paragraph, but after a while I raised
my head to study the book and then the notebook. I'd written
what was in the notebook, but the content was exactly the same
as what was in the book. I was so delighted with this that I began

to repeat the same process every night until the early hours in
the morning.

I no longer attended classes. I paced the hallways like someone
who's a fugitive from his own soul, often not concerned in the
slightest where and when classes were being held; not allowing
myself a moment's peace, I scoured the canteen, then the library,
the classrooms, only to end up back at the canteen, and each
time I observed that Janan was present in none of these places a
deep ache in my viscera made me suffer intensely.

As time went by, I became used to the ache and succeeded in
living with it and, to a certain extent, I even held it at bay. Perhaps walking at full speed or smoking was of some help, but even
more crucial was finding small ways to distract myself, such as a
story someone related, the purple-colored new drawing pen, the
fragility of the trees seen through a window, a new visage encountered by chance in the street. These things could relieve me
even if only briefly from sensing the pain of frustration and loneliness that radiated from my belly through my whole body. Whenever I went into some spot where I might chance upon Janan,
such as the canteen, I would not immediately exhaust all the
possibilities by scanning the place precipitously, but I would first
glance over to a corner where some girls in blue jeans smoking
cigarettes were talking away, and in the meantime I would fantasize that Janan was sitting somewhere just beyond or behind
me. I would soon come to believe the fantasy so thoroughly that
I was loath to turn and look behind me for fear she would vanish;
instead, I would take my time surveying the space between those
students standing in front of the cashier and those sitting at the
table where, not long before, Janan had set the book down in
front of me, thereby gaining a few more moments of happiness
in the warmth of Janan's presence stirring just behind me, and
coming to believe in my vision all the more. Yet, when I turned
my head and saw that neither Janan nor a sign of her presence

was anywhere around, the vision coursing like a sweet substance through my veins yielded up to a poison that seared my stomach. I had heard and read so many times that love is such sweet torment. It was during this period that I so often came across this kind of bunk mostly in books on palmistry, or in the home and lifestyle pages in the paper, right next to the horoscopes, pictures of salads, and recipes for face creams. Because of the leaden ache in the pit of my stomach, the miserable loneliness and jealousy I felt had severed me so thoroughly from humanity and rendered me so totally without hope that I resorted not only to astrology and the like for relief but also to blind faith in certain signs, such as: if the number of stairs leading up was odd, then Janan was upstairs; if the first person out the door was female, it meant I would see Janan that day; if the train departed at the count of seven, she would find me and we would talk; if I was the first one off the ferry, today was the day she would come.

I was the first person off the ferry. I didn't step on the cracks in the sidewalk. I calculated correctly that there were an odd number of bottle caps on the café floor. I had tea with an apprentice welder who wore a matching purple sweater and overcoat. I was lucky enough to be able to spell her name with the letters on the license plates of the first five taxicabs that I encountered. I was successful going in one end of the Karaköy underground passage and out the other, holding my breath. I counted up to nine thousand without losing my place while I stared at the windows of their place in Nişantaşı. I discarded friends who weren't aware that not only did her name mean *soulmate* but it also signified God. Taking the cue from the fact that our names rhymed, I had our wedding invitations printed in my imagination, adorning them with a smart rhyme like the ones that come out of New Life brand caramel candies. I succeeded in predicting the number of lighted windows I counted for an entire week at three in the morning, without exceeding the margin of five percent error that

I allowed myself. I repeated Fuzuli's famous line of poetry, *Janan yok ise jan gerekmez*, to thirty-nine people, subjecting them to my interpretation, "If the soulmate is absent there is no need for the soul." I called up and asked after her under twenty-eight different guises, each time using a different voice; and I would not go home before I said *Janan* thirty-nine times, forming her name in my imagination with the letters I extracted from billboards, posters, flashing neon signs, in the show windows of pharmacies, kebab and lottery shops. Still, Janan did not come.

I was returning home one midnight, having patiently won the numerical and fortuitous games I played, double or nothing, which brought Janan a little closer to me in my fondest dreams, when I noticed lights burning in my room. Either my mother was worried that I was so late, or else she was looking for something; but a completely different picture appeared in my mind.

I imagined myself sitting at my table, up there in my room where I saw the lights. I imagined it with such passion and force of will that I thought I could almost see for a brief moment my own head in the faint orange glow of my table lamp, against the little segment of dingy white wall that was barely visible between the parted drapes. At the same moment, such an amazing feeling of freedom manifested itself in the electric sensation I experienced that I was amazed. It had been so simple all along, I said to myself: the man in the room that I saw out of another's eyes must remain there in that room; I, on the other hand, must run away from home, away from the room, away from everything, including my mother's smell, my bed, my twenty-two years of lived life. New life could begin only by my leaving that room; if I were to keep leaving that room in the morning only to return to it at night, I could never reach Janan nor that land.

When I entered my room, I looked at my bed as if I were seeing someone else's belongings, the books that were piled on one corner of my table, the nudie magazines I had not touched since I first saw Janan, the carton of cigarettes drying on the radiator, the change I kept in a dish, my key ring, my wardrobe that didn't close right; and regarding all my stuff that bound me to my old world, I understood I had to make good my escape.

Later, when I was reading and copying the book, I perceived that what I was writing signaled a certain tendency in the world. It seemed I should not be in one place but simultaneously in every place. My room was somewhere; it was one place. It was not everywhere. "Why go to Taşkışla in the morning," I asked myself, "when Janan won't be there?" There were other places Janan would not be either, places where I had been going in vain but where I would no longer go. I would only go where the text took me, where Janan and the new life must be. As I copied down all that the book imparted, the knowledge of the places where I must go gradually filtered into me, and I was gratified that I was gradually becoming someone else. Much later, when I was reviewing the pages I had filled like a traveler satisfied with the progress he has made, I could see with clarity the new human being into whom I was in the process of being transformed.

I was the person who oriented himself on the road leading to the new life he sought by sitting down and copying the book sentence by sentence into his notebook. I was the person who had read a book that changed his whole life, who had fallen in love, and who had a feeling he was progressing on the road to a new life. I was the person whose mother tapped on his door and said, "You sit up all night writing, but please don't smoke, at least." I was the person who rose from the table past the witching hour when the only noises heard in the district are the dogs howling across great distances, and took a final look at the book he had been poring over for many nights and the pages he had filled under its influence. I was the person who removed his savings from his sock drawer and, without turning off the lights in his room, stood at his mother's bedroom door listening fondly to the

sound of her breathing. It was I, Angel, who long past the midnight hour slipped out of his own house like a timorous stranger
and blended into the darkness in the streets. I was the one on
the sidewalk, his eyes fixed on his own lighted windows as if he
were contemplating with tears and pathos someone else's fragile
and depleted life. It was me who was running to his new life
eagerly, listening to the reverberations of his own footsteps in the
silence of the night.

The only light in the neighborhood still burning was the ghastly
glow in the windows of Uncle Railman Rıfkı's house. I was up on
the garden wall in an instant and looking in between the partially
closed curtains to see under the feeble light his wife, Aunt Ratibe,
sitting up and smoking. In one of Uncle Rıfkı's stories for children, there's an intrepid hero who, like myself, takes to the disconsolate streets of his own childhood in search of the Land of
Gold, hearkening to the call of obscure venues, the clamor of
faraway countries, and the roaring sound in trees that remained
invisible. Wearing on my back the overcoat my dead father who
retired from the State Railroads left me, I walked into the heart
of darkness.

The night concealed me, it kept me and showed me the way.
I proceeded into the inner organs of the city that vibrated steadily,
its concrete highways rigid as the arteries of a paralyzed patient,
its neon boulevards reverberating with the whine of rowdy trucks
carrying meat, milk, and canned food. I consecrated the garbage
pails that belched the swill in their maws out on the wet sidewalks
that reflected the lights; I asked the gruesome trees that never
stand still for directions; I blinked seeing fellow citizens in dimly
lit stores who still sat up at cash registers going over their accounts; I steered clear of the police on duty in front of precinct
stations; I smiled forlornly at drunks, vagrants, unbelievers, and
outcasts who had no tidings of a glowing new life; I exchanged
dark glances with Checker Cab drivers who sneaked up on me

like sleepless sinners in the stillness of blinking red lights; I was not deceived by the beautiful women smiling down on me from soap billboards, nor did I put my trust in the good-looking men in the cigarette advertisements, nor even in the statues of Atatürk, or the early editions of tomorrow's papers being scrambled up by drunks and insomniacs, or the lottery man drinking tea at an all-night café, nor his friend who waved and called out to me, "Take a load off, young man." The innermost stench of the rotting city led me to the bus terminal that reeked of the sea and hamburgers, latrines and exhaust, gasoline and filth.

Trying to avoid becoming intoxicated by the plastic lettering on top of bus line offices that promised me new venues, new hearts, new lives, and hundreds of colorful cities and towns, I took myself into a small restaurant. There, I turned away from the semolina cakes, the puddings and salads being displayed in the ample refrigerated case, wondering in whose stomachs and how many hundreds of miles away they would finally be digested. Right now they were just standing there in neat rows like the plastic letters in the names of towns and bus companies. And then I forgot for whom I had begun to wait. Perhaps I was waiting for you, Angel, to pull me away, tenderly and graciously cautioning me, putting me gently on the right track. But there was no one in the restaurant aside from a mother holding a child and a couple of obdurate travelers who were stuffing their sleepy faces. My eyes were searching for signs of the new life when a sign on the wall warned: "Do not tamper with the light," and another announced: "There is a charge for using the facilities," and yet a third proclaimed in stern and deliberate lettering: "No alcoholic beverages allowed." I had an impression that dark crows were taking wing across the windows of my mind; then I seemed to have a presentiment that my death would follow from this point of departure. I wish I could describe to you, Angel, the grief in that restaurant slowly closing in upon itself, but I was so terribly tired; I heard the whine of the centuries resonating in my ears like the sleepless woods; I loved the turbulent spirit gurgling in the engines of dauntless buses that each took off to another clime; I heard Janan call out to me from a place far away where she was searching for the access point that would take her to the threshold. Yet I was silent, a passive spectator who was willing, due to a technical difficulty, to watch a film without the sound because my head had dropped on the table and I had fallen asleep.

I slept on I don't know for how long. When I woke up I was still in the same restaurant but in the presence of a different clientele, yet I felt I was now capable of communicating to the angel the point of departure for the great journey that would take me to unique experiences. Across from me were three young men who were boisterously settling their money and bus fare accounts. A thoroughly forlorn old man had placed his coat and his plastic bag on the table next to his soup bowl in which he was stirring and smelling his own grievous life; and a waiter read the paper, yawning in the dimly lit area where the tables were lined up. Next to me the frosted glass wall extended all the way from the ceiling down to the dirty floor tiles, behind it was the dark blue night, and in the dark were the revving bus engines that invited me to another realm.

I boarded one randomly at an indeterminate hour. It wasn't yet morning but the day broke as we progressed, the sun rose, and my eyes were filled with light and sleep. Then, it seems, I dozed off.

I got on buses, I got off buses; I loitered in bus terminals only to board more buses, sleeping in my seat, turning my days into nights, embarking and disembarking in small towns, traveling for days in the dark, and I said to myself: the young traveler was so determined to find the unknown realm, he let himself be transported without respite on roads that would take him to the threshold.

4 IT WAS A COLD WINTER'S NIGHT, O ANGEL, AND I HAD been traveling for days; I was on one of the several buses I took each day, not knowing where I departed from, where I was destined, or how fast I was going. I was sitting on the tired and noisy bus, somewhere back on the right-hand side in the darkened interior, half asleep and half awake, more dreaming than sleeping, and closer to the ghosts in the darkness outside than to my own dreams. I could see through my half-closed eyelids a single puny tree on the interminable steppe lit by the cross-eyed headlights on high beam, the boulder with a cologne ad painted on it, the power poles, the threatening headlights of the trucks that we encountered sporadically, but I was also watching the movie on the video screen placed high above the driver's seat. Whenever the female lead spoke, the screen took on a purplish hue like Janan's winter coat, and when the fast-talking, impetuous male actor came back with his rejoinder, the screen turned that dull blue which had at some time or other penetrated somehow into my very marrow. As it often happens, I was thinking of you, and remembering you, when that purple and that dull blue came together in the same frame; and yet, alas, they did not kiss.

It was at that very moment, in the third week of my journey

as I was watching the movie, that I remember being overwhelmed
by an astonishingly powerful feeling of incompleteness, of apprehension and expectation. I was nervously tapping my cigarette
ash into the ashtray, the lid of which I would very soon close
with a sharp and decisive blow of my forehead. The angry impatience rising inside me against the indecisiveness of the lovers
who still had not managed to kiss turned into a deeper and more
significant feeling of edginess. I had a sense of something profound and authentic approaching, there it comes, now!—like the
magical silence that falls over everyone including the audience
the moment before the king is crowned. In that silence preced-
ing the coronation the only sound heard is the flutter of the
wings of a pair of doves flying across the royal scene. Then I
heard the old man next to me moan, and I turned toward him.
His bald head was peacefully bouncing on the dark, frozen window on which it rested, the same head that contained the raging
pains he had described to me a hundred miles and a couple of
miserable towns back which were carbon copies of each other. I
conjectured that maybe the doctor at the hospital he was going
to see when he got there in the morning had advised that he
press his head against icy-cold panes as a remedy for his brain
tumor; but turning my eyes back to the dark highway, I was
gripped by a panic that I had not felt in days. What was this
deep and irresistible anticipation? Why now this impatient urgency that overwhelmed me?

I was jolted by the crashing sound of a distinct force that
wrenched my inner organs. I was heaved out of my seat and was
about to tumble over into the one in front when I was rammed
into components of steel, tin, aluminum, and glass, angrily striking objects and being hit, hurt, crumpled. At that very instant, I
fell back once more into the same bus seat as someone who was
altogether different.

Yet neither was the bus any longer the same bus. I could see through a blue fog from where I still sat in confusion that the driver's station plus the seats immediately behind it had disintegrated into smithereens and disappeared.

It must have been this that I had been looking for; it was what I wanted. How aware I was of what I discovered in my heart! Peace, sleep, death, time! I was both here and there, in peace and waging a bloody war, insomniac as a restless ghost and also interminably somnolent, present in an eternal night and also in time that flowed away inexorably. Consequently, I went into slow motion, just as in the movies, and rose from my seat, skirted the corpse of the young bus attendant who had migrated into the land of the dead, still holding a bottle in his hand. I went out the rear exit and stepped into the dark garden of the night.

One end of this arid and limitless garden was the asphalt highway that now lay covered with shards of glass, the other end a realm from which there was no return. I proceeded fearlessly into the velvet night, convinced that this was the halcyon land which had for weeks wafted balmy as paradise in my imagination. It was as if I were sleepwalking, but I was awake, walking but with my feet not touching the ground. Perhaps I had no feet, but perhaps I no longer remember since I was there all by myself. I was there by myself and I was myself alone, my numbed body and my consciousness. I was brimming with my own being.

I sat down somewhere next to a rock in the paradisical darkness and stretched out on the ground. Stars here and there above me and an actual rock beside me. I touched it with longing, feeling the unbelievable pleasure of a touch that was real. Once upon a time, there was a real world where a touch was a touch, smells were smells, and sounds were sounds. Can it be, O star, that the other time has given this present time a glimpse of itself? I could see my own life in the dark. I read a book and found you. If this be death, then I am born again. I am here, in this world, a brand-new being with no memory and no past. I am like some new

attractive TV star appearing in a new serial, or childishly astonished like a fugitive who sees the stars for the first time after years
of being incarcerated in a dungeon. I heard the call of silence,
the like of which I had never before experienced, and I kept asking: Why buses, nights, towns? Why all these roads, bridges,
faces? Why solitude that like a hawk overwhelms the night? Why
words that get caught in appearances? Why time that has no
return? I could hear the crackling in the earth and the ticking of
my watch. Time is three-dimensional silence, the book said. I said
to myself: So I am to die without understanding the three dimensions in the slightest, without comprehending life, the world,
and the book, without, even, seeing you once more, Janan. That
was how I was talking to the stars, these brand-new stars, when a
childish thought came to me childishly: I was still too much of a
child to die. And feeling the warmth of the blood that trickled
from my forehead down on my hands, I felt the happiness of
discovering, once again, the tactual, olfactory, and visual properties of things. I regarded this world, happy and loving you, Janan.

Back where I left the unfortunate bus on the spot where it had
rammed with all its might into a cement truck, a cloud of cement
dust hung like a miraculous umbrella over the dying. A stubborn
blue light was leaking out of the bus. Hapless passengers who were
still alive and others who would not stay alive much longer were
coming out the rear exit, cautiously as if stepping on the surface
of a strange planet. Mom, Mom, you're still in there, but I got
out. Mom, Mom, blood is filling my pockets like coins. I wished
to communicate with them, with the avuncular man crawling
along the ground, his hat on his head, a plastic bag in his hand;
the fastidious soldier who was bent over carefully examining the
rip in his trousers; the old lady who had abandoned herself to
jubilant chatter now that she had been granted the chance to
address God directly. I wished to impart the significance of this
unique and impeccable time to the virulent insurance agent who

was counting the stars, to the dumbfounded daughter of the mother who was pleading with the dead driver, to the men with mustaches who were strangers to each other yet holding hands and dancing for the joy of being alive, swaying gently like people who have fallen in love at first sight. I wished I could tell them that this unique moment was a felicity granted all too rarely to God's creatures like us, saying that you, O Angel, would appear only once in a lifetime in this wondrous time beneath the miraculous umbrella of cement dust, and ask them why it was that now we were all so very happy. You, mother and son clutching each other hard like a pair of dauntless lovers and freely weeping for the first time in your lives, you, the sweet woman who has discovered that blood is redder than lipstick and death kinder than life, you, the spared child standing over your dead father clutching your doll and watching the stars, I ask you: Who was it that granted us this fulfillment, this contentment, this happiness? The voice inside me gave one word as an answer: Departure . . . departure . . . But I had already understood I was not yet to die. The elderly woman who was soon to expire asked me the whereabouts of the cabin attendant to get her luggage out of the hold immediately because, although her face was crimson with blood, she was hoping to get to the next town where she was to catch the train in the morning. I was left holding her blood-soaked train ticket.

I boarded the bus through the rear to avoid looking at the front-row passengers whose dead faces had been plastered on the windshield. I became aware of the sound of the motor running, reminding me of the horrible engine noise on all the buses I had ridden; what I heard was not deathly silence but living voices that were grappling with recollections, desires, and ghosts. The bus attendant was still holding the same bottle and a teary-eyed mother her peacefully sleeping baby. It was cold outside. I too sat down, feeling the pain in my legs. My seatmate with the aching

brain had left this world along with the rash crowd in the front
rows, but he was still sitting patiently. His eyes had been closed
while he slept, now they were open in death. Two men appeared
out of somewhere in the front, and lifting a bloody body roughly
over their shoulders, they carried it out into the cold.

It was then that I became aware of the most magical coincidence or impeccable fortune: the TV screen over the driver's seat
was still intact and the lovers on the video were finally in each
other's arms. I wiped the blood off my forehead, my face and
neck with my handkerchief, and I flipped up the lid of the ashtray
which I had slammed down with my forehead only a little while
ago; I lit up contentedly and began watching the film.

They kissed and kissed again, sucking lipstick and life. I wondered why in my childhood I used to hold my breath during the
kissing scenes, why I used to swing my legs and focus on a point
on the screen that was slightly above the lovers. Ah, the kiss! How
well I had retained the memory of the taste that had touched my
lips that day in the white light that came through the icy win-
dowpanes. Only one kiss in my entire lifetime. I wept repeating
Janan's name.

When the film came to an end, I first noticed the headlights
then the truck itself standing respectfully in the presence of the
unhappy scene where the cold corpses were chilled even further
by the cold outside. As it happened, there was a fat wallet in the
pocket of my seatmate, whose blank eyes were still fixed on the
blank video screen. His given name was Mahmut, his last name
Mahler. His identification papers. The photo of his soldier son
who looked like me. And a dilapidated news item about cockfight-
ing clipped from the *Denizli Post*, 1966. The money would see
me through many weeks ahead. The marriage certificate too
might come in handy. Thanks.

We prudent survivors were transported to town stretched out
like the meek dead beside us, trying to keep warm against the

cold in the truck bed, contemplating the stars. Stay calm, the stars seemed to tell us, as if we were not calm; see how well we bide our time. Vibrating in concert with the truck where I was lying down watching some rushing clouds and anxious trees intermediate between us and the velvet night, I considered that this animated, dimly lit revelry in which the living were locked in a close embrace with the dead was a scene fit for a perfect Cinemascope film in which my dear angel, whom I imagined as being humorous and cheerful, would descend from the sky and reveal to me my life's and heart's secrets; however, the scene I had appropriated from one of Uncle Rıfkı's illustrated story lines failed to materialize. Thus, I was left alone with the North Star, the Big Dipper, and the symbol Π, counting the dark power poles and tree branches that flowed over us. Then it occurred to me that this was not a perfect moment after all, that something was missing. But as long as I had a new soul in my body, a new life before me, wads of money in my pocket, and these stars just out in the sky, what of it? I would seek out the missing element.

What was it that made one's life incomplete?

A missing leg, answered the green-eyed nurse who put some stitches on my knee. I was told not to resist. All right, will you marry me, then? There are no fractures or hairline cracks in the leg or the foot. All right, then, will you make love to me? A few horrible stitches on my forehead too. Tears of pain in my eyes, I knew what had been awry all along; I should have put it together seeing the ring on the ring finger of the attending nurse. She was probably betrothed to someone working in Germany. I was a new being, but not altogether new. It was in this condition that I left the hospital and the sleepy nurse.

I arrived at the New Light Hotel just as the summons to morning prayer was being called, and I asked the night clerk for the best room in the house. I masturbated looking at an old *Hürriyet* I found in a dusty closet in the room. It was a color print sup-

plement of the Sunday edition in which the proprietress of a
Nişantaşı restaurant in Istanbul had exposed parts of her anatomy
for the camera, as well as both her neutered cats and all the
furniture she had ordered from Milan. I fell asleep.

The town called Şirinyer where I stayed almost sixty hours,
thirty-three of which were spent sleeping at the New Light Hotel,
was as charming a place as its given name. 1. The barbershop: on
the counter sits a stick of OP brand shaving soap in an aluminum
wrap. 2. Youth Reading Room: they shuffle kings of hearts and
spades made of paper pulp, watching the Atatürk statue on the
square where distracted old men hang out, watching the passing
tractors and my slightly limping person, as well as the TV, which
runs constantly, keeping an eye out for women, soccer players,
murders, soaps, and kissing scenes. 3. At the tobacconist's with
the Marlboro sign: besides cigarettes, it has old cassettes of karate
and soft porno films, National Lottery and Sport Toto tickets,
pulp novels, rat poison, and a calendar on the wall with a smiling
beauty who reminds me of my Janan. 4. The restaurant: beans,
meatballs; edible. 5. Post Office: I phone home. Mother cannot
comprehend, cries. Şirinyer Coffeehouse: I sat down and once
more began reading with pleasure the short news item in *Hürriyet*
that I had been carrying on me about the happy traffic accident
(TWELVE DEAD!) which I had by now memorized, when a man in
his mid-thirties or early forties who seemed to be a cross between
a hired killer and an undercover cop approached me from behind
like a shadow; and having read for me the brand name of the
watch he pulled out of his pocket (Zenith), he versified:

> If wine excuses love in a mad poem,
> Does not death fit the same theorem?
> Drunk on the wine of hazard
> You are thirsty like a buzzard.

He did not wait for my response but went out of the café, leaving behind him a dense smell of OP brand shaving soap.

On my walks that always took me impatiently to the bus depot, I wondered why every nice little town must have its own merry little madman. Our friend with the penchant for wine and rhyme was present in neither of the two taverns in town where I had begun to feel the aforementioned intoxicating thirst as deeply as my thoughts of love for you, Janan. Somnolent drivers, fatigued buses, unshaven cabin attendants! Take me to that unknown realm where I want to go! Take me to death's door, unconscious and my forehead bleeding, so I may become someone else! That was my state of mind when I left the town called Şirinyer on the long back row of a dilapidated Maigrus bus, with a couple of stitches on my body and a dead man's fat wallet in my pocket.

Night! A long, very long and windy night. Dark villages and even darker sheepfolds, immortal trees, sorry service stations, empty restaurants, silent mountains, and anxious rabbits went past the dark mirror of my window. At times I would study a distant light flickering beneath the stars, and contemplating the sort of life I imagined being led moment to moment under that light, I would find a place in it for Janan and myself; and when the bus sped away from the flickering light, I wished I were under that roof instead of sitting in my uncontrollably vibrating seat. My eyes would sometimes regard the passengers on buses that we encountered at service stations, rest stops, crossroads where trees respectfully wait on each other, or on narrow bridges, and I would imagine that I saw Janan sitting among them; and totally taken over by my imagination, I would fantasize catching up with the other bus, boarding it, and taking Janan in my arms. But sometimes I felt so hopeless and so weary that I wished I were the man I saw through the half-closed curtains who was sitting at a table and smoking when our angry bus went by past midnight through the narrow streets of some secluded town.

But I still knew that I really wanted to be someplace else, in a time other than this, like that felicitous moment of being when one has not yet chosen between life and death, there among the dead who died in the heartrending eruption of chance . . . Before ascending to the seven spheres of heaven, trying to accustom my eyes to the obscure sight with pools of blood and shards of broken glass at the threshold of that realm from which there is no return, I might contemplate with pleasure whether to enter, or not. Should I turn back? Or proceed? What were mornings like in the nether world? What would it be like to abandon this journey altogether and lose oneself in that bottomless night? I would shiver thinking about the unique time in that realm where I might shed my being and perhaps unite with Janan, and I would feel in my legs and in my stitched forehead the urgency to achieve the unexpected happiness that would follow.

Ah, you who ride the night buses! My abject brethren! I know you too are seeking the hour of zero gravity. Ah, to be neither here nor there! To become someone else and roam the peaceful garden that exists between the two worlds! How well I know that the soccer fan in the leather jacket is not waiting for the game to start but anticipating the hour of hazard when bleeding copiously he becomes a blood-red hero. And I also know that the elderly woman who keeps taking something out of her plastic bag and stuffing it in her mouth is not in reality dying to reunite with her sisters and nieces but to reach the threshold of the nether world. The surveyor who has one eye on the road and the other on his dreams is not reckoning the cadastration of the town hall but calculating the point in the crossroads where all towns become history. And I am sure that the pasty-faced high school kid dozing in his seat up front is not dreaming of kissing his sweetheart but of the forceful impact when he kisses the windshield with passion and vehemence. Is it not the same rapture that besets us, after all? Whenever the driver slams on the brakes or the bus whips around in the wind, we open our eyes instantly to stare into the dark road, trying to figure out if the zero hour is upon us. No, not yet!

I spent eighty-nine nights in bus seats without once hearing the tolling of the blissful hour in my soul. There was one time when the bus came to a screeching halt and bumped into a poultry truck, but not even a single one of the bewildered chickens received a bloody nose let alone any of the drowsy passengers. Another night, the bus was skidding pleasurably on an ice-covered highway when I looked out of my frozen window and felt the radiance of coming face to face with God. I was about to discover the single element common to all existence, love, life, and time, but the prankish bus hung on the edge of the dark void, suspended.

I had read somewhere that luck is not blind, just illiterate. Luck, I mused, is a palliative for those who don't know probability and statistics. The rear exit was where I descended on earth, where I returned to life; the rear exit is where I meet the hurly-burly life in bus terminals: Hello there, roasted-seed vendors, cassette-tape peddlers, bingo captains, elderly fellows with suitcases, elderly dames with plastic bags, hello! So as not to leave the matter to luck, I looked for the least safe bus, chose the route with the most curves, and canvassed the personnel coffee shops for the driver who was the most sleep-deprived, for bus lines with names like SAFEWAY, TRUE SAFEWAY, EXPRESS SAFEWAY, FLYING SAFEWAY, GREASED LIGHTNING. Bus attendants poured bottles of cologne on my hands, but none had the fragrance of the face I was seeking; they brought around arrowroot biscuits on fake silver trays, but none tasted like those my mother served at tea. I ate domestic chocolates made without real cocoa, but my legs didn't get cramps like they used to when I was a kid. Sometimes the attendant offered all manner of candy and caramels in baskets, but among brands like Golden, Mabel, Fruito, I never came

across any of those Uncle Rıfkı liked, the ones called New Life
Caramels. I counted the miles in my sleep and dreamed when I
was awake. I scrunched into my seat, I shrank and shrank and
turned into a wrinkle, I wedged my legs into the seat, I dreamed
that I made love to my seatmate. When I awoke, I found his bald
pate on my shoulder, his pitiful hand in my lap. Every night I
initially played the part of the reserved neighbor to some hapless
passenger, then quite the fellow conversationalist, but by morning
we would be on such intimate terms that I was his brazen confidant. Cigarette? Where are you going? What's your line of work?
On one bus I was a junior traveling insurance salesman; on another, where it was freezingly cold, I claimed I was soon to marry
my cousin who was the love of my life. Behaving like someone
who watches UFOs, I divulged to a grandfatherly type that I was
anticipating an angel; another time I said my boss and I would
be happy to fix all your broken timepieces. Mine is a Movado,
said the elderly man with the false teeth; it never misses. While
the owner slept with his mouth open, I thought I heard the ticking of the watch that kept perfect time. What is time? An accident! What is life? Time! What is accident? A life, a new life!
Submitting to this simple logic, which I was surprised no one had
proposed before, I resolved to forego bus terminals, O Angel, and
go straight to the scenes of accidents.

I observed passengers who had been cruelly speared into the
front seats when their bus had heedlessly and treacherously
slammed into the back of a truck loaded with steel bars the tips
of which projected out. I saw a driver who in an effort to miss a
tabby cat had driven his clumsy bus into a ravine; his corpse was
so jammed in, it couldn't be pried out. I saw heads that had been
ripped to pieces, bodies that were rent, hands sundered; I saw
drivers who had tenderly taken the wheel into their guts, brains
that had exploded like heads of cabbage, bloody ears that still

wore earrings, eyeglasses both broken and intact, mirrors, florid bowels carefully laid out on newspapers, combs, squashed fruit, coins, broken teeth, baby bottles, shoes—all manner of matter and spirit that had been eagerly sacrificed to the moment of truth.

One cold spring morning I was tipped off by the traffic police and caught up with a pair of buses that had butted heads in the silence of the steppe. Already half an hour had passed since the moment of ardent and blissful collision that had tumultuously exploded, but the magic that makes life meaningful and bearable still hung in the air. I was standing between vehicles that belonged to the police and to the gendarmerie, studying the black tires of one of the buses that had turned over, when I caught the pleasant whiff of new life and death. My legs trembling and the stitches on my forehead smarting, I pressed forward with determination as if I had an appointment, making my way among the bewildered survivors in the misty dusk.

I climbed into the bus, the door handle of which was somewhat hard to reach, and I was going past all the upended seats, gratified to be stepping on eyeglasses, glassware, chains, and fruit that had succumbed to gravity and spilled on the ceiling, when it seemed that I remembered something. I used to be someone else once, and that someone used to desire to become me. I had dreamed of a life where time was blissfully concentrated and compressed and where colors flowed in my mind like waterfalls, hadn't I? The book I had left behind on my table came to my mind, and I imagined the book staring at the ceiling like the dead staring open-mouthed at the sky. I imagined my mother keeping the book on my table among all the things left over from my previous life which had been interrupted. I was imagining myself say, Look, Mom, what I am searching for among shards of glass, drops of blood, and the dead is the threshold of another kind of life, when I spied a wallet. Before expiring, a body had climbed over the seat and up toward the window, but it had come to rest at the point of equilibrium, and presented to full view the wallet in its back pocket.

I took the wallet and slipped it in my own pocket, but this was not what I had recalled only a moment ago and yet pretended not to remember. What was on my mind was the other bus; where I stood looking through the shattered glass and the cute little curtains that wafted gently in the windows, I now read the Marlboro-red and lethal blue lettering on the other bus that said SAFEST SAFEWAY.

I jumped out of one of the window frames in which the glass had been totally smashed and began to run, stepping on bloody shards of broken glass strewn between the bodies that the gendarmes had yet to carry away. I was not mistaken, the other bus was indeed the same SAFEST SAFEWAY that had safely carried me from a trifling city to an obscure town. I climbed into this old acquaintance and sat in the same seat where I had ridden six weeks ago, and I began to wait like a patient passenger whose trust in this world is optimistic. What was I waiting for? Perhaps for a wind, an appointed hour, or perhaps for a wayfarer. Twilight began to fade. I felt the presence of other living or dead souls who like me were ensconced in the seats, and I heard them calling out to some enigmatic spirits; they were gasping as if talking to beauties in their nightmares or else, in their dreams of paradise, they were having a spat with death. Then my attentive soul sensed something even more profound: I focused on the driver's station where everything had vanished except for the radio, where, along with the sighs and cries, there was music playing that was enveloped in a sweetly exquisite aura.

Silence fell for a brief moment, and I observed that the light was growing denser. In the mist I saw the blissful ghosts of the dead and the dying. You have gone as far as you may, thou wayfarer! But I think you can go farther! You are pleasantly swaying in anticipation, not knowing whether there is another door and another secret garden where life and death, meaning and motion, time and chance, light and happiness come together. Suddenly that same impatient desire rose once more from deeper depths and besieged my entire body, the desire to be both here and there. It seemed as if I heard several words, I shivered, and it was then, my beauty, that you came through the door, my Janan, clad in that same white dress you were wearing in the corridor at Taşkışla Hall where I saw you last. Your face was drenched in blood.

I did not ask you, "What are you doing here?" And you, Janan, neither did you ask me what I was doing here. We knew.

I took you by the hand and seated you next to me, in seat No. 38. And with the checkered handkerchief I'd got in Şirinyer I tenderly wiped the blood off your face and your forehead. Then, my sweetheart, I held your hand, and for a while we sat thus silently. It was getting lighter; the ambulances arrived, and on the dead driver's radio they were playing and singing our song.

5 WE CAUGHT THE FIRST BUS OUT OF TOWN SOON AFTER Janan had had four stitches on her forehead in Rumi's moribund Konya, where we walked along the low garden walls, somber buildings, and treeless avenues, conscious of the mechanical rise and fall of our feet on the pavement. I sort of remember the next three towns: one was the capital of chimney stacks, the other the capital of lentil soup, and the last, the capital city of bad taste. But after that, as we were driven from town to town, sleeping and waking on buses, everything blurred together. I saw walls where the plaster had crumbled off, where posters left over from the youth of antediluvian performers were still being displayed; I saw bridges that had been swept away by floods, and refugees from Afghanistan peddling Holy Korans no bigger than my thumb. I must have seen other things besides Janan's light brown hair falling on her shoulders, such as the multitudes at bus terminals, the purple mountains, glossy plastic billboards, frisky dogs playfully chasing our bus out of town, abject peddlers hawking their wares through the bus. At some obscure rest stop when Janan had lost hope of finding any clue for what she called her "investigations," she set up repasts on our laps with foodstuffs she bought from these peddlers, such as hard-boiled eggs, meat

pies, peeled cucumbers, and some no-name provincial soda pop. Then it was morning, then night, then a cloudy morning, then the bus changed gears, then a night darker than dark was upon us, and the video screen above the driver's seat radiated red-orange light the color of cheap lipstick, when Janan began to relate her story.

Janan's "relationship" (her word) with Mehmet had begun a year and a half ago. She had a vague apprehension of having perhaps seen him before in Taşkışla Hall milling about among students of architecture and engineering, but the first time she had actually noticed him was at a reception being held for a relative who had recently returned from Germany at a hotel in Taksim. Around midnight, she and her parents had gone down to the lobby, where the pale, tall, and slender man behind the reception desk had made an impression on her mind. "Perhaps because I couldn't figure out just where I had seen him before," Janan said, giving me an affectionate smile, but I knew it was not the case.

When school started in the fall, she had seen him again in the hallways in Taşkışla, and soon after they had "fallen in love." They took long walks together in the streets of Istanbul, went to the movies, frequented student canteens and cafés. "At the beginning we didn't talk too much about things," Janan said, using the voice she reserved for serious explanations. But it wasn't because Mehmet was shy or didn't like talking. The longer she knew him, the longer she shared her life with him, the more she observed how gregarious, tenacious, articulate, even aggressive he could be. "His silence came from sadness," she said one night, not looking at me but at the chase scene on the TV screen, and then she added, with the hint of a smile on her lips, "It came from grief." The police cars speeding on the screen that had been flying over each other and off bridges into rivers had now crashed together and tangled into a knot.

Janan had tried hard to untangle the knot of his grief and sorrow, and she had been successful to a certain degree in penetrating into the life that lay behind it. Mehmet had initially mentioned a previous life when he was someone else and lived in a mansion somewhere in some province. But as he grew bolder, he had said he had left that life behind him, that he desired a new life, and that his past meant nothing to him. He was once someone else, but then he had willed himself to become another person. Since Janan knew only his new self, he advised her to relate only to his present identity and leave his past alone. The terrors he had encountered on his quest were not part of his previous existence but part of the new life that he had once been seeking ardently. "That was the life . . ." Janan had said to me in some dingy bus terminal where we had been amicably, even playfully, arguing about which bus to take, sitting at a table over a can of ten-year-old food which she had managed to locate on the shelves of some mice-infested grocery in this shabby town, as well as the watch movement discovered in an old clock repair shop and the children's comics on the dusty shelves in the Sport Toto shop. ". . . That was the life he had encountered in the book."

It was the first time we had mentioned the book in the nineteen days after we ran into each other on the crashed bus. Janan told me that getting Mehmet to discuss the book was as difficult as getting him to talk about the reasons for his melancholy and the life he had left behind him. There had been times when they had been dejectedly walking the streets of Istanbul, or having tea at some café on the Bosphorus, or studying together, when she had demanded the book from him, asking him for that magical object, but he would refuse her in no uncertain terms, telling her that it was not right for a girl like Janan even to imagine the land of perdition, heartbreak, and bloodshed because in that twilight land illuminated by the book, Death, Love, and Terror wandered like hapless ghosts in the guise of downtrodden, heartbroken men with frozen faces who packed guns.

It was through her perseverance and protestations of anxiety that Janan had been able to beguile Mehmet, even if only modestly. "Perhaps he wanted me to read the book and rescue him from its enchantment and its virulence," she said. "After all, I was sure by then that he loved me." Then, while our bus waited patiently at a railroad crossing for a train that seemed to be in no hurry to go by, "Or perhaps," she added, "he unconsciously wished that we could enter together into that life which was still viable in some corner of his mind." Clattering like the trains whose locomotives screamed through my old neighborhood, a string of boxcars loaded with wheat, machinery, and broken glass went by our bus window, one after the other, like illegal and chastened ghosts from another country.

Janan and I said little about the influence that the book exerted on us. The influence was so powerful, so indisputable, and so right that talking about it would turn the book's content into a kind of prattling, idle chatter. The book was something whose necessity was so indisputable in both our lives that it existed palpably between us, basic like sunlight and water. We had set out on the road in response to the light that surged from its pages into our faces, and we attempted to progress on this road by virtue of our instincts, but without wishing to know for sure where it was that we were headed.

Even so, we often disputed long and hard over which bus to take. There was an instance when the metallic voice announced the time of departure and the destination on the loudspeaker in the passengers' lounge (which was too much of a cavernous hanger for a town that small), inspiring in Janan such a longing to go there that, despite my opposition, we had complied with her desire. Another time we followed a young man carrying a plastic suitcase to the bus lanes, flanked by his teary-eyed mother and his cigarette-puffing father, just because the young man's size and his slight stoop reminded her of Mehmet, and we boarded his bus, where a sign informed us that Turkish Airlines was the bus line's main competition, only to observe our young man get off three towns and two dirty rivers later and make his way to some barracks surrounded by a barbed-wire stockade and observation posts, where the lettering on the ramparts proclaimed that HAPPINESS IS BEING A TURK. We took many and sundry buses that went to the very heart of the steppes, sometimes just because Janan took a fancy to some felt-green and brick-red bus, or else, look! how the tail of the R in GREASED LIGHTNING on the side of the bus seems to have become tapered from the vibrations and speed, zigzagging like a bolt of lightning. When Janan's investigations proved inconclusive in dirty terminals and sleepy marketplaces in the dusty towns where we arrived, I would question her as to why and wherefore we were traveling; and reminding her that the money I had lifted from the pockets of dead passengers was dwindling, I would pretend that I was trying to comprehend the illogical logic of our investigations.

Janan was not at all surprised when I told her about looking out of the window in the classroom in Taşkışla Hall and seeing Mehmet get shot. According to her, life was full of distinct, even intentional, convergences that some obtuse fools called "coincidences." Shortly after Mehmet was shot, Janan had sensed that something extraordinary had taken place from the movements of the fellow who ran the hamburger stand across the street, and remembering she had heard gunshots, she intuited all that had transpired and run to Mehmet, who lay wounded. If it were up to some others, they might consider it coincidental that there was a cab immediately on the spot where Mehmet had been shot, and the fact that they were taken to the Kasımpaşa Naval Hospital was merely contingent on the fact that the cabby had recently done his military service in the navy. The wound in Mehmet's shoulder was not too serious, and he was to be discharged in a

day or two, but when Janan arrived at the hospital the next morning, she found that he had taken off and vanished.

"I went to the hotel, gave Taşkışla Hall a quick once-over,
stopped at his favorite haunts, then waited at home for his phone
call, although I knew it was all in vain," she said with a cool clarity
that left me full of admiration. "But I realized he had gone back
there, to that realm; he had long since returned to the book."

I was her "traveling companion" on her journey to that realm;
we were to "support" each other in rediscovering that place. It
was not wrong to think that in our quest for the new life two
heads were "better" than one. We were not merely traveling companions but soulmates; we were each other's unconditional support; we were as creative as Marie and Ali who started a campfire
with a pair of eyeglasses; and so it was that for weeks we sat next
to each other on night buses, pressing our bodies together.

Some nights, long after the second film on the VCR came to
an end resounding with the high-spirited noises of gunshots and
exploding helicopters, long after we tired and seedy passengers
departed for the land of dreams, our breaths resigned to death on
our restless journey as we sat over jogging wheels, I would be
shaken awake by a ditch, or a sudden braking, and I would stare
long and hard at Janan sleeping like a baby next to the window,
her head resting on the short curtains she rolled together to make
a pillow, her light brown hair making a sweet mound on this
pillow that fell to her shoulders. Her long beautiful arms sometimes reached toward my eager knees like a pair of fragile branches
that were parallel; sometimes one arm steadied the hand that held
her head like a second pillow, the other hand gracefully holding
the elbow of the steadying arm. When I looked into her face I
saw there a pain that creased her brow, sometimes her light brown
eyebrows were so furrowed that question marks that alarmed me
appeared in the middle of her forehead. Then I'd see a radiance

in her pale complexion, and I would dream of a velvet paradise where roses were blooming and squirrels gamboling in the sunset, calling me to the wondrous country where her cheekbone met her slender throat, or if her head was bent forward, on the inaccessible spot where her hair fell on the nape of her neck. I would behold that golden realm in her face and, if she had managed to smile even just a little in her sleep, on her lips that were so very full and so very pale, and sometimes lightly chapped because she so often bit those lips, and I would say to myself: I was not taught it at school, and I did not read it in any book, but how sweet it is, O Angel, to watch the beloved sleep!

We did talk about the angel and also about Death who seemed to be the angel's dignified and ponderous stepbrother, but we did it through words that were fragile and flimsy like the friable things Janan bargained for at market stalls, the corner hardware, or sleepy dry-goods stores and, after playing with them for a bit, left behind at terminal cafés or on bus seats. Death was everywhere, especially There because it radiated out from That Place. We were looking for clues to get us There and find Mehmet, but we left tracks behind us. We had learned all this from the book—just as we had learned about unique moments of accident, the threshold where the other world was visible, about cinema vestibules, New Life Caramels, assassins who might kill Mehmet and maybe even us, about hotel marquees where my steps were arrested, about prolonged silences, about nights and badly lit restaurants. I must put it like this: After all that was said and done, we boarded some bus once again; after all that was said and done, we set out once more on the road; sometimes even before night fell, the bus attendant would be checking the tickets, the passengers making acquaintances, and the children and the more anxious passengers watching the smooth asphalt mountain road as if watching the video screen, when a sudden gleam would appear in Janan's eyes and she would begin to speak.

"When I was young, sometimes I would get up in the middle of the night," she said on one occasion. "I would part the curtains and look outside. There would be a man walking in the street, a drunk, a hunchback, a fat man, the night watchman. Always a man . . . I was afraid, and I liked my bed, but I wished I were out there too."

Later that night, she said, "I learned about boys playing hide-and-seek with my brother's friends at our summer place. Or in middle school, watching them look at something they took out of their desks. Or when I was much younger, when we were right in the middle of the game and they suddenly had to pee, the way they wiggled their legs."

And later still, "I was nine years old. I fell down at the seashore and wounded my knee. My mother shrieked and cried. We went to see the hotel doctor. What a pretty girl you are, he said, what a sweet girl. He washed my wound with peroxide, saying, what a smart girl. The way he looked at my hair, I had an idea the doctor liked looking at me. He had enchanted eyes that regarded me from another world. His lids were slightly heavy, making him appear somewhat somnolent perhaps, but still, he saw me fully and everything around me."

On another night, we were talking again of the angel. "The angel's eyes are everywhere," she said. "On everything, always present. Yet, wretched humans that we are, we still suffer from the absence of those eyes. Is it because we are forgetful? Because our will is slack? Or because we cannot love life? I know that I will look out the bus window some day, or some night on the road, going from town to town, and my eyes will meet the eyes of the angel. I must learn how to look, so that I may see. I have faith in buses. And I also have faith in the angel . . . sometimes . . . no, always. Yes, always. Well, sometimes.

"The angel I am looking for comes out of the book. There the angel seemed to be someone else's idea, like a guest of some sort, but still I identified with him. I am sure that the moment I see him, life's mystery will become manifested to me. I felt his presence at the sites of accidents and also riding on the bus. Everything that Mehmet has said has come true. Wherever Mehmet goes, Death radiates brilliantly around him, you know? Perhaps it is so because he carries the book inside him. But I have also heard accident victims mention the angel when they knew absolutely nothing about the book or the new life. I am on his trail. I am putting together the signs he has left behind.

"One rainy night, Mehmet told me the people who want to kill him were on the move. They could be anywhere at all, they could even be listening to us this very minute. Don't take this the wrong way, but you yourself could be one of them. Many times one does exactly the opposite of what one thinks, or thinks one is doing. You are on the road to that realm, but you are turning inwards. You think you are reading the book, yet you are rewriting it. When you imagine you are helping, you inflict harm. Most people want neither a new life nor a new world. So they kill the book's author."

This was how Janan first brought up the writer, or the old man to whom she referred to as the "author," talking to me in a language that was none too clear but spoken in a style that excited me, not because of the content but because of the mysterious quality of what she said. She was sitting in one of the front-row seats on a fairly new bus, her eyes were fixed on the luminescent white median line on the asphalt road; but, for some odd reason, what was absent in the purple night were the oncoming headlights belonging to other buses, trucks, and cars.

"I know that when Mehmet and the old writer talked, they understood everything in each other's eyes. Mehmet had been looking for him and had looked him up. When they met, they didn't talk very much, they were quiet; they argued a little and then fell silent. The old man had either written the book when he was young or else he called the time he'd written it his youth. A young man's book, he had said sadly. Later, 'they' had terrorized the old man and made him renounce what he'd written with his own hand, looking into his own soul. Nothing surprising about that. Not even about 'their' killing him in the end . . . Nor about it being Mehmet's turn now that the old man is dead . . . But we will find Mehmet before the killers do . . . What is significant is this: There are others who have read the book and who believe in it. I have met them walking around towns, bus terminals, shops; I know them, I recognize them from their eyes. The faces of those who have read the book and have faith in it are distinct; they all have the same melancholy desire in their eyes, as you too will understand some day, maybe you already do. If you comprehend the mystery, and if you are making progress toward it, Life is awesome."

If we were in some depressing, fly-infested restaurant at a desolate rest stop when Janan was telling me all this, we would be smoking cigarettes with the complimentary tea served by some sleepy busboy, and spooning up the strawberry compote that had a plastic taste. If we were vibrating in the front seats of a ramshackle bus, my eyes would be fixed on Janan's full lips and generous mouth, but her eyes were always fixed on the uneven headlights of trucks that went by occasionally. If we were in a jam-packed bus terminal among the multitudes carrying plastic bags, cardboard suitcases, and gunnysacks, Janan would suddenly cut short what she was saying and, oops! she'd bolt from the table and disappear, leaving me stone-cold and alone in the crush of people.

Sometimes I would count the minutes for hours on end, only to find her in a second-hand shop in the back alley of some town where we were waiting to catch a bus; she would be anxiously studying a broken flatiron or one of those old coal-burning stoves that are no longer made. Sometimes she'd turn to me with a

mysterious smile on her face and an odd provincial newspaper in
her hand, and she would read to me the municipal ordinance
passed to prevent livestock from using the main street on their
way home in the evening, or the notice put in by the Crescent
Gas dealership, advertising the innovations in the local store
brought in fresh from Istanbul. Many a time I found her chatting
away intimately with some people in the crowd; she'd be in deep
conversation with some elderly woman wearing a kerchief, or re-
peatedly kissing the little duck-faced girl on her lap, or expending
her surprising knowledge concerning bus lines and terminals to
help out ill-willed strangers who reeked of OP shaving soap. When
I came up to her hesitantly and all out of breath, she would act
as if we were out on the road just to solve other people's difficulties. "This dear woman was to meet her son here after he got
discharged from the army," she would inform me, "but he wasn't
on the bus from Van." We inquired about bus schedules on behalf of other people, we exchanged their tickets for them, we
calmed down their crying children, we kept an eye on their cases
and bundles when they went to the toilet. "May God reward you,"
a plump older woman with gold teeth had once said, and then
turning to me, she had raised her eyebrow and added, "You do
know your wife is awfully pretty, don't you?"

Once the lights and the luminous video screen had been turned
off after midnight, and all movement on the bus ceased other
than the smoke that rose quivering from the cigarettes of the
most melancholic and wakeful of the passengers, our bodies gradually moved together on our gently swaying seats. I felt your hair
on my face, Janan, your slender hands on my knees and, on my
neck, your breath that smelled of slumber. The tires spun around
and the diesel engine kept repeating its constant moan, and time
pervaded the space between us like a dark, warm, and heavy liq-

uid. A nascent sensitivity to this primordial time in the bones of our benumbed, lethargic, stiffened legs stirred our flesh with desire.

Sometimes, when my arm burst into flames at the very touch of her arm, sometimes waiting all night for her head to fall on my shoulder (please God let it!), sometimes going rigid in my seat for fear of disturbing the strands of her hair on my throat, I counted her breaths reverently and with awe, wondering about the meaning of some sorrow fleeting by on her brow. When her face, pale in a sudden flash of light, was startled awake under my gaze, how thrilled I was that she did not glance out the window in her initial confusion to see where she was, but looking into my reassuring eyes, she smiled. I kept vigil all the night long, making sure her head did not lean against the icy window and get chilled. I took off the maroon jacket I bought in Erzinjan and laid it over her knees. When the driver careened exuberantly down mountain roads, I guarded her contorted sleeping form, lest she be thrown out of the seat and get hurt. Sometimes, though, somewhere in the thick of my vigil, listening to engine noises, passengers' sighs and yearnings for death, my eyes focused on some spot between the smooth skin of her neck and the convolutions of her tender ears, I lost myself in a childhood reverie of a boat ride or a snowball fight which then melted into dreams of the marital bliss that would one day be our life.

And then, hours later, when I was bidden awake by a prankish ray of sunlight that was as cold and refracted as cut glass, I realized that the lavender-scented sultry garden cradling my head had all along been her neck; and remaining there quietly a while longer between sleep and wakefulness, I blinked my greetings to the resplendent morning outside, the mauve mountains and incipient signs of the new life, only to behold with grief how very remote from me were her eyes.

"Love," she began saying one evening like some adept voice-over narrator, blowing fire into the word that stuck in my throat like a hot coal, "points the way, empties you of the stuff of life, carries you at last to the mystery of creation. I understand it now. We are on the way There.

"The moment I saw Mehmet," she went on, oblivious to Clint Eastwood staring at her from the cover of some old magazine left on a table in a bus terminal somewhere, "I knew my whole life would change. Before I saw him, I had a life, but after I knew him, my life was altered. It was as if everything around me had changed its color and shape—human beings, beds, lamps, ash-trays, streets, clouds, chimneys, everything but everything. It was with awe and wonder that I set out to discover this new world. I bought the book thinking I no longer needed books and fictions. To really know the world that opened to me, I had to do the work of looking, of seeing each and every thing with my own eyes. But once I read the book itself, I apprehended instantly what lay be-hind everything that I must see. I encouraged Mehmet, who had returned disconsolate from the country where he'd gone in search of the new life, and I convinced him that together we'd make it there. Back in those days, we read the book over and over again, but each time with new eyes. Sometimes we spent weeks on a passage, other times everything was clear as a bell the instant we read it. We went to the movies, read other books and newspapers, walked through the streets. The times when the book was on our minds, when we knew it by heart, the streets in Istanbul glowed with such an extraordinary luminescence that the city belonged to us. We had a way of knowing that the old man we saw on a street corner leaning on his cane planned to idle away his time at the coffeehouse until it was time to pick up his grandchild after school. We knew that the mare pulling the last cart of the three carts that went by was the mother of the two skinny horses that pulled the first two. We knew the reason why more men were now wearing blue socks; we knew how to decipher train timetables read upside down, or that the suitcase the fat and sweaty man who boarded the bus carried was full of underwear taken from the house he'd just robbed. We'd go in a café to read the book again and then discuss it for hours. It was love. Sometimes I thought love was the only way of apprehending a distant world, like in the movies, and being transported there.

"But then," she had said one rainy night without taking her eyes off the kissing scene on the video screen, "there were things I knew nothing about, things that I would never know." And after four or five slippery miles when the kissing scene was replaced by one where a bus which looked like ours was traveling across a charming landscape that was so different, she had added, "Now we are going to that place that is unknown to us."

When the clothes we were wearing became stiff with dirt and dust, and the history of all the peoples who had stirred up the dust on this terrain since the days of the Crusaders had settled layer after layer on our skin, we would go shopping at random in a random town before we changed buses. Janan would buy herself some of those long poplin skirts that made her look like some well-meaning provincial school teacher, and I would get the sort of shirts worn by pale imitations of former selves. Later if we managed to look past the provincial administration building, the statue of Atatürk, the Arçelik appliance dealership, the pharmacy and the mosque, noticing the delicate white streak left behind by some jet in the crystal-blue sky, seen beyond the sailcloth banners of the Koran school and a circumcision party that was approaching, we would stop where we were, carrying in our hands our paper-wrapped packages and plastic bags, and for a moment we would look up at the sky with ardor before asking some faded bureaucrat wearing a faded tie for directions to the local public bath.

Since the baths were reserved for women in the mornings, I would while away the time in the streets and in coffeehouses;

and when I went past the town hotel, I dreamed of telling Janan that we needed to spend at least one night on solid ground, in a hotel, for instance, instead of riding the tires again and sleeping on the bus. And some evenings when I managed to tell her what I had been dreaming of, Janan would show me the fruits of the investigations she conducted in the afternoon while I was in the baths: bound volumes of old photo romance magazines, children's comics which were even older, samples of bubblegum I didn't remember ever chewing, and a hairpin the significance of which was not immediately apparent. "I'll tell you on the bus," she would say, giving me that special smile that appeared on her face when the film on the VCR was one she had already seen.

One night when, instead of the tawdry video film that was usually shown on our bus, a serious and sober announcer had appeared on the TV screen to give some death notices, Janan had said, "I am making my way to Mehmet's other life, yet he was not Mehmet but someone else in that other life." Querulous red neon lights reflected on her face as we sped by a filling station.

"Mehmet didn't divulge much else about the person he used to be, other than mentioning his sisters, a mansion, a mulberry tree, and that he used to have another name and identity. Once he told me how in his childhood he liked reading the periodical called *Children's Weekly*. Did you ever read *Children's Weekly?*" Her slender fingers ran over the yellowing editions of bound periodicals stuck in the space between our legs and the ashtray, and watching me look through the pages without looking at them herself, she said, "The reason why I collect these is because Mehmet claimed that everybody would eventually return to a place within these pages. These pages constitute his childhood. They are what make up the book. Do you understand?" I did not fully understand, and sometimes I did not understand at all, but Janan addressed me in such a way that I felt I did indeed understand. "Like you," Janan said, "Mehmet too read the book and apprehended that his whole life would change; and he pushed his apprehension all the way to its logical end. He had been studying medicine, but he quit it in order to devote all his time to the life in the book. He understood that he must abandon his past totally if he was to become a totally new being. So he cut off all relations with his father and his family . . . But it was not easy to become free of them. He told me that he had actually achieved the freedom to move toward his new life by virtue of a traffic accident. True: accidents are departures, and departures are accidents. The angel becomes visible at the magical moment of departure, and it is then that we perceive the real meaning of the turmoil called life. Only then can we ever go back home."

Hearing these words, I would catch myself dreaming of the mother I had left behind, my room, my things, my bed; and feeling insidiously rational and commensurably guilty, I would construct fantasies of joining together what was in my dreams with Janan's dreams of the new life.

6 THE TV SET WAS ALWAYS PLACED SOMEWHERE ABOVE the driver's seat, and some evenings we did not speak but kept our eyes on the screen. Since we had not read the papers for months, the TV—which would be bedecked with boxes, doilies, velvet drapes, varnished woodwork, amulets, evil-eye beads, decals, ornaments, and elevated to the status of a present-day altar—was the only window, other than the bus windows, we had on the world. We watched karate films in which nimble heroes bounce around kicking in simultaneously the faces of hundreds of derelicts, and their slow-motion domestic imitations which are made using clumsy actors. We also saw American films like the one where a smart and engaging black hero puts one over on the police as well as on the mobsters, or aviation films in which good-looking young men perform daredevil acrobatics with their flying machines, and horror films where pretty young girls are scared stiff by vampires and ghosts. In domestic films, which were mostly about kindly affluent people who just could not manage to find suitable and sincere husbands for their ladylike daughters, all heroes, no matter whether male or female, seemed to have spent time being singers at some point of their lives, and they continuously misunderstood each other so thoroughly that these mis-

understandings eventually turned into a kind of understanding. We had become so used to seeing the same faces and bodies in stereotypic roles as the patient postman, the cruel rapist, the kindhearted but plain-looking sister, the bass-voiced judge, the lamebrain, or the intelligent matron, that when we saw at a rest stop the kindhearted sister sitting with the cruel rapist and calmly having rice and red lentil soup along with the rest of the sleepy night passengers in the MEMORY LANE RESTAURANT where the walls were hung with pictures of mosques, Atatürk, wrestlers, and movie stars, we were convinced we were being tricked. While Janan recalled one by one which of the famous actresses in the photographs on the walls had played victims assaulted by the rapist in the films we had seen, I remember absentmindedly regarding the other clients in the gaudy restaurant, thinking we were all passengers on an uncanny ship having soup in the bright and chilly dining room and sailing toward death.

We saw so many fight scenes on the screen, so many broken windows, glasses, doors, so many cars and planes that disappeared from sight and went up in flames, so many houses, armies, happy families, bad guys, love letters, skyscrapers, treasures that were swallowed up in raging infernos. We saw all the blood that spurted out of wounds, faces, slashed throats, and viewed endless chase scenes where hundreds and thousands of cars tore after each other, negotiating curves with great speed and then blissfully crashing into each other. We watched tens of thousands of desperadoes, male and female, foreign and domestic, with mustache and without mustache, who fired at each other without respite. "I didn't think the guy would be so easily duped," Janan would say after one videotape came to a stop and before the next one appeared on the screen. And after the second video ended and gave way to black stains on the blank screen, she would add, "Still, life is beautiful if you are on the road to somewhere." Or, "I don't believe any of it, I am not taken in, but I still love it." Or, the

happy ending in the movie lingering on her face, she would murmur between sleep and wakefulness, "I will dream of connubial
bliss."

At the end of the third month of our journeys, Janan and I
must have seen more than a thousand kissing scenes. With each
kiss, silence fell on the seats, no matter what small town or remote
city the bus was destined for, no matter who the passengers were,
be they the sort who travel with baskets full of eggs or bureaucrats
carrying briefcases; I would become aware of Janan's hands on her
knees or her lap, and for a moment I yearned to do something
significant that was profoundly forceful and tough. I even succeeded one rainy summer's eve in doing something I was not
totally aware that I wanted to do, or something close to it.

The darkened bus was half full; we were sitting somewhere in
the middle; and on the video screen it was raining in a tropical
scene that was very distant and foreign. I had instinctively brought
my face closer to the window, thereby closer to Janan, and I noticed it was raining outside. My Janan was smiling at me when I
kissed her on the lips as they do in the movies and on TV, or as
I imagined they did; I kissed her as she struggled, O Angel, with
all my might, desire, and fury, drawing blood.

"No, my dear, no!" she said to me. "You look so like him but
you are not him. He is somewhere else."

Was the pink glow on her face a reflection of the most remote,
the most fly-spotted, the most accursed of Turkish Petrol neon
signs? Or of an incredible dawn breaking in the nether world?
There was blood on the girl's lips, books tell us concerning situations like this, and the heroes in the movies respond by turning
the tables over, breaking windows, and smashing their cars into
walls. I anticipated the taste of the kiss on my lips, but I was
confounded. It was perhaps a creative thought that came to my
mind: I am not here, I told myself; if I am not here, what difference does it make? But then the bus began vibrating with renewed

ardor and I felt more alive than ever. The agony between my legs grew more acute, making me yearn to strain, explode, and then abate. Then the yearning must have gone even deeper; it must have become the whole world, a new world. I anticipated it without knowing what would happen; I was waiting, my eyes moist, my body sweating: I was hankering for something without knowing what it was, when everything blissfully exploded, not too fast, not too slowly, and then abated and dissolved.

We first heard that magnificent pandemonium and then the moment of peaceful silence that follows an accident. I realized the TV set too had exploded into pieces along with the driver; and when the cries and moans commenced, I took Janan by the hand and led her safely and skillfully down to the face of the earth.

Standing in the pouring rain, I realized the bus had not sustained total damage. There were two or three dead besides our driver. But the other bus, HASTY SPEEDWAY, had folded in half over its dead driver's body and rolled into a muddy field, and it was teeming with the dead and the dying. As if stepping down into the center of life, we descended into the cornfield where the bus had rolled, and we approached it feeling enchanted.

When we drew near, we saw a girl who was struggling to get out a window that had burst open; she was working her way out feet first; her blue jeans were covered in blood. An arm still reached into the bus where she was holding someone's hand—we craned our heads in to see that the hand belonged to a young man who was too exhausted to move. The girl in the blue jeans freed herself with our help, but not for a moment did she ever let go his hand. She then bent over the hand and kept on tugging at it, struggling to pull out the young man. But we could see that he was wedged in between chrome and painted metal that had been squashed together like cardboard. He was upside down, looking at us and the dark and rainy creation outside when he died.

Rain washed the blood down her long hair, her eyes and her face. She seemed to be about our age. Her face, which had been invigorated by the rain, carried a childlike expression rather than the look of someone who had come face to face with death. Wet young woman, we were so sorry for you. In the light provided by our bus, she regarded for a moment the dead young man sitting in his seat.

"My father . . ." she said. "Father will be furious now." She let go of the dead man's hand, then she took Janan's face between her two hands, and cradling Janan's face as if she were an innocent sister she'd known for hundreds of years, "Angel," she said, "I found you at last, finally here, after all the journeys in the rain." Her blood-streaked sweet face was turned toward Janan, glowing with admiration, longing, and bliss. "The gaze that always fol-lowed me, which seemed to appear in the most unlikely places only to disappear, and which made itself sought all the more for disappearing, was all along your gaze," she said. "You know how we set out on the road by bus and traveled from town to town, reading the book again and again, just to meet your gaze, Angel, just to gaze back into your eyes."

Janan smiled lightly, a little surprised, a little uncertain, but pleased and saddened by the hidden geometry in the girl's mis-apprehension.

"Keep smiling at me," said the dying girl in the blue jeans. (I had fathomed, O Angel, she was meant to die.) "Smile at me so that I may see in your face for once the radiance of that other world; it reminds me of the warmth in the bakery on a snowy day where I stopped by after school with my satchel in my hand and got a sesame seed bun; it reminds me of the joy of leaping from the jetty into the sea on a hot summer day. Your smile reminds me of my first kiss, my first embrace, the walnut tree I climbed by myself all the way to the top, the summer's eve when I tran-scended myself, the night I was blissfully drunk, the feeling of being under my quilt, the eyes of the beautiful boy who looked at me with love. All these memories exist in that other realm where I too long to be. Help me to get there, help me so that I may blissfully accept myself dwindling with each breath I take."

Janan smiled at her sweetly.

"Ah, you Angels!" the girl said, standing in the cornfield that resounded with cries of death and memory. "How terrifying you are! How pitiless, and yet how beautiful! While every word, every object, every memory gradually drains us and turns us into dust, everything touched by you and your inexhaustible radiance tranquilly remains outside of time. So, ever since my ill-fated lover and I read the book, we have long sought your gaze out of bus windows. I now see that it is your gaze, Angel, that is the unique moment that the book had promised, this moment of transition between the two realms; now that I am neither here nor there, I understand what is meant by departure; and how happy I am to comprehend the meaning of peace, death, and time. Keep smiling at me, Angel, smile."

I could not remember for a time what happened next. What befell me was something like when you lose your head at the end of a pleasant bout of drunkenness, and in the morning you say, "And at that point the film broke." I remember it was the sound that went off first, and I could almost see how Janan and the girl were gazing at each other. It must be that the image went off as well as the sound because what I saw next failed to become part of my recollections, and it evaporated without being recorded by any memory trace.

I vaguely remember the girl in blue jeans mentioning something about water, but I cannot recall how we crossed the cornfield to arrive at a river bank, or if in fact it was a river or a muddy stream, and I couldn't tell the source of blue light in which I can see the drops of rain falling on a body of water and making concentric circles.

I saw the girl in blue jeans a while later again taking Janan's face between her hands. She was whispering something to Janan, but I could not hear, or the words that were being whispered as if in a dream did not reach me. Feeling vaguely guilty, I thought I should leave the two of them alone. I took a couple of steps on the river bank, but my feet were mired in the marshland mud, and a team of frogs frightened by my unsteady steps jumped with a "plop" into the water. A crumpled cigarette pack slowly sailed toward me; it was a Maltepe pack, being swayed now and then by the tiny raindrops that hit it on either side; then, confidently proud, it ostentatiously proceeded on to the land of uncertainty. There was nothing else clearly visible in my obscure field of vision aside from the cigarette pack and the shadows of Janan and the girl I thought I could see moving. Mom, Mom, I kissed her and I saw myself die, I was saying to myself when I heard Janan call.

"Help me," she said. "I want to wash her face to keep her father from seeing the blood."

I stood behind her and held up the girl. Her shoulders were fragile, her armpits nice and warm. I watched my fill of the motherly care and grace in Janan's gestures, washing the girl's face, scooping water by the handful from the pool where I had seen the cigarette pack sail, tenderly cleaning the wound on her forehead; but I had a sense that the girl's bleeding would not stop. The girl said that when she was little, this was how her grandmother bathed her; she used to be afraid of water once, but now that she was older she liked it, yet she was dying.

"I have things to tell you before I die," she said. "Help me to the bus."

There was now an irresolute crowd, like those seen at the end of a wild and exhausting night of festivities, milling around the bus that had turned over and folded on itself. A couple of people were slowly moving about without any apparent aim, perhaps they were moving dead bodies like so much baggage. A woman carrying a plastic bag had opened her umbrella and stood waiting as if for another bus. The passengers on our killer bus, as well as some of the passengers on the bus that had been ravaged, were trying to pull out into the rain some of the living who had been trapped among the baggage and the corpses in the mangled bus. The hand that the girl who was soon to die had held was still there just as she had left it.

The girl seemed to approach the bus not out of sorrow but more out of a sense of duty and necessity. "He was my boyfriend," she said. "I was the one who read the book first, and I was spellbound, and scared. It was a mistake giving him the book to read. He too was spellbound, but that was not sufficient for him; he wanted to go to that land. I kept telling him it was only a book, but he would not be persuaded. I loved him. So we embarked on the road, traveling from town to town, touching life's appearances, looking for what is hidden under its colors, searching for reality but not finding it. When we began having fights, I left him to his investigations and returned home to my parents and waited. My beloved returned to me at last, but he had become someone else. He told me the book had led astray too many people, taken too many unlucky persons off the course of their lives, and it was the source of too many evils. Now he had sworn an oath to avenge himself on the book for being the cause of much disappointment and so many broken lives. I told him the book was innocent, explaining to him that there were a great many books much like it. I told him what was important is your own perception, what you read into it, but I couldn't make him listen. He had already been stricken by the vengeful rage that besets unfortunates who have been deceived. He brought up the subject of Doctor Fine, touching on his struggle against the book, against foreign cultures that annihilate us, against the newfangled stuff that comes from the West, and his all-out battle against printed matter. He mentioned all manner of timepieces, and antique objects, canary

cages, hand grinders, windlasses. I did not understand any of it,
but I loved him. He was beset with a deep resentment, but he was
still the life of my life. That was why I was following him to the
town called Güdül where he said there was a secret convention being held by dealers united under the cause of 'our goals.' His
henchmen were supposed to locate us and convey us to Doctor
Fine, but now you have to go there in our stead. Stop the betrayal
of life and the book. Doctor Fine is expecting us—two young
cookstove dealers who have committed themselves to the struggle. Our identification papers are in my boyfriend's breast pocket.
The man who comes to get us will smell of OP shaving soap."

Her face was again streaked with blood; she kissed and caressed
the hand she was holding, and she began to weep. Janan took her
by the shoulders.

"I too am to blame," said the girl. "I don't deserve your love.
I was persuaded by my lover to follow him, I betrayed the book.
He had to die without getting to see you because he was more
to blame. My father will be very angry, but I am happy I am dying
in your arms."

Janan assured her she would not die. Yet we were willing to
believe in the reality of her death, given that the dying never
disclosed their impending demise in all the movies that we had
seen. In her role as the angel, Janan joined the girl's hand with
the dead young man's as in those films, then the girl died, hand
in hand with her lover.

Janan drew near to the dead young man who was regarding the
world upside down and stuck her head into the bus where the
window had been smashed. She looked through his pockets and
then emerged into the rain with a pleased smile on her face,
holding up our new identification papers.

How I loved seeing Janan's elated smile! I could see the two
dark triangles on either corner of her full lips where they softly
met her beautiful teeth. The two darling triangles that formed in

the corners of her mouth when she laughed! She had kissed me once, and I had kissed her once; now I yearned for us to kiss once more standing in the rain, but she took a small step away from me.

"In our new life together, your name is Ali Kara," she said, reading the identification cards in her hand, "and mine is Efsun Kara. We even have a marriage certificate." Then, using the instructive tones of an affectionate and sympathetic teacher of English, she added, smiling, "Mr. and Mrs. Kara are on their way to a dealers' convention in the town of Güdül."

7 AFTER A PERIOD OF ENDLESS SUMMER RAINS, TWO DIF-
ferent towns, and three buses, we arrived in the town
called Güdül. We had just left the muddy terminal and were
approaching the narrow sidewalks in the shopping district when
I looked up to the sky and saw something odd, a cloth banner
summoning children to summer Koran school. In the window of
the State Monopolies and Sport Toto dealer, placed between
gaudy bottles of liqueurs there were three stuffed rats smiling with
their teeth bared. The photographs that had been posted on the
door of the pharmacy looked like the kind mourners wear on their
lapels at funerals occasioned by political assassinations, showing
the dates of birth and death of the deceased below faces that
reminded Janan of the proper upper-class characters in the old
domestic films. We went in a store and bought a plastic suitcase
and nylon shirts, hoping to pass ourselves off as two proper young
dealers. The chestnut trees along the sidewalks that took us up
to the hotel had been planted in surprisingly even rows. Janan
read the sign under one of the trees advertising *"Circumcisions
performed the good old way, not by laser,"* and she said: "They are
expecting us." I kept the papers of the deceased Ali and Efsun
Kara ready in my pocket, but the slightly built hotel clerk with

the Hitler mustache gave only a casual glance at the marriage certificate.

"Are you here for the dealers' convention?" he said. "They're all at the high school building for the opening session. Any other luggage besides this case?"

"Our luggage burned in the fire on a bus," I said, "so did the other passengers. Where is this high school?"

"Buses have a way of burning, sir," the clerk said. "The boy will take you to the high school."

Janan spoke to the boy in a sweet way that she never used with me. "What's with those dark glasses?" she teased him. "They turn your world black, don't they?"

"They don't either!" the boy said. "Because I am Michael Jackson."

"What does your mother say to that?" Janan said. "Look what a nice vest she has knit for you!"

"None of my mother's business!" said the boy.

By the time we reached the Kenan Evren High School, the name of which was up in a flashing neon sign, we had gleaned these pertinent facts from Michael Jackson: He was in the sixth grade; his father worked at the movie theater which belonged to the same owner as the hotel, but he was busy with the convention; all the town was busy with the convention; there were some people who were against all this business; after all, the district governor had given voice to something that went like this: "I won't let disgrace be associated with any town where I am the governor!"

There, in the exhibits set up in the cafeteria of the Kenan Evren High School, we saw the displays of a device that cloaks time, a magic glass that transforms black-and-white into color, the first Turkish-made gizmo that detects pork in any given product, an unscented shaving lotion, scissors that automatically clip news-paper coupons, a heater that lights whenever the owner steps into the house, a windup clock that provides the answer to the problem of the call to prayer, that is, whether it should be broadcast by loudspeakers or by a muezzin calling from the minaret by the powers of his own lungs. This clock automatically settled the Westernization-versus-Islamization question through a modern device: Instead of the usual cuckoo bird, two other figures had been employed, a tiny imam who appeared on the lower balcony at the proper time for prayer to announce three times that "God is Great!" and a minute toy gentleman wearing a tie but no mustache who showed up in the upper balcony on the hour, asserting that "Happiness is being a Turk, a Turk, a Turk."

When we saw a version of the camera obscura, we too had to agree with the suspicion that the inventions must entirely be the work of local high school students in the area, although the fathers, uncles, and teachers milling in the crowd must also have had a finger in creating all these science projects. Hundreds of pocket mirrors had been lined up across from each other in the space between an automobile tire and the inner rim, thereby creating a labyrinth of reflections. When the lid was closed on light from external objects that entered from an aperture into the labyrinth of mirrors, the captive light image was forced to go round and round, being reflected in the mirrors until the end of time. Then, whenever you felt like it, you could fit your eye to the aperture and see the virtual image that had been imprisoned there in the chamber, be it a plane tree, or the shrewish school teacher taking in the science fair, the fat appliance dealer, a pimply student, the land-deeds official tossing down a glass of lemonade, the portrait of General Evren, a toothless janitor smiling into the device, a shady character, your own eye, and even the beautiful and intellectually curious Janan whose skin was still fresh in spite of her travels on the bus.

We observed other things at the fair aside from the devices; for example, the white-collar gentleman in the checked jacket making a speech. The crowd was comprised of small groups that gave us, as well as each other, appraising looks. A small redheaded girl with a ribbon in her hair was going over the poem she was soon to recite, nestled in her kerchiefed mother's skirt. Janan drew close to me; she was wearing the pistachio-green print skirt we had bought in Kastamonu. I loved her, O Angel, I loved her very much, as you know so very well. We bought iced yogurt drinks at a stand and stood on the edge of the crowd in the dusty afternoon light in the cafeteria, feeling dazed, tired, and sleepy, just taking in the scene. What we were watching seemed to make up a kind of music of existence, or a science of life. Then we saw a television set of sorts which we approached for a closer examination.

"This novel television happens to be Doctor Fine's contribution," said a man who wore a bow tie. Was he a Freemason? I had read in the paper that Freemasons sported bow ties. "Who do I have the pleasure of meeting?" he said, carefully examining my forehead, perhaps to avoid staring at Janan more than necessary.

"Ali and Efsun Kara," I said.

"You are so young! It gives us hope to see such young people among all these disgruntled entrepreneurs."

"We are not here to represent youth, sir," I said, "but to represent new life."

"We aren't disgruntled, we have true faith," said a large person, a pleasant avuncular man, proper enough for a high school girl to ask him the time.

So we joined the assembly. The girl with the ribbon in her hair recited her poem, mumbling her way through it like a light summer breeze. A young man handsome enough to play the singer in a domestic film discussed the region with the categorical fastidiousness of a military man, talking about Seljuk minarets, storks, the new power station under construction, and the high milk pro-

duction of the local cows. As students explained their projects
placed on the cafeteria tables, their fathers or teachers stood next
to them and gazed proudly into the audience. We met the others
in the room who were having either yogurt drinks or lemonade,
bumping into each other and shaking hands. I caught a whiff of
alcohol, and of OP shaving soap, but where did the smell come
from, or from whom? We took another look at Doctor Fine's
television. The talk was mostly about this Doctor Fine, but he
himself was nowhere around.

When evening fell, we all left the high school building, men
leading the women, and made our way to a restaurant. A tacit
sense of hostility was palpable in the streets throughout the town.
We were being observed from the doorways of barber shops and
grocery stores which were still open for business, the coffeehouse
where the TV was going, and the lighted windows of the government building. One of the storks mentioned by the handsome
fellow was watching us enter the restaurant from the tower in the
square where it was perched. Was it with curiosity? Or hostility?

The restaurant was a proper place with an aquarium and flower
pots, the walls were hung with pictures of eminent Turks, a historical submarine that had gone down in honor, soccer players
with lopsided heads, purple figs, golden pears, and frolicking
sheep. When the place had quickly filled with the dealers and
their wives, high school students and teachers, and all those who
loved and had faith in us, I felt as if I had been anticipating this
congregation and preparing for a night such as this all these many
months. I began drinking along with others but then ended up
drinking more than anyone else. I sat with the men, clinking raki
glasses with those who kept coming to sit next to me, talking
hungrily of honor, the missing meaning of life, of things that had
been lost.

Well, it was because they brought up the subject first, but I
found myself in such total agreement with a friendly man that

we were both terribly surprised; he had pulled a pack of playing cards out of his pocket and proudly showed me the face cards on which he had drawn with his own hand, changing the king into "sheik" and the jack into "disciple," and explained at length the reason why it was high time that cards like these should be distributed in the hundred and seventy thousand coffeehouses where card games are played in our country at close to two and a half million card tables.

Hope was among us in some form this evening, but was hope the same as the angel? It is a form of light, they said. They said: we dwindle a little each time we draw a breath. They said: we are digging up the things we have buried. One of them showed a picture of a stove. Another fellow said: A bicycle that fits our size perfectly. The man with the bow tie produced a bottle of liquid: works like toothpaste. A toothless old man regretted that he was forced to abstain from drink but he told us his dream: He tells us, never fear; you won't disappear. Who was He? Doctor Fine who was privy to abstruse matters had not yet put in an appearance. Why was he not here? If truth be told, a voice said, had Doctor Fine met this fine young man, he would have loved him like his own son. Whose voice was it? He had disappeared by the time I turned around. Ssssh! they said; don't throw around Doctor Fine's name! When the angel appears on TV sooner or later, there will be hell to pay. All this is the district governor's doing, all this fear, they said; but he is not totally against us either. The richest man in Turkey, Vehbi Koç himself, could very well arrive here as our invited guest. Why not? someone commented; Koç is after all the king of all us entrepreneurs.

I remember being kissed on the cheeks, congratulated for being so young, and after I explained to them about TV screens, colors and time, being hugged for being so candid. You just wait, said the pleasant man who ran the State Monopolies store; our television screen will be the final curtain for those who are after us;

the new screen means, after all, the new life. People kept coming
to sit next to me; I also kept changing seats and telling people all
about accidents, death, peace, the book, and that moment . . . I
sensed I had gone too far when I began saying, "Love . . ." I rose
to see Janan where she sat being interviewed by school teachers
and teachers' wives. I sat down and said, "Time is an accident;
we are here in this world by accident." They called out to a farmer
who wore a leather jacket, telling me here was the fellow I must
hear out, seeing how I was interested in time. "You give me too
much credit," the fellow said, breathing like an old man although
he did not seem very old, and he produced from the inner pocket
of his jacket his "modest" invention. It was just a pocket watch,
but one sensitive to bliss; it stopped when you were happy so that
your blissful hour could persist for all eternity; and conversely,
when you were in despair, the small and big hand speeded up
tremendously, making you remark how quickly time had passed
and how your sorrows had ended in the blink of an eye. Then at
night while you slept peacefully, the watch—this little object that
patiently ticked away in the palm of the man, who was quite old—
adjusted time by subtracting it from your lifetime, and when you
rose in the morning along with everybody else, you were not any
older.

   "Time," I said and stared for a moment at the fish gliding ever
so slowly in the aquarium. Someone came up to me like a shadow.
"They accuse us," he said, "of being hostile to Western culture.
In fact, it's not true. Did you know, for example, that leftover
Crusaders lived for centuries in the rock-cut dwellings in Cappadocia?" Who was the speaking fish who spoke to me when I
had been only talking to the fish? When I turned around, he was
gone. At first I said to myself it had been just a shadow, then I
was frightened when I caught a whiff of that formidable smell:
OP shaving soap.

   As soon as I sank into a chair, an avuncular man with a handlebar mustache began interrogating me, nervously winding around one of his fingers the chain of his key ring: Who were my folks, how did I vote, which invention had caught my fancy, what would be my decision in the morning? I was still thinking about the fish and I was going to offer him another glass of raki when I heard voices, voices, voices. I kept quiet and then found myself next to the good-natured Monopolies dealer. He told me he no longer feared anyone, not even the district governor who had a problem with the stuffed rats in his shop window. Why was there only one company selling liquor in this country, a state monopoly? I remembered something which frightened me, and the fear made me say the first thing that came to my mind. "If life is a journey," I said, "I have been on the road for six months, and I learned a thing or two which, with your permission, I would like to impart." I had read a book, and I had lost my whole world. I had set out on the road to find a new world. What had I found? It felt as if you were about to say, O Angel, what it was that I had found. I fell silent for a moment and pondered, but I didn't know what I was saying when I blurted out: "Angel." And, as if waking up from a dream, I began to look for you in the crowd, suddenly having remembered: Love. There she was among appliance dealers and their wives, the man with the bow tie and his daughters, it was Janan dancing with some presumptuous overgrown high school boy to the music from a radio somewhere while school teachers and senile geriatric cases looked on temperately.

I sat down and smoked a cigarette. If only I knew how to dance . . . like the bride and groom in the movies. I had some coffee. Time according to the watch that gauged happiness must have been going full speed ahead. Another cigarette. Applause for the dancing couples. More coffee. Janan went back to be with the women. Yet another coffee.

I pressed myself close to Janan on our way back to the hotel like all the provincials and district appliance dealers who had

taken their wives' arms. Who was that high school boy? How does
he know you? The stork must be watching us from the tower
where it was perched. We had just been given the key for Room
19 by the night clerk as if we were really husband and wife, when
someone who looked like he knew what he was doing and was
more determined than anyone else thrust his large and sweaty
body between us and waylaid me.

"Mr. Kara," he said, "if you have a moment . . ."

Police! I thought; he is on to us that we inherited the identifications and the marriage certificate from the victims of a traffic
accident.

"I wonder if it's possible for us to talk?" the man went on. He
acted as if he wanted to talk man to man. How delicately Janan
left us alone, how graceful she was in her print skirt, going up the
stairs with the key to Room 19 in her hand!

The man was not a native of the town of Güdül, but I forgot
his name as soon as he mentioned it; let us say his name was Mr.
Owl, based on the fact that he was talking to me so late at night,
but perhaps Owl was associated in my mind with the caged canary
in the lobby which had been hopping up and down and against
the wires when Mr. Owl began to speak.

"They are wining and dining us now," he said, "but tomorrow
they will ask us to vote. Have you thought about it? Tonight I
canvassed not only the dealers from this district but each and
every one that came from all over the country. All hell might
break loose tomorrow, so I want you to think about it now. Have
you thought it through? You are the youngest dealer among us.
Who has your vote?"

"Who do you think I should vote for?"

"Not for Doctor Fine, that's for sure! Believe me, brother—if
I may call you brother—it's all nothing but a misadventure. Can
angels be said to commit sin? Is it possible to deal with all the
difficulties that trouble us? There is no way that we can be our-

selves any longer, a fact that even the well-known columnist Jelal
Salik realized, which led to his suicide; it's someone else who's
writing the column under his name. Every rock you lift, there
they are, the Americans. Sure it's sad to realize we will never be
ourselves again, but mature assessment may save us from disaster.
So our sons and grandsons no longer understand us, so what?
Civilizations come and civilizations go. What are you going to
do? Believe you are all set when your civilization is on the move?
And then, when things begin to run down, grab your gun like
some loudmouth kid? Who do you kill when it's the whole population assuming a different guise? How can the angel be an ac-
cessory to the crime? Besides, who is this angel anyway? What's
this business of collecting old stoves, compasses, children's magazines, clothespins? Why is the angel supposedly against books
and print? We all try to live meaningful lives, but we are all
stymied at some point. Who among us can be himself? Who's
the lucky person that hears the angels whisper? It's all speculation,
empty words meant to dupe the unwary. Things are getting out
of hand. Have you heard? They say Koç is on his way, Vehbi Koç.
The authorities won't let it happen. The innocent will suffer along
with the guilty. The demonstration of Doctor Fine's television
has been put off until tomorrow. Why do you suppose he's getting
special treatment? He's the one herding us into this misadventure.
They say he will explain the Cola affair; it's madness; this is not
why we came to this convention."

He was ready to say more, but a man wearing a scarlet tie
came into the space, which didn't deserve to be called a lobby.
Owl said, "They will be all night now, tackling and blocking,"
and he took off. I saw him follow another dealer out into the
dark night.

I stood at the foot of the stairs where Janan had gone up. I felt
feverish, my legs were shaking; perhaps it was the alcohol or the
coffee, but I was having palpitations and there was perspiration

on my forehead. I didn't go up the stairs but ran to the phone
booth in the corner, dialed, the line was busy, I dialed again, got
the wrong number, I dialed your number, Mom: "Mom, I said,
I'm getting married, Mom, do you hear me? I am getting married
tonight, in a little while, now, in fact we're already married, she's
upstairs in the room, there's a staircase, I married an angel, Mom,
don't cry, I swear I will come home, don't you cry, Mom, I will
come back with an angel on my arm."

Why hadn't I realized before that there was a mirror right behind the canary cage? It was odd seeing it as I went up the stairs.

Room 19, it was the room where Janan opened the door,
greeted me holding a cigarette in her hand, then went back to
the open window where she had been watching the town square;
the room seemed like someone else's hometown which had suddenly become hospitable to us. Quiet. Warm. Low light. Twin
beds.

The town's somber light came through the open window, defining Janan's long neck and her hair, and a nervous and impatient
wisp of cigarette smoke (or did it only seem so?) rose out of
Janan's mouth, which I couldn't see, up toward a kind of dolorous
darkness that insomniacs, restless sleepers, and the dead in the
town of Güdül had for many years been breathing into the sky.
A drunk laughed downstairs; someone, perhaps a dealer, slammed
a door. I saw Janan toss her cigarette out the window without
putting it out, and then like a child she watched the cigarette's
orange tip doing somersaults as it fell. I too went to the window
and glanced down into the street and the town square, but without seeing anything. Then we both looked out the window for a
long time as if contemplating the cover of a new book.

"You too were drinking, weren't you?" I said.

"I was drinking," Janan said congenially.

"How long will this go on?"

"Do you mean the road?" Janan said lightly, indicating the

route leading from the town square to the cemetery before it reached the bus terminal.

"Where do you think it will end?"

"I don't know," said Janan. "But I want to go as far as it goes. Isn't that better than sitting around waiting?"

"The money is almost all gone," I said.

The dark corners in the road Janan had pointed out a moment ago were now completely lit by the powerful headlights of some vehicle which drove into the town square and parked in a vacant space.

"We will never get there," I said.

"You're even more drunk than I am," said Janan.

The man who emerged from the car locked the door and walked toward the hotel without becoming aware of us; he first stepped on Janan's cigarette stub like someone thoughtlessly squashing out someone else's life, and then he entered the Hotel Trump.

A prolonged silence fell over Güdül, as if this charming little town were completely deserted. A few dogs exchanged barks in the distance, then everything grew silent once more. The leaves of the plane and chestnut trees on the square moved in the breeze now and then, but there was no sound of rustling. We must have stood silently at the window for a long time, looking out like children anticipating something that was going to be fun. It was some sort of perceptual illusion, but though I was aware of every second I couldn't say if time was passing or if it was on hold.

It was much later when Janan said, "No! Please don't touch me! I have never been with a man."

As sometimes happens in real life or when remembering the past, I felt for a moment as if the situation and the town I was seeing out the window were not actual but in my imagination. Perhaps the small town of Güdül I saw before me was not a real town, perhaps I was only looking at the picture of a town on a stamp, like one issued by the postal service administration in their homeland series. Just as with the towns on those stamps, the town square made Güdül appear to be more like a souvenir than a place with streets to walk in, where a pack of cigarettes could be bought or dusty windows inspected.

Fantasytown, I reflected; Souvenir City. I knew that my eyes were searching for that indelible objective correlative for a bitter memory that can never be forgotten, which arises from someplace very deep and arrives of its own volition. I scanned the dark space under the trees next to the square, the tractor fenders gleaming in light that came from a mysterious source, the lettering in the names of the pharmacy and the bank partially obscured from sight, the back of an old man in the street, and some windows in particular. Then, like some cinematography enthusiast who has located the vantage point of the camera and the photographer who filmed the town square, I began to see my own image looking out of the second-story window in the Hotel Trump. I was standing there and looking out of a window in this remote and secluded hotel, and you were stretched out on the bed next to the window, when I zoomed in on the images in my head, starting with the countryside, the route we traveled, the town, the town square, the hotel, the window, the two of us—just like the camera in the opening scenes of foreign films we saw on the buses, zooming in on the city first, then the neighborhood, then a yard, a house, a window. It seemed as if all the towns, villages, films, filling stations, and passengers that I imagined and remembered inadequately had been fused with the pain and longing I felt somewhere deep inside me, but I couldn't determine whether the sorrow of the towns, broken-down objects, and passengers had infected me, or if I was the one who spread the sorrow in my heart all over the country and the map.

The purple wallpaper around the window reminded me of a map. The trade name on the electric heater in the corner was VESUVIUS, the regional dealer for which I had met earlier in the evening. The faucet in the sink on the wall across from me was dripping. The mirror on the door to the closet was ajar, reflecting the bedside table between the two beds and the little lamp that stood on top of it. The light from the lamp softly washed over the sleeping form of Janan, who had lain down on the bedspread with purple leaves without taking off her dusty clothes.

Her light brown hair had turned somewhat auburn. How was it that I hadn't noticed the reddish highlights?

Then I thought there were a great many things I still had to notice. My mind was brightly lit like the restaurants at rest stops where we got off to have some soup, but it also was, at the same time, in total disarray. Weary thoughts crossed the confusion in my mind, changing gears, huffing and puffing like the sleepy phantom trucks that kept going by one of those crossroads restaurants, and I could hear immediately behind me the girl of my dreams breathe as she slept dreaming of someone else.

Lay yourself down beside her and wrap her in your arms! After all this time together, bodies can't help longing for one another. Who was this Doctor Fine anyway? When I could no longer bear it and turned around to behold her beautiful legs, I remembered, brothers (brothers, brothers!), that they were conspiring out there in the still of the night, and lying in wait for me. A moth that had seeped in from the stillness was circling the light bulb, painfully shedding itself in flakes. Kiss her long and hard until both our bodies are consumed with fire. Did I hear the sound of music? Or was my mind playing the piece called "The Call of the Night" that had been requested by the listeners? As any young man my age whose sexual passion remains ungratified knows all too well, the call of the night is actually nothing more than finding oneself in some dark dismal alley and howling bitterly in the night in the company of a couple of hopeless characters in the same predicament, bringing down invectives on other people and making bombs that will blow them up, and—have pity on us, O Angel—

cursing those who deal in the international conspiracy that has condemned us to this miserable existence. I believe gossip of this sort is called "history."

I watched Janan sleep for half an hour, perhaps forty-five minutes, all right, all right, an hour at most. Then I opened the door and stepped out, locked the door, and pocketed the key. My Janan remained inside. And I, I had been turned down and exiled.

Walk up and down the street, then go back and embrace her. Smoke a cigarette, go back and embrace her. Find someplace open, get soused, take courage, go back and embrace her.

The conspirators in the night pounced on me as I descended the stairs. "So you're Ali Kara," one of them said. "My congratulations, you made it all the way here, and you are so young." "Join us," said the second thug who was about the same age, same height, and wore roughly the same narrow tie and the same black jacket, "and we'll let you know what's going to happen when the ruckus starts tomorrow."

They held their cigarettes as if the red tips were gunpoints aimed at my forehead, and they smiled provocatively. "Not to scare you or anything," added the first, "but we just wanted to warn you." I could see that they were conducting some sort of gossip session in the middle of the night, doing the footwork to catch converts.

We went out into the street where the stork was no longer keeping watch, and we passed by the shop window with the liqueur bottles and the stuffed rats. We went into a back alley where we had only taken a few steps when a door was opened and we were confronted with a dense tavern smell reeking of raki. We sat down at a table covered with a filthy oilcloth and in quick succession tossed down a couple of glasses of raki—in lieu of medication, please!—and soon I learned quite a few things about my new acquaintances as well as the subject of life and happiness.

The one who first accosted me, let's call him Mr. Sıtkı, was a

beer salesman from Seydişehir who told me his story as to why
there was no contradiction between his occupation and his creed
because it was all too obvious, if you thought about it, that beer
was not really an alcoholic beverage like raki. He called for a bottle
of Ephesus beer and pouring it into a glass demonstrated that the
bubbles were nothing but carbonation. My second buddy paid
scant attention to such dilemmas, sensibilities, and distinctions,
perhaps because he was a sewing machine dealer, plunging instead
into the heart of things like those drunk and sleepless truck drivers
who in the middle of the night blindly meet up with purblind
power poles.

Here was peace; peace existed here, in this peaceful town, here
in this tiny tavern. We were here and now, three faithful cronies
in the heart of life, sharing a table. When we thought over everything that happened to us and all that would happen tomorrow,
we were well aware how precious was this unique moment which
existed in between our victorious past and our gruesome and miserable future. We swore we would always tell each other the truth.
We hugged and kissed. We laughed with tears in our eyes. We
exalted the magnificence of the world and life. We raised our
glasses in honor of a party of crazy dealers and a coterie of mindful
subversives who were in the tavern. This was life in its essence;
it was neither one thing nor the other, neither in heaven nor in
hell. It was right here, in the present, in the moment, life in all
its glory. What madman had the nerve to contradict us? Where
was the idiot who would put us down? Who had the right to call
us pitiful and wretched trash? We had no desire to live in Istanbul, nor in Paris or New York. Let them have their discos and
dollars, their skyscrapers and supersonic transports. Let them have
their radio and their color TV, hey, we have ours, don't we? But
we have something they don't have: heart. We have heart. Look,
look how the light of life seeps into my very heart!

I remember gathering my wits for a moment, O Angel,

and wondering why, if all you have to do is drink down the pan-
acea against unhappiness, then why isn't everybody drinking? Out
of the tavern and into the summer night with his bosom friends,
the person walking under the pseudonym of Ali Kara keeps asking:
Why all this pain, all this sorrow and misery? Why, oh why?

In the second floor of the Hotel Trump a bedside lamp casts
reddish highlights on Janan's hair.

Then I remember being pulled into a milieu of the Republic,
Atatürk, and legal stamps. It was in the government building,
where we went all the way to the inner sanctum, the office that
belonged to the district governor, who kissed me on the forehead.
He was one of us. He told us an edict had been dispatched from
Ankara, no nose was to be bloodied tomorrow. He had already
singled me out, he trusted me, and if I felt like it, I might as well
go ahead and read the missive which was still damp out of the
brand-new duplicating machine.

"Esteemed denizens of Güdül, notables, brothers, sisters,
mothers, fathers, and devout young members of the Imam-
Preacher School. Some people are apparently oblivious to the fact
that they are in our town as our guests. What is it that they want?
Are they here to insult everything that is held sacred in our town?
Our devotion to our religion, our prophet, our sheiks, and the
statue of Atatürk has for centuries been demonstrated amply in
our mosques and on our holy holidays. Not only do we refuse to
drink wine, we will not succumb to drinking Coca-Cola. We wor-
ship Allah, not the Cross, or America, or Satan. We cannot understand why our peaceful town has been chosen as the
convention site for these certified madmen, copycat versions of
Marie and Ali, and the Jewish agent Max Rulo, whose only aim
is belittling our Field Marshall Fevzi Çakmak. Who is the angel?
And who has the temerity to put the angel up for ridicule on
TV? Are we to watch idly while insolence is perpetrated against
our conscientious firefighters and our Hadji Stork who has

watched over our town for the last twenty years? Was it for this that Atatürk chased out the Greek army? If we do not put these impudent so-called guests in their place, if we don't teach the lesson they deserve to the derelicts who are responsible for inviting these people to our town, how are we to face ourselves tomorrow? There will be a rally at ten in the Firehouse Square. We prefer death to life without honor."

I read the announcement once more. If it were to be read backwards, or if an anagram were formed by the capital letters, would one get an entirely different version? Apparently not. The district governor said that the fire trucks had been loading up water from the stream since morning. There was a possibility, however small, that things could get out of control tomorrow, fires could get out of hand, and in the heat the mob might not be so easily deterred by the pressure hoses. The mayor had assured our supporters that the mayor's office would provide full cooperation, and the gendarme units dispatched from the provincial capital were to put an immediate lid on any and all disturbance that might ensue. "When things calm down and provocateurs and enemies of the Republic and the nation are unmasked," said the district governor, "let's see who is left around to deface soap ads and billboards featuring women. Let's see who swaggers out of the tailor shop dead drunk, cursing the governor up and down, not to mention the stork."

It was decided that the tailor shop had to be seen by me, the staunch young man. After the governor had me read the opposition's statement penned by two school teachers who were semisecret members of the Caucus for the Promotion of Modern Civilization, he assigned a janitor to me, telling him to take the young man to the tailor shop.

"The governor has been pushing us to work overtime," said the janitor, who was known as Uncle Hasan, once we were out in the street. Two members of the secret police were busy ripping out the cloth banner for the Koran school, working as quietly as a pair of thieves in the dark blue night. "We're all hard at work on behalf of the nation and the state."

In the tailor shop, there was a television set on a stand with a video player under it, sharing the space with sewing machines, bolts of cloth, and mirrors. Two fellows slightly older than me were working on the set, wielding screwdrivers, trip wires, and such. A man sat in a purple chair in the corner watching them, as well as his own image in the full-length mirror across from him; he looked me up and down first and then turned his questioning eyes to the janitor.

"The Honorable District Governor sends him," said Uncle Hasan. "He entrusts this young man to your care."

The man who was sitting in the purple chair was the same one who had parked his car in front of the hotel before stepping on the butt of Janan's cigarette. He smiled at me affectionately and asked me to sit down. Half an hour later he reached to turn on the VCR.

The image of a television screen appeared on the screen, within which was the image of yet another screen. Then I saw a blue light, something that was associated with death, but at this juncture death must have been quite a distance away. The blue light wandered aimlessly across the vast steppe where we had been riding on the buses. Then it was morning, dawn breaking on a scene that was like those on calendars. The images might have referred to the dawn of creation. How wonderful it was to get drunk in an unfamiliar town and, while my sweetheart was fast asleep in a hotel room, to sit with my mysterious buddies in some tailor shop, and without having to so much as wonder about the meaning of life, watch it being suddenly revealed through images.

Why is it that one thinks through words, but suffers through images? "I want! I want!" I said to myself without quite knowing

what it was that I wanted. Then a white light appeared on the
screen, the appearance of which the two young fellows who were
working on the set perhaps realized by seeing the radiance that
surged on my face; and facing the screen themselves, they turned
up the volume. Presently the light was transformed into the angel.

"I am so far away," said a voice. "I am so far away that I always
am among you. Listen to me in the sound of your own inner
voice. Move your lips in keeping with mine."

I mumbled, trying to sound natural, like some unfortunate re-
cording artist dubbing someone else's botched-up translation into
the sound track.

"Time cannot be endured," I said, speaking in that voice, "as
Janan sleeps, as morning approaches. But I could still grit my
teeth and bear it."

Then there was a silence. It seemed as if I could see what was
in my mind on the screen; it was immaterial therefore whether
my eyes were open or closed since the images in my mind and in
the world outside were identical. Presently I spoke again.

"God created the universe when he wished to see the reflection
of his own infinite attributes, re-creating his own image which he
beheld in his mirror. So the Moon, which frightens us when it
shines into the forest, materialized over the images that we see
so abundantly on the TV and movie screen such as the morning
on the steppe, the brilliant sky, spanking-clean water washing
rocky shores. The Moon was all alone back then in the dark sky
like a television set that plays for itself in the living room when
the power comes back on while the family is fast asleep in the
night. The Moon and all of creation existed back then, but there
was no one to see them. Like an unreflecting mirror which is
devoid of silver backing, things were devoid of spirit. You know
what it is like, having watched so much of it. Now take another
look at this spiritless universe so it may serve you as a lesson."

"There, boss!" said the fellow with the drill. "That's exactly when the bomb goes off!"

I surmised from their conversation that they had placed a bomb in the television set. Could I have been mistaken? No, I was right; it was some sort of image bomb which would explode when the angel's dazzling radiance appeared on the screen. I knew I was right because along with the curiosity I had for the technical details of an image bomb, a feeling of guilt vexed my mind. On the other hand, I kept thinking, "It must be thus." Maybe it would go like this: In the morning when the dealers were totally lost in the magical images on the screen and involved in discussions about the angel, light, and time, the bomb would explode nice and warm as in traffic accidents; and time, having welled up in these people who were dying to live, to fight, and to conspire, would violently expand over the scene and freeze the frame. I realized then that I did not want to die of a bomb or a heart attack, but in an actual traffic accident. Perhaps I thought the angel might appear to me at the moment of impact and whisper in my ear the secret of life. When, oh when, O Angel?

I could still see some images on the screen. Some sort of light that was perhaps devoid of color, or perhaps it was the angel, but I couldn't tell for sure. Being able to see the aftermath of a bomb was like reviewing life after death. I was so excited about taking advantage of this unique opportunity that I caught myself providing the words for the image on the screen. Was I only repeating what someone else had said? Or was it a moment of fellow feeling as in the union of souls in the great beyond? Here is what we were saying:

"When God blew his soul into the creation, Adam's eye beheld it. We then saw matter in its true guise, yes, just like children might, but not in the unreflecting mirror that we see now. We were such joyful children back then, naming what we saw and seeing what we named! Back then, time was time, hazard was hazard, and life was life. It was a state of true happiness, but Satan was displeased by our happiness; and he who is Satan conceived of the Great Conspiracy. One of the pawns of the Great Conspirator was a man named Gutenberg, known to be a printer and emulated by many, who reproduced words in a manner that outstripped the production of the industrious hand, the patient finger, the fastidious pen; and words, words, words broke loose like a strand of beads and scattered far and yonder. Like hungry and frenzied cockroaches, words invaded the wrapping on bars of soap, on cartons of eggs, on our doors and out in the street. So words and matter, which had formerly been inseparable, now turned against each other. And when asked by moonlight what is time, life, grief, fate, pain, we were confused like a student who stays up all night before an exam learning his lessons by rote, although we had once known the answers in our hearts. Time, said a fool, is a noise. Accident, said another, is fate. Life, a third said, is a book. We were confused, as you see, waiting for the angel to whisper the right answer in our ears."

"Ali, my son," interrupted the man in the purple chair, "do you believe in God?"

I thought it over.

"My Janan awaits me," I said, "in a hotel room."

"God is everyone's *janan*," he said, "so go unite with your beloved. But get a shave in the morning. At the Venus Barbershop."

I went out into the warm summer's night. Like an accident, I said to myself, the bomb is also a mirage; you never know when it will appear. Miserable losers that we were, it was obvious that we had lost the gamble called history; now we were reduced to bombing each other for centuries to come, hoping to convince ourselves that we are winners and get a taste of victory, blowing up our souls and our bodies to high heaven with bombs we place in gear housings, in volumes of the Koran, and in boxes of candy made for the love of God, books, history, and the world. I was just thinking that it was not such a bad scenario when I saw Janan's light.

I went in the hotel and up to the room. Mom, I was really drunk. I lay down next to my Janan and fell asleep, believing I had her in my arms.

When I woke in the morning, I watched my Janan sleeping beside me. Her face had the same anxiety and attentiveness with which she watched the video screen when she was sitting on a bus; she had raised her chestnut-colored eyebrows as if in anticipation of an astonishing dream sequence. The faucet in the sink was still dripping. A dusty ray of sunlight seeped in through the curtains, becoming honey-colored where it fell on her legs, and Janan mumbled a question in her sleep. When she turned over, I left the room quietly.

I felt the cool morning on my forehead on my way to the barbershop called Venus, where I saw the man I met last night, the same man who had stepped on Janan's cigarette. He was getting a shave, his face foaming with lather. I smelled the shaving cream when I sat down to wait, it was with apprehension that I recognized the smell. Our eyes met in the mirror, and we smiled at each other. Obviously this was the man who would conduct us to Doctor Fine.

8 ON THE WAY TO DOCTOR FINE, JANAN SAT IN THE BACK of the '61 Chevrolet with fins, petulantly fanning herself with a copy of the *Güdül Post* like a haughty Spanish princess, while I sat up front taking account of ghostly villages, wornout bridges, and weary towns. Our driver who smelled of OP shaving cream was not talkative, he liked to fool with the radio listening to the same news over again and weather reports that contradicted each other. Rain showers were predicted for Central Anatolia, or not. There were scattered torrential rainstorms in parts of the Aegean region, or it was partly cloudy, or it was sunny. We traveled for six hours under partially cloudy skies, driving through ominous downpours that arrived out of pirate films and the land of fairy tales. After a final shower that battered the roof of the Chevrolet mercilessly, we suddenly found ourselves in a storybook place that was totally different.

The gloomy rhythm of the windshield wipers had come to an end. The sun in this geometrically conceived land was brilliant and it was setting in the butterfly vent of the left window. Crystal-clear, lucid, and tranquil realm, relinquish to us your secrets! The trees with raindrops on their leaves were perceptibly trees. Birds and butterflies crossed our path like calm and collected birds and butterflies without any intention of flying into the windshield. I was about to ask where the storybook giant was lurking in this place that existed outside of time. Behind what tree were the pink dwarves and the purple witch? I was about to point out the absence of signs or lettering anywhere, when a truck with a bumper sticker that said "Think before you pass" glided by smoothly on the shimmering highway. We passed through a small town, then turned left and drove into a gravel road; we climbed hills, went by a lost village or two obliterated by the dusk, caught glimpses of dark woods, and finally stopped in front of Doctor Fine's domicile.

It was a wood structure that looked like one of those provincial mansions that get converted into inns with names like Welcome Palace, Celestial Palace, Pleasure Palace, or Comfort Palace when the big family that lived there is dissolved due to death, misfortune, or migration, but there were no signs of local fire engines being kept around this place, nor any dusty tractors, or some restaurant called the City Grill. Only solitude. There were four windows upstairs instead of the customary six in mansions such as these, and the light in the third window cast an orange glow on the lower branches of the three plane trees in the front of the house. The silhouette of a mulberry tree was just visible in the dark. There was movement in the curtains, a window banging, footsteps, a bell; shadows shifted, the door was opened, and the person who welcomed us was Doctor Fine himself.

He was tall, good-looking, in his late sixties or early seventies, and he wore glasses. He had the kind of face you could not remember later in your room whether it was bespectacled, as you cannot remember if some men you know quite well wear mustaches or not. He had great presence. Later in our room, Janan said, "I am scared," but she seemed to me more curious than frightened.

We ate dinner with the whole family at a very long table by

the light of kerosene lamps that cast long shadows. He had three daughters. The youngest daughter, called Rosebud, was dreamy and content but still unmarried although it was high time she were. The middle daughter, Rosabelle, seemed closer to her doctor husband, who sat across from me breathing noisily through his nose, than to her father. And the eldest, beautiful Rosamund, had been divorced for some time, as I gleaned from the conversation of her two well-behaved daughters, who were six and seven. The mother of the three rosy daughters was a small woman who practiced emotional extortion; not only her eyes but her whole demeanor said: Watch it, should you displease me, I shall burst into tears. At the other end of the table sat a lawyer from town—I didn't catch what town—who told a story concerning a land dispute that pivoted on partisanship, politics, bribery, and death, and he was quite pleased when Doctor Fine fulfilled his expectations by listening to his story with curiosity, his eyes approving the lawyer although they deplored the events. Sitting next to me was one of those old men who's happy to be spending the last years of his life witnessing the lively state of affairs in the bosom of a large family that is powerful and well-respected. It was not clear what relation the old man was to the family, but he augmented his happiness with a small transistor radio he had placed next to his plate. He put his ear several times right on the radio to listen—perhaps he was hard of hearing—and then he turned toward Doctor Fine and me, smiling to reveal his false teeth and saying, "No news from Güdül!" Then, as if it were a natural conclusion to his statement, he added, "The doctor loves philosophical discussions, and he adores young individuals like you. It is amazing though how much you look like his son!"

A lengthy silence ensued. I thought the mother would burst into tears, and I recognized irritation flashing in Doctor Fine's eyes. A grandfather clock somewhere outside the dining room struck nine, reminding us that time and life are transitory.

It slowly dawned on me as I ran my eyes over the table, the room and the objects, the people and the food that there were signs and traces right here among us in the mansion of some dream or else of a deeply felt life and memories. During those long evenings Janan and I spent on a bus, after the attendant slipped a second videotape into the machine at the insistence of some of the more enthusiastic passengers, for a few minutes we would be seized by an enchantment that was weary and hesitant, or a feeling of irresolution that was sharp but aimless, abandoning ourselves to a game we couldn't quite perceive the meaning of in terms of its contingency and necessity; and confused to be reliving the same moment in a different seat and from a different vantage point, we felt we were about to discover the secret of the concealed and incalculable geometry called life; and just as we were eagerly figuring out the deep meaning behind the tree shadows, the dim image of the man with the gun, the video-red apples, and the mechanical sounds on the screen, we would realize that, goodness, we had already seen this movie!

The same feeling stayed with me even after dinner. For a while we listened to the old fellow's radio, which was tuned to the same radio theater hour that I never missed in my childhood. Rosebud brought us sweets from a bygone era, Lion brand coconut candies and New Life Caramels in a silver dish that was identical to the one at Uncle Rıfkı's. Rosabelle offered us coffee, and the mother inquired if we wished for anything else. On the side tables and on the shelves of the mirror-backed breakfront there were copies of the photo romances that are sold all over the country. And whether Doctor Fine was drinking his coffee or winding the clock on the wall, he was the very picture of the fine and affectionate father in the model family on National Lottery tickets. The signs of a certain patriarchal refinement and a logical order that could not easily be named were infused in all the objects that graced the room, such as curtains which had borders embroidered with carnations and tulips, old-fashioned kerosene stoves and kerosene lamps which were as moribund as the light they cast. Doctor Fine took me by the hand to show me the barometer on the wall, asking me to tap thrice on the fine and delicate crystal face. When I tapped it and the needle moved, he said paternally, "Tomorrow the weather will be rough again."

On the wall next to the barometer there apparently was an old photograph in a large frame, the portrait of a young person, which Janan mentioned when we went back to our room. But I had not registered it. Like some dispassionate person whose life slips away from him, like someone who sleeps through movies and gives books careless readings, I asked her whose picture it was that she saw in the frame.

"Mehmet's," Janan said. We were standing in the light of the kerosene lamps we had been handed to bring up to the room. "You still don't get it? Doctor Fine is Mehmet's father."

I remember hearing clanging noises in my mind that sounded like an unfortunate public telephone in which the token will not fall. Then everything fell into place and I felt more angry than surprised, realizing the incontrovertible truth which was like a storm subsiding at the break of dawn. It happens to most of us at some time or other. When we have sat and watched a movie for a whole hour thinking we know what is going on before we realize that we were the only fool in the theater who has completely missed the point, we become enraged.

"So what was his other name?"

"Nahit," she said, nodding knowingly like a person who has faith in astrology. "It means the evening star, apparently, the planet Venus."

I was about to say that if I had a name like that and a father to match, I too would want to take on a different identity, when I realized tears were streaming from Janan's eyes.

I don't even want to remember the rest of the night. My role was to console Janan, who was weeping for Nahit alias Mehmet, and perhaps this was not too much to ask, but I was reduced to having to remind Janan that we already knew that Mehmet-Nahit had not actually died in a traffic accident; he had only made it appear as if he had. We were sure to find Mehmet walking in the wondrous streets somewhere in the heart of the steppe, and he would have transformed the wisdom he gleaned from the book into his own existence in the wondrous realm where new life is possible.

Even though this conviction was actually stronger in Janan than in me, anxiety created violent storms in my dolorous beauty's soul; so I was forced to explain to her at length why I thought we were on the right track. Look how we had managed to sneak away from the dealers' convention without getting into any trouble! And look how we had managed to follow an internal logic that only appeared coincidental, ending up in this mansion where the object of our quest had spent his childhood, in this very room that was full of his traces. The reader who senses the sarcasm in my tone perhaps perceives that the scales had fallen off my eyes, that the enchantment that invaded my whole being and illuminated my soul—how shall I put it?—had changed direction. While Janan was grief-stricken merely because Mehmet-Nahit was assumed to be dead, I was despondent because I now understood that our bus trips would never again be the same.

After a breakfast of bread, honey, ricotta cheese, and tea with the three sisters, we saw the museum of sorts on the second floor that Doctor Fine had dedicated to the memory of his fourth child, and only son, who was burned to death in a bus accident. "My father wishes for you to see this," Rosamund said, putting a very large key surprisingly easily into a small keyhole.

The door opened into a magical silence. The smell of old magazines and newspapers. Low light filtered through the curtains. Nahit's bed and coverlet embroidered with flowers. Photographs of Mehmet's childhood, adolescence, and his Nahit period hanging on the walls inside frames.

My heart had speeded up under a strange compulsion and it was beating wildly. Rosamund whispered to point out Nahit's primary and secondary school report cards, his honor roll certificates. In hushed tones, all A's. Little Nahit's still muddy soccer shoes, his short pants with suspenders. A Japanese make kaleidoscope ordered from an Ankara store called Jonquil. In the dimly lit room, finding correspondences to my own childhood gave me shivers, and I was feeling as scared as Janan had said she was, when Rosamund pulled aside the curtains and whispered that during his years in medical school her darling brother used to stay up all night reading and smoking whenever he was home, and then in the morning he would open this window to gaze at the mulberry tree.

There was a silence. Then Janan asked what books Mehmet-Nahit had been reading during that period. The eldest sister had a brief attack of uncertainty and indecision. "My father didn't think it was appropriate to keep those on the premises," she said, and then she smiled as if consoling herself. "But these can be looked at," she said, "the stuff he read in his childhood."

She was pointing to the bookcase next to the bed, which was full of children's magazines and comic books. I didn't want to come any closer to the bookcase because I wished to avoid over-identifying with the child who had once read these publications, besides I was afraid Janan might become emotional and burst into tears in this unnerving museum; yet my resistance was broken when my hand reached out of its own volition to touch the picture on the cover of one of the magazines neatly stacked in the case, the colors on their spines looking quite familiar although somewhat faded.

The picture on the cover showed a twelve-year-old kid who was clinging with one hand to the thick trunk of a tree, on which the leaves had been drawn painstakingly but due to the bad printing job the green had bled outside the lines, while with the other hand he had grabbed the hand of a blond kid who was the same age as himself, saving him at the last minute before he fell into a bottomless ravine. Both of the child heroes wore expressions of terror. In the background was a wild American landscape rendered in grays and blues, with a vulture circling in anticipation of a disaster and spilled blood.

I sounded out the syllables of the title the way I used to when I was a child: NEBî IN NEBRASKA. I flipped through the comic book, which was one of Uncle Rıfkı's earlier efforts, remembering the adventures that took place within the pages.

Young Nebî is appointed by the Sultan to represent Muslim children at the Chicago World's Fair. There, a kid called Tom who happens to be an American Indian tells Nebî about his problem, so they go to Nebraska together to solve it. White men who have their eyes on the lands where Tom's forefathers have for centuries hunted buffalo are encouraging Tom's Indian tribe to become addicted to alcohol, handing guns as well as bottles of whiskey to tribal youths with a penchant for bad behavior. The conspiracy Nebî and Tom bring to light is absolutely merciless: getting peaceful Indians drunk enough so they will revolt, then getting the federal army to squash the rebels and drive them off the land. The rich hotel and bar owner who tries to push Tom into the sheer ravine falls into it himself and dies, so the children save the tribe from falling into the trap.

Janan was looking through MARY AND ALI because the title sounded familiar to her; it was about the adventures of a boy from Istanbul who had also gone to America. He arrives at Boston harbor on the steamship he has embarked on in Galata in search of adventure; at the docks he meets Mary, who is weeping with great big sobs and looking at the Atlantic Ocean because her stepmother has turned her out of her own home; the two kids set out on the road west in search of her absent father. They pass through St. Louis, which looks like the illustrations in Tom Mix comics; they make their way through the white forests of Iowa where Uncle Rıfkı has placed in dark corners the shadows of wolves; and they arrive at a sun-drenched paradise, having left behind them all the errant cowboys, bandits that attack railway cars, and Indians who circle wagon trains. In the green and bright valley, Mary understands that true happiness is not finding her father but comprehending the Sufi virtues of Peace, Resignation, and Patience which she has learned from Ali; and heeding a sense of duty, she returns to be with her brother back in Boston. As for Ali, he thinks to himself, "When you come to think of it, injustice and wickedness exist everywhere in the world"; and looking back at America from the deck of the clipper he has boarded feeling homesick for Istanbul, he says, "What is important is to live in such a way that the goodness inside you is kept intact."

Instead of growing despondent as I imagined she might, Janan had cheered up considerably turning the ink-smelling pages that reminded me of the dark and cold winter nights of my childhood. I told her I too had read the same comics as a child. Assuming she had not perceived the sarcasm in my words, I added that it was one more thing Mehmet alias Nahit and I had in common. I suppose I was behaving like some obsessive lover who thinks because his love is not requited his beloved must be insensitive. But I did not feel at all like telling her that the illustrator and writer who created these comics was someone I used to call Uncle Rıfkı. I did tell her of one instance when the author had felt like telling us readers why he was compelled to create these comic-book characters.

"Dear Children," Uncle Rıfkı had put in a brief note at the beginning of one of his comic books, "wherever I see you after school, be it in train compartments or in the street in my modest neighborhood, I always see you reading about Tom Mix or Billy the Kid's adventures in cowboy magazines. I too love those brave and honest cowboys and Texas rangers. So I thought that if I told you the story of a Turkish kid among American cowboys, you might like it. Besides, this way you will be exposed not only to heroes who are Christians, but through the adventures of your plucky Turkish compatriots you will also come to cherish the ethics and the national values that our forefathers have bequeathed to us. If it is exciting to you that a kid from a poor neighborhood in Istanbul can draw a gun as fast as Billy the Kid or be as honest as Tom Mix, just you wait until you read our next adventure."

Patiently, carefully, and as quietly as Mary and Ali had contemplated the wonders they met in the Wild Wild West, Janan and I studied for a long time the heroes Uncle Rıfkı had drawn in a world that was black and white, the dusky mountains, the terrifying woods, the cities teeming with odd inventions and habits. In law offices, in harbors full of schooners, in distant train stations, and among gold rushers, we met swashbucklers who sent greetings to the Sultan and the Turks, Negroes who had been freed from slavery and had embraced Islam, Indian chiefs who consulted shamans who were Central Asian Turks on their methods of making yurts, as well as farmers and their children who were so pure and good-hearted they were like angels. After reading some pages of a gory adventure where gunslingers mow each other down like flies, where good and evil bollix up the heroes by trading places time after time, or where the ethics of the Orient are compared to the rationalism of the Occident, one of the good and brave heroes gets shot in the back by a craven bullet, and just as he dies at daybreak he has an intimation that he is at the threshold of encountering an angel. But Uncle Rıfkı had not rendered the angel on the page.

I put together the issues in which a string of adventures related how Pertev from Istanbul and Peter from Boston become fast friends and turn America upside down, and I showed my favorite scenes to Janan: young Pertev with Peter's help foils a crooked gambler who robs a town blind by virtue of a system of mirrors he has rigged up; then he runs the gambler out of town with the aid of townsmen who swear off poker and gambling. When crude oil comes gushing out right in the middle of a church, and the townspeople, who are divided among themselves, are ready to come to blows and fall into the trap of either oil billionaires or exploiters of piety, Peter saves the day by giving an Atatürk-style speech on secularization, enlightened by ideas of Westernization which he has learned from Pertev. Not only that, young Pertev provides the initial electric idea that leads to the discovery of the light bulb by Edison, whom he meets when young Edison made his living selling newspapers in railway cars, by telling Edison that angels are created of light, that angels have a kind of mysterious electricity.

But then, of all his works, *Heroes of the Railroad* was the one that most strongly reflected Uncle Rıfkı's own enthusiasms and yearnings. In this story we see Pertev and Peter supporting the initiative to build a railroad from East to West across America. The railroad that would connect the country coast to coast was a matter of life and death for America, just like it was for Turkey in the thirties, but there were a great many enemies of the endeavor, such as the Wells Fargo Company or the minions of Mobil Oil, clergymen who refused to let the railway through their land holdings, or international rivals like Russia, sabotaging the railway men's enlightened efforts by inciting the Indians, or instigating workers' strikes, and encouraging young men to slash railway car seats with razors and knives, just as it was done on Istanbul commuter trains.

"Should the railroad proposition fail," Peter was saying anxiously in one of the balloons, "the development of our country will be curtailed, and what people call accident will be a matter of fate. We must fight to the end, Pertev!"

How I used to love those big exclamation marks that followed boldface ejaculations that filled up the balloons! "Look out!" Pertev would shout out to Peter, warning him to dodge the knife before some treacherous villain stabbed him in the back. "Behind you!" Peter would shout out to Pertev, who, without even bothering to look back, would swing his fist, which would connect with the chin of some enemy of the railways. Sometimes Uncle Rıfkı would mediate directly, inserting among the pictures small boxes into which he wrote in letters as spindly as his own legs words like SUDDENLY or NOW WHAT and ALL OF A SUDDEN, punctuating them with huge exclamation marks, at which point, as borne out by my own experience, Mehmet alias Nahit would be drawn into the story.

Janan and I had been watching for sentences that took exclamation points when we read this one: "The things written in the book are now left behind me!" It was spoken by a character who had dedicated himself to the war against illiteracy and said to Pertev and Peter when they visited him in his hut where, disappointed with his failed life, he had secluded himself.

I pulled myself together when I realized Janan was becoming alienated from these pages where all Americans of good will were blond and freckled, all the evil ones had crooked mouths, where everyone thanked each other for every little thing, where vultures always picked all the corpses to shreds, and where cactus juice saved the lives of people who were dying of thirst.

Instead of fantasizing that I might start life anew as another Nahit, I said to myself I had better disabuse Janan of her false dreams. She was getting sentimental looking at Nahit's middle-school reports and the picture on his identification card. Just then Rosebud came in the room suddenly, like Uncle Rıfkı coming to

the aid of his characters cornered by ill luck and adversity by
inserting the small box that said SUDDENLY! She informed us that
her father was expecting us.

I had absolutely no idea what would happen to us next, neither
did I have the least notion on what to base my calculations in
order to get closer to Janan. Coming out of the museum dedicated to the Nahit period of Mehmet's life, two instinctive
thoughts occurred to me: I wanted to leave the scene, or I wanted
to become Nahit.

9 LATER, WHEN THE TWO OF US WENT ON A LONG WALK on his estate, Doctor Fine generously offered me a choice between the two alternative lives, both of which I wanted. It is entirely coincidental when fathers seem to know, as if they were gods in possession of an infinite memory and books of records, the thoughts on their sons' minds. In reality, they are merely projecting their own unrealized desires on their sons, or on perfect strangers that remind them of their sons. That's all there is to it.

I had been given to understand that once I had been shown the museum, Doctor Fine wanted us to go on a walk together and have a talk. We walked along the edges of fields where the wheat was waving in the breezes; we crossed fallow ground where a few sheep and cows were nuzzling the scarce herbage under apple trees on which the fruit was small and unripe. Doctor Fine showed me dens that had been excavated by moles; he drew my attention to tracks made by wild boars, and explained how the thrushes called fieldfares flying from the southern outskirts of the town toward the fruit orchards could be recognized by the small irregular beat of their wings. He explained a great many things besides, speaking in a voice that was instructive, patient, and not too far from being affectionate.

He was not really a doctor. His cronies when he was doing his military service had nicknamed him Doctor just because he was cognizant of details that came in handy for small repairs, such as the eight-thread nut required for a certain bolt or the cranking speed of a field telephone. He had identified with the nickname because he loved equipment and enjoyed taking care of it, and because he had recognized that discovering the unique properties of each object constitutes the highest good. He had not studied medicine but the law in accordance with the wishes of his father, who had been a deputy member of parliament, and he had pursued a law practice in town; but when his father died and he inherited all the trees and lands to which he pointed with his index finger, he had decided to live as he pleased. Just as he pleased! Among products he had chosen himself, products he was accustomed to, products he himself knew. He had opened the store in town with this goal in mind.

We were going up a hill that was partially warmed by rather hesitant sunlight when Doctor Fine divulged to me that objects had the capacity to remember. Just like ourselves, objects also had the faculty to record what happened to them and preserve their memories, but most of us were not even aware of it. "Substances inquire after each other, come to an agreement, whisper to one another, and strike up a harmony, constituting the music we call the world," said Doctor Fine. "Those who are attentive hear it, see it, and comprehend it." He could tell fieldfares had been nesting around the area by looking at the limy stains on the dried branch he had picked up; and having studied the signs in the mud, he explained to me how the branch had been broken two weeks ago by a certain storm.

It seems that he sold merchandise he brought not only from Istanbul and Ankara but from manufacturers all over Anatolia, such as whetting stones that never wore down, handwoven rugs, locks made out of hammered iron, sweet-smelling wicks for ker-

osene stoves, simple versions of refrigeration, beanies made of fine
grade felt, RONSON trademark flintstones, door handles, stoves
made out of recycled gasoline barrels, small aquariums—anything
at all that made sense to him, or anything that was sensible. The
years he spent in the store where all sorts of basic human needs
were supplied in a humane way had been the happiest years of
his life. When he was granted a son after he had fathered three
daughters, his happiness had been complete. He asked my age,
and I told him. He said when his son died he had been the same
age as me.

From somewhere below the hill there came the sounds of children who were not visible to us. When the sun disappeared behind several insistent and dark clouds that traveled fast, we could
see in the distance kids playing soccer on a bald playing field.
There was a time lapse between seeing the ball being kicked and
the moment we heard the sound. Doctor Fine said there were
some among the children who perpetrated petty theft, and that
the downfall of all great civilizations and the disintegration of
their memories was first signaled by the moral degradation of the
young. The young had the capacity to forget the old as quickly
and painlessly as they could imagine the new. He added that the
kids lived in town.

When he was talking about his son, I felt enraged. Why were
fathers so full of pride? How could they be so unconsciously cruel?
I realized that his lenses made his eyes behind his glasses look
unusually small. I remembered his son too had the same eyes.

His son was very intelligent, in fact, brilliant. Not only had he
begun to read at the age of four and a half, he could make out
the letters and read the newspaper even when it was held upside
down. He thought up rules for children's games he invented; he
beat his father at chess; he instantly committed to memory a
three-stanza poem after a couple of readings. I realized these were
only the stories of a father who had lost his son but who himself

was not a good chess player, yet I still took the bait. When he
told me how he and Nahit rode horseback, I too imagined myself
riding with them; when he spoke of Nahit's devout religious prac-
tices during his years in middle school, I imagined getting up
during Ramadan with the old grandma in the dead of night and
having a bite to eat before the fast from daybreak to sundown
began; in just the way his father told me that Nahit had responded, I too had been pained and angry in the face of the
poverty, ignorance, and stupidity that was all around me; yes, I
had! Listening to Doctor Fine, I remembered how I too was a
young man who, in spite of his brilliant qualities, still had a deep
inner life like Nahit. Yes, sometimes when others were smoking
and drinking at some gathering, busy trying to make jokes and
attract attention that was all too brief, Nahit would withdraw into
a corner and be lost in sensitive thoughts that softened the severe
expression in his eyes. Yes, he would intuit most unexpectedly
the merit of some nondescript person whom he would encourage
and make friends with, be it the son of the janitor at the high
school, or the idiot-poet projectionist at the movie theater who
always got the reels mixed up. But these friendships did not mean
that he had abandoned his own world; after all, everyone wanted
to be his friend, his buddy, or some sort of close companion to
him. He was honest and handsome, he gave his elders respect,
and his juniors . . .

I kept thinking of Janan. I was tuned to her like a television
set constantly on the same channel, but now I was thinking of
her sitting in a different kind of chair, perhaps because I was
seeing myself in a different light.

"Then suddenly, he turned against me," said Doctor Fine when
we had reached the top of the hill. "Just because he had read
some book."

The cypress trees on top of the hill were moving in a wind that
was cool and light but carried no scent. Beyond the cypresses

there was an outcropping of rocks and stones. At first I had thought it was a graveyard, but when we got there and began to walk among the large, carefully dressed stones, Doctor Fine explained that it was the ruins of a Seljuk fort. He pointed out the slopes across from us, and a dark hill with its cypresses that was actually a graveyard, all the fields golden with wheat, the heights obscured by rain clouds where the winds blew heavily, and an entire village as well. All was his now, including the fort.

Why would a young man turn his back on all this land that was alive with life, all these cypresses, these poplars, these wonderful apple orchards and conifers, all the food for thought that his father had provided for him, as well as the storeful of merchandise that was in complete accord with all the above mentioned? Why would a young man write his father that he never wanted to see him again, telling him not to send anyone after him, or have him followed? Why would he want to disappear? There was one particular look that appeared at times on Doctor Fine's face, and I could never figure out whether it meant that he wanted to stick a needle in me, others like me, or the world as a whole, or whether he was just a disgruntled and oblivious man who had renounced this whole damn world. "It's all a conspiracy," he said. There was a great conspiracy against him, his way of thinking, the products to which he had devoted his life, against everything that was vital for this country.

He asked me to listen carefully to what he was going to tell me. I must make sure I did not think that the things he had to say were the ravings of a senile old man stuck in some out-of-the-way town, or fantasies prompted by the pain felt by a father who had lost his son. I said I was sure. I listened carefully, although I slipped away as anyone might when my mind wandered, thinking of his son or Janan.

He discussed for a while the memory of objects; as if he were talking about something tangible, he explained with passionate conviction the concept of time fixed fast inside matter. The Great Conspiracy had taken hold around the same time he had first become aware of the presence of a magical, necessary, and poetic concept of time that was transmitted to us from objects when we came into contact using or touching some simple thing like a spoon or a pair of scissors. Speaking specifically, it was around the time that their humdrum sidewalks had been besieged by vendors who sold the sort of dull and flat stuff that was displayed in the odorless, colorless stores. At first he had paid scant attention to either the CRESCENT GAS dealer who sold the bottled gas that powered those gas burners, those thingamajigs with knobs, or the AEG dealer who sold refrigerators that were white as synthetic snow. But when, instead of the nice creamy yogurt that we are all familiar with, vendors began to bring around some sort of yogurt called PERT (he said it as if he were saying DIRT), or instead of the traditional cool yogurt drinks or sour cherry sherbets, drivers wearing open-neck shirts brought, on trim and spanking-clean trucks, the imitation stuff called Mr. Turk Cola which was soon replaced by the real Coca-Cola being sold by honest-to-goodness gentlemen with ties around their necks, out of some stupid impulse he had thought of getting a dealership himself, such as for that UHU glue licensed under the German trademark of a darling little owl that promised it could stick together anything you wanted, rather than our glues that are made out of pine resin, or else something to take the place of our clay soap like Lux hand soap, which had a scent as polluting as its box. But as soon as he put these articles in his store which was so serene that it seemed to exist in a former time, he realized that not only could he no longer tell the time, he didn't know what time it was. Not only he but also his merchandise had been distressed—much like nightingales who are perturbed by the presumptuous finches in the next cage—by the presence of these lackluster, prosaic objects; and that is why he had abandoned the idea of a dealership.

He was unconcerned that only old men and flies dropped by his store, he continued stocking only those products which had traditionally been available to his forefathers.

Like those people who lose their minds from drinking Coca-Cola but do not realize it, given that the whole populace has gone crazy on Coca-Cola, he too might have come to disregard or even accept the Great Conspiracy; after all, he did have dealings and friendships with some of the dealers who were the tools. Not only that, his merchandise resisted the Dealer's Conspiracy, perhaps due to the magical harmony objects establish between themselves, including everything in his store, all of them his sort of things—his flatirons, his lighters, his odor-free stoves, his bird cages, his wooden ashtrays, clothespins, fans, his whatnots. There were others like him who had closed ranks against the conspiracy, such as the dark and dapper fellow from Konya, a retired general from Sivas, dealers who were heartbroken but still true believers from Trabzon and, you name it, even from Teheran, Damascus, Edirne, and the Balkans, who had joined him in forming an organization of heartsick dealers who arranged for their own kind of merchandise. He had received right about that time those letters from his son who was away in Istanbul studying medicine. "Don't look for me; don't have me followed; I am dropping out." Doctor Fine repeated sarcastically his dead son's rebellious words, the words that had angered him.

He had soon understood that when the powers who were involved in the Great Conspiracy could not contend with his store, his ideas, and his taste, they had tried to go the way of winning over his son in order to undermine him. "Me, Doctor Fine!" he said with pride. So he had gone against what his son had requested in his letter, hoping to turn the whole business around. He had hired someone to tail his son, asking him to keep Nahit under surveillance and write reports on his behavior. Then realizing that one spy was not enough, he had sent a second of his

minions after his son, and then a third. They too wrote their
reports. And so had others he dispatched after them. Reading the
reports, he was once more convinced of the reality of the Great
Conspiracy, fostered by those who wanted to destroy our country
and our spirit, and to eradicate our collective memory.

"When you read the reports yourself, you will see what I
mean," he said. "Everything and everybody that is involved with
them must be tracked down. I have undertaken the work that
should rightfully be done by the government. I am up to it. I now
have many sympathizers, many heartsick individuals who have put
their total trust in me."

The vista before us which we could see like a postcard, and
which was all Doctor Fine's property, was now covered over by
dove-gray clouds. Starting at the hill where the graveyard was located, the clear and brilliant view was disappearing inside some
sort of pale, saffron-colored oscillation. "It's raining there," said
Doctor Fine, "but it won't come here." He had spoken it like a
god who was standing on a hill and regarding the creation that
was animated by his own volition, but at the same time his voice
possessed a note of irony, or even self-deprecatory humor, which
indicated he was well aware of how he had spoken. I decided his
son didn't possess a single iota of this kind of subtle humor. I was
beginning to like Doctor Fine.

Thin, fragile lightning bolts were flashing back and forth in the
clouds when Doctor Fine repeated once more that what had
turned his son against him had been a book. His son had read a
book one day and thought his whole world had changed. "Ali, my
boy," he said to me, "you are also the son of a dealer, and you
are also in your early twenties. Tell me, is this possible in this day
and age? Can a book change someone's whole life?" I kept quiet,
regarding Doctor Fine out of the corner of my eye. "By what
power can such a strong spell be cast in this day and age?" He
was not merely trying to strengthen his own conviction, but for

the first time he truly wanted an answer from me. I kept quiet
out of fear. For a moment I thought he was coming at me instead
of walking toward the ruins of the fort. But he suddenly stopped
and picked something off the ground.

"Come see what I found," he said. He showed me what was in
the palm of his hand. "A four-leaf clover," he said, smiling.

In order to counteract the book and literature in general, Doctor Fine had soldered his relations with the dapper fellow from
Konya, the retired general in Sivas, the gentleman called Halis in
Trabzon, and his other heartsick friends who hailed from Damascus, Edirne, and the Balkans. In response to the Great Conspiracy, they began to trade with each other exclusively and to
confide in others whose hearts had also been broken, and to organize—carefully, humanely, modestly—against the tools of the
Great Conspiracy. Doctor Fine had requested that all his friends
preserve the products that were real to them, products which were
like the extensions of their hands and arms and which like poetry
made their souls complete, "in other words, whatever object it
was that rendered them whole"—like their hourglass-shaped tea
glasses, their oil censers, their pencil boxes, their quilts—as a
measure to prevent being rendered helpless like hopeless boobs
who had lost their collective memory, which was "our greatest
treasure," so that despite having suffered through all the misery
and oblivion foisted on us, we might establish victoriously anew
"the sovereignty of our own unadulterated annals of time which
were in danger of being annihilated." And everyone had squirreled
away to the best of his ability old adding machines, stoves, dye-
free soap, mosquito netting, grandfather clocks, etc., in their
stores, and if keeping these products in the stores was prohibited
by the state terrorism called the laws of the land, then in their
houses, their basements, even in pits dug in their gardens.

Since Doctor Fine was pacing up and down, at times he put
some distance between us, disappearing behind some cypresses

among the ruins of the fort, which required that I wait for him. But when I saw him walk toward a hill that was concealed behind some tall brush and the cypresses, I ran to catch up. First we went down a slight grade that was covered with bracken and thistles, then we started up the hill, which was quite steep. Doctor Fine led the way, stopping to wait for me at times so I would not miss hearing his narrative.

Considering that the pawns and tools of the Great Conspiracy assail us, either knowingly or unknowingly, through books and literature, he said to his friends, we ought to take precautions against printed matter. "What literature?" he asked me, leaping from one rock to another like some nimble Boy Scout. "What book?" He had reflected on it. He fell silent for a while, as if to demonstrate how meticulously and in what great detail he had reflected upon it, and how long the process had taken him. He explained it as he helped me out of a patch of brambles where I was caught by the cuffs of my trousers. "The culprit is not only that particular book, the book that snared my son, but all the books that have been printed by printing presses; they are all enemies of the annals of our time, our former existence."

He was not against literature that was scripted by hand, which was an integral part of the hand holding the pen—the kind of literature that moved the hand, and in expressing the sorrows, the curiosity and affections of the soul, pleased and enlightened the mind. Nor was he against the kind of books that informed the farmer how to deal with his mice, steered in the right direction some absentminded person who had lost his way, reminded the misguided of their own traditions, or informed and educated the naïve child about the nature of the world through illustrated adventures; he was all for these kinds of books which were as necessary now as they had once been, and it would be a good thing if they were written in greater numbers. The books Doctor Fine opposed were those that had lost their glow, clarity, and truth but

pretended to be glowing, clear, and true. These were the books
that promised us the serenity and enchantment of paradise within
the limitations set by the world, those which the pawns of the
Great Conspiracy mass-produced and disseminated—at this point
a field mouse zipped past us and was gone in the blink of an
eye—in their concerted effort to make us forget the poetry of our
lives. "Where's the proof?" he said, looking at me suspiciously as
if I were the one who had asked the question. "Where's the
proof?" He was climbing quickly among spindly trees and rocks
covered with bird droppings.

For the proof, I must read the records kept by his men all over
the country, the spies he had dispatched to do the investigations
in Istanbul. After reading the book, his son had lost his bearings;
not only had he turned his back on his family—which one could
attribute to youthful rebellion—but he had closed his eyes to the
wealth of life, that is, the "unmanifested symmetry of time," carried away by some kind of "blindness" against the "totality of
details reposited in each object," having succumbed to some kind
of "death wish."

"Can one book accomplish all this?" asked Doctor Fine. "That
book is merely a tool in the hands of the Great Conspiracy."

Still, he underestimated neither the book nor the writer. I
would see for myself, when I read the reports his friends and spies
had made and the records they had kept, that the use made of
the book was not consistent with the writer's aims. The writer
had been a poor retired bureaucrat, a weak personality who didn't
even have the courage of his own convictions. "The sort of weak
personality we are required to produce by those who infect us
with the plague of forgetfulness that blows here on the winds from
the West, erasing our collective memory. Someone feeble, someone wishy-washy, a nothing! He is gone, destroyed, rubbed out."
Doctor Fine made it clear that he didn't feel in the least sorry
for the writer's death.

For quite some time we climbed up a goat path without speaking. Silken thunderbolts flashed through the rain clouds that kept changing places without either approaching or departing; but the thunderclaps were inaudible, as if we were watching a TV set with the sound set on mute. When we got to the top of the hill, we could see not only Doctor Fine's holdings but also the town that stood neatly on the plain like a table set by an industrious housewife, the red tile roofs, the mosque with the slim minarets, the streets spreading out freely, and outside the town limits, the sharp boundaries of the wheat fields and fruit orchards.

"In the morning I get up and greet the day before the day has a chance to wake me," Doctor Fine said, studying the view. "The sun comes up from behind the mountains, but one knows by the swallows that in other places the sun has already been up for hours. Sometimes in the mornings I walk all the way up here to welcome the sun who greets me. Nature is bestilled; bees and snakes are not yet stirring about. The earth and I ask each other why we are here at this hour, for what purpose, for what grand purpose. Very few mortals think these things through in concert with nature. If human beings think at all, there are only a few pitiful ideas in their heads which they have acquired from others but think are original with them; they never discover something by contemplating nature themselves. They are all feeble, wishy-washy, fragile.

"Even before I discovered the Great Conspiracy that came from the West, I had already comprehended the fact that to remain unvanquished one must have strength and determination," said Doctor Fine. "Our melancholy streets, long-suffering trees, ghostly lights held out nothing to me but indifference; so I put my stuff in order, pulled my time concept together, refusing to submit either to history or those who want to govern it. Why should I submit? I trust in myself. It was because I trusted in myself that others too put their trust in my willpower and the poetic justice of my life. I made sure they were bonded to me, so they too discovered the annals of our own time. We were bonded to each other. We communicated through ciphers, corresponded like lovers, held clandestine meetings. This first dealers' convention in Güdül, my dear boy Ali, is the fruit of a long and hard struggle, well-planned action that has required the patience of digging a well with a needle, and organization that has been meticulously constructed like a spider's web. No matter what, the West can no longer deter us."

After a silence he added this information: Hours after my pretty young wife and I had left Güdül, fires had broken out all over town. It was not coincidental that the fire department had been unable to cope despite the help they received from the government. No wonder that the tears, the flashes of anger, to be seen in the eyes of the insurgents, that rabble roused by the newspapers, were the same as those of his heartsick friends who had intuited that they had been robbed of their souls, their poetry, their memory. Had I known that cars had been set on fire, that guns had been discharged, and that one person—one of their own—had lost his life? The whole thing had been instigated by the district governor himself with the aid of the local political parties, when he forbade the convention of the heartsick dealers to continue on the pretext that it threatened law and order.

"It's a done deal," said Doctor Fine. "I am not about to acquiesce. I was the one who requested that the subject of angels be debated on the floor. I was also the one who put in the request for building the television set that reflected our hearts and our childhood, I was the one who had that device built. I was the one who demanded that all wicked things, like the book that took my son away from me, be chased back to the hole they emerged from, back to the evil pit where they seethe and roil. We found out that hundreds of our young people had 'their whole lives changed' through this sort of subterfuge every year, 'their worlds deranged'

by having a book or two put in their hands. I gave everything
thorough consideration. It is not coincidental that I did not attend the convention. That the convention brought me a young
man like you is not a mere stroke of good fortune, either. Everything has been falling in place just as I premeditated it. When
my son was taken from me by the traffic accident, he was the
same age as yourself. This is the fourteenth of the month. I lost
my son on the fourteenth."

When Doctor Fine opened his large fist, I saw there the four-
leaf clover. He picked it up by the stem and studied it before he
let it drift away on a light breeze. Air was wafting from the direction of the rain clouds but so imperceptibly that I felt it only
by the coolness on my face. Dove-gray clouds tarried where they
were situated, as if by indecision. Light that had a yellowish cast
seemed to simmer somewhere in the distance beyond the town.
Doctor Fine said it was "now" raining over there. When we
reached the rocky cliffs on the other side of the hill, we saw that
the clouds over the graveyard had scattered. A kite had nested
among the rocks which were rough in places; the moment it realized we were approaching, it fluttered off in alarm and began
to soar, defining a wide arc over Doctor Fine's territory. Silently,
respectfully, and with a kind of admiration, we watched the bird
glide in the air.

"This land has the power and wealth," Doctor Fine said, "to
support the great movement inspired by the single-minded grand
idea that I have been nurturing all these years. If my son had had
the strength and the willpower to resist the ruse perpetrated by
the Great Conspiracy and had not allowed himself to be taken in
by a mere book despite his great intellect, he would have felt the
creativity and strength I feel today, surveying the land from these
heights. I know that you yourself have perceived today the same
inspiration, the same horizon. I knew from the beginning that
what was communicated to me about your resolution was not in

the least exaggerated. When I found out your age, I had no remaining reservations; there was not even any necessity to dig up your background. Even though you are only at the age when my son was so mercilessly and underhandedly taken from me, you have already comprehended everything thoroughly enough to want to take part in the dealers' convention. Our acquaintance of a single day has already shown me that a manifest destiny aborted in one individual can be reactivated through another. It was not for nothing that I gave you access to the little museum I established in memory of my son. You and your wife are the only persons who have visited it aside from his mother and his sisters. You were able to appreciate your own self there, your own past and your future. And now you are becoming cognizant of our next step as you contemplate me, Doctor Fine. Become my son. Take his place. Carry on my work after me. I am growing old, but my passions have not in the least abated. I want to be sure that the movement will survive. I have connections in the government. Those who report to me are still active. I am keeping track of hundreds of young people who have been hoodwinked. I will make the dossiers available to you, all of them without any exception, even the records of my son's activities. Just read them. So many young people have been taken off the course of their lives! It's not necessary that you renounce your own father, your family. I also want you to see my gun collection. Just say 'Yes!' Say yes to your destiny. I am not a decadent person, I am aware of everything. I didn't get a male heir for years on end, I suffered; when they took him away from me, I suffered even more; but nothing can be more painful than leaving behind my inheritance without someone to inherit it."

The thunder clouds were being scattered here and there, and sunlight flooded Doctor Fine's realm like the lights that illuminate a stage set. When a piece of land was momentarily brightened up, colors changed quickly in the level ground covered with apple and oleaster trees, the graveyard where he told me his son was buried, the arid earth around a sheep pen; and we observed a conical beam of light swiftly proceed over the fields like a restless spirit which does not respect boundaries, only to vanish. When I realized that we could see most of the area we had covered on our walk from this vantage point, I looked back, observing the rocky cliff, the goat path, the cypresses, the first hill, the woods and the wheat fields, and, astonished as an airplane passenger seeing his own house from above for the first time, I recognized Doctor Fine's mansion. It stood in the middle of an ample plain that was surrounded by trees; and I saw there in that clearing five miniature individuals walking toward the pinewood and the road to town, recognizing one of them as Janan by the maroon print cotton dress she had bought recently—no, not just by that fact alone, but by her walk, her stance, her delicacy, her grace—no, by the beating of my own heart. Then suddenly, materializing afar in the distance beyond the mountains at the edge of Doctor Fine's wondrous realm, I saw a spectacular rainbow.

"Others observe nature," Doctor Fine said, "only to see there their own limitations, their own inadequacies, their own fears. Then, fearful of their own frailties, they ascribe their fear to nature's boundlessness, its grandness. As for me, I observe in nature a powerful statement which speaks to me, reminding me of my own willpower that I must sustain; I see there a rich manuscript which I read resolutely, mercilessly, fearlessly. Similar to great eras and great states, great men too are those who can accumulate in themselves power so great that it is at the point of exploding. When the time is ripe, when opportunities present themselves, when history gets rewritten, this great power moves as pitilessly and decisively as the great man who has been mobilized. Then fate is also set mercilessly into motion. On that great day, no quarter shall be given to public opinion, to newspapers, or to current ideas, none to petty morality and insignificant consumer products, like their bottled gas and Lux Soap, their Coca-Cola and Marlboros with which the West has duped our pitiful compatriots."

"When can I read the records, sir?" I asked.

There was a long silence. The rainbow shimmered brilliantly on Doctor Fine's dusty and spotted spectacles like two symmetrical rainbows.

"I am a genius," said Doctor Fine.

10 WE RETURNED TO THE MANSION. FOLLOWING A quiet lunch with the family, Doctor Fine let me into his study, unlocking it with a key very similar to the one with which Rosamund had in the morning opened Mehmet's childhood room. Showing me the notebooks he pulled out of drawers and dossiers he brought down from cabinets, he told me that he did not disregard the possibility that the directive which had commissioned these intelligence reports and testimonials might one day materialize in the form of a state. If his efforts were successful, as attested to by the espionage network he had organized, Doctor Fine meant to found a new state.

The reports had in fact been meticulously dated and filed, which made it easy for me to get to the heart of the matter. Doctor Fine had kept the identities of the informants he sent after his son secret from each other, supplying each agent with a code name that was a watch trademark. Although most of these watches were made in the West, Doctor Fine considered them "ours," given that they had been keeping our time for over a century.

The initial informant, code name Zenith, had filed his first report four years ago in March. Nahit—he had not yet assumed

a new identity—was then a student at the University of Istanbul
in Çapa, in his third year of the six-year program of studies leading to an M.D. degree that begins in Turkey right after high
school. Zenith had determined that ever since school started in
the fall, this third-year student had been a terrible failure in his
classes; then he went on to summarize his investigations: "The
subject's failure in school the last few months is the direct result
of his rarely venturing out of his dormitory, cutting his classes,
and not even showing up for his practicum hours at the clinic
and the hospital." The dossier was chock-full of reports, showing
in great detail what time Nahit left the student dormitory and
went into which fast-food place, kebab or pudding shop, what
bank and what barber he patronized. Each and every time Mehmet took care of his errands, he did not tarry but returned swiftly
back to his dormitory, and each and every time Zenith concluded
his intelligence report he asked Doctor Fine for more money to
continue his "investigations."

The next agent after Zenith that Doctor Fine had assigned was
Movado, who apparently was a supervisor at the student dormitory in Kadırga; and like most supervisors of student housing, he
had ties to the police. I imagined that this experienced man, who
was able to keep an eye on Mehmet hour by hour, had probably
written reports on other students previously for the benefit of
anxious parents in the provinces or for the National Bureau of
Investigation, seeing how he had sketched the balance of power
in the dormitory so astutely that his assessment had a professional
edge, sharp and succinct. Conclusion: Nahit had no association
with the student factions who were struggling to gain ascendancy
in the dormitory; two of these factions were fundamentalist ex-
tremists, one had ties to a Nakshi-bend Sufi order, and the ori-
entation of the last was moderately leftist. Our young man kept
to himself, had no brushes with the factions, lived quietly with
three compatriots with whom he shared a room, and he read and

read without even raising his head, reading nothing but one particular book as if he were some hafiz ("if I may use the term, my worthy sir") employed from morning to night in memorizing the Koran. Other dormitory staff whose grasp of political and ideological matters Movado trusted completely, the police, and our young man's roommates as well had ascertained this book was not of the type that young fundamentalists or politicos committed to memory. To show he did not take the situation too seriously, Movado had added a few observations such as the young man sitting for hours at his desk reading in his room and then absentmindedly staring out the window, or smiling good-naturedly or making some perfunctory remark in response to the teasing he took in the refectory, or not shaving every morning as usual; and he had gone on to give his patron the assurance that in his experience this sort of youthful fancy was nothing but a "passing phase," not unlike always watching the same porno film, or listening a thousand times to the same cassette, or always ordering the same dish of braised leeks with ground meat.

Seeing how Omega, the third agent, who went on duty in May, was more in pursuit of the book than of Nahit, he must have received a directive on the subject from Doctor Fine. This showed that his father had accurately determined that in fact what took Mehmet, that is Nahit, off the track had been the book.

Omega had surveyed many of the booksellers in Istanbul including the sidewalk stall that had sold me my copy some three and a half years later. As a result of his patient probing, he had come across the book at two different sidewalk stalls, and the information he gleaned from the booksellers had sent him to a secondhand bookstore, where the facts he received had led him to draw these conclusions: A small number of these books, maybe 150 to 200 copies, had been made available from an unknown source, most probably sold by weight to some junk dealer when some musty warehouse had either been cleared out or gone out

of business, and from there the books had ended up at a couple
of sidewalk stalls and the shop in the secondhand bookstore district. The supplier who bought books by weight had a falling out
with his partner, closed his business, and left Istanbul. It had not
been possible to find him and get a fix on the original purveyor.
The idea that the police might have had a hand in the redistri-
bution of the book had been suggested to Omega by the owner
of the shop in the secondhand bookstore district. The book had
at one time been published legitimately, only to be confiscated
by the prosecutor's office and placed in a warehouse that belonged
to Internal Security, and from there, as happens so often, the
confiscated books were probably pinched by some impecunious
police officer and sold by weight to a junk dealer, thereby once
more going back into circulation.

When diligent Omega had not come across any other work by
the same author at the library, and what's more had not found
the name in the phone book, he had offered this speculation:
"Although our citizens who cannot even afford a telephone have
the temerity to write books, I respectfully submit my opinion that
this book has been published under a pseudonym."

Mehmet, who had spent the whole summer reading the book
again and again, had in the fall begun the investigations that
would take him to the original source of the book. The new man
his father added to the three already on his tail had been named
after a brand of Soviet-made watches and clocks popular in Istanbul during the early years of the Turkish Republic: Serkisof.

Serkisof, after verifying that Mehmet had totally immersed
himself in reading at the Beyazıt National Library, had initially
given Doctor Fine the good news that the young man was merely
studying to make up his incomplete work at school. Then, realizing that our young man had been reading children's comics such
as *Pertev and Peter* or *Ali and Mary*, Serkisof had abandoned his
optimistic conclusion and had put forth this conjecture by way

of consolation: Perhaps by returning to his childhood memories, the young man was hoping to pull himself out of his depression.

According to the reports, during the month of October Mehmet had been paying visits to Babıali publishers who had once produced or were still producing children's comics, as well as the sort of unscrupulous writers—like Neşati, for example—who had scribbled for such magazines. Serkisof, who assumed Doctor Fine was having the young man investigated to find out his ideological and political leanings, said the following about certain people: "I tell you, sir, no matter how interested they pretend they are in politics, and no matter how often they hold forth about the political and ideological issues of the day, these polemicists do not have any real convictions. They write for the money, and if they can't get that, they write to annoy people they don't like."

I saw in both Serkisof's and Omega's reports that one autumn morning Mehmet had visited the personnel department of the State Railroad Administration in Haydar-Pasha. Of the two investigators, who were not aware of each other, Omega was the one who had come up with the correct information: "The young man wanted to obtain information on a retired official."

I flipped quickly through the pages of reports that had been put in binders. My eyes were scanning for the names of my own neighborhood, my street, my childhood. My heart began to beat fast when I read that Mehmet had walked in my street and had one evening studied the second-story window in some house. It was as if those who prepared the wondrous world where I was soon to be summoned had decided to make things easier for me by displaying their skill right under my nose, but the high school student that I was back then had never been any the wiser.

Mehmet had met Uncle Rıfkı the following day, which was the conclusion I personally drew from the material. Both the agents who were following Mehmet had verified that the young man had entered 28 Silver Poplar Street in Erenköy and stayed five, more like six minutes, but neither had found out whom he had visited in what apartment. Omega, who was the more diligent of the two watches, had at least pumped the errand boy at the corner grocery and received information on the three families who lived in the building. I assume this was the first time ever that Doctor Fine had got wind of Uncle Rıfkı.

After his interview with the gentleman called Rıfkı, Mehmet had a crisis that even Zenith didn't fail to notice. Movado had noted that the young man did not stir from his room at all, not even to go down to the refectory, and was not seen reading the book, not even once. According to Serkisof, his forays out of the dormitory were irregular as well as aimless. He had spent an entire night trudging around the back streets in Sultan-Ahmet and sat smoking in a park for hours. Another evening Omega had observed him with a bunch of grapes in a paper sack which he had taken out one by one to scrutinize as if the grapes were jewels before chewing them each very slowly; he had gone on doing this for four hours before returning to his dormitory. His hair and beard had grown too long, he paid no attention to his appearance. The informants all felt they needed more pay, complaining about the irregular hours kept by the young man.

. One afternoon in November, Mehmet had taken the ferry to Haydar-Pasha, then gone to Erenköy on the train, where he had walked around the streets for a long time. According to Omega, who was on his tail, the young man had pounded the streets in the whole district, had gone by my window three times—most probably while I was sitting inside—and by the time it began to get dark, he had taken up his post across from 28 Silver Poplar Street and begun to watch the windows. Mehmet, who had kept watch for a couple of hours in the dark under a light rain without getting the signal he wanted from the lighted windows, according to Omega, had gotten terribly drunk at one of the taverns in Kadıköy before returning to his dormitory. Later, Omega and Serkisof had both mentioned that the young man had made the same trip six more times; Serkisof, who was the more astute, had correctly identified the person in the room with the lighted window that the young man had watched.

Mehmet's second interview with Uncle Rıfkı had taken place right under Serkisof's eyes. Serkisof, who had peeped into the lighted window from the opposite sidewalk first and then standing on a low garden wall, had in several subsequent letters given alternate interpretations of the interview—which he sometimes called a rendezvous—but his initial impressions had been more accurate, considering that these were more closely founded on the facts and what he had actually seen.

At first the old writer and the young man had sat without speaking for seven or eight minutes in armchairs placed across from each other, with a television set between them on which a cowboy film was being shown. The old man's wife had at some point brought them coffee. Then Mehmet had risen to his feet, and gesturing wildly he had spoken with such passion and rage that Serkisof had thought the young man was about to raise his hand against the old fellow. The gentleman called Rıfkı, who at first had only been smiling sadly, had also risen to his feet himself in response to the increased force of the young man's words, and he had counterblasted the young man just as impetuously. And then both of them sat back in their armchairs, followed by their faithful shadows mimicking them on the walls, and they had patiently listened to each other before falling silent and sorrowfully watching the TV for a while, only to strike up a conversation again, with the old man holding forth and the young man listening, then both of them falling silent once more and looking out the window without ever becoming aware of Serkisof.

But the shrew next door, who spied Serkisof peeping into the window, began to screech with all her might, "Help! Damn you, you lousy pervert," forcing the unfortunate investigator to leave

on the double, without being able to observe the last three
minutes of the interview which in his subsequent letters he conjectured had to do with a secret organization, a political fraternity
of international dimensions; he also offered a conspiracy theory.

The next file indicated that during that period Doctor Fine
wanted his son followed assiduously, and his investigators had
responded by bombarding him with reports. After his interview
with the gentleman called Rıfkı, Mehmet, who seemed half crazed
to Omega and extraordinarily saddened and resolute according to
Serkisof, had bought all the available copies of the book and tried
distributing "the work" in all sorts of possible places all over town,
such as at the Kadırga student dormitory (Movado), in student
hangouts (Zenith and Serkisof), and in bus stops and movie foyers
and on ferry gangplanks (Omega). He was only partially successful
in this task. Movado was all too aware that the young man was
reckless in his efforts to influence other students in his dormitory;
it had also been established that in and around other student
hangouts the subject attempted rallying other young people
around him, but having always been a loner up to this point, he
was not sufficiently effective. I had just read that he had been
able to enlist a few students he met at the refectory and in
school—where he showed up just for this end—and that he had
successfully cajoled them into reading the book, when I came
across the following news clipping:

MURDER IN ERENKÖY (Ankara News Agency): Rıfkı Ray, a
former chief inspector retired from the State Railroads Administration, was shot and killed around nine o'clock last
night by an unknown person. On his way to his coffeehouse
from his apartment on Silver Poplar Street, he was accosted
by someone who fired on him three times. The assailant,
whose identity it has not been possible to establish immediately, departed the scene. Found dead on the spot as a

result of the wounds he sustained, Ray (67) had served ac-
tively with the State Railroads Administration in various ca-
pacities until retiring from his last post as chief inspector.
Ray's death has been deplored in circles where he was much
appreciated.

I raised my head from the files, remembering: My father had
returned home very late, looking distraught. Everyone had cried
at the funeral. There had been gossip that the murder had been
a crime of passion. Who was the jealous guy? Rifling through
Doctor Fine's meticulous files, I tried to discover him. Was he
the serviceable Serkisof? Flimsy Zenith? Punctual Omega?

In another file, I found out that the investigations Doctor Fine
had commissioned at tremendous expense had reached a different
conclusion. An agent called Hamilton Watch who in all probability also worked for the National Investigation Bureau had sent
a short letter providing Doctor Fine with the following information:

Rıfkı Ray was the author of the book. He had written the book
twelve years ago, but, diffident amateur that he was, he had not
been able to muster the courage to publish the book under his
own name. National Bureau of Investigation agents, who always
had an ear trained on tales carried by fathers and teachers moti-
vated by fear for their sons' and students' futures during those
troubled times, had got wind that the book had led some youths
astray; and dragging the writer's identity out of the publishing
house, they let the matter take its course in the able hands of the
prosecutor in charge of the press. The prosecutor had the book
impounded quietly twelve years ago, but it had not been necessary
to put the fear of God into the greenhorn writer by threatening
to prosecute him. When the author, one Rıfkı Ray, a retired State
Railroads inspector, was initially summoned to the prosecutor's
office, he had expressed, using language that almost openly dis-

played his satisfaction, that not only was he not against the con-
fiscation of his book, he would not contest the action; besides, he
had signed without further ado the statement he himself had
suggested that he make, and had never again written another
book. Hamilton's report had been written eleven days before Uncle Rıfkı was killed.

Considering what Mehmet's reaction was, it was clear that he
had found out about Uncle Rıfkı's death within a short period of
time. According to Movado, "the obsessive young man" who was
in a bad way had shut himself in his room and, as if in a religious
trance, he had begun to read the book continuously from morning
to night. Then both Serkisof and Movado, who observed him
leave his quarters, pretty much agreed that our youth's activities
did not show any rhyme or reason. One day he would hang around
the back streets in Zeyrek like an idle bum, then the next day he
would watch porno movies all afternoon in some Beyoğlu theater.
Serkisof indicated that he left the dormitory sometimes in the
middle of the night but was unable to ascertain the destination.
Zenith had seen him in a terrible condition in the middle of the
day; his beard and hair were overgrown, his appearance was di-
sheveled, and he was staring at the people in the street "like an
owl spooked by daylight." He stayed away completely from his
acquaintances, from the student locales and hallways in school
where he used to try pushing the book. He had no relationship
with any female, nor did he seem to try anything in that direction.
Movado, the dormitory supervisor, had found several nudie magazines when he had gone through Mehmet's room in his absence,
but he added that this was stuff of which most normal students
availed themselves. In the light of the work Zenith and Omega
did without knowledge of each other, it was obvious that Mehmet
was for a period drinking quite hard. Later, following a brawl he
was involved in set off by some taunting in a students' beer hall
called the Three Merry Crows, he had come to prefer the more

out-of-the-way and run-down taverns located in back alleys. For a period, he had tried renewing contact with other students and crazies he had met in taverns, but it was of no avail. After that, he had loitered for hours in front of book stalls, looking for the soulmate who might show up to buy and read the book. He had located the few young people whom he had once managed to befriend and prevail on to read the book, but according to Zenith he was so ill-tempered that he would soon pick a fight. Omega had been able to eavesdrop on an argument that took place at a tavern situated in some Aksaray back alley, and he was successful in overhearing our young man, who no longer appeared so young, enthusiastically spout about the world in the book, arriving there, the threshold, stillness, the unique moment, and hazard. But these enthusiasms must also have been temporary because, as Movado had indicated, Mehmet, who was so unkempt, dirty, and messy that he had become a nuisance to his friends—if in fact he had any friends left—was no longer reading the book. "If you ask me, sir," Movado had written regarding our young man's aimless ramblings and walks that ended nowhere, "this young man is searching for something that will lighten his burden, and although I am not entirely sure I know what he is looking for, I don't think he knows it for sure either."

On one of those days on which he aimlessly walked the streets of Istanbul, our young man, whom Serkisof was following closely, had found the "something" that might relieve his grief and bring peace to his soul at the bus terminal. That is, he had found the bus. Without packing a suitcase, without buying a ticket that indicated a destination, he had spontaneously boarded some departing bus at random; and Serkisof, who was thrown for a moment, had also jumped on the next Magirus bus and taken off in pursuit.

From then on they had traveled on the same buses for weeks without a destination, from town to town, terminal to terminal,

from one bus to the next, Serkisof always in hot pursuit. The
records written in a cramped hand which Serkisof had kept while
sitting in vibrating bus seats were heartfelt testimonials to the
magic and vibrancy of these precarious and aimless journeys. They
had observed travelers who had lost their luggage and their way,
lunatics who had lost track of time; they had met retired souls
selling calendars, gung-ho boys going off to the army, young men
announcing the Judgment Day. They had sat down in terminal
restaurants and taken their meals with young engaged couples,
repair shop apprentices, soccer players, purveyors of contraband
cigarettes, hired killers, primary school teachers, movie theater
managers; and they had slept pressed against hundreds of people
curled up in bus seats and waiting rooms. They had not spent
even a single night in a hotel. They had never established a per-
manent bond or any sort of friendship. They had not traveled
even once where they had known their destination.

"All we do, actually, is to get off one bus and get on another,"
Serkisof had written. "We are expecting something, perhaps a
miracle, or some kind of light, perhaps an angel, or an accident;
I just don't know what, but this is all that comes to me . . . It is
as if we are looking for some sign that will take us to an uncharted
realm, but so far we have had no luck. The fact that we have not
had even the slightest mishap so far indicates that perhaps an
angel is keeping watch over us. I can't tell if the young man remains altogether unaware of my motives. I don't know if I can
last it out to the bitter end."

He had not been able to last it out. A week after Serkisof had
written the halting letter, Mehmet had left his soup half finished
at a rest stop where they had stopped at midnight and he had
bolted into a BLUE SAFEWAY bus, leaving Serkisof, who had been
spooning up a bowl of the same soup, to stare in amazement while
Mehmet got away and disappeared. So he had calmly finished his
soup, and he had reported it to Doctor Fine, saying that in all

honesty he was not in the least embarrassed. What should he do next?

After that, neither Serkisof, who had been told to continue with his investigations, nor Doctor Fine had been able to learn anything further about Mehmet's activities for some weeks.

Until the moment Serkisof encountered the corpse of another young man whom he took to be Mehmet, for more than a month he had been killing time at bus terminals, traffic bureaus, and driver hangouts, hurrying to the sites of traffic accidents where his instincts led him to look for our young man among the dead. I understood from other letters written on other buses that Doctor Fine had also dispatched other watches after his son. One of these letters was being written when the bus Zenith was on had plowed into the rear of a horse cart, and Zenith's punctilious heart had stopped from the loss of blood; it had been the management of the PROMPT SAFEWAY bus company that had mailed Doctor Fine the bloodstained letter, which remained unfinished.

It had taken Serkisof four hours to reach the traffic accident where Mehmet had victoriously brought to a close his life as Nahit. A SAFETY EXPRESS bus had rear-ended a tanker truck carrying printer's ink, and for a while the bus, which was rife with screams, had glowed under a pitch-black substance, only to go up in the middle of the night, consumed by brilliant flames. Serkisof had written that he had been unable to make a positive identification of "the poor obsessive boy who had been burned beyond recognition," and the only evidence he had in hand was the young man's identification card, which, as luck would have it, had not been consumed. Those who had lived through the incident had verified that the dead young man had been sitting in seat number 37. Had Nahit been in number 38, he would have survived without a scratch. Serkisof, having learned from a survivor that the young man in seat 38 was about the same age, a student of architecture called Mehmet who was studying at the Technical Uni-

versity in Istanbul, had tracked the young man down to his home
in Kayseri to hear about Nahit's last hours, but he had been unable to get hold of the young man called Mehmet. Considering
that he ought to have gone to see his parents after the horrible
accident he had survived, but hadn't, Serkisof surmised the young
Mehmet must have been terribly affected by the mishap; yet he
was not Serkisof's immediate problem. Now that the subject
whom he had followed all these months was dead, he was waiting
for further orders and money from Doctor Fine. After all, his
investigations had revealed that the whole of Anatolia, not to
mention the Middle East and the Balkans, was seething with enraged young people who had read books of this sort.

   After the news of his son's death and then the charcoaled
body's arrival home, Doctor Fine was so beside himself with anger
that he fired the surviving watches. The fact that Uncle Rıfkı had
been killed did not lessen his ire but only clouded its focus, dif-
fusing it against the whole of society. In the days following the
funeral Doctor Fine hired seven new investigators with the aid of
a well-connected retired police officer who took care of Doctor
Fine's affairs in Istanbul; and he bestowed code names on the
new crew taken from all sorts of watches. Besides that, he had
further developed his ties to the heartsick dealers whose common
enemy was the Great Conspiracy; and he had begun to receive
from them occasional tips. These persons—whose businesses had
failed because of competition from specific international companies that were in such things as heaters, ice cream, refrigerators,
soda pop, usury, and hamburgers—suspected and reviled young
people who read not only Uncle Rıfkı's book but, in general, any
books that seemed to these dealers odd, different, or foreign; and
if they received encouragement from Doctor Fine, they were all
too keen on tailing these youths and keeping an eye on them,
gladly making it their duty to write paranoid and irate reports.

   Just to see if someone who had read the book in a provincial town, or in some stuffy dormitory, or in a dinky neighborhood like mine, had been informed on by one of Doctor Fine's spies, I skimmed through these reports while eating the dinner Rosebud had brought on a tray, saying, "Father did not think you would want to interrupt your work." In the pages I quickly flipped through eager to chance upon a soulmate, I came across a couple of intriguing incidents that made my hair stand on end; but I could not make out to what extent these people were my soulmates.

Upon reading the book, a student of veterinary medicine, for example, whose father labored as a coal miner in Zonguldak, had ceased to attend to anything other than basic human requirements like eating and sleeping, and spent all his time reading the book. This young man would some days read one single page over and over a thousand times, thereby failing to do anything else with his time. One alcoholic high school math teacher, who did not conceal his suicidal tendencies, kept spending the last ten minutes of every class period—that is, until his students rose up in arms—with readings from the book which he accompanied with irritating peals of laughter. As for a young man from Erzurum who was studying economics, he had papered the walls of his room with pages from the book, which had led to a terrible fight with his roommates when one of them claimed there was a slur against Prophet Mohammad in the pages; whereupon a dorm resident who was half blind had climbed on a chair trying to read the corner between the stovepipe and the ceiling with a magnifying glass, which had resulted in some heartsick handyman getting wind of the book and reporting the incident back to Doctor Fine; but I could not be sure if the book that had ruined the life of the student from Erzurum with debates over "whether or not he should be turned in to the prosecutor" was in fact the one written by Uncle Rıfkı.

As it turns out, the book was traveling like a loose mine by

virtue of a hundred or a hundred and fifty copies which were
changing hands through chance meetings, or being mentioned by
half-curious readers, or attracting attention in bookstalls; or similar books which performed the same magical function were sometimes instilling in one of the readers a current of excitement or
some sort of inspiration. Some went into solitude with the book,
but at the threshold of a serious breakdown they were able to
open up to the world and shake off their affliction. There were
also those who had crises or tantrums upon reading the book,
accusing their friends and lovers of being oblivious to the world
in the book, of not knowing or desiring the book, and thereby
criticizing them mercilessly for not being anything like the persons in the book's universe. There was another set of organizer
types who read the book in order to apply themselves to humanity
rather than to the text. These enthusiasts settled down to search
for others like themselves who had read the book, and if they
were unsuccessful in this task—which was always the case—they
prevailed on others to read the book, hoping to engage in activism
shared by the people they had ensnared. Neither these activists
nor the informants who informed on them had any idea as to
what sort of activism these people held in common.

During the next couple of hours, as I pieced out the facts from
news clips that had been filed meticulously among the informants' letters, I learned that five such readers who had been inspired by the book had been killed by Doctor Fine's watches. It
was not clear what watch had committed which murders at what
time and for what reason. It was just that the short news items
clipped from the newspapers had been placed in chronological
order among the records of denunciation. There were, however,
some details available on a couple of the killings. Since one of
the murdered persons was a student of journalism who had done
translations for the foreign news service of the *Sun* papers, the
Journalists Association for Patriotic Action pretended to have

taken an interest in the incident, announcing that the Turkish press would never bow down before senseless terrorism. The other killing involved a waiter who had been gunned down when his hands were full of empty bottles of a popular yogurt drink; Islamic Youth Raiders had disclosed that the dead waiter had been a member, declaring at their press conference that the homicide had been perpetrated by the agents of the CIA and Coca-Cola.

11 THE PLEASURE OF READING, WHICH NATTY OLDER gentlemen complain is lacking in our culture, must be in the musical harmony I heard reading the documents and murder reports in Doctor Fine's mad and orderly archive. On my arms I felt the cool night air, in my ears I heard night music that was not actually playing; meanwhile, I tried to figure out what I must do to act like a young person who had decided to be resolute in the face of the wonders he has come across at his tender age. Since I had decided to be a responsible young person who prepared for his future, I pulled a piece of paper out of Doctor Fine's stock and began to write down small clues that might come in handy.

I left the archive room when I was still hearing that music in my ears, at an hour when I felt deep inside me how cold and calculating were both the world and the philosophically inclined patriarch of the house. It was as if I could hear the encouraging provocation of some blithe spirit. I felt something tingling inside like that playful feeling people like me get when we leave the theater after seeing a fun and upbeat movie, a feeling which is as light as the music that goes through our heads. You know what

I mean: we identify with the hero, as if we were the guy with the clever jokes, the spontaneous levity, the incredible ready wit.

"May I have this dance?" I was about to ask Janan, who was watching me with concern.

She was sitting at the dinner table with the three rosy sisters, looking at some balls of yarn in all manner of colors which had spilled out from a wicker basket on the table top like ripe apples and oranges out of a cornucopia of felicity and plenty. Next to these were the knitting and embroidery patterns that came with the magazine called *Home and Women* that my mother also used to take at one time, flowers to needlepoint, cute little ducks, cats, dogs, besides the mosque motifs which must have been contributed by the publisher, who lifted all the rest from German women's magazines and foisted it on Turkish women. I too studied all that color in the light of the kerosene lamps, remembering that the actual life drama I had just been reading about had been constructed with equally vivid raw materials. Then turning to Rosamund's two little daughters who came up to their mother, melting into this scene of family happiness, yawning and blinking their eyes, I said to them, "What, your mother hasn't put you to bed yet?"

They were taken aback and a little frightened when they nestled against their mother. My mood was improving. I could even have regaled Rosebud and Rosabelle, who were eyeing me suspiciously, with something like, "You are both blooms that have not yet faded."

Yet I didn't manage to say anything until I entered the quarters reserved for receiving male guests. "Sir," I said to Doctor Fine, "I read your son's story with great sorrow."

"It has all been documented," he replied.

He introduced me to two semiobscured men in the darkened room. No, these gentlemen were not watches, seeing how they weren't ticking. One was a notary, but since in murky situations like this my mind does not record things, I didn't get what the other one did; I was more concerned with how Doctor Fine had introduced me: I was a young man destined to do great things, who was levelheaded, serious, and passionate; I could already be considered to be very close to him. There was nothing about me that smelled of those pseudo longhairs who aped characters in American films. He had great trust in me, very great.

How quickly I identified with all the praise! I didn't know what to do with my hands, but I wanted to look refined, so I bent my head down as befits a modest young man like me and changed the subject, all too aware that my changing the subject would be observed and appreciated.

"How quiet it is here at night, sir," I said.

"Yet there's a rustling in the mulberry tree," said Doctor Fine, "even when the night is all quiet and there's not even a hint of a breeze. Listen."

We all listened. I was more discomfited by the chilling darkness in the room than by the tree rustling out there somewhere. Listening to the silence I realized that since I had come to this house I hadn't once heard people speak in anything but whispers.

Doctor Fine took me aside. "We were just sitting down to play a few hands of bezique," he said. "Now I want you to tell me, my son, which would you prefer to see? My guns, or my timepieces?"

"I'd like to see the timepieces, sir," I said without a thought.

In the next room, which was even darker, all three of us were shown two old-time Zenith table models that banged away like gunshots. We saw the drawer horologe made by the Galata clockmakers' colony, which was encased in wood, played a tune of its own accord, and had to be wound only once a week; according to Doctor Fine, there was one just like it in the harem section of the Topkapı Palace. Then we were trying to figure out in which

Levantine port lived Simon S. Simonien who had made and
signed the pendulum clock with the carved walnut cabinet, when
we made out the words "à Smyrne" on the enameled dial. We
noted that the Universal clock that sported a moon and a calendar
showed the days of the full moon. When Doctor Fine took a huge
key and wound the pendulum of the skeleton clock, the dial of
which had been fashioned like a Mevlevi turban at the instigation
of Sultan Selim the Third, we tensed, realizing that it was the
inner organs of the skeleton that were being wound up. We remembered having seen and heard in so many places ever since
our childhood the Junghans pendulum wall clocks that still
clicked sadly like caged canaries in so many houses. It gave us
shivers to see the locomotive and under it the words Made in
USSR on the dial of the crude Serkisof clock.

"For our people, the ticking of clocks is not just a means of
apprising the mundane, but the resonance that brings us in line
with our inner world, like the sound of splashing water in fountains in the courtyards of our mosques," Doctor Fine said. "We
pray five times a day; then in Ramadan, we have the time for
iftar, the breaking of fast at sundown, and the time for *sahur*, the
meal taken just before sunup. Our timetables and timepieces are
our vehicles to reach God, not the means of rushing to keep up
with the world as they are in the West. There never was a nation
on earth as devoted to timepieces as we have been; we were the
greatest patrons of European clock makers. Timepieces are the
only product of theirs that has been acceptable to our souls.
That is why clocks are the only things other than guns that cannot
be classified as foreign or domestic. For us there are two venues
that lead to God. Armaments are the vehicles of Jihad; timepieces
are the vehicles for prayer. They have managed to silence our
guns. Now they have hatched these trains so that our time will
also be silenced. Everyone knows that the greatest enemy of the
timetable for prayers is the timetable for trains. My dead son

was well aware of this fact, and that's why he spent months on buses to retrieve our lost time. Those who wanted to estrange him from me used the bus to take the life of my son and heir, but Doctor Fine is not naïve enough to be duped by their machinations. Remember this: when our people get some money together, the first thing they buy is always a watch."

Perhaps Doctor Fine was going to continue whispering his harangue, but he was interrupted by an English-made ormolu Prior clock fitted with an enameled dial, ornamented with ruby roses, and graced by the sound of a nightingale, which began to play the melody of the old Ottoman song, "My Scribe."

While his bezique buddies pricked their ears to the sweet song about the scribe's excursion to Üsküdar, Doctor Fine whispered into my ear: "Have you come to a decision, my child?"

At the same instant I saw through the open door in the next room Janan's shimmering reflection in the mirror on the console, and I was distracted.

"I need to do some more work in the archives, sir," I said.

I said it in order to avoid making a decision rather than in the hope of coming to one. I was passing through the next room when I felt the eyes of the three roses on me, the fastidious Rosebud, high-strung Rosabelle, and Rosamund who had come back from putting her daughters to bed. How curious and how determined were Janan's honey-colored eyes! I felt as if I had achieved something important, as I suspect many a man feels when he is associated with a beautiful and lively woman.

Yet how far I was from being that man! Here I was, sitting in Doctor Fine's archives, with files upon files of intelligence reports in front of me, and having jealously internalized the beauty of Janan's visage augmented by the mirror on the console in the other room, I was turning the pages rapidly with the hope that my increasing jealousy might finally impel me to come to a decision.

I did not have to continue my research for too long. After the funeral of the luckless youth from Kayseri whom Doctor Fine had buried believing that he was his son, he had phased out the remaining old watches Movado, Omega, and Serkisof, and Zenith was dead. Seiko, the most reliable and timely of the new watches Doctor Fine had hired in order to track down every soul who had ever read the book, had managed to put his finger on a certain Mehmet and his girlfriend Janan, students of architecture whom he had come across during his forays into the student dormitories, cafés, clubs, and school lounges in the hope of encountering someone who was familiar with the book. His discovery had taken place sixteen months earlier. It was in the spring. Janan and Mehmet were in love, and they carried a book which they read to each other intimately. They had no clue as to the existence of Seiko, who continued to watch them, even though not too closely, for some eight months.

Seiko had submitted to Doctor Fine twenty-two reports, written at random intervals during the eight months from the time he discovered the pair until I read the book and Mehmet was shot at the minibus stop. It was with patience and mounting jealousy that I read these reports again and again, way past the midnight hour, trying to absorb the poisonous conclusions I drew by virtue of the logic provided by the archive where I was working.

1. What Janan told me looking out the window in Room 19 where we spent the night in the town of Güdül, saying something to the effect that no man had ever touched her, was not true. Seiko, who had followed them not only in the spring but also throughout the summer when he had observed the two young people go into the hotel where Mehmet worked, had determined that they had stayed in his room for many hours. It's not that I did not suspect this, but when someone else has witnessed what we merely suspected, and has written it down, one feels even more foolish.

2. No one including Seiko had suspected that Mehmet might be the new identity Nahit assumed after closing out his former life, not his father, not the management at the hotel where he worked, not the registrar's office at the school of architecture.

3. The lovers displayed no social anomaly to attract attention other than their being in love. If the last ten days of Seiko's surveillance were discounted, they had not even attempted to pass their copy of the book to others. Besides, they did not read the book all the time, which was the reason why Seiko had not made a point of watching what it was that they did with the book. They appeared to be a couple of university students headed for an ordinary marital life. Their association with classmates was well-balanced, their grades fine, their enthusiasms prudent. They had no relationship with any political group, and had no zealous involvement that was worth noting. Seiko had even written that, among all those who had read the book, Mehmet was the most even-tempered, the least obsessive and passionate of the lot. Perhaps that was why Seiko was caught by surprise later; he might even have been pleased with the way things turned out.

4. Seiko envied them. When I made comparisons with his other reports, I initially noticed that he described Janan in language that was overly considered and poetic. "Reading the book, the young woman knits her brows delicately, and her countenance assumes a limpid grace and dignity." "She then made the gesture that is special to her, pulling her hair with one tiny swoop behind her ears." "Sometimes if she is reading the book standing in line at the cafeteria, she sticks out her upper lip slightly, and her eyes begin to glimmer so, one imagines two large teardrops may appear any moment in the corners of those beautiful eyes." And what about these astonishing lines? "Well, sir, the young woman's visage over the book became so tender after a half hour's reading, and the expression on her face was so strange and unparalleled, that for a moment I thought the magical light did

not stream in the windows but surged from the pages of the book into this angelic countenance." In contrast to Janan's celestial virtues the young man in her company was seen as being too much of the world. "This thing is nothing more than an affair of the heart between the daughter of a fine family and a penniless young man whose antecedents are obscure." "Our young man is forever the one who's more cautious, anxious, and parsimonious." "The young woman has the inclination to open up to friends, to get close to them, and even to share the book, but the hotel clerk keeps her in check." "Obviously he avoids her circle of friends because he himself comes from a low-class family." "Come to think of it, it's hard to imagine what the young woman sees in this cold and lackluster fellow." "He is far too arrogant for a mere hotel clerk." "He's one of those crafty people who manage to seem wise because they're tight-lipped and uncommunicative." "Effete upstart!" "He has nothing to recommend him, I must say." I was beginning to like this Seiko. If only I could rely on his accuracy. He did, however, persuade me of something else.

5. How happy they were! After class, they went up to a Beyoğlu theater, and they held hands all through a movie called *Endless Nights*. They sat at a corner table in the student canteen, watching people and talking animatedly to each other. Always together, whether window shopping in uptown Beyoğlu, or taking the bus, or going to class and on outings throughout the city, or sitting up on stools at sandwich bars, knee to knee, watching themselves eat their sandwiches in the mirror; and there they are again, reading the book the young woman has pulled out of her tote bag. And then there was that summer's day! Seiko began following Mehmet from the moment he left the hotel; and then observing him meet Janan, who was carrying a plastic bag, he assumed that something was up and took off after them. They rode the ferry to Princess Island, rented a rowboat and went swimming; they hired a hansom cab, had corn on the cob and ice cream; and

when they got back to town, they went up to the young man's room. It was difficult reading all this. They had spats and their share of arguments, and at times Seiko read these as bad signs, but until the fall there had been no real strain between them.

6. Seiko must have been the person who pulled the gun out of the pink plastic bag and shot Mehmet on that snowy December day in the vicinity of the minibus stop. But I was not entirely sure of it. Yet his anger and jealousy attested to that. Remembering the image of the shadowy person whom I'd seen out of the window sprinting away through the snow-covered park, I imagined Seiko must be around thirty years old, an ambitious officer who was a graduate of the police academy, who moonlighted doing private investigation jobs in order to supplement his income, someone who considered students of architecture "effete." Well then, what was his assessment of me?

7. I was an abject victim of entrapment. Seiko had reached this conclusion so handily that he had even felt somewhat sorry for me. And yet he had been unable to deduce that the source of the strain between the young woman and the young man had been Janan's desire to do something with the book. But then, it must have been on Janan's insistence that they decided to draft someone into whose hands they would put the book. They had looked over the students in the halls of the Technical University like headhunters for a private firm sifting through the talent pool for the right candidate to fill a vacant position. It was not at all clear why I was the one they had chosen. But soon Seiko had accurately determined that they had indeed been watching me, following me, and talking about me. Then, the scene of my falling into the trap had gone even more easily than their singling me out. How easy? Well, Janan had walked close to me several times in the hallway, carrying the book in her hand. She had once given me a sweet smile. Then it was with great relish that she had indeed set me up: She had become aware of me watching her in line at the

canteen, and pretending that she had to put down what she had in her hand so that she could rifle through her bag for her wallet, she had placed the book on the table before me; and after ten seconds or so, her delicate hand had spirited it away. Then assured that I, the poor fish, had taken the bait, the two of them had placed the book free of charge at the sidewalk stall which they had already determined was on my route, so that I would see the book on my way home and recognizing it bemusedly—"Ah, there's that book!"—I would buy it. Which is exactly what happened. Saddened by the situation on my account, Seiko accurately made this observation about me: "a dreamy kid with nothing special to recommend him."

Not only did I not mind it too much, since he had pretty much the same assessment of Mehmet, I even found enough consolation in it to work up the courage to ask myself this question: Why had I not ever confessed to myself that I had bought and read the book as a means of getting to the beautiful girl?

What was truly unbearable, however, was the fact that while I was gazing at Janan with open admiration, staring at her without even being aware that I was staring, while the book lighted on my table like a timid magic bird—that is, while I was living the most entrancing moment of my life—not only was Mehmet watching the two of us, in the distance there was Seiko, watching all three of us.

"The coincidence that I loved and accepted with joy, thinking it was life itself, turns out to be mere fiction constructed by someone else," said the hoodwinked hero, deciding to leave the room for the purpose of seeing Doctor Fine's arsenal. But he still had to figure out a few more things and do some more research, that is, he needed to put in another hour's work.

I worked as hard as I could and came up with an inventory of all the young Mehmets who were seen reading the book, which had been made by Doctor Fine's punctilious watches and the heart-

sick dealers all over Anatolia. Seeing that Serkisof had not disclosed our Mehmet's surname, I ended up with a fairly long list
which I did not yet know how to evaluate.

It was quite late, but I was certain Doctor Fine was waiting up
for me. I walked toward the room where the games of bezique
were played against the background ticking of all the clocks. Janan
and Doctor Fine's daughters had retired to their rooms, and the
bezique cronies had long gone home. Doctor Fine had retreated
into the farthest corner of the room, where he was reading sunk
deep in an overstuffed chair as if to shield himself from the light
of the kerosene lamps.

When he became aware of my presence, he slipped a letter
opener inlaid with mother-of-pearl into the book he had been
reading, closed it, and rose to his feet, saying he was ready and
had been waiting up for me. I might want to rest a bit first, in
case my eyes were too fatigued from all that reading. But he was
certain that I was pleased with all that I had read and gleaned.
Wasn't life just rife with sly sonsobitches and mind-boggling hap-
penstances? And yet he was resolved that it was his duty to bring
order to all this chaos.

"The dossiers and the indexes have been prepared by Rosabelle
with the care of a girl working at an embroidery frame," he said.
"As for Rosebud, it is as much a pleasure for her to direct the
correspondence as it is to be a dutiful daughter, writing the letters
to my obedient watches in line with my general wishes and responses. Every afternoon we take tea listening to Rosamund's
beautiful voice read us the letters we receive. Sometimes we work
in this room, sometimes we move into the archive room where
you have been studying. On warm spring days and in the summer,
we sit for hours around the table under the mulberry tree. For a
man who likes solitude as I do, those are hours spent in true
happiness."

My mind kept searching for appropriate words to praise all this

love and devotion, all this care and refinement, and all this peace
and order. Having seen the cover of the book he put down when
he saw me, I knew he had been reading a volume of *Zagor*. Did
he have any knowledge that Uncle Rıfkı, whose death he had
ordered, had at one time attempted a nationalistic version of this
illustrated novel? But I was in no mind to fuss with the finer
points of these coincidences.

"May I see the guns now, sir?"

His fond response was spoken with an affectionate tone that
gave me confidence: I was welcome to call him Doctor, or else
Father.

Doctor Fine showed me a Browning semiautomatic pistol
which had been imported by the department of internal security
from Belgium in 1956 on a contract bid, explaining that until
recently these had been issued only to top echelon police. Then
he told me about the time the German-make Parabellum pistol,
which could be converted into a rifle by virtue of the wooden
holster that doubled as a stock, had gone off by accident, and the
9-millimeter bullet had pierced through two massive Hungarian
draft horses, then gone in one window of the house and out the
other, and lodged in the trunk of the mulberry; he went on to say
that it was, however, an awkward firearm to carry. If I wanted
something practical and reliable, he recommended the Smith &
Wesson with a safety grip. And then there was the shiny Colt
revolver that would thrill any gun enthusiast, which did not have
a safety, so even if one were to freeze up, all one had to remember
was to pull the trigger; and yet one might possibly feel too much
like an American cowboy carrying one of these babies. So our
attention was directed to a series of the German-made Walthers,
which was the one make that had been successfully absorbed into
our national consciousness, and its patented domestic look-alike,
the Kırıkkale model. These guns were special in my eyes too by
virtue of their widespread use in the last forty years, having been

tried hundreds of thousands of times by gun enthusiasts ranging
from army officers to night watchmen, from bread bakers to po-
licemen, on the bodies of many a rebel, thief, Casanova, politi-
cian, and starving citizen.

On Doctor Fine's assurance that there was nary a difference
between the Walther and the Kırıkkale and after he had asserted
several times that they were both part of our bodies as well as our
souls, I settled on a Walther 9-millimeter with a hammer, a gun
that could be easily concealed and did not need to be fired at
close range to do the trick. And, of course, there was no need for
me to say anything before Doctor Fine made me a present of the
gun as well as a couple of clips, kissing me on the forehead, which
was the fitting gesture that lightly alluded to our forefathers' obsession with guns. He said that he still had some more work to
do, but I ought to go to bed now and get my rest.

Sleep was the last thing on my mind. Walking the seventeen
steps from the gun cabinet to our room, seventeen different scenarios went through my head. I had stored all of them in one corner of my mind as I read, and had at the last moment settled on
the synthesis that fit in with the final scene. I remember knocking
three times on the door Janan had locked, reviewing once again
the wonder wrought by my mind which had been intoxicated by
so much reading, but I have no notion of what that synthesis was.
As soon as I knocked on the door, a voice inside me said "Password!" perhaps because I thought Janan might have asked for the
password, so I came back with: "Long live the Sultan!"

When Janan turned the lock and then opened the door, I was
unnerved by the expression on her face which was half-cheerful,
no, half-sad, no, totally mysterious, and I felt like some amateur
actor who forgets the lines he had been memorizing for weeks the
moment he steps into the lights. It was not all that difficult to
calculate that someone who had his wits about him would trust
his instincts in a situation like this rather than trying to come up

with a bunch of derelict words that he barely remembers. Which is what I did. I tried to forget that I was a prey, at best, who had fallen into a trap.

I kissed Janan on the lips like some young husband back from a long trip. Here we were at last, after all the unforeseen dangers, at home in our room. I loved her so much I thought nothing else was important. If life presented a rough spot or two, I was the seasoned traveler who had the courage to take things in my stride. Her lips smelled of mulberries. The two of us, we were the two people who were meant to hold on to each other, turning our backs on the summons of a dogmatic and unattainable life and all those who tried to distress us with their self-sacrifices, all those esteemed and passionate fools who try projecting their obsessions on the world, all the people who have slipped off the course of their lives, lured by ideas that have been thought of some place far away. When two people have shared great dreams, when they've been comrades from morning to night for months on end, when they've covered such great distances together, what could possibly be the impediment to their forgetting the world in an embrace, O Angel? And most of all, what could stop them from becoming their authentic selves and finding that unique moment of truth?

The ghost of the third lover.

Please let me again kiss you on the lips, for the ghost who remains a mere name in all those intelligence reports shuns becoming an actual person. Whereas I am here and, look, I know time is slowly running out. Look how all those highways we traveled exist as themselves without being in the least aware of us once we have traveled over them, stretching out full of themselves, made of stones and asphalt and warmth on summer nights under the stars. Let us too, here, without further ado lie down together . . . Please, sweetheart, when my hands touch your beautiful shoulders, your slender and fragile arms, when I come so

close to you, look how slowly and joyfully we approach that
unique time so sought after by all the voyagers who travel on the
bus. When I press my lips on that semitransparent skin between
your ear and your hair, when the electricity of your hair gives
fright to the birds that suddenly swoop past my forehead and face,
raising the scent of autumn in the air, and when your breast
stiffens like a stubborn bird taking wing in my palm, look, I see
in your eyes how full and right is the unattainable time that rea-
wakens between us: now we are neither here nor there, not in the
land you have been dreaming about, not on some bus or in a dim
hotel room somewhere, not even in some sort of future that can
only exist within the pages of a book. Now we are here in this
room, as if existing in a time that is open-ended, you with your
sighs and I with my hurried kisses, we are holding on to each
other, awaiting a miracle that might happen. A time for fullness!
Embrace me, so that time will not flow away, come, embrace me,
my soul, so that the miracle will not end. Please, don't resist, but
remember: the nights in bus seats when our bodies would slowly
lose themselves in each other, when our dreams and our hair
tangled together; remember before you turn away your lips, remember seeing the inside of houses in the back streets of small
towns we passed through, our heads pressed against the cold and
dark windowpane; remember all the films we watched hand in
hand: the bullets that poured like rain, blondes descending staircases, all the cool dudes you so adored. Remember all the kisses
we watched quietly as if we were committing a sin, forgetting a
crime, dreaming of a different land. Remember those lips drawing
together while the eyes were averted from the camera; remember
how we were able to sit completely still for a moment even as the
bus tires revolved seven and a half times per minute. But she did
not remember. I kissed her hopelessly for the last time. The bed
had been rumpled. Was it possible that she felt on me the hard

form of the Walther? Janan had stretched out on the bed, staring at the ceiling thoughtfully as if contemplating the stars. Even so, I couldn't help saying, "Janan, were we not happy on our bus trips? Let us go back to riding the buses."

Of course, it made no sense.

"What were you reading?" she asked me. "What have you found out today?"

"Many things about life," I said, using the language of dubbed films and the tone of soap operas. "Very useful things really. There are so many who have read the book, all rushing toward some place or other . . . Everything is confused and the light that the book inspires in people is as dazzling as death. Life is so astounding."

I had a feeling I could go on in this vein; if I could not create miracles through love, then I could at least do it by speaking the sort of words that fascinate children. Forgive my naïveté, Angel, and the trickery I resorted to out of my need, for this was the first time in seventy days that I had felt this close to Janan, lying beside her on the bed; as anyone who has done a bit of reading knows, imitating childlike wonderment is the immediate ruse attempted by people like me who have had the doors of true love slammed in their faces. On a night it rained like a deluge as we rode from Afyon to Kütahya on a bus that leaked in torrents through the ceiling and the windows, the film we saw was *False Paradise*; but Seiko had recently informed me—had he not?— that Janan had watched the same film in happier and calmer circumstances a year before that, her hand in the hand of her lover.

"So who's the angel?" she asked me now.

"Appears to be related to the book," I said. "We are not the only ones who know about it. There are others pursuing the angel."

"So who does the angel appear to?"

"Those who have faith in the book, those who read it with care."

"Then what?"

"Then you keep reading until you become transformed. One morning you wake up and people who see you say, my, my, this girl has turned into an angel in the light that emanates from the book. Then it means that the angel must have been a girl all along. It makes you wonder then how such an angel could lure someone into a trap. Is it possible for angels to pull nasty stunts?"

"Don't know."

"I don't either. I am also doing some thinking, and searching." That is what I said, Angel, perhaps because I was loath to step out of line into zones of danger and uncertainty, thinking that the only piece of heaven I was sure of was the bed where I was lying next to Janan. Let the unique moment have its reign. There was a faint smell of woodwork in the room, and also a cool scent that was reminiscent of the sort of soap and chewing gum we bought when we were children but no longer do because the packaging is so poor.

I, who had neither the ability to delve deep into the book nor to rise to Janan's level of seriousness, I felt that in the wee hours of the night I might be able to come up with the words that would mediate some points. So I told Janan that the most horrifying thing was time itself; without knowing it, we had embarked on this journey to escape time. That was the reason why we were in constant motion, looking for the moment when time stood still. Which was the unique moment of fulfillment. When we got close to it, we could sense the time of departure, our own eyes having witnessed, along with the dead and the dying, the miracle of this incredible zone. The seeds of the wisdom in the book also existed in their most childlike form in the comics we had thumbed through all morning, and it was high time we used our heads and got the point. There was nothing there, in that distant place. The beginning and the end of our journey was wherever we happened to be. He was right: the road and all the dark rooms were rife with killers carrying guns. Death seeped into life through the book, through books.

I held her, saying, Sweetheart, let's do stay here, in this beautiful room, cherishing it. Look, a table, a clock, a lamp, a window. When we rise in the morning, the mulberry tree will be there for us to admire. So what if he is there and we are here? Here's the windowsill, the table leg, the wick in the lamp: light and scent. The world is so simple! Do forget the book. He too wants us to forget it. To be is to be embracing you. But Janan was not having any of it.

"Where is Mehmet?"

She was looking at the ceiling with rapt attention, as if the answer to her question was inscribed there. She knit her brows. Her forehead seemed higher. Her lips twitched for a split second as if about to reveal a secret. Under the parchment-colored light in the room her skin had assumed a pink hue which I had never before seen. What with decent meals and a place to sleep in peaceful surroundings after all those nights traveling on some bus, at last Janan had some color in her face. I mentioned this to her, hoping that, like some girls who will marry out of a sudden longing for a happily settled married life, she would marry me.

"I am getting sick, that's why," she said. "I was chilled in the rain. I'm running a fever."

How beautiful she was! She was stretched out and staring at the ceiling, and I was lying next to her, admiring the color in her face, keeping my hand pressed as objectively as a doctor's on her noble forehead. My hand remained there as if to make sure she would not escape from me. I was reviewing my childhood memories, how she had completely transformed ordinary objects in the sphere of the pleasure of touch, like beds, rooms, smells. Other thoughts and calculations were also running through my head. When she turned her face slightly, her eyes questioning me, I pulled my hand away from her forehead and told her the truth.

"You do have a fever."

Suddenly a lot of possibilities that were not part of my plans appeared before me. I went down to the kitchen at one in the morning. Negotiating among hulking pots and phantoms in the half light, I came upon a saucepan in which I made tea with the dried linden flowers I found in a jar, imagining all the while how I was going to tell Janan that the best way to ward off a cold was to crawl under the blanket with someone. And later, as I rifled through the medicine bottles on the sideboard where Janan had directed me, looking for an aspirin, I was thinking that if I too were to get sick, then we wouldn't have to leave the room for days. A curtain moved and some slippers sounded on the floor. The shadow of Doctor Fine's wife appeared first and then her nervous self. "No, ma'am," I said, "it's nothing serious; she has just caught a cold."

She took me upstairs. She had me take down a heavy blanket from a storage space, and slipping a duvet cover over it, she said: "The poor sweetheart, she's an angel! Don't give her any trouble, you hear? You take care." Then she mentioned something else which would always stay in my mind: How beautiful was my wife's neck!

Back in the room I gazed at her neck for a long time. Had I not noticed it before? Yes, I had and I loved it. But now the length of her neck seemed so striking, I could think of nothing else for quite some time. I watched her drink her linden tea slowly and then take her aspirin, wrapping herself in the blanket like some good-natured child expecting to "get well."

There were long stretches of silence. Shielding my eyes with my hands, I looked out the window. The mulberry tree stirred ever so slightly. Dear One, our mulberry tree rustles even in the faintest breeze. Silence. Janan was trembling, and how quickly time was passing.

So it didn't take long for our room to acquire that special climate and character known as a "sick room." I paced up and down, apprehensive that the table, the glass, the side table were being gradually transformed into objects that were overly familiar, overly intimate. The hour struck three. Will you sit here next to me on the edge of the bed? she asked. I gripped her feet through the blanket. She smiled, telling me I was so sweet. She closed her eyes, pretending to be asleep. No, she actually fell asleep, slept. Was she asleep? She was asleep.

I found myself pacing. Looking at the time, pouring water out of the pitcher, gazing at Janan, floundering. Taking an aspirin for the hell of it. Placing my hand on her forehead to gauge her temperature again and again whenever she opened her eyes.

Time which flowed as if under the compulsion of timepieces came to a stop at a certain point, the semitransparent membrane in which I was being enveloped was torn open, and Janan sat up in bed. All of a sudden we found ourselves hotly discussing bus attendants who were really auxiliary bus drivers; one of them had once said that someday he was going to commandeer the driver's seat and drive the bus to a yet unexplored land. And then there was the one who said, help yourselves to the chewing gum, provided for our valued passengers with the compliments of the bus company; and then unable to hold his tongue, he had added, but don't chew too much, brother, because the gum is laced with opium so that the passengers will sleep like babies, thinking their peaceful sleep is due to good shock absorbers, the skill of the driver who never passes on the right, and the superiority of our vehicles and our bus company. Then how about the one we came across on two different bus lines, Janan, do you remember what he said?—it was so good to laugh! Brother, he said, the first time I laid eyes on you both I just knew you had

eloped together, now I see from your ring that you two got
hitched, sister, congratulations.

Will you marry me? We had seen so many scenes come alive
with the brilliance of these words: when the lovers are walking
under the trees, arms around each other, or when they are under
a lamppost, or in a car—in the back seat, naturally—or on the
bridge that spans the Bosphorus, or in the rain produced under
the influence of foreign films, or when the boy and the girl are
suddenly left alone by the charming uncle or friends whose intentions are good, or when the rich guy pops the question to the
seductive female as he goes splash into the swimming pool: Will
you marry me? Since I had never seen a scene in a sick room
where the girl with the beautiful neck gets asked the question, I
didn't believe my words could awaken in Janan a feeling as magical as those in the movies. Besides, my mind was on a dauntless
mosquito that was working the room.

I looked at the time and got anxious. I checked her temperature
and became worried. Let me see your tongue, I said; she stuck it
out; it was pink and came to a point. I leaned over her and took
her tongue in my mouth. We remained like that for a while,
Angel.

"Don't, dear heart," she said. "You are very sweet, but let's
not."

She fell asleep. I lay down next to her, hanging on the edge of
the bed, and began counting her breaths. Later, as the day was
about to break, I was thinking a lot of things and then thinking
again: I'll say to her, Janan, I'd do anything for you, Janan, don't
you understand how much I love you . . . Stuff like that which
always had the same gist. For a while I thought I'd make up some
lie and drag her back to the buses, but I already knew approxi-
mately where I had to go; besides, after becoming acquainted with
Doctor Fine's merciless watches and spending a night in this

room with Janan, I was aware that I had begun to be afraid of death.

You know it all too well, Angel, the poor kid was lying next to his beloved, listening to her breathing until daybreak, gazing at Janan's regular but distinctive chin, her arms showing out of the nightgown Rosebud had loaned her, her hair spreading on the pillow, and the mulberry tree gradually becoming resplendent with daylight.

Then everything speeded up. There was clattering in the house, footsteps cautiously going by our door, the sound of a window being slammed in the wind that had started up again, the mooing of a cow, the growl of a car, a cough, and a knock on our door. A clean-shaven middle-aged person with a large medical bag, looking more like a doctor than anything else, entered the room followed by a whiff of toasted bread. His lips were gory red as if he had recently been sucking blood, and there was an ugly sore on the side of his mouth. I was gripped by a fantasy that he was going to strip Janan, who was burning with fever, and use those lips to kiss her neck and back. He was taking his stethoscope out of his hateful bag when I snatched my Walther from where I had concealed it and left the house without paying any attention to the worried mother of the house standing by the door.

Before anyone could see me I rushed out to the terrain with which Doctor Fine had acquainted me. In a deserted spot surrounded by poplars where I was sure that I would neither be observed nor the wind bear any tales, I took out my gun and fired rounds in rapid succession. That was how I used up some of the rounds that had been Doctor Fine's gift, doing a short target practice which was not only curtailed by its parsimony, it was so inept that it was pitiful. I had not managed to hit the trunk of the poplar I had aimed at, not even in one out of three shots at four paces. I remember being somewhat hesitant, helplessly trying to pull my thoughts together as I observed the hurried clouds that arrived from the north. The sorrows of young Walther . . .

Up ahead there was a rocky outcrop that was high enough to afford a partial overview of Doctor Fine's estate. I climbed up there, sat down, and instead of being lost in patrician thoughts contemplating the vastness and the wealth of the landscape, I wondered in what miserable place my own life would end. A long time went by but none of the angels, books, muses, and wise peasants who in times of dire distress come to the aid of prophets, film stars, saints, and political leaders put in an appearance on my behalf.

There was no help for it but to return to the mansion. The gory-lipped mad doctor had already drunk my Janan's blood with relish and was now sitting with the mother and drinking the tea made by the rosy daughters. When he saw me, his eyes gleamed at the prospect of giving me advice.

"Young man!" he began. My wife had caught a cold, she was suffering from the flu; more important, she was on the verge of a serious debilitation due to fatigue, neglect, and lack of sleep. What was I up to, getting her so dead tired? How was it that I treated her so roughly? The mother and the daughters eyed the newlywed young husband with disapprobation.

"I gave her some heavy-duty medicine," said the doctor. "She is not to stir out of bed for an entire week."

A whole week! I was thinking to myself that seven days were more than enough for me, when the quack, having had his tea and stuffed a couple of almond macaroons in his face, was finally ready to get the hell out. Janan was asleep in bed, so I removed a few of the paraphernalia I thought I might need, the notes I had taken in the archives, and the money. I kissed Janan on the neck. I left the room with the haste of a volunteer on his way to save his country. I told Rosebud and her mother that I had some urgent business that could not wait and a responsibility that I could not shirk. I entrusted my wife to them. They said they would look after her as if she were the bride of their own son. I indicated with special insistence that I would be back within five days, and without looking back, not even once, to see the land of witches, phantoms, and bandits I was leaving behind me, without even a glance at the grave of the young man from Kayseri who was interred there in lieu of Doctor Fine's son, I made my way to town and the bus terminal.

12 ON THE ROAD AGAIN! HEY THERE, YOU OLD TER-
minals, you rickety buses, you sad voyagers, hello!
You know how it goes, when you are deprived of the rituals of
some commonplace habit you have become addicted to without
even being aware that you have a habit, you are gripped by the
sorrow of a feeling that life is not what it used to be. I had assumed I would be free of this sorrow riding on an old Magirus
bus that carried me away from the town of Çatık which was under
Doctor Fine's clandestine reign, and toward the rest of civilization. After all, here I was on a bus at last, albeit one that was
coughing, sneezing, and out of breath like an old geezer moaning
up the mountain roads. Yet in the heart of the storybook land I
left behind Janan was burning with a fever in the room where she
lay, and in the same room was the mosquito I hadn't managed
to dispatch, lying low, waiting for nightfall. I went over my papers
and plans once more, so that I might conclude my business as
soon as possible and return victoriously to start my new life.

Around midnight when I opened my eyes between sleep and
wakefulness and removed my head from the vibrating window of
yet another bus, I had the happy thought that it might be here
perhaps that I would first come face to face with you, O Angel.

Yet how distant from me was the inspiration that unites the purity of spirit with the magic of the unique moment. I knew it would not be soon that I saw you out of some bus window. Flowing past were dark plains, gruesome ravines, rivers the color of quicksilver, deserted gas stations, and billboards with missing letters advertising cigarettes or cologne, but all that was on my mind were evil schemes, selfish thoughts, death, and the book; I neither saw the pomegranate-color light on the video screen which might have fueled my imagination, nor heard the heartrending snores of the restless butcher who was returning home after the daily massacre at the slaughterhouse.

In the mountain town of Alacaelli, where around daybreak the bus dropped me off, the season had skipped autumn, let alone the end of summer, and it was already winter. In the tiny coffeehouse where I went to wait for the government offices to open, the boy who washed the glasses, made the tea, and who did not seem to have any forehead since his hairline began almost at his eyebrows, asked me if I was one of the folks who came to hear the Sheikh. Just to pass the time, I told him yes. He favored me with strong tea and treated himself to the pleasure of sharing with me that, aside from the miracles the Sheikh performed, such as curing the sick or bestowing fecundity on barren women, his real talent was for bending a fork by just laying eyes on it, or opening a Pepsi-Cola bottle by simply touching the cap.

When I left the coffeehouse, winter was gone, autumn had again been skipped, and a hot and fly-infested summer day was already in progress. Like someone mature and steadfast who solves problems by immediately tackling them, I went directly to the post office, and feeling a vague excitement, I carefully looked over the sleepy male and female clerks reading the newspaper at their desks or smoking and drinking tea, leaning on the counters. The sisterly-looking female clerk I thought was a likely candidate turned out to be a real witch, making me sweat bullets before she would tell me Mr. Mehmet Buldum had just left to deliver the mail—what relation did you say you were? Why don't you wait here? But, sir, these are working hours, could you come later? I was forced to say I was an army buddy who had come all the way from Istanbul and I had considerable influence at the Postal Service General Directorate. By then, Mehmet Buldum, who had left—just now, a little while ago, presently—had found enough time to vanish into the neighborhoods and streets where I ran around hopelessly, getting the names of streets confused.

Even so, questioning everyone and anyone—Hello there, has Mehmet the mailman been here yet?—I kept getting lost in the narrow streets of the main neighborhood. A calico cat was lazily licking itself in the sun. A youngish and kind of pretty matron, who was out on the balcony airing out the sheets, quilts, and pillows, exchanged stares with some municipal workers who had climbed up a ladder they had leaned against a power pole. I saw a child with black eyes; he knew at once that I was a stranger. "What's up?" he said with a cocky air. If Janan were with me, she would immediately make friends with this smarty-pants and start up a witty banter, and I would be left to reflect that the reason I was so head over heels in love with her was not only because she was so beautiful, so irresistible, so mysterious, but because she would just as soon talk to this kid.

I sat down at a sidewalk table that belonged to the Emerald Coffeehouse across the street from the post office, which was placed under a chestnut tree, facing the Atatürk statue. A little while later I found myself reading the *Alacaelli Post*: the local pharmacy had brought in from Istanbul a new drug against constipation, sold under the trademark of *Stlops*; the coach snagged from the Bolu Sport soccer team had arrived in town to train the Alacaelli Brick Youth Sport, who considered themselves serious contenders for the coming season. So there is a brick works in town, I was thinking to myself, when I saw Mehmet Buldum enter the town hall huffing and puffing, a sizable mail pouch slung across his shoulders, and I was greatly disappointed. This heavy-footed and dog-weary Mehmet was nothing like the Mehmet that Janan could not get out of her mind.

My work here was done, and considering that there was many a youthful Mehmet waiting for me on my list, I ought to leave this peaceful place alone and quick get out of town. But the devil made me wait for Mehmet Buldum to come out of the town hall.

He was walking across the street to the shady sidewalk with the rapid and short stride of the postman when I stopped him, addressing him by name, and while he looked at me in bewilderment, I hugged and kissed him, chiding him for still not recognizing his dearest army buddy. He sat down with me at the table out of a feeling of guilt, and falling for my merciless sport of "at least come up with my name," he started making useless guesses. I stopped him sharply a while later, and offering him the pseudonym I made up on the spot, I made it known to him that there were important people I knew in the Postal Service Directorate. He was the true-blue sort of friend, it seems; he wasn't even interested in the possibility of moving up the ranks in the Postal Service. He was so tired and sweating blood carrying the heavy mailbag in the heat, he eyed with gratitude the bottle of ice-cold soda pop the waiter brought and swiftly opened, but he wished to escape as soon as possible this dubious army buddy and the shame that not remembering the guy in the least had brought upon him. Perhaps it was due to the lack of sleep, but I felt a clear sense of revenge that sweetly went to my head.

"I hear you've read a book!" I said, taking a sip of my tea with high seriousness. "I hear you have been reading this book, is that right? I hear sometimes you don't care who sees you reading it."

His face went ashen. He had understood the subject all too well.

"Where did you get that book?"

But he was able to recover quickly. He had accompanied a relative to a hospital in Istanbul, where he had seen the book in a sidewalk stall, and fooled by the title which made him think it was a book on health care, he had bought it; but then he couldn't bear to throw it away, so he had given it to the relative in the hospital.

We paused for a while. A sparrow lighted on one of the two extra chairs at the table and then hopped to the next.

I studied the mailman, whose name was written on his pocket in small careful letters. He was about my age, perhaps a little older. He had come across the same book that had taken my life off track and turned my world upside down, and he had felt the impact, had a jolt—the exact nature of which I did not know, or I couldn't decide whether I cared to know or not. We had something in common that had made us into either fellow victims or winners, and this fact irritated me.

Having noticed that he didn't underestimate the subject by tossing it aside laconically as he had done with the cap of the soda pop, I felt the book had a special place in his heart. What kind of a man was he? His hands were extraordinarily beautiful, with long refined fingers. His skin could almost be called delicate; he had a sensitive face, and almond-shaped eyes that signaled he was growing somewhat cross and apprehensive. Could it be said that he had been snared by the book like me? Had his whole world also been changed? Did he drown in sorrow some nights too when the book made him feel so miserably alone in the world?

"Anyway," I said. "I am so glad, my friend, but it's time for my bus."

Forgive my crudeness, Angel, for I suddenly felt I was capable of doing something that was not part of my plan. I might have shown the misery of my own heart to him as if exposing a wound, just to get this man to lay bare his soul. It wasn't because I hated the rituals of sincerity that end up with getting drunk together, sadness, tears, and a feeling of brotherhood that's not entirely convincing—in fact, I like doing it with guys from the neighborhood in some dingy tavern—it was because I did not wish to think about anything but Janan. I wanted to be alone as soon as possible to distract myself with dreams of the happy connubial life Janan and I could one day attain. I had just risen from the table when my army buddy said, "There is no bus scheduled to leave at this time from anywhere around this town."

Take that! He was no fool! Pleased to have hit the nail on the head, he was stroking the pop bottle with his pretty hands.

I couldn't decide whether I should pull out my gun and put holes through his delicate skin, or become his best friend, his confidant, his fate mate. Perhaps I might settle on a middle course, such as shooting him in the shoulder, only to regret it and rush him to the hospital; and then at night, his shoulder in bandages, we would open and read one by one all the letters in his mailbag, having a madly entertaining time.

"Doesn't matter," I said finally. I left the money to pay for the bill on the table with a jaunty air. Then I turned and left. I don't know from what film I had pinched this gesture, but it hadn't played too badly.

I walked rapidly like a man who means business, a go-getter; he was probably watching me walk away. I went around the Atatürk statue and up the shady narrow sidewalk, and toward the bus terminal. Terminal is just a figure of speech. If there were a bus unlucky enough to have to spend the night in the miserable town of Alacaelli—my mailman friend had called it a "city"—I didn't think there would even be some sort of hut to shelter the bus from the snow and the rain. A proud man who was condemned to sell tickets in a closet of a room for the rest of his life was pleased to tell me there was no bus before noon. Naturally,

I did not bother telling him that his bald head was exactly the same color orange as the legs of the beauty on the Goodyear Tire calendar behind him.

Why am I so angry, I kept asking; why have I become so ill-tempered? Tell me why, O Angel, whoever you are, wherever you come from, tell me! Take care of me, at least, warn me not to go off half-cocked with anger; let me set things right as best I can, taking care of the world's ills and misfortunes like some family man intent on protecting his nest; let me reunite with my Janan who is burning with a fever.

But the anger inside me knew no bounds. Was this what happened to every twenty-three-year-old youth who began carrying around a Walther?

I glanced at my notes; it was easy finding the street and the shop in question: Salvation Sundries. The handmade tablecloths, gloves, baby shoes, lace, and prayer beads that had been displayed with care in the tiny window, patiently alluding to the poetry of another time, would have warmed the cockles of Doctor Fine's heart. I was just going in when I saw the man behind the counter reading the *Alacaelli Post,* and I felt uncertain about confronting him; so I turned back. Was everyone in the town of Alacaelli really so self-confident? Or did it only seem like that to me?

I sat in some coffeehouse feeling slightly defeated, I drank a bottle of the local soda pop and marshaled the armies of my mind. I went and bought a pair of dark glasses I had seen in the pharmacy window when I had walked by it on the shady sidewalk. The industrious proprietor had already clipped the ad about the laxative in the paper and pasted it on the window.

Once I donned the dark glasses, it was a breeze venturing into Salvation Sundries, having myself been transformed into one of those self-confident fellows. Speaking in a bass voice, I asked to see the gloves. That's how my mother did it. She never said, "I am looking for some leather gloves for myself," or "I need some medium-size wool gloves for my son away in the army." She'd demand, "I'd like to see the gloves!" creating a commotion in the store that was beneficial to her purpose.

But my command must have been music to the ears of the fellow who obviously was both the owner and the clerk. With a careful grace that was reminiscent of a fastidious housewife, and an orderliness approaching the obsession for hierarchy displayed by a soldier determined to make staff officer, he showed me his entire line of inventory, which he took out of drawers, handmade satchels, and the window. He seemed to be in his sixties, there was stubble on his face, and his voice was assured enough not to betray his fetish for gloves. He showed me the small women's gloves made of handspun wool, each finger of which was festively knit in three different colors of yarn; then he turned the coarse wool gloves favored by shepherds inside out to show the Maraş-make goat-hair felt that reinforced the palm; no artificial dyes had been used in the yarns, which he personally picked out himself and had peasant women knit into gloves according to his speci-fications. He had the fingertips lined, considering that was the place where woolen gloves were so easily frayed. If I wanted a flower design on the wrist, I should go for the pair that had been graced with the purest walnut dye and lace along the edge; or else, if I had something very special in mind, would I please take off my dark glasses and take a look at this wonder made of dogskin that came from the Sivas breed *kangal*.

I looked and put my glasses back on.

"Orphan Panic," I said—that was the pseudonym he used in letters he sent Doctor Fine informing on people. "I was sent by Doctor Fine. He is not at all pleased with you."

"Why is that?" he said with equanimity, as if I had merely taken objection to the color of some glove.

"Mehmet the Mailman is an inoffensive citizen. Why would you want to harm such a person, informing on him?"

"Not so inoffensive," he said. And with the same voice he used displaying the gloves, he explained: The fellow kept reading the book, and he did it in a way that attracted attention. It was obvious what he had on his mind were dark and ugly ideas that had to do with the book and the evil the book was intended to disseminate. One time he had been caught in a widow's home where he had entered without even knocking under the pretext of delivering a letter. Another time he was seen sitting knee to knee, cheek to cheek, with a school kid at a coffeehouse, presumably reading the child a comic book. One of those illustrated stories, of course, the sort that appraises bandits, reprobates, and thieves by the same measurement as the saints and prophets. "Isn't that enough?" he asked me.

Feeling somewhat uncertain, I kept silent.

"If today in this town,"—yes, he said town—"the virtue of living an ascetic life is considered shameful, and ladies who put henna on their fingers are belittled, it's because of the stuff brought in from America by that mailman, the buses, and the television sets in the coffeehouses. What bus brought you here?"

I told him.

"Doctor Fine," he said, "is indubitably a great human being. Following his orders gives me peace of mind, I thank God. But young man, you go and tell him not to set some kid on me again." He was putting away the gloves. "Also tell him this: I witnessed that mailman at the Mustafa Pasha Mosque, masturbating in the latrine."

"With those pretty hands too," I said and left.

I had thought I would feel better once I got outside, but as soon as I set foot in the stone-paved street that lay flat out under the sun like a hot plate, I remembered with horror that I still had another two and a half hours to kill in this town.

I waited, feeling sort of faint, fatigued, and mostly sleep-deprived, my stomach full of all the glasses of regular tea, linden tea, and soda pop I had consumed, my memory full of short local news items from the *Alacaelli Post*, my field of vision full of the red-tile roof of the town hall and the red and purple colors in the shiny plastic sign of the Farmers Bank that appeared and disappeared before my eyes like a mirage, my ears full of birds twittering, the hum of generators, and coughing. Finally when the bus swerved in and parked with pizzazz, I eagerly grabbed at the door, but I was pushed and shoved away. People behind me pulled me back—without feeling the Walther, thank God—getting me out of the holy Sheikh's way. He went by me swaying solemnly, an enlightened expression on his rosy face, carrying himself with dignity as if he were full of grief for those of us who lived in depravity, but he seemed extremely pleased with himself at all the attention he was getting. What's the use of reaching for my gun? I said to myself, feeling the gun in my belt against my belly. I boarded the bus not giving a damn about anybody.

I had a feeling the bus would never leave and Janan and the whole world along with her would forget me sitting and waiting in seat 38, in the meantime I couldn't help watching the crowd that welcomed the Sheikh, and I saw the busboy from the coffeehouse when his turn came to kiss the Sheikh's hand. He had just finished kissing the Sheikh's hand properly and was raising it with the utmost care up to his forehead when the bus started up. It was then that I noticed the heartsick shopkeeper's head among the heads in the undulating crush of humanity. He was making his way through the crowd like an assassin resolved to kill some political leader, but as the bus pulled away, I realized he hadn't really been trying to get to the Sheikh, but to me.

The town was left behind us when I said to myself, Forget it. The sun kept collaring me in my seat like an ingenious detective after each turn in the road or moment of shade from a tree, and it was relentlessly baking my neck and arm like a loaf of bread, but I kept repeating, Forget it, let it go. As the shiftless bus trav-

eled, making nasal sounds over this yellow arid wasteland where
there was no house or chimney, no tree or rock, and my sleepless
eyes were dazzled in the light, I realized that, let alone forgetting
it, something had gone very deeply into my consciousness. During
the five hours I had spent in that town, where I had gone on
account of the given name of my mailman buddy Mehmet whom
the heartsick shopkeeper had turned in, something had already
been defined—how shall I put it?—which colored and harmo-
nized the scenes and people I would observe in all the towns I
was to visit in the spirit of an amateur detective.

Thirty-six hours after I left Alacaelli, for example, it was midnight and I was waiting at the depot for my next bus in a dusty
and smoky town made over from a village that seemed to have
come out of some fantasy, chewing on a cheese-filled *pida* to stop
the gnawing in my stomach as well as to kill time which would
not pass, when I felt a malignant shadow approaching me from
behind. Was it the shopkeeper who fancied gloves? No. His soul!
No, a heartsick and angry dealer? No. I was thinking maybe it was
Seiko when, bang, the door to the latrine slammed, and the ap-
parition was altogether transformed from Seiko wearing a raincoat
into a harmless avuncular man in a raincoat. And when he was
joined by a traditional lady wearing a scarf on her head and their
daughter, I wondered where in the world I got an image of Seiko
in a dun-colored raincoat. Was it perhaps because I had seen in
the crowd my heartsick shopkeeper friend whose raincoat was of
the same color?

The threat put in an appearance another time, not as the ghost
of Seiko but in the form of an entire mill. I had slept soundly on
a fairly quiet bus and then continued sleeping like a top on a
second one that was not only stable but had better shock absorbers, and then in the morning, at the flour mill where I went directly to get a quick result interviewing the young bookkeeper who
had been denounced by a baklava chef, I had made up the lie

that I had been his buddy in the army. Since all the Mehmets I
was tracking down were roughly twenty-five years old, the army
buddy pretext which always came in handy must have sounded
convincing to the worker I first spoke to, who was white from
head to toe with flour dust; his eyes lit up with camaraderie,
brotherhood, and surprise as if he too had done his military duty
in the same squadron, and he went directly into the management
office. I withdrew to a corner, and for some reason I felt an odd
sense of threat in the air. A huge shaft powered by the electric
motor that ran this flour mill turned ominously over my head,
and white and scary ghosts of the workers with brilliant tips of
their cigarettes in their mouths moved very slowly in the dim
white light. I sensed that the ghosts were observing me with hostility and talking among themselves, pointing at me, but in the
corner where I had withdrawn I tried to appear as if I was not
concerned. A little later when I thought that I was being menaced
by the dark flywheel I had seen through chinks in the wall of flour
sacks, one of the busy ghosts, limping slightly, came up to me
and inquired who was I to break wind here. He couldn't hear me
over the din of the machinery so I was forced to shout, telling
him that I had not broken wind. No, he said, he had only said
what wind brings you here. Once again I explained loudly that I
had been very fond of my army buddy; Mehmet had a great sense
of humor and was a true-blue friend. I was on a tour of Anatolia
selling life and casualty insurance when I had remembered that
Mehmet worked here. The floury ghost questioned me about the
insurance business: were the people in this business a bunch of
thieves, low-life three-card sharpers, masons, gun-toting queers—
perhaps I was mishearing him because of all the noise—and other
evil-minded enemies of the flag and the mosque? There was no
help for it but to explain, which I did at length; he listened with
a friendly look on his face. We progressed to the view that all
professions have their share of good and bad: there were honest

individuals in this world, as well as the swindling sonsobitches
you didn't know what they were after. Just then, I inquired again
about my army buddy Mehmet, what was keeping him? "Take a
look, fella!" the ghost said to me, and pulling up his pant leg, he
showed his odd-looking leg. "Mehmet Okur is not some sort of
cheat who'd think of going in the army with a leg like this, you
got that?" So, who the hell was I?

It was not out of helplessness but surprise that for a moment
I could not come up with an answer to that question. It must be
a mix-up of addresses resulting from a confusion in my mind, I
said, knowing full well that was not at all convincing.

I was lucky to slip away without getting walloped, and later,
eating a delicious slice of melt-in-the-mouth Anatolian *börek* at
the establishment of our heartsick pastry chef informant, I
thought how lame Mehmet did not look like someone who had
read the book, but my experience taught me how wrong it is to
assume one can know what lies in the hearts of men.

Let's take, for example, the town of Incir Paşa where all the
streets smelled of tobacco; it was not only the traduced young
fireman who had read the book, but the whole municipal fire
team had read it with a kind of seriousness that was surprising.
The town was busy preparing for the Liberation Day festivities
marking the day Greek occupation forces were thrown out, when
I had the opportunity to watch, in the company of some children
and one chummy mastiff dog, these firefighting confreres wearing
steel helmets with ornaments on top that were tiny gas jets, running lockstep across the training grounds with flames leaping from
the tops of their heads, singing flawlessly in unison the song that
goes "Fire, fire, our homeland is on fire." Afterwards we all sat
down together to a meal of braised goat meat. The firemen in
their bright yellow and red short-sleeved uniform shirts occasionally mumbled some words they quoted from the book, either as
a joke or else to acknowledge my presence. As to the book, they

showed me later that they kept it in the cab of their only fire
truck as if it were the holy Koran. Was it me who had misread
the book? Or was it the firemen who believed that angels—not
one solitary angel—descended from heaven on summer nights
brilliantly lit with stars, sniffed the smell of tobacco, and showed
the grief-stricken and the careworn the road to happiness?

I had my picture taken by the town photographer in one town;
in another, I had the doctor listen to my lungs; in a third, I didn't
buy the ring I tried on at the local goldsmith; and each time I
left these sad, dusty, and ramshackle places, I fantasized about
the day when Janan and I would come here and actually have our
picture taken, or get her two beautiful clusters of lung taken care
of, or buy the ring that would bind us till death do us part, and
not merely to find out about the photographer Mehmet, or Dr.
Mehmet, or Mehmet the goldsmith, who they really were, and
why they read the book with such passion.

Then I would go around the town for a while, chide the town
pigeons for dropping on the Atatürk statue, consult my watch,
check my Walther, and then make my way to the bus terminal,
which was the moment when I sometimes had an apprehension
that those evil men, the fellows in raincoats, that punctilious
Seiko and the ghosts of watches, were after me. Might that tall
and thin shadow possibly be Movado from the National Bureau
of Intelligence? Because the moment he saw me, he got off the
Adana bus which he had just boarded. Yes, it had to be him;
that's who it was, and I had better quick change my destination,
which is what I did; and I hid in some foul-smelling john, and
hoping without hope to see the angel in the window of the IM-
MEDIATE SAFEWAY bus I boarded on the sly, I felt the presence
of a pair of eyes that made the hair on the back of my neck stand
up, which made me conclude that it must be Serkisof this time
who had me under his perfidious watch. So, in the Formica-
paneled restaurants at the rest stops where we halted in the mid-

dle of the night, I would leave my tea half finished and make for
the cornfields to wait until the departure time of the bus, watching the stars in the dark blue velvet sky; or, during the day, I
would go into some local store wearing a white outfit and a smiling face, and leave the store in a red shirt, a purple jacket, cor-
duroy pants, and a scowling face; several times I found myself
running in a swelter through the local crowds toward the bus
terminal.

After all the running around, when I was convinced that I had
lost the armed ghost tailing me, or had concluded that there was
indeed no earthly reason for Doctor Fine's watches to shoot me
full of holes, then the evil eyes that watched me from afar would
be replaced by friendly townspeople regarding me with eyes that
were pleased to see me among themselves.

One time, just to make sure the Mehmet in question who had
gone to see his uncle in Istanbul was not our Mehmet, I accompanied the garrulous lady who lived in the apartment across from
his on her way back from market day. In her mesh string bags
and the plastic pouches we carried together, chubby eggplants,
lush tomatoes, and pointed peppers gleamed robustly under the
sun, and she went on about how wonderful it was to look up one's
army buddy, and how very lovely life was, not at all troubled that
my wife was lying sick at home.

Perhaps life was like that. In the garden of the Tasty Treats
Restaurant in the town of Kara Çalı, I sat at a table under a grand
plane tree and had a delightful kebab redolent with thyme, served
on a bed of creamed purée of smoked eggplant. The light wind,
which turned the leaves this way and that, brought from the
kitchen an aroma of pastry dough that was as pleasant as cherished memories. In a troubled town near Afyon the name of which
I don't recall, my legs had carried me out of their own volition,
as they so often did, to a candy store where I stopped dead in my
tracks on seeing a mamma who was as round and smooth as the

sparkling jars that were full of candies the color of old rose and the skin of tangerines, and I turned to the cash register, shaken. The mamma's smaller and paler version, who seemed to be sweet sixteen, a peerless little beauty with tiny hands, tiny mouth, high cheekbones, and slightly slanted eyes, looked up from the photo-romance magazine she was reading and smiled frankly, unbeliev-able as it was, giving me the eye like those liberated vamps in American films.

One night, I was waiting for the bus in a terminal that was lit with soft lights as in the peaceful and quiet living room of a fashionable home in Istanbul, sitting there with three reserve of-ficers I had met and playing a card game that they had made up and elaborated among themselves which they called Shah Trumped. They had cut the cards out of Yenice cigarette boxes on which they had drawn the pictures of shahs, dragons, sultans, djins, lovers, angels; and the angels, which were female counter-parts of jokers, each represented either the girl next door, or some-one's one and only love, or some domestic movie star or cabaret singer who could only be slept with in these fellows' masturbatory dreams, as was the case for the one among them who was the biggest prankster. They let me designate the fourth angel, and they showed me the courtesy of not even asking me who it rep-resented, which is something even intelligent and considerate friends are seldom capable of doing.

There was one scene of bliss that particularly distressed me to witness during the period I was listening to all the bunk that the heartsick informers fed me, gleaning whatever I could from all those many Mehmets, each tucked away in his inaccessible corner, doors closed, the hedges thorny, walls covered with ivy, and the road winding—or else, I was fleeing to avoid all those raincoated, evil imaginary watches after me at the bus terminals, town squares, and terminal restaurants.

It was the fifth day I was on the road. I had drunk the raki offered me in a tea glass by the publisher of the *Çorum Free Press*, so that I might all the better understand the poems of his that he read me; and I had learned that the publisher would no longer print excerpts from his book in the "home and family" section because he had understood it neither helped the railroad problem nor furthered the building of the Çorum-Amasya line; then in the next town, after having spent six hours running around looking for addresses and trails, I had been furious to discover that for the sake of worming some money out of Doctor Fine, some local heartsick informer had invented a nonexistent reader of the book and placed him on a nonexistent street; and I had beat it to Amasya where night falls quickly, the city being situated between craggy and steep mountains. I was halfway through the Mehmets on my list, so far to no avail, and my legs were twitching with the anxiety of imagining Janan still burning with fever in bed, so I had been planning to get on the first bus to the Black Sea coast immediately after going to the requisite address in town, inquiring after my army buddy, only to find out he was not that Mehmet.

I crossed a bridge spanning a murky stream—which turned out to be the renowned Green River which was not in the least green—and went into a neighborhood situated below tombs cut into the rock on the face of a cliff. The old and stately mansions indicated that at one time people who had seen better times— who knows what pashas or landed agas—had once lived in this dusty quarter. I knocked on the door of one of these mansions and inquired after my army buddy; they told me he was out driving his car, but they let me in and presented to me scenes from a blissfully happy family life.

1. The patriarch, a lawyer who took the cases of the poor pro bono, saw to the door his client whose troubles grieved him deeply; and taking a volume of jurisprudence out of his magnificent library, he settled down to review it. 2. When the matriarch

who was apprised of the case introduced me to the distracted
father, the sister with the impish eyes, the grandmother wearing
her reading glasses, and the little brother who was studying his
stamp collection—the homeland series—they were all excited
and overjoyed, exhibiting the kind of true Turkish hospitality ex-
tolled so much in travel books written by Western explorers.
3. The mother and the impish girl questioned me affably while
they waited for the oven to brown the delicious-smelling *börek*
Aunt Süveyde had made, then they had a discussion about André
Maurois' novel *Climats*. 4. Their hardworking son Mehmet who
had spent the whole day taking care of things at their apple orchard told me candidly that he didn't remember me at all from
the time he spent doing his military duty, but he expended considerable goodwill looking for topics of conversation we might
have in common, and eventually he came across the subject, so
we had a chance to discuss how detrimental it had been for the
country that political incentive for building railroads and encouraging village farm cooperatives had been dropped.

When I left the blissful mansion to drown in the darkness of
the street, I thought to myself these people probably never got
laid. I had known as soon as I knocked on the door and saw them
that the Mehmet in question did not live here. So why had I
stayed to get myself charmed by the picture of bliss that came
right out of the commercials advertising homes on credit? Because
of the Walther, I said to myself, feeling the presence of my gun
in my belt. I wondered if I should just turn around and spray my
9-millimeter rounds into the peaceful windows of the mansion;
but I knew it wasn't a real thought, it was more of a whisper to
put to sleep the black wolf deep in the dark forest of my mind.
Sleep, black wolf, sleep. Ah, yes, let's go to sleep. A store, a store
window, an advertisement: My feet, which were as meek as a lamb
that fears the wolf, were taking me somewhere now. Where? Pleasure Theater, Spring Pharmacy, Death Dry-Fruits and Nuts. Why

is the salesboy smoking and staring at me like that? Then a grocery store, a pastry shop, and eventually I found myself looking at the Humble-Steel refrigerators in a good-size window, the Crescent Gas stoves, bread boxes, armchairs, sofas, enameled steel cookware, lamps, Modern brand stoves, and when I saw the lucky dog with the thick coat, that is, the figurine of the dog perched on the Humble-Steel brand radio, I knew I could no longer control myself.

That's how I stood in front of a store window in the city of Amasya stuck between two mountains, Angel, and I wept, breaking into big sobs. You ask a child why he is crying; he weeps because of a deep wound inside him but he tells you he's crying because he has lost his blue pencil sharpener; that was the kind of grief that overcame me looking at all the stuff in the window. What was the sense in turning into a murderer for naught? To live with that pain in my soul for the rest of my life? I might buy some roasted seeds in the dry-fruits-and-nuts store, or look into the mirror of some grocer to see myself, or be living the life of bliss replete with refrigerators and stoves, but still the accursed sinister voice inside me, the black wolf, would snarl and accuse me of my guilt. Whereas I, Angel, I had so completely believed in life once and in good works. Now, caught between Janan whom I couldn't trust, and Mehmet whom I would kill in a minute if I could trust her, I had nothing to hold on to but my Walther and the dreams of a blissful life up on cloud nine that depended on schemes which were intricate beyond belief and sinister to the extreme. The images of refrigerators, orange juice machines, armchairs bought on time flowed by parading in my mind, accompanied by a soundless wail.

The elderly man in domestic films who assuages the pain of the sniffling little boy or beautiful weeping woman came to my aid momentarily, me the tough rooster. "Son," he said, "why are you crying, my boy? Is something the matter? Don't cry."

This bearded clever uncle was either on his way to the mosque to pray, or else to throttle someone.

I said, "Sir, my father died yesterday."

He must have suspected something. "Who are your folks, son?" he said. "You're surely not from here."

"My stepfather never wanted us coming around," I said and I wondered if I should also say: Sir, I am going to Mecca on pilgrimage, but I missed my bus. Can you loan me some money?

Acting as if I were dying of grief, I walked into the darkness, dying of grief. Still, it had helped to come up with a couple of lies out of the blue. Later, I was amply soothed on the TRUSTED SAFEWAY bus I could always trust, seeing on the video screen a dainty lady driving her car pitilessly and without any hesitation into a crowd of evil guys. I arrived on the shore of the Black Sea by morning, and I called my mother from the Black Sea Grocery and told her I was about to conclude my affairs and come home with her angelic daughter-in-law. If she insists on crying, let her cry out of happiness. I sat down in a pastry shop in the old shopping district, and opening my notes, I made some calculations to finish the job as soon as possible.

The reader of the book in Samsun was a young doctor doing his residency at the Social Security Hospital. As soon as I determined he was not that Mehmet, something hit me for no explicable reason, perhaps it was his clean-shaven face, or his physically fit and self-confident manner. Unlike people like me whose lives had slipped off the track, this man had found a sound way to absorb the book into his system and he could live with it in peace as well as with passion. I hated him immediately. How could the very book that had changed my world and screwed up my destiny have affected this man as if it were a vitamin pill? I knew I would die of curiosity if I didn't ask, so I brought up the subject with the wide-shouldered doctor and his nurse, who looked like a third-class Kim Novak with her large eyes and chiseled features, pointing at the book that was sitting in all its deceptive innocence among the pharmaceutical catalogues on the desk, as if it too was something about pharmacy.

"Oh, the doctor just loves to read!" chuckled this willing and able Kim Novak.

When the nurse left, the doctor locked the door behind her. He sat in his chair with the deliberation of a mature man. And while we smoked man to man, he explained everything.

There was a time in his early youth when under the influence of his family he had been religious, he went to the mosque on Fridays and fasted during the month of Ramadan. Then he had fallen in love with a girl; a while later he had lost his faith; following that, he had become a Marxist. He had felt an emptiness in his soul after these storms had abated, having left there their mark. But when he'd seen the book in a friend's library and read it, "everything had fallen into place." He now comprehended the place of death in our lives; he had accepted its reality like an undeniable tree in the garden, or a friend in the street; he quit being rebellious. He had comprehended the importance of his childhood. He had learned to remember and love all the little things from the past, like bubble gum and comics, and the proper place in his life for his first love as well as for the first book he had ever read. He had always loved his wild homeland anyway, and those mad and sad buses too. As to the angel, he had understood this miraculous angel's existence through reason and believed it by virtue of his emotions. After all this synthesis, he knew the angel would find him someday, and together they would ascend to the heavens; he would, for example, land a job in Germany.

He had told me all this as if he were explaining to me how to effect a cure by giving me a prescription for bliss. The doctor rose, having assured himself that his patient had understood the prescription, and all that was left for the incurable patient was to see himself to the door. I was just leaving when he said, as if telling me to take the pills after meals, "I always underline as I read; I recommend you do the same."

I took the first bus going south, Angel, as if I were running away. I told myself never again! I would never again venture to the coast of the Black Sea, adding that Janan and I would have never been happy on the Black Sea, as if there had been such a clear-cut and boldly painted fantasy among my plans involving my future happiness. Dark villages, dark sheep pens, deathless trees, sad filling stations, empty restaurants, silent mountains, and anxious rabbits went through the looking-glass of my window. I told myself I had seen similar things before; in the film that was playing on the screen, it was only long after the nice young man with good intentions discovered he had been badly deceived that he first took the bad guys to task and then turned the gun on them. Before he killed them, he interrogated them one by one, getting them to beg for mercy, considered forgiving them, hesitating long enough to give them the chance to do something treacherous; and it was only after we, the viewers, also decided that the bad guy was a blackguard who deserved to be put out of his misery that gunshots were heard on the screen placed above the driver's seat. That is when I looked out of the window like someone who finds seeing bloodshed and killing distasteful, feeling as if I were hearing the lyrics of a curious song made up of gunshots, the noise of the engine and the tires; and I wondered, Angel, why I had not asked the handsome doctor, when he was prescribing me the book, your identity.

The lyrics went like this: "Doctor, Doctor, give me the news . . ." Who is the angel? asks the young patient. The angel? says the doctor full of himself, takes a map, spreads it on the table, and as if showing the pitiful patient the X-rays of his hopeless organs, he points out the Mount of Meaning, and the City of the Unique Moment; and if this is the Valley of Naïveté, and this the Point of Accident, then this here has to be Death. Must one love meeting Death, Doctor, as one does the angel?

According to my notes, next on my list of people who had read the book was the local newspaper distributor in the town of Ikizler. Ten minutes after I got off the bus, I saw him sitting in his store in the middle of the shopping district, scratching his thick and short body through his shirt with pleasure—nothing like Janan's lover; being the ready and able detective that I am, I was out of there in ten minutes on the first bus out of town. Two buses and four hours later, my next suspect in the capital of the province put me through even less trouble; there he was in the barber shop right across from the bus terminal, regarding the lucky passengers get off the bus with a deep sadness in his eyes, a dustpan in one hand and a spanking-clean apron in the other, waiting on his boss who was industriously shaving someone. I felt like singing a verse that went through my head, "Come, brother, come with us / let's you and I on the bus / go to a land that's fabulous." I wanted to push through to the end before my muse left me. So, in the next town which was an hour's ride on the bus, thinking that the unemployed suspect was very suspect indeed, I was forced to inspect the old birdcages, flashlights, scissors, cigarette holders made of rosewood, and oddly enough, gloves, parasols, and a Browning that the heartsick informant had hidden in a dry well in his backyard. This dealer with a broken heart and broken tooth presented me with a Serkisof watch as an insignificant expression of his respect and admiration for Doctor Fine. As he was explaining how he and his three friends met after Friday prayer in the backroom of the pastry shop to discuss the Day of Independence, I reflected that not only the evening but also autumn was suddenly upon us. My mind was overcast with dark and low clouds when a light went on in the house next door, and suddenly among the autumn leaves the honey-colored shoulders of a well-built half-naked woman appeared in the window, only to disappear like a shudder. Following that, I saw black horses galloping through the sky, Angel, and impatient monsters, gas pumps, dreams of bliss, closed movie theaters, other buses, other people, other towns.

Later on that evening, I felt more upbeat than disappointed talking to the cassette tape dealer even after I understood he was not the Mehmet in question, skipping from subject to subject talking about the good cheer his wares provided for people, about the rainy season being over, about the sadness of the town I had come from, when I heard a dolorous train whistle and became anxious. I had to immediately leave this town, which did not have even a name in my memory, and return to the dear velvet night where the bus would take me.

I was walking toward the bus terminal, which was in the direction of the train whistle, when I saw myself in the rearview mirror on a bright and shiny bicycle parked on the sidewalk. There I am, with my concealed gun, my new purple jacket, the Serkisof watch presented for Doctor Fine in the pocket, blue jeans on my legs, my clumsy hands, my fleeting strides; then the shops and windows backed off and were gone, and what I saw in the night was a circus tent which had a picture of an angel over the entrance way. The angel was a hybrid between a Persian miniature and domestic film star, but still, my heart leapt. Not only does this student who cuts his classes smoke, sir, but look how he sneaks into the circus tent!

I bought a ticket and entered the tent, where it smelled of mold, sweat, and earth, sat down and, having decided to take time off from everything, I began to wait along with some crazy conscripts who had failed to return to their squadrons, a few fellows out to kill some time, sad and elderly persons, and a couple of children and their families who seemed to be in the wrong place. This was not like the circuses I saw on television; there were no marvelous trapeze artists, no bears riding bicycles, not even some domestic jugglers. A man pulled off a dirty gray cloth and materialized a radio, which was then levitated to dematerialize into music. We heard a piece of à la turca music, then the young woman who was singing it appeared and sang a second song with her plaintive voice and left. Our tickets were numbered, there would be a drawing, we were to sit patiently; that's what we were told.

The woman who had sung before put in another appearance; this time she was an angel, she had lined the corners of her eyes, which made them appear slanted. She had on a modest two-piece swimsuit like the kind my mother wore to Süreyya Beach. Then around her neck was an odd piece of apparel, something I assumed at first was some sort of a strange shawl until I saw that it was a snake she had wrapped around her neck, flinging the two ends over her delicate shoulders. Was I seeing some sort of unusual light that I had never seen before? Or was I merely anticipating such a light? Or perhaps I was only imagining it. I was so happy to be there in that tent watching the angel and the snake with the other twenty-five people or so, I thought tears would pour out of my eyes.

Later, when the woman was having a conversation with the snake, I thought of something. Sometimes you suddenly remember a distant memory seemingly long forgotten, and you wonder why of all times you're remembering it now and your mind becomes utterly confused; that's how I felt, but it was more a feeling of peace than confusion. One time my father and I were visiting Uncle Rıfkı. "I could live anywhere at all, provided trains go there, even if it is a whistle stop at the end of the world," he had told us. "I cannot even imagine a life where one cannot hear a train whistle before dropping off to sleep." I could easily imagine spending the rest of my life here in this town, with these people. Nothing can be worth more than the peace that comes from oblivion. Those are the things I thought as I beheld the angel speaking sweetly to the snake.

The lights went down for a moment, the angel withdrew from the stage. When the lights went up again, it was announced that there would be a ten-minute intermission. I had a mind to go out and mill around with my fellow townspeople with whom I was to spend my whole life.

I was just threading my way among wooden chairs when I saw someone sitting three or four rows from the so-called stage which was nothing more than a rise in the ground, reading the *Viran Bağ Post*, and my heart began to beat wildly. It was *that* Mehmet, Janan's lover, Doctor Fine's son who was presumed dead; he had crossed his legs and, in full possession of the peace I so longed for, he was reading his paper, oblivious to the world.

13 WHEN I STEPPED OUTSIDE THE TENT, A LIGHT WIND blew into my collar, down my back and then all over my body, giving me goose bumps. My prospective fellow citizens changed into mistrustful enemies. My heart kept beating wildly, I felt the weight of the gun in my belt, and it wasn't just my cigarette I was sending up in smoke but the whole world.

A bell rang, I looked in: still reading his paper. I returned to the tent with the rest of the audience. I sat down three rows directly behind him. The "program" began. I felt dizzy. I don't remember what I saw, what I didn't see, what I heard, what I listened to. My mind was on the back of a neck. It was a clean-shaven humble neck that belonged to a decent human being.

Quite a while later I watched the lottery being drawn from a purple pouch; then the winning number was announced. A toothless old man leapt up on the stage, overjoyed. The angel, who was wearing the same two-piece bathing suit and a bridal veil, congratulated him. Without further ado, the man who sold the tickets showed up with a huge chandelier in his hand.

"My God!" cried the toothless old man. "It's the Pleiades with Seven Branches!"

Listening to the audience in the back shouting their protests,

I realized the same man must win the lottery every time, and the chandelier must be the same one that reappeared every evening under its plastic wraps.

The angel had in her hand a cordless microphone, or some sort of fake microphone that did not amplify her voice. "What are your feelings?" she said. "How does it feel to be so lucky? Are you excited?"

"I am very excited, very happy, God bless you!" the old man said to the microphone. "Life is something beautiful. Despite all the troubles and sorrows that abound, I am neither afraid nor ashamed of being so happy."

A few people applauded him.

"Where are you going to hang your chandelier?" asked the angel.

"This was a stroke of fortune," said the old man, leaning over the microphone as if it were viable. "I am in love. Also my fiancée loves me very much. We will soon get married and move into our new house. That's where we will hang this piece with seven branches."

Some applause was offered. Then I heard shouts of "Kiss, kiss."

Everyone fell silent when the angel bussed the old man on the cheeks. The old man took advantage of the silence and slipped away carrying the chandelier.

"But the rest of us never win anything!" said an angry voice in the back.

"Quiet!" said the angel. "Now listen to me." The same odd silence that had ensued during the kiss again fell over the audience. "Your lucky number too will come up one of these days, don't you forget it! Your hour of happiness will also strike," the angel said. "Do not become impatient, do not be cross with your life, cease and desist envying others! If you learn to love your life, you will know the course of action you are to take for your happiness. Whether you have lost your way or not, you will see me then." She raised one eyebrow seductively. "After all, the Angel of Desire is here every evening, here in the charming town of Viran Bağ!"

The magical lighting that illuminated her went down. A naked light bulb lit up. Keeping a distance between myself and my quarry, I left with the crowd. The wind had risen. I looked left and right; there was a bottleneck up ahead, so I found myself standing a couple of steps behind him.

"How was it, Osman? Did you enjoy it?" said a man who was wearing a melon hat.

"Oh, so-so," said he. He sped along, his newspaper tucked under his arm.

Why had I never considered the possibility that he would resign his identity as Mehmet just as he had fled from being Nahit? And what about this particular name he'd adopted for his new pseudonym? If I could have considered it, would I have considered it? I didn't even consider it. I stayed behind, waiting for him to put some distance between us. I took pains studying his lean body with a slight stoop. Yes, this was the guy all right, the one with whom my Janan was madly in love. I began to follow him.

The town of Viran Bağ had more streets lined with trees than any of the small towns where I had been. My quarry was moving right along; when he came to a street light, he seemed to step onto a dimly lit stage; then, approaching a chestnut or linden tree, he would vanish into a darkness where the leaves and the wind were in commotion. We went past the town square, past the New World Theater, went through a strip of neon lights that belonged to the pastry shop, post office, pharmacy, teahouse which cast consecutively a pale yellow, then sort of orange, then blue, then reddish hue on my quarry's white shirt; and presently we entered an alley. When I became aware of the impeccable perspective presented by the three-story row houses, the street lights, and the rustling trees, I shivered with the thrill of the chase which I imagined was a turn-on for all those Serkisof, Zenith, and Seiko types, and I began to approach my quarry's undistinctive white shirt quickly with the object of getting the job done.

Then all hell broke loose, there was a crash; I was forced to skulk into a corner, unnerved for a moment, fearing that one of those watches was tailing me. But it was only a window that had slammed in the wind, smashing the pane; and my quarry turned around in the dark and paused briefly; I assumed he was going to proceed without having seen me when, before I could even release my Walther's safety, he suddenly pulled out his key, opened the door, and disappeared into one of the row houses. I waited around until a light went on in a window on the second floor.

Then I took stock of myself, feeling all alone in the world like a murderer, or an aspiring murderer. One street down from the street that had respectfully submitted to the rules of perspective, the modest neon letters of the Ease Inn swayed back and forth in the wind, promising me a little patience, a little advice, a little peace, a bed, and a long night in which to think over my life, my decision to become a killer, and my Janan. There was no help for it but to go in, and I asked for a room with a TV just because the clerk had inquired if I wanted one.

I went in the room and turned on the TV; when the black-and-white picture came on, I told myself I had made a good choice. I would not be spending the night with the abjectness of an incorrigible murderer, but I would be in the company of my black-and-white friends gleefully joshing away because they rubbed people out so often they considered it trivial. I increased the volume. I felt relieved when men with pistols started to yell at each other, and American-make cars began to speed along, gliding into the curves in the road; I looked out on the world outside my window, calmly watching the chestnut trees snarling in the wind.

I was nowhere and everywhere; and that is why it seemed to me I was in the nonexistent center of the world. From the window

of my cutesy-cute and deadly-dead hotel room which was located
in this center, I could see the lights in the room of the man I
wanted to kill. I could not actually see him, but I was pleased
that he was over there for now, and I was over here for the night;
besides, my friends on TV had already commenced spraying each
other with bullets. A little while after my quarry's lights went out,
I too dropped off to sleep without reflecting on the meaning of
life, love, and the book, but listening to the sound of gunshots.

In the morning I got up, bathed, shaved, and left without turning off the TV set, which was forecasting rain for the entire country. I had neither checked my Walther nor checked myself in the
mirror with irritation like some young man inducing himself to
kill for love and the love of a book. In my purple jacket I must
have looked like an optimistic university student, traveling from
town to town during his summer vacation, trying to sell door to
door the New World Encyclopedia. A university student who fit
the description would expect to have a long chat on life and
literature with a bibliophile he chanced upon in the provinces,
would he not? I had already known for some time that I couldn't
kill him right off the bat. I went up a flight of stairs, I rang the
bell, rrringg! but no, some electrical mechanism went twitter-
twitter, imitating a canary. The latest fads somehow make their
way even to towns like Viran Bağ, and killers find their victims
even if they have to go to the ends of the earth. In situations like
this in films, victims assume an attitude that implies their om-
niscience and say, "I knew you would come." But it didn't happen
like that.

He was amazed. Yet he was not amazed by his amazement but
experienced it as something not quite out of the ordinary. His
face had nice features, all right, although not as deeply meaningful as I had imagined they would be on this occasion, and he was
indeed—oh, all right—handsome.

"Osman, I have come," I said.

Silence.

Then we both composed ourselves. He looked at me for a moment and then at the door with embarrassment, as if he had no intention of letting me in, and he said, "Let's leave together."

He put on a dun-colored jacket which was not bullet-proof, and together we stepped out into the street which was an excuse for a street. A distrustful dog on the sidewalk looked us over and the turtledoves on top of a chestnut tree fell silent. Look, Janan, we two have become good friends! He was slightly shorter than me and I was thinking that there must be something in my walking style that was reminiscent of his, which is the most obvious personal attribute of guys like us—that is, the confluence of the way the shoulders go up and down and the forward motion of the strides—when he asked me if I had eaten anything by way of breakfast. Would I like something to eat? There was a café at the station. How about some tea?

He bought a couple of warm savory buns at the bakery, stopped by a grocery and had a quarter pound of *kaşar* cheese sliced and wrapped in wax paper. Presently, we were hailed by the angel in the poster on the circus entrance. We went in the café, where he ordered two teas; we stepped out the back door into a courtyard garden with a view of the station and sat down. The turtledoves, which had perched either in the chestnut tree or in the eaves, kept right on sighing without paying us any heed. The cool morning air was soft, it was silent, and in the distance there was music on a radio that was barely audible.

"Every morning before I begin working, I come and have my tea here," he said as he unwrapped the cheese. "This place is nice in the spring. And also when it's snowing. In the morning I like watching the crows walk in the snow on the platform, and the trees lined with snow. The other nice café is the Homeland on the square, a good-size place which has a large stove that gives a lot of heat. I read my paper there, listen to the radio if it's on, and sometimes I just sit there, doing nothing.

"My new life is ordered, disciplined, and punctual . . . Every morning I leave the café before nine and return to my worktable. By the time the clock strikes nine, I will have my coffee prepared and already be hard at work, writing. What I do might appear simple, but it requires great care. I keep rewriting the book without missing a single comma, a single letter, or a period. I want everything to be identical, right down to the last period and comma. And this can only be achieved through inspiration and desire that is analogous to the original author's. Someone else might call what I do copying, but my work goes beyond simple duplication. Whenever I am writing, I feel and I understand every letter, every word, every sentence as if each and every one were my own novel discovery. So, this is how I work arduously from nine in the morning until one o'clock, doing nothing else, and nothing can keep me from working. I generally put out better work in the morning.

"Then I go out for lunch. There are two restaurants in this town. Asım's place tends to be crowded. The food in the Railway Restaurant is heavy and the place serves alcohol. I go in one sometimes, and sometimes the other. And there are times when I have some bread and cheese at some café, and times I don't leave home at all. I never have anything alcoholic at noon. I might have a little nap sometimes, but that's all. The important thing is to sit down to work by two-thirty. I work straight through to six-thirty or seven. If the work is going well, I may keep at it even longer. If one likes what he is writing and is pleased with his vocation, he should not miss the opportunity to write all he can. Life is short, this is how things are, and you know the rest. Don't let your tea get cold now.

"After a day's work, I view with satisfaction whatever I have done, and I go out again. I like to chat with a couple of people while I look through the papers or catch some TV. It is a necessity for me because I live alone and intend to continue living alone. I like to meet people, chew the fat, toss down a few, hear a couple of stories, and perhaps even tell one. Then I sometimes go to the movies, or see some program on TV; there are some evenings when I play cards at the coffeehouse, and others when I return home early, bringing the daily papers with me."

"You were at the tent theater last night," I said.

"These people showed up about a month ago and stayed on. Some of the townspeople still go to see them."

"The woman there," I said, "she looked a little like an angel."

"She is no angel," he said. "She sleeps with the town biggies, and any soldier boy who comes up with the cash. Got that?"

There was silence. The expression "Got that?" swept me away from the easy chair of sarcastic anger where I had been luxuriating with the hedonism of a drunk and placed me on a hard and uncomfortable wooden chair where I was perched uneasily in a garden overlooking the train station.

"What it says in the book," he said, "is all behind me now."

"But you are still writing the book all day," I said.

"I do it for the money."

He said it without seeming to feel either victorious or ashamed, but more as if he were apologizing for having to spell it out. He was writing the book over and over into ordinary school notebooks in longhand. Since he worked eight to ten hours a day on the average, hitting about three pages per hour, he was done with a handwritten edition of a three-hundred-page book within ten days, easy. There were people here who paid "reasonable" wages for this sort of labor, such as notables in town, traditionalists, folks who liked him, those who admired his effort, conviction, devotion, patience, or felt a kind of happiness that a fool who insisted on his folly lived contentedly among themselves . . . What's more,

the fact that he had dedicated his life to such a modest enterprise
had created around him unwittingly—and he said this with great
hesitation—a "flimsy legend" of sorts. They respected him, per-
ceiving in his work an aspect—he too said "how shall I put it?"—
which was sacred.

He explained all this at my insistence in response to my probing
questions; otherwise, he didn't at all appear to enjoy talking about
himself. After speaking of his gratitude to his customers, the
goodwill of enthusiasts who bought handwritten versions of the
book, and the respect they accorded him, he said, "Anyway, I am
providing them with a service. I offer them something that's real.
A book written by hand word for word, written with conviction,
body and soul. They compensate me with a day's wages for a day's
work. In the final reckoning, everyone's life goes along the same
lines."

We were silent. Eating the fresh savory bun with the slices of
kaşar cheese, I thought his life had now fallen into place; his life
was, to quote the book, "on track." Like me, he had set out on
the road that began with the book, but through his quest, the
voyages and adventures replete with death, love, and disaster, he
had achieved what I could not; he had found the equilibrium
where things would remain in stasis for good; he had discovered
his inner peace. I was taking careful bites of the slices of cheese
and relishing the last swallow of tea in the bottom of the tea
glass, when I sensed that he must repeat daily his routine of small
gestures involving his hands, fingers, mouth, chin, and head. The
composure that came from the equilibrium he had discovered had
granted him infinite time, whereas I, inquisitive and unhappy, was
swinging my legs under the table.

Jealousy towered inside me momentarily, the desire to perpe-
trate something evil. But I became aware of something even more
dreadful. If I pulled out my gun and shot him in the pupil of his
eye, I still would not have affected this man who had arrived at

the stillness of eternal time through the act of writing. He would only proceed on his way, albeit in a different form, within time that was at a standstill. My restless soul which did not know respite was struggling to get somewhere or other, like some bus driver who had forgotten his destination.

I asked him many things. His responses of "yes," "no," "naturally" were so short that I realized with every instance that I had already known the answer myself. He was contented with his life. He expected nothing more. He still loved the book and believed it. He felt no rancor toward anyone. He had understood the meaning of life. But he couldn't explain what it was. He had naturally been surprised to see me. He didn't think he could teach anything to anyone. Everyone had a life of his own and, according to him, all lives had equal validity. He liked solitude, but this in itself was not all that essential because he happened to enjoy company quite a lot, too. He had loved Janan very much. Yes, he had fallen in love with her. But then he had succeeded in escaping from her. He was not surprised that I had managed to find him. I was to take his deepest regards to Janan. Writing was the sole activity of his life, but not his sole happiness. He knew he had to work like everybody else. He could enjoy doing other work. Yes, if it provided a livelihood, he could do any kind of work. Looking at the world, so to speak, actually seeing the world in its true guise, gave him great pleasure.

A locomotive was maneuvering in the station. We watched it. Our heads followed it going past us huffing and puffing, putting out great billows of smoke, elderly, tired, but still sound, making metallic noises and moaning noises like some rinky-dink municipal band.

When the locomotive disappeared into a grove of almond trees, there was melancholy in the eyes of the man whose heart I shortly planned to plug with a bullet in hopes of finding in Janan the repose he had found in rewriting the book over and over again.

Caught up for a moment in the spirit of brotherhood, I was observing the childlike pensiveness in these eyes when I understood
why Janan had loved this man so very much. My perception
seemed so right and true that I revered Janan for her love; but
only moments later, the overly burdensome feeling of reverence
gave place to a feeling of jealousy which I fell into as if tumbling
down a well.

The killer then asked his victim why he had settled on the name
of Osman, which was also the killer's name, at the time he had
decided to join oblivion in this obscure little town.

"I don't know," said the pseudo-Osman without noticing the
clouds of jealousy in the eyes of the real Osman; then, smiling
sweetly, he added, "I had immediately liked you when I first met
you, perhaps that was why."

He observed with attentiveness that verged on esteem the locomotive that was returning from the almond orchard on a different track. The killer could have sworn that his victim, who was
engrossed in the locomotive brightly shimmering in the sunlight,
had become totally oblivious to the whole world. But not quite.
The cool morning air was being replaced by the oppressiveness of
a warm and sunny day.

"It's past nine o'clock," said my rival. "Time for me to get to
work . . . Where are you off to?"

Knowing full well what I was doing, anxious and hapless but
not without thought, I begged someone in all sincerity for the
first time in my life: please, stay a while longer; let's talk a little
longer; let's get to know each other better.

He was surprised and perhaps a little worried, but he had understood me. Not the gun in my belt, but my thirst. He smiled
so indulgently that even the feeling of equal footing I thought
the Walther afforded me was blasted into smithereens. That is
how the unfortunate traveler who was able to reach merely the
frontiers of his own misery rather than reaching the heart of life

was gripped by enough anxiety to question the wise master at this frontier about the meaning of everything from life to the book, time, writing, and the angel.

I kept questioning him as to what all this meant, and he kept asking me what it was that I meant by "all this." That is when I questioned him as to what might be the initial question to ask, so that I might put it to him. And he kept telling me I had to discover that place which had no beginning and no end. So then, perhaps there was not even a question to ask him. No, there was not. So what was there? What a person was depended on how he looked at things. Sometimes there was a stillness from which one attempted to retrieve something. Other times, one sat and had tea and a pleasant conversation in a café in the morning, as we were presently doing, watching the locomotive and the train, and listening to the cooing of the turtledoves. Perhaps these things were not everything, but they were not, after all, nothing. Well, then, was there not a place beyond, a new realm to be seen after all that travel? If there was a place beyond, it was within the text; but he had determined that it was futile to search for what he discovered in the text outside of the text, in actual life. After all, the world was at least as limitless, flawed, and incomplete as the text.

In that case, why had we both been so affected by the book? He told me that was a question only a person who was not in the least affected by the book might ask. The world was full of such people, but was I one of them? I no longer knew what kind of person I was. I was someone who had prodigally squandered and lost the core of his soul on the road, trying to make Janan fall in love with him, to locate that realm, and to dispatch his rival. I did not ask him about this, O Angel, I asked him who you are.

"I have never encountered the angel the book talks about," he said to me. "It might be that you behold the angel at the moment of death, in the window of some bus."

How beautiful was his smile, so merciless. I would kill him. But not just yet. First I must drag it out of him how I might find and retrieve the focal point of my lost soul. But the misery I had fallen into would absolutely not allow me to ask the right questions. The ordinary morning in Eastern Anatolia for which the radio weather forecast was partially cloudy with scattered showers, the bright light in the peaceful train station, the pair of hens scratching around absentmindedly at one end of the platform, a pair of happy young men chatting and carrying cases of soda pop out of a hand wagon into the station snack bar, the stationmaster who was smoking a cigarette—all these had impressed the existing day as it progressed into my consciousness so completely there was no room left in my scattered brain to ask a proper question on the subject of life or the book.

We were silent for a long time. I kept wondering which question to put to him. And perhaps he was wondering how he was going to peel himself away from me and my questions. We stayed some more. Presently, the moment of reckoning put in an appearance. He paid for the tea. He threw his arms around me and kissed me on the cheeks. How delighted he had been to see me! How I hated him! Well, no, I liked him. But why should I like him? I meant to kill him.

But not just yet. He would pass the tent theater on his way home to the room where he performed his crackpot task, in that rat's nest on the street which had submitted to the order and composure of the rules of perspective. I would take the shortcut along the railroad tracks and catch up with him, and I would kill him under the gaze of the Angel of Desire whom he had disparaged.

I let the self-satisfied bastard go. I felt irritated with Janan for bringing herself to love him. But just glancing at his pensive and vulnerable shadow in the distance was enough to know Janan was right. How indecisive was this Osman, the protagonist of the book you are reading! And how pitiful! He knew in the depths of his being that the man he wanted to hate was "right." He also knew he couldn't quite bring himself to kill him yet. I sat moping for a couple of hours on the dilapidated café chair, swinging my legs, thinking over what other traps Uncle Rıfkı might have set for me in the course of the rest of my life.

Toward noon I returned, crestfallen, back to the Ease Inn, looking for all the world like a prospective murderer. The clerk was pleased enough with the guest from Istanbul who was staying an extra night to offer him tea. So I listened to his military service reminiscences for an extremely long time because I was afraid of the solitude in my room; when the subject turned to me, I was content with telling him I had an "account to settle" but hadn't yet been able to "finish the job."

As soon as I stepped into the room, I turned on the TV, which had been turned off. On the black-and-white screen, a shadow was walking along a white wall, pointing a gun, and upon reaching the corner, emptied the clip into the target. I wondered if Janan and I hadn't seen the color version of the same scene on some bus. I sat down on the edge of the bed, waiting patiently to see the rest of the homicide scenes. Presently, I found myself staring out my window into his window. There he was writing, although I could not quite make out if the shadow I saw was indeed him. But there he sat writing in peace just to give me grief. I sat and was lost watching TV for a while, but when I rose I had already forgotten what it was that I had seen. Then I found myself watching his window again. He had reached the point of stillness at the end of the road, and I was stuck among black-and-white shadows that fired on each other. He had arrived and crossed to the other side; he was in possession of the wisdom of the new life which was concealed from me; and I had nothing but the vague hope that I might yet possess Janan.

Why don't these films ever show us how sorry these pathetic

killers are, mired in their own bathos in some hotel room? If I were the director, I would show the messed-up bedspread, the chipped paint on the window frames, the filthy curtains, the dirty and wrinkled shirt on the man studying to be a murderer, the insides of the pockets of his purple jacket that he keeps poking through, the way he sits on the edge of the bed with his back hunched, wondering whether to masturbate to pass the time.

For quite a while I started up open discussions with the many voices in my head on the following themes: Why do sensitive and beautiful women always fall in love with abject men whose lives have gone off the track? If I did manage to become a murderer and if the traces of murder could always be read in my eyes for the rest of my life, would I have the appearance of a miserable man, or a pensive man? Could Janan ever truly love me, even if it were only half of what she feels for the man I will soon dispatch? Could I do what Nahit-Mehmet-Osman had done, give myself over to writing again and again Uncle Rıfkı's book into school notebooks?

Once the sun disappeared behind the street in perspective, and the cool of the evening and long shadows began wandering around the streets insidiously like a cat, I started to watch his window without any respite. I could not see him, but thinking that I did, I focused my gaze on the window and the room behind it without paying the slightest attention to the occasional person in the street, trying to believe that I could indeed see someone there.

I don't know how long this went on. It was still not quite dark and the light in his room was not yet on, when I found myself in the street under his window, calling out to him. Someone appeared in the blurred window and disappeared at once upon seeing me. I went into the building, climbed the stairs in a rage; the door opened without my having to set the doorbell twittering; but for a moment I could not see him there.

I went into the flat. A green felt cloth had been spread on the table. On it I saw an open notebook, and the book. Pencils, erasers, cigarette pack, shreds of tobacco, a watch next to the ashtray, matches, a cup of coffee that had gone cold. There, these were the tools of the trade that belonged to a pitiful person condemned to write for the rest of his life.

He came out from somewhere inside the flat. I began reading what he had written because I was loath to look into his face. "Sometimes I miss a comma," he said, "or write the wrong letter or word. That's when I realize I am writing without conviction or feeling, so I stop. Returning to work with the same concentration sometimes takes hours, even days. I wait patiently for the inspiration to come because I don't wish to write a single word the power of which I don't feel inside me."

"Listen to me," I said coolly, as if I were talking about someone else instead of myself. "I cannot be myself. I cannot be anything. Help me. Help me get this room, the book, and what you are writing out of my mind, so I can return to my old life in peace."

Like some mature guy who had caught a glimpse of what life and the world was about, he said he knew what I meant. I suppose he thought he understood everything. Why didn't I just shoot him then and there? Well, because he had said, "Let's go to the Railway Restaurant and talk."

When we sat down at the restaurant, he informed me that there was a train at a quarter to nine. After I left, he would take in a movie. So he had already made up his mind to send me packing.

"When I met Janan, I had already given up on proselytizing for the book," he said. "Like everybody else, I wanted a life. But I had to have more books than anyone else. Besides, all that I had lived through hoping to reach the world that the book had opened for me would provide me with extra advantages. But Janan inflamed me. She promised she would unlock me to life. She was convinced of the existence of a garden that I concealed from her, not telling her although I knew it was somewhere behind me, or beyond me. She demanded the key to that garden with such conviction that I was forced to talk about the book and eventually to give it to her. She read the book, read it again, and again. I was seduced by her devotion to the book, by her passionate desire for the world that she perceived in it. For a period of time, I was oblivious to the stillness in the book or—how shall I put it?—the internal music of the text. As in the days when I had first read the book, I was carried away stupidly by the hope of hearing the music in the streets, or someplace far away, or wherever in the world it happened to be. Passing the book to someone else was her idea just then. I was frightened by how quickly you read and fell for the book. I was about to forget the nature of the book when, thank God, they shot me."

Naturally I asked him what he thought was the nature of the book.

"A good book is something that reminds us of the whole world," he said. "Perhaps that's how every book is, or what each and every book ought to be." He paused. "The book is part of something the presence and duration of which I sense through what the book says, without it actually existing in the book," he said, but I could see he wasn't pleased with how he expressed it. "Perhaps it is something that has been distilled from the stillness or the noise of the world, but it's not the stillness or the noise itself." Then he said I might think he was talking nonsense, so he would try putting it into different words. "A good book is a piece of writing that implies things that don't exist, a kind of absence, or death . . . But it is futile to look outside the book for a realm that is located beyond the words." He said he had realized this while writing and rewriting the book, that he had learned it and he had learned it well. It was useless to look for the new life and the new realm beyond the text. He had richly deserved to be punished for having done just that. "But my killer turned out to be inept," he said. "He merely wounded me in the shoulder."

I told him I had been watching him from a window in Taşkışla Hall when he was shot in the vicinity of the minibus stop.

"All my travels, my expeditions, my bus trips have shown me that some sort of plot has been formed against the book," he said. "Some madman wants anyone who has a serious interest in the book dead. Who he is and why he's doing it, I just don't know. It is as if he is doing it to strengthen my resolve not to broach the subject of the book to anyone else. I don't want to bring damnation on anyone, or cause someone's life to slip off course. I ran away from Janan. Not only did I know we would never find the realm she desired, I had understood all too well that along with me she too might be caught in the glare of death that radiates from the book."

I brought up Uncle Rıfkı to ambush him and take him by surprise for a moment, in order to drag out of him the information he was withholding from me. I said this man might very well be the author. I mentioned that I had known him in my childhood when I used to read madly his illustrated fictions. After reading the book, I had once more carefully examined these comics, for example, *Pertev and Peter*, where I had seen that many of the topics had already been promulgated.

"Was this disappointing for you?"

"No," I said. "Tell me about meeting him."

What he told me completed in a logical fashion the information provided in Serkisof's reports. After having read the book thousands of times, he had seemed to remember something reminiscent of it in the children's comics he had read. He had located these comics in the libraries, and pinpointing the astonishing similarities, he had detected the identity of the author. He had been unable to talk to Rıfkı Ray much the first time, having been forestalled by the wife. During the interview that took place at the entrance, Rıfkı Ray had tried closing the subject as soon as he realized the strange young man at his door was interested in the book, responding to Mehmet's entreaties by saying that he had no further concern with the subject himself. A touching interview could have possibly taken place there at the door between the youthful fan and the elderly writer, but for Rıfkı Ray's wife— that's Aunt Ratibe, I interjected—who had interfered, as I had done just now, and had pulled her husband inside, slamming the door in the face of this uninvited guest who was a fan.

"I was so disappointed, I couldn't believe it," said my rival whom I couldn't decide whether I should call Nahit, or Mehmet, or Osman. "For a while I kept going back to the neighborhood and spying on him from a distance. Then one day I screwed up my courage again and rang the doorbell."

Rıfkı Ray had this time responded to him more positively. He had said that he still had no further interest in the book, but the insistent young man might stay and have some coffee. He had inquired where in the world the young man had obtained and read the book which had been published so many years before, and wanted to know why he had chosen this book when there were so many wonderful books to read; where was our young man going to school, and what did he want to do with his life, etc., etc. "Although I demanded several times that he reveal to me the secrets of the book, he didn't take me seriously," said our erstwhile Mehmet. "He was right, though. Now I know he had no secret to reveal."

He had insisted because he hadn't understood this back then. The old man had explained that he had been in deep trouble on account of the book, he had been pressured by the police and the prosecutor. "It all happened just because I thought I might provide some diversion and entertainment for a few grownups as I have diverted and entertained the kids," he had said. And if that

were not enough, Uncle Railman Rıfkı had gone on to say, "I
certainly could not allow my whole life to be destroyed for the
sake of a book I wrote to amuse myself." Nahit hadn't realized in
his anger then how grief-stricken the old man had become when
he explained that he had repudiated the book and had promised
the prosecutor he would neither get another edition printed nor
would he ever write anything more in that vein; but now, when
he was neither Nahit nor Mehmet, but Osman, he understood
the old man's grief so well he was mortified every time he remembered his own tactlessness.

As any young man who was bonded to the book with deep
conviction might end up doing, he had accused the old writer of
irresponsibility, vicissitude, treachery, and cowardice. "I was trembling with anger, yelling and insulting him, but he was understanding and indulgent." At some point, Uncle Rıfkı had also
risen to his feet and said, "You will understand it some day, but
you might be too old by then for it to be of any use." "I have
understood it," said the man whom Janan loved madly, "but I
can't tell if I am of any use or not. Besides I think the people
who murdered the old man were the minions of that madman
who was having me followed."

The prospective killer asked the prospective victim whether
causing the murder of someone was an unbearable burden for
him to carry the rest of his life. The prospective victim said nothing, but the prospective murderer saw the sorrow in his eyes and
feared for his own future. They were drinking raki at a slow pace
like a pair of gentlemen; and among the pictures of trains, scenes
of the homeland, and photographs of film stars, the portrait of
Atatürk was smiling down with the assurance of having safe-
guarded the Republic by entrusting it to the crowd getting drunk
in the tavern.

I consulted my watch. There was an hour and a quarter before
the time of departure for the scheduled train on which he wanted

to ship me off, and there was a feeling between us that we had managed to talk things over more than enough; as it says in books, "whatever needed to be said had been said." We kept quiet for quite a while like a pair of old friends who aren't troubled by silence falling between them, feeling it might be empty; on the contrary, we considered the silence, at least as far as I was concerned, the most eloquent form of conversation.

Even so, although I fluctuated between admiring him enough to emulate him and wanting to finish him off in order to possess Janan, I thought for a moment I'd tell him that the madman who was having the author and the readers of the book killed was none other than his own father, Doctor Fine. I wanted to inflict this pain on him, just because I felt oppressed, that's all. But I didn't tell him. All right, all right, I thought to myself; you never know, of course; don't upset the apple cart.

He must have had an inkling of my thoughts, or at least picked up some sort of vague echo concerning them, so he related to me the story of the bus accident that had led him to shake off the men his father had set after him. His face lit up for the first time. He had known at once that the young man sitting next to him on the bus that was covered in black ink had died in the accident. He had picked the identification card out of the pocket of this youth whose name was Mehmet and appropriated it. When the bus began to go up in flames, he got out. After the fire died down, he had this bright idea. He slipped his own identification card into the pocket of the burned body, and moving it into his own seat, he fled away to his new life. His eyes gleamed like a kid's when he was telling me about all this; but, naturally, I kept it to myself that I saw the same joyous face now as in his childhood photographs that I had seen in the museum his father had dedicated to his memory.

Another silence, and silence, and silence. Waiter, bring us some stuffed eggplant.

Just to pass the time, you know. For the hell of it, we went into generalizing on the topic of our situation, that is, our lives, his eye on his watch, my eye on his, expressing back and forth this sort of stuff: Well, life was like that. Actually, everything was quite simple. A fanatical old guy who wrote for the railway magazine and who despised bus travel and bus accidents had written some sort of a book, inspired by the children's comics he had penned himself. Then, some years later, optimistic young men such as ourselves who had read those comics in our childhood happened to read the book, and believing that our whole lives were changed from top to bottom, we slipped off the course of our lives. The magic in this book! The miracle of life! How had it happened?

I mentioned once more that I had known Railman Uncle Rıfkı in my childhood.

"Seems strange to hear that, somehow," he said.

But we knew nothing was strange. Everything was like that, and that's how everything was.

"It's even more so in the town of Viran Bağ," said my dear mate.

This must have jogged my memory. "You know," I said, deliberately enunciating each syllable and staring in his face, "many times I was under the impression that the book was about me, that the story was my story."

Silence. Death rattle of a soul giving up the ghost, a tavern, a town, a world. Clattering of knives and forks. Evening news on TV. Twenty-five more minutes.

"You know," I said again, "I have come across New Life brand caramels in many places during my Anatolian sojourn. Many years ago, they were available in Istanbul too. But they are still out there in remote places, in the bottom of tin boxes and candy jars."

"You are really after the Original Cause, aren't you?" said my rival, who had had his fill of scenes from the other life. "You are

questing for things that are pure, uncorrupted, and clear. But
there is no prime mover. It's futile to search for the key, the word,
the source, the original of which we are all mere copies."

So it was no longer because I wanted to possess Janan, but
because he did not believe in you, O Angel, that on my way to
the station I contemplated plugging him.

For some reason he broke the fractured silences by saying some
things, but I could not even give my undivided attention to this
good-looking sorrowful man.

"When I was a kid, reading seemed like a career to me which
one might take up someday in the future along with other professions.

"Rousseau, who worked as a music copyist, knew what it meant
to write over and over what other people had created."

Presently, not only the silences but everything else also seemed
fractured. Someone had turned off the TV and tuned the radio
to an intensely melancholic song about love-sickness and separa-
tion. How many times in one's life has mutual silence given one
such pleasure? He had just asked for the bill when a middle-aged
uninvited guest plopped himself down at our table and looked
me over. When he understood I was Osman's army buddy Osman, "We are very fond of our Osman here," he said, making
conversation. "So you were army buddies!" Then carefully, as if
he were revealing a secret, he mentioned a customer who had
turned up for a handwritten copy of the book. When I realized
my clever companion paid a commission to go-betweens such as
this one, once more, for the last time, I realized you had to love
the guy.

I assumed the parting scene, aside from the report of my
Walther, would go along the lines of the conclusion in *Pertev and
Peter*, but it turned out I was wrong. In that final adventure, when
the two bosom friends who have gone through many a battle
together realize that they are in love with the same girl with the

same goal, they sit down and solve the problem amicably. Pertev, who is more sensitive and taciturn, knows that the girl will be happier with Peter whose nature is optimistic and outgoing, so he quietly relinquishes the girl to Peter; and, accompanied by sniffling from teary-eyed readers like me, the heroes take their leave of each other at the train station which they had once heroically defended. In our case, we had a literary agent sitting between us who didn't give two hoots about outpourings of sensitivity or spleen.

Together, the three of us walked to the station. I bought my ticket. I picked out a couple of savory buns like those I had in the morning. Pertev had them weigh for me a kilo of the famous large white grapes grown in Viran Bağ. While I selected some humor magazines, he went into the can to wash the grapes. The agent and I stared at each other. The train took two days to arrive in Istanbul. When Pertev returned, the stationmaster signaled the go-ahead with a firm but graceful gesture that reminded me of my father. We kissed each other on the cheeks and parted.

The rest was more in keeping with the suspense videotapes Janan loved watching on the bus, rather than with Uncle Rıfkı's comics. The frenzied young man who has made up his mind to kill for love flings the plastic bag full of wet grapes and the magazines into a corner in the compartment, and before the train gathers speed, he leaps out of the railway car on the farthest side of the platform. Making sure he has not been observed, he stays at a distance and watches with eagle eyes his victim and Mr. Ten Percent. The two talk for a while and then amble together through the sad and deserted streets before taking leave of each other in front of the post office. The killer observes his victim go into the New World Theater, and he lights a cigarette. We never know what the killer is thinking in this genre of film, but we watch him throw down the cigarette he has finished smoking, as I just did, and step on the butt, buy a ticket for the feature called

Endless Nights, and walk into the theater with steps that appear confident, but before he enters the hall, we see him check out the bathroom, making sure he has an escape route.

The rest was fractured like the silences that accompany the night. I pulled out my Walther, released the safety, and entered the theater hall where the film was playing. It was hot and humid in there, and the ceiling was low. My silhouette carrying the gun appeared on the screen and the Technicolor film was projected on my purple jacket. The light from the projector glared into my eyes, but the seats were fairly empty, so I immediately located my victim.

Perhaps he was surprised, perhaps he did not understand, perhaps he didn't recognize me, perhaps he had expected it, but he stayed seated.

"You find someone of my ilk, you give him a book you make sure he will read, you cause him to slip off the course of his life," I said, but more to myself.

To make completely sure I hit him, I fired three times at point blank range into his chest and his face which I could not see. Following the Walther's report, I announced to the viewers sitting in the dark, "I killed a man."

While I was walking out of there, still watching my own silhouette on the screen and *Endless Nights* playing all around it, someone kept shouting, "Projectionist! Projectionist."

I boarded the first bus out of town, where I considered many a life-and-death question. I also wondered why in our language the same French loanword, *makinist*, designates both the person who runs films and the person who runs railway engines.

14 I CHANGED BUSES TWICE, SPENDING THE SLEEPLESS night of the assassin, and then, in the cracked mirror of a rest-stop washroom, caught a glimpse of myself. No one would believe me if I said the person I saw in the mirror resembled the ghost of the assassinated more than he did the assassin. But the inner peace that the one now dead had found through writing was very far indeed from the one in the washroom, the one later riding on restlessly, carried along over the wheels of a bus.

Early in the morning before returning to Doctor Fine's mansion I went into the town barbershop and had a haircut and a shave, so that I might present myself to my Janan in the guise of the good-natured and dauntless young man who for the sake of building a happy family nest had gone through many an ordeal successfully and had come face to face with death. When I set foot on Doctor Fine's property and saw the windows of the mansion, the thought of Janan waiting for me in her warm bed set my heart pounding, thump-thump, for two measures, and a sparrow in the plane tree went twitter-twitter in counterpoint.

Rosebud opened the door. I didn't register the surprise on her face, perhaps because only half a day before I had bumped off

her brother in the middle of a movie. Maybe that was why I hadn't
noticed her raising her troubled eyebrows, why I hardly listened
to what she was saying; instead, as if I were in my own father's
house, I walked directly to our room, the room where I had left
my Janan in her sickbed. I opened the door without knocking so
that I could surprise my sweetheart. When I saw that the bed in
the corner was unoccupied, completely empty, I began to understand what Rosebud had been telling me as I entered the room.

Janan had burned with a fever for three whole days, but then
she had recuperated. When she was up and about, she had gone
down to town and made a phone call to Istanbul, talked to her
mother, and when there was no word from me for several days
she had suddenly decided to go home.

My eyes stared out of the window of the unoccupied room at
the mulberry tree in the backyard shimmering in the morning
light, but now and then I couldn't help glancing back at the bed,
which had been meticulously made. The copy of the *Güdül Post*
she had used like a fan on the way here had been placed on the
deserted bed. A voice inside me declared that my Janan had already understood that I was a lousy murderer, and that I would
never see her again, so I might just as well close the door and
throw myself on the bed that still smelled of Janan and cry my
eyes out until I fell asleep. Another voice spoke in opposition to
the first one, saying a killer must act like a killer and behave cold-
bloodedly and without undue agitation: Janan was undoubtedly
waiting for me at her parents' place in Nişantaşı. Before leaving
the room, I saw that treacherous mosquito at the edge of the
windowsill and, yes, I dispatched it with one swipe of my hand. I
was sure the blood in the mosquito's belly which was smeared on
the love line in my palm must be Janan's sweet blood.

I had to get together with Janan back in Istanbul, but before
beating it out of the mansion in the heart of the counterplot
against the Great Conspiracy, I thought it would be beneficial

and in the interests of Janan's and my future together to see Doctor Fine. Doctor Fine was sitting at a table placed a little past the mulberry tree, where he was eating a bunch of grapes with much gusto, looking up from the book in front of him at the hills where we had hiked together.

Placid as a pair of people who have all the time in the world, he and I talked about life's cruelty, about how nature actually determined man's fate surreptitiously, about the way serenity and stillness were instilled into the human heart by the compressed concept we called time, about how one could not relish the pleasure of even these juicy grapes unless one exercised great willpower and resolution, about the high level of consciousness and desire necessary to reach the source of real life that was free of any trace of travesty, and whether it was a sign of the great order in the universe or the ludic manifestation of some random coincidence which had brought a humble porcupine to scurry past us rustling. Killing a man must endow one with maturity; I was able to link the admiration that I continued to feel for Doctor Fine, much to my amazement, with the feeling of sympathy and tolerance that suddenly rose from the depths of my being like a latent disease. For this reason, when he suggested that I accompany him on his visit to the grave of his dead son, I was able to refuse him firmly without offending him: The long days of concentrated effort had really tuckered me out; I should by all means go back home to my wife and rest up, during which time I must pull my wits together and decide whether to accept the great responsibility that he had offered to me.

When Doctor Fine inquired if I had had a chance to try out the present he had given me, I told him I had certainly put the Walther to a test and was terribly pleased with its performance; then remembering the Serkisof watch in my pocket, I pulled it out. I placed it next to the golden bowl that held the grapes, conveying to him that this was the expression of the respect and admiration that a dealer with a broken heart and broken teeth felt for him.

"All these heartsick unfortunates, these wretches, these weaklings!" he said, casting a sidelong glance at the watch. "They want to live the life they are accustomed to and keep their cherished objects. For that end, they bond themselves passionately to someone like me. Just because I give them hope for a just world! How cruel the external powers have proved to be in their determination to destroy our lives and our memories! Before you make your decision back in Istanbul, consider how you might be able to help with these people's broken lives."

I considered for a moment the prospect of finding Janan in Istanbul quickly, sweet-talking her back here to the mansion, where we might live happily ever after in the heart of the Great Counterconspiracy . . .

"Before returning to your charming wife," Doctor Fine said, employing the language of French novels in translation, "please divest yourself of that purple jacket that makes you look more like an assassin than a hero, eh?"

I immediately headed back by bus to Istanbul. Morning prayer was being called when my mother opened the door; I offered her no word of explanation about the Eldorado I had been seeking nor her angelic daughter-in-law.

"Don't you ever leave your mother like that!" she said, turning on the gas heater and running hot water in the bathtub.

We breakfasted quietly as in the old days, mother and son. I realized my mother, like many mothers whose sons are swept into political and fundamentalist currents, was keeping her mouth shut, thinking I had been attracted to some magnetic pole in the hinterland, and that if she asked, I might tell her something that would terrify her. When my mother's quick and light hand rested for a moment next to the red currant jam, I saw the spots on the back of her hand, making me think I had returned to my old life.

Was it possible for everything to go on as if nothing had happened?

After breakfast I sat at my desk and looked for a long time at the book, which was open at the place where I had left it. But what I was doing could not be called reading, it was something more like remembering, or some kind of suffering . . .

I was just leaving to go find Janan when my mother accosted me.

"Swear you'll be back by nightfall."

I did. I swore for two whole months every time I left home in the morning, but Janan could be found nowhere. I went to Nişantaşı, I pounded the streets, waited in front of their door, I rang their bell, I crossed bridges, took ferryboats, went to the movies, made phone calls, but I got no word. I convinced myself she would show up at Taşkışla Hall when classes started at the end of October, but she did not come. I walked the hallways in the building all day long; sometimes, thinking that a shadow which looked like hers went by the windows that looked on the hallway, I bolted out of class and broke into a run, and sometimes I went into a vacant classroom and lost in thought watched the foot traffic on the sidewalk and in the street.

It was on the day central heating was first turned on and people lit their stoves that, armed with a scenario that I had cleverly concocted, I rang the doorbell of my "missing classmate's" parents' apartment, and I managed to disgrace myself totally giving them the bullshit I had prepared in great detail. Not only did they not provide me with any information on Janan's whereabouts, they offered no clue as to where any information might be obtained. Even so, on the second visit I made to their place one Sunday afternoon when color TV was amiably gurgling away with a soccer match, I deduced from their attempt to get information out of me by questioning my motives that they knew a lot they were not telling. I got nowhere trying to pump information out of their relatives whose names I located in the phone book. The only conclusion that could be drawn from the conversations I had with all the testy uncles, inquisitive aunts, cautious maids, and snotty nephews and nieces was that Janan was at the university studying architecture.

As to her classmates in the school of architecture, they had long come to believe the myths they had dreamed up themselves in connection with Janan as well as with the news of Mehmet being shot in the vicinity of the minibus stop. I heard some say that Mehmet had been shot due to some settling of accounts between the dope pushers at the hotel where he worked, and I also heard it whispered that he had fallen victim to fanatic fundamentalists. There were those who said that Janan had been sent to school somewhere in Europe, a stratagem upper-class families often resort to with daughters who fall for some shady character, but the bit of investigative work I did at the registrar's office proved that this was not the case.

It's best that I don't even talk about the ingenious details of the snooping I did for months and years, nor about the cold-blooded calculations worthy of a murderer, and the colors reminiscent of an unfortunate's dreams. In essence, Janan was nowhere around, I had no news of her, nor did I come across her trail. I took the course of studies that I'd missed for a semester, and then also completed the next one. Neither I nor Doctor Fine's minions got back in touch. I had no idea whether they were still busy with their assassinations. Along with Janan they too had absconded from my dreams as well as from my nightmares. Then it was summer; then the new academic year began in the fall, which I completed, and also the one after that. Then I headed off to do my military service.

Two months before I was done with my patriotic duty, I had word that my mother had died. I was granted a furlough and made it to Istanbul in time for the funeral. My mother was interred. After the night I spent at some friends', I went home; and when

I felt the emptiness of the place, I became apprehensive. I was looking at the pots and pans hanging on the kitchen wall when I heard the refrigerator sighing sadly and lamenting through its familiar hum. I had been left all alone in this life. I lay down on my mother's bed and wept a little, then I turned on the TV and sat across from it like my mom, watching it for quite some time with resignation and some sort of joy of living. Before I went to sleep, I took the book out of its hiding place; I placed it on the desk and I began to read, hoping to be as affected as I was on the day when I had first read it. Although I did not sense a light surging on my face, or feel my body sever itself and pull away from the chair where I sat reading the book, I felt an inner peace.

That is how I began to read the book anew. But I no longer imagined with each new reading that my life was being swept away by a powerful wind toward an unknown realm. I was trying to capture the concealed pattern of a long-settled account, or the finer points of the story, the internal logic which I had not perceived while I was living through it. You do understand, don't you? Even before I was done with my military duty, I had already become an old man.

And so I devoted myself to other books in the same way. I did not read to assuage the desire for a soul other than the one which coiled inside me at the hour of dusk, or to fan the joy of connecting felicitously with the secret festival taking place in a metaphysical world, or even—oh, I don't know—to hasten toward a new life within which I might meet up with Janan. I read to face up to my lot in life with wisdom, with sobriety, like a gentleman, as well as to endure Janan's absence, which I felt profoundly. I harbored no hope that the Angel of Desire would ever offer me a candelabra with seven branches as a consolation prize with which to grace my home with Janan. At times, when I lifted my head from a book I read into the wee hours of the night with some sort of spiritual equilibrium and equanimity, I would become aware of the profound silence in the neighborhood, and that was when suddenly before my eyes appeared the image of Janan sleeping beside me on those bus rides which I had thought would never come to an end.

On one of those trips, which was refreshed in my imagination in full color like a dream of paradise each time I remembered it, I had observed that Janan's forehead and temples were covered in perspiration and her hair was wet and stuck together due to the air on the bus being unexpectedly hot, and I was dabbing the beads of perspiration with a Kütahya tile-design handkerchief I had bought in the town with the same name, when I perceived in my beloved's face—thanks to the mauve light from a filling station that was momentarily reflected on us—an expression of intense happiness and surprise. Later, at a rest-stop restaurant, Janan had cheered up sitting in her sweat-drenched State-store-bought print cotton dress and drinking down several glasses of tea, and she was all smiles telling me that she had dreamed of her father placing kisses on her forehead, but a while later she had realized it wasn't her father but a messenger from a realm created out of light. After she smiled, she often pulled her hair behind her ears with a supple gesture which each time she did it melted a piece of my heart, my soul, my mind before disappearing into the dark night.

I can almost see some of my readers scowling with sorrow, having understood that I am making do with what remains of those nights in my mind, heart, and soul. Patient Reader, sympathetic Reader, sensitive Reader, weep for me if you can, but don't you forget that the person for whom you expend your tears is none other than an assassin. Or else, if there are mitigating circumstances in the courts of law even for common murderers that call for compassion, empathy, and benevolence, then I wish these to be included in this book with which I am so involved.

Even though I was married some time later, I knew now that

everything I would ever do until the end of my life, which I did
not think was too distant, would have something great or small
to do with Janan. Before getting married and then even years after
my bride was easily ensconced in the condominium apartment
inherited from my father and vacated by my mother, I went on
extended bus trips with the hope of chancing upon Janan. I had
ascertained on these trips over the years that the buses gradually
became larger and larger, that they took on an antiseptic smell
inside, that the hydraulic systems installed in the doors automatically opened and closed them at the touch of a button, that the
drivers had peeled off their faded and sweaty shirtsleeves and were
now clad in pilot garb with epaulettes, that the tough-guy bus
attendants were now so gentrified they shaved every day, that the
rest stops were better lighted and fancier and yet they were monotonously all the same, that the highways were now wider and
all were paved with asphalt; but I never came across a trace of
Janan, let alone Janan herself. It was too much to ask to find her
and her trail. But what wouldn't I have given for some object that
came out of those wonderful nights I spent in her company, or
an elderly lady with whom we once had tea and conversation, or
even a bit of light that I was sure had reflected from her face
onto mine! But taking the cue from the new highways which were
rife with traffic signs, blinking lights, and merciless billboards, and
where the recent paving obscured youthful memories, everything
seemed busily anxious to forget us and our memories as soon as
possible.

It was following one of these depressing trips that I learned
Janan had married and had left the country. Your hero who is
married and has a child, who is a good family man and a murderer, was returning home in the evening from his job at the city
planning office—his briefcase in his hand, inside the case a Swiss-
license chocolate bar for the child, clouds of gloom in his heart,
a frozen look of weariness on his face—and he was standing on

the crowded Kadıköy ferryboat when he suddenly came face to face with a garrulous classmate from the engineering department. "As to Janan," the garrulous woman said, recounting all the marriages made by the females in our year, "she married a doctor from Samsun, and they settled down in Germany." When I shifted my eyes away from the woman to look out of the portholes, hoping to forestall further bad news she might yet impart, I observed that fog had descended over Istanbul and the Bosphorus, which was a rare condition for the city. "Is it fog?" the murderer asked himself. "Or is it the stagnancy of my unfortunate soul?"

It didn't prove necessary to investigate too long before I found out that Janan's husband was none other than the handsome doctor with wide shoulders who worked at the Samsun Social Security Hospital, the man who, in total contrast to other readers, had managed to find a sound method of absorbing the book into his system and living in peace and happiness. I even took up drinking to keep my merciless memory from relentlessly reminding me of the worrisome details of the man-to-man conversation on the meaning of the book and life that the doctor and I had many years ago in his consultation room at the hospital; but the drinking did not prove to be too smart.

After the household quieted down and all that remained from the bustle of the day was my daughter's toy fire truck with two missing wheels, and her blue teddy bear standing on his head to watch television upside down, I would come in with the raki highball I had mixed carefully in the kitchen myself and I would sit beside the teddy bear courteously, turn on the TV set, turn down the volume, and settling on a series of images that didn't seem too terribly vulgar, I would watch TV in a fog, attempting to discriminate the colors of the clouds in my head.

Don't you pity yourself! Don't believe how unique your identity and your existence is in reality. Don't complain about how the intense love you feel has not been appreciated. I read a book once upon a time, you know; I fell in love with a girl; I once experienced something profound. They did not understand me . . . they vanished . . . what do you suppose they're doing now? Janan is in Germany . . . on Bahnhofstrasse . . . I wonder how she is . . . the doctor husband . . . don't dwell on it. He comes home in the evening . . . Janan meets him at the door . . . nice home . . . new car . . . and two children . . . don't dwell on it . . . the husband's a chump. Suppose I am sent to Germany as part of a research delegation, suppose some evening we run into each other at the consulate . . . well hello . . . are you happy . . . I loved you so much back then. And now? I still love you very much . . . I love you . . . I'm ready to give up everything . . . I'll stay in Germany . . . I love you so much . . . I became a murderer for your sake . . . no don't say anything . . . how beautiful you are . . . Don't dwell on it. No one can love you as much as me. Do you remember the time when the bus had a flat, when in the middle of the night a drunk wedding party had showed up, and so . . . Don't dwell on it.

Sometimes I would drink myself into a stupor, and when I woke up hours later and sat up on the sofa, I would notice that the little blue bear that had been standing on his head was now sitting upright and watching TV, and I would be amazed: During what vulnerable moment had I sat him properly in his chair? And sometimes I would be absentmindedly watching the video clip of a foreign song on the screen, and I would remember having heard one of these songs when Janan and I were sitting together on a bus, our bodies pressing gently on each other, and I felt the warmth of her fragile shoulder on mine: Look at me, look at me sit here and weep, listening to the music we once heard together which has burst into color on TV. Another time, I had heard the child coughing, for some reason, before her mother had, and gathering the wakeful little girl in my arms, I had carried her into the living room, and while she watched the colors on the screen, I

began examining with awe her hand that was an impeccable miniature copy of a grownup's hand, down to the last tiny but amazingly detailed curve of her fingers and fingernails, and I was
engaged in reflecting on the book called life, when my daughter
said, "The man went pouf!"

We had watched with concern the hopeless face of the unfortunate man down in a pool of blood after a serious beating whose
life had gone "pouf."

Sensitive readers following my adventures should not assume
that I had let myself go, that my life too had already gone "pouf,"
seeing how I stayed up half the night getting drunk. Like most
men who live in this corner of the world, I too had become a
broken man before the age of thirty-five, and yet I had been able
to pull myself together and, by virtue of reading, to bring some
order into my mind.

I read voraciously, not only the book that changed my whole
life but other books as well. But when I read, I never attempted
to assign some deep meaning to my broken life, or to look for
some sort of consolation, not even to search for some beautiful
and admirable aspect of sorrow. Can one feel anything but love
and admiration for Chekhov, that talented, consumptive, modest
Russian? But I feel sad for readers who try giving an esthetic
dimension to their broken and sorry lives with sentiment which
they call Chekhovian, bragging about their misery in an effort to
render it beautiful and sublime; and I despise exploitive writers
who make a career out of accommodating these readers' need for
consolation. This is why I have left off reading many a contemporary novel or story halfway through. Ah, the poor man who talks
to his horse to alleviate his loneliness! Oh woe, the decrepit nobleman who keeps watering his potted plants which are his only
love. Pity the sensitive fellow who sits among his shabby furniture,
waiting for something that will never come, say, a letter, or an
old flame, or his inconsiderate daughter. The writers who pinch

rough drafts of Chekhovian protagonists in order to present them in other lands and climes, exposing to us their wounds and pains, have this message in common: Look at us, look at all the woe and agony we suffer! Look how sensitive, how refined, how special we are! Our anguish has elevated us to a more sensitive and refined state than you. You too want to transform your wretchedness into a triumph, or even into a sense of superiority, don't you? In that case, trust us, and believe it when we tell you that our pains are more gratifying than life's ordinary pleasures.

So, Reader, place your faith neither in a character like me, who is not all that sensitive, nor in my anguish and the violence of the story I have to tell; but believe that the world is a cruel place. Besides, this newfangled plaything called the novel, which is the greatest invention of Western culture, is none of our culture's business. That the reader hears the clumsiness of my voice within these pages is not because I am speaking raucously from a plane which has been polluted by books and vulgarized by gross thoughts; it results rather from the fact that I still have not quite figured out how to inhabit this foreign toy.

This is what I mean to say: I became something of a bookworm from reading so much in order to forget Janan, to comprehend what befell me, to dream the colors of the new life I never achieved, and to pass the time pleasantly and wisely—although not quite so wisely all the time—but I was never carried away by any intellectual pretensions. More important, I never looked down on those who were. I loved reading just as I loved going to the movies, or thumbing through newspapers and magazines. I didn't do these things to gain some sort of advantage, or as a means to an end, or maybe to think of myself as someone superior, or more knowledgeable, or more profound than others. I could even say that being a bookworm had taught me a kind of humility. I enjoyed reading books but I didn't like discussing them with anyone else, as I later learned that Uncle Rıfkı had not liked to do. If books awakened in me an urge to talk, the conversation often took place between the voices in my head. Sometimes I sensed that the books I read in rapid succession had set up some sort of murmur among themselves, transforming my head into an orchestra pit where different musical instruments sounded out, and I would realize that I could endure this life because of these musicales going on in my head.

Consider, for example, that it occurred to me I could put together an anthology inspired by the music whispered to me on the subject of love in that magnetic and painful stillness that began after my wife and daughter went to sleep, and I was left to view with awe and wonder the kaleidoscopic colors flowing on television as I reflected on Janan, the book that brought us together, the new life, the angel, accident, time. Whatever was said on the subject of love in the papers, books, magazines, on the radio, TV, by columnists, opinion editors, and novelists stuck fast in my brain because my life had gone off the track at a young age on account of love—if you notice, Reader, I am sentient enough not to claim it happened on account of the book.

What is Love?

Love is submitting. Love is the cause of love. Love is understanding. Love is a kind of music. Love and the Gentle Heart are identical. Love is the poetry of sorrow. Love is the tender soul looking in the mirror. Love is evanescent. Love is never having to say you are sorry. Love is a process of crystalization. Love is giving. Love is sharing a stick of gum. You can never tell about Love. Love is an empty word. Love is being reunited with God. Love is bitter. Love is encountering the angel. Love is a vale of tears. Love is waiting for the phone to ring. Love is the whole world. Love is holding hands in the movie theater. Love is intoxicating. Love is a monster.

Love is blind. Love is listening to your heart. Love is a sacred silence. Love is the subject of songs. Love is good for the skin.
   I acquired these pearls without letting myself be taken over
completely by blind faith, but also without being swept away by
a cynicism that would leave my soul homeless—that is, exactly
the way I view television, getting duped while being fully aware
that I am being duped, or not being duped yet wanting to be
duped. So here I am adding my own ideas on the subject which
come from my own limited but intense experience.
   Love is the urgency to hold fast to another and to be together
in the same place. It's the desire to keep the world out by embracing another. It is the yearning to find a safe harbor for the
human soul.
   You see, I was not able to say anything new. But still, I did
manage to say something! I no longer care if it's new or not.
Contrary to what some pretentious fools think, it's better to say
a couple of words rather than remain silent. What good is it to
keep our mouths shut, for heaven's sake? Why passively watch
life grinding down our bodies and souls like a merciless train
slowly proceeding to its destination? I knew a man who was about
my own age who implied that silence was preferable to struggling
against the force of evil that stalks and riddles us with holes. I
say implied because he never came out and said it, but sitting at
a table like a good boy, he kept writing in a notebook from morning to night someone else's words in silence. Sometimes I would
imagine he was not dead but still kept writing away, and I would
fear that his silence might expand inside me into the shape of a
gruesome terror.
   I had pumped those bullets into his chest and face, but had I
really managed to kill him? I had only fired three rounds, and
what's more, I was somewhat blinded by the light from the projecting machine in the dark movie house.

The times I believed he was not dead, I would imagine him still copying the book in his rooms. What an unbearable idea that was! While I tried creating a whole world with which to console myself, what with my well-meaning wife, my sweet daughter, my TV, newspapers, books, my work at City Hall, my co-workers and office mates, gossip, coffee, cigarettes, protecting myself surrounded by concrete objects, he was able to surrender himself resolutely to utter silence. In the middle of the night, I would be thinking of the stillness to which he devoted himself with faith and humility, when I would picture him rewriting the book, and miracle of miracles, I would sense that while he patiently did the same thing over and over at his table, silence would begin speaking to him. The enigma I could not arrive at but intuited through my aspirations and passion existed within that silence and darkness; and as long as the man Janan loved kept writing, I imagined that the authentic whispers in the depths of the night, which were totally inaudible to someone like myself, would acquire a voice of their own.

15 I WAS SO STRICKEN ONE NIGHT WITH A TERRIBLE desire to hear the whispering that I turned off the TV, and without waking my wife who went to bed early I removed the book quietly from my night stand, and I sat down at the table where we ate our supper every evening watching TV; and I began to read the book with renewed ardor. That is how I remembered first reading the book many years ago in the same room where my daughter now slept. My desire for the same light to surge from the pages and illuminate my face was so intense, I felt for a moment the image of the new world stir inside me. I sensed some movement, some sort of urgency, a stirring that might impart the secret of the whispering that would take me to the heart of the book.

As on the night when I had first read the book, I again found myself walking in neighborhood streets. On this fall night, the streets were dark and wet; on the sidewalks there were a few people on their way home. When I reached the square at Erenköy Station, I observed the window displays of the familiar grocery stores, the ramshackle trucks, the battered tarpaulin with which the greengrocer had covered his orange and apple crates on the sidewalk, the blue light that exuded from the butcher's window, the large old-fashioned stove in the pharmacy, and I was satisfied that everything was in its usual place. There were a couple of young men watching color TV in the student hangout where, in my university days, I used to get together with my pals from the neighborhood. As I walked through the streets, I could see the colored light of the same TV program seeping through the half-drawn curtains in the living rooms of families who were still up, light that was sometimes blue, or green, or reddish, as it was reflected on the plane trees, on the wet light poles, and on the iron railing on the balconies.

I was proceeding with my eyes on the television light emanating through half-drawn curtains when I stopped in front of Uncle Rıfkı's old place and stared for quite some time at the windows on the second floor. I felt a momentary sense of being free and venturesome, as if Janan and I had randomly got off some bus we had taken at random. I could see in between the curtains the room lit by the light from the television set but not Uncle Rıfkı's widow whose form I could imagine sitting in her chair. The room was lighted in keeping with the images on the screen, sometimes a gaudy pink, sometimes a ghastly yellow. I was seized by a notion that the secret of the book and my life lay there in that room.

I raised myself up peremptorily on the wall between the front yard and the sidewalk. I saw Aunt Ratibe's head and the TV set she was watching. She had sat herself down at a forty-five degree angle to her dead husband's empty chair, and she was watching TV with her head hunched between her shoulders just like my mother used to do, but unlike my mother she was not knitting but smoking up a storm. I watched her for quite a long time, remembering two other persons who had climbed on this wall previously and peeped in the window.

I pushed the button at the entrance which said Rıfkı Ray. The woman called down from the window that opened presently.

"Who is it?"

"It's me, Aunt Ratibe," I said, stepping back a few steps so that she could see me in the light cast by the street lamp. "It's me, Railman Akif's son, Osman."

"Heavens, it's Osman!" she said, withdrawing inside. She pushed the buzzer and the door was opened.

She greeted me with smiles at the apartment door and kissed me on my cheeks. "Let's have the top of your head too," she said. When I bent my head down, she kissed me there, smelling my hair exaggeratedly as she used to do when I was a child.

Her gesture first reminded me of the sorrow she and Uncle Rıfkı shared all their lives together, the fact that they never had a child; then I remembered that ever since my mother died, for the last seven years no one had treated me as if I were a child. Suddenly I felt so at ease that as we walked in, I wanted to say something before she began to ask questions.

"Aunt Ratibe, I was going by when I saw your light; I know the hour is late, but I thought I would stop and say hello."

"Good for you!" she said. "Take the seat across from the TV. I just can't get to sleep at night, so I watch this stuff. See that woman at the typewriter, she's a real snake. Terrible things keep happening to our young man, that's the cop. These people are going to blow up the whole town . . . Can I get you some tea?"

But she didn't immediately leave the room to make the tea; for a while we watched TV together. "Look at that shameless hussy," she said, pointing at an American beauty in red. The beauty took off some of her clothes, she and some guy kissed for a long time; and we watched them make love through the clouds of cigarette smoke that Aunt Ratibe and I put out. Presently, she too vanished out of sight along with many of the cars on the screen, bridges, guns, nights, cops, and beauties. I had absolutely no recollection of seeing this flick with Janan, but I felt the memories of all the movies Janan and I had watched together flipping through my consciousness, excruciating me.

When Aunt Ratibe turned up with the tea, I realized the necessity of finding something or other in this place if I were ever
to solve the secrets of the book and my broken life and thereby
perhaps ease some of the pain I suffered. Was the canary dozing
in his cage in the corner the same bird that impatiently hopped
up and down in my childhood when Uncle Rıfkı entertained me
in this room? Or was it a new one bought and caged following
the demise of that one, and the ones after that? Meticulously
framed pictures of railway cars and locomotives were still hanging
in their former places, but in my childhood I had always seen
them in cheerful daylight, listening to Uncle Rıfkı's jokes and
trying to solve his puzzles, so it made me sad seeing these tired
and long-retired vehicles in their neglected and dusty frames in
the light from the TV set. In one half of the mirrored breakfront,
there were cordial sets and half a bottle of raspberry liqueur. Next
to these between railroad service medals and a locomotive-shaped
lighter stood Uncle Rıfkı's conductor's punch, which he used to
let me play with when my father and I visited him. When I saw
the thirty books or so in the other half of the breakfront where
miniature railway cars, a fake crystal ashtray, and twenty-five years'
worth of train schedules were reflected in the mirror on the back,
my heart began to pound loudly.

These had to be the books Uncle Rıfkı must have been reading
during the years when he wrote *The New Life*. A wave of excitement overtook me as if I had come across a tangible trace of Janan
after all these years and all these bus trips.

We were having our tea watching television when Aunt Ratibe
asked after my daughter, then she questioned me as to my wife's
person. I was mumbling something or other, feeling guilty about
not having invited her to the wedding, telling her that my wife's
family actually lived on our street, when I remembered that I had
first laid eyes on the girl who was later to become my wife during
the first few hours when I first read the book. Which of these

coincidences, then, was the more intrinsic and astonishing? Was it that I had first seen that dolorous girl I was to marry years later on the first day I had ever read the book? Or that I remembered the coincidence and discovered years after my marriage the concealed pattern in my life while sitting in Uncle Rıfkı's chair? She was the daughter of the family that had moved into the vacant apartment across the street from ours, whom I saw eating their evening meal watching TV under the light of a powerful naked bulb. I remembered observing that the girl's hair was light brown, the TV screen green.

I was transported by a sweet confusion involving life, coincidence, and memory, but Aunt Ratibe and I kept talking about neighborhood gossip, the new butcher shop, my barber, old movies, and a friend of mine who left the neighborhood after expanding his father's shoe business into a shoe factory and getting rich. While we were having a fractured conversation which was interrupted by silences, revolving around the topic "Life is so fractured," the TV abounded in gunshots, passionate lovemaking, shouts and screams, planes falling out of the sky, exploding gas tankers, all sending the message, "No matter what, things must be smashed and broken"; and yet we did not assume it pertained to us.

In the wee hours of the morning when the moaning, the murmurs in the night, and death throes were replaced by an educational film on the lives of red and black crabs on Christmas Island in the Indian Ocean, I, the crackerjack detective, approached the topic sideways like the sensible crab on the screen.

"How wonderful things were back in the good old days," I had the temerity to say.

"Life is wonderful for the young," Aunt Ratibe said. But she had nothing wonderful to say about her youth which she had spent with her husband—perhaps because I questioned her on the children's comics, the spirit of railmanship, Uncle Rıfkı's fic-

tion and his illustrated romances. "Your Uncle Rıfkı took the pleasure out of our youth with his hobby, scribbling and doodling."

Actually, she had initially responded positively to the idea of
his writing for the *Rail* magazine and putting a lot of effort into
the publication. For one thing, this way Uncle Rıfkı was somewhat
spared the long trips railway inspectors have to make, and Aunt
Ratibe didn't have to wait all alone for days on end, her eye on
the door, for her husband to come home. Pretty soon, he had
come up with the idea of putting illustrated adventures at the
end of the magazine for the children of railway enthusiasts, so
that the children would come to believe in the cause of the railways which were to be our country's salvation. "Some children
really loved them, didn't they?" Aunt Ratibe said, smiling for the
first time; so I told her how transported I was, reading the adventures, and that I knew the *Pertev and Peter* series almost by heart.

"But he should have left it at that!" she interrupted me. "He
should not have taken it so seriously." According to her, when
the illustrated adventure supplement enjoyed quite a success, her
husband's mistake had been deciding to put out a separate children's magazine, having fallen for the proposal made by some
shrewd Babıali publisher. "From then on, he had to work day and
night; he'd return dead tired from some tour of inspection or his
job at the directorate, only to head immediately to his desk where
he worked until daybreak."

These magazines had become popular reading for a while, but
after their initial success, they had soon lost their appeal in favor
of all those illustrated historical romances, such as *Kaan, Karaoğlan,* and *Hakan,* created in response to the fad for Turkish war-
riors battling the Byzantines. "*Pertev and Peter* caught on for a
while, so we made a bit of money," Aunt Ratibe said. "But the
one who made a real fortune was, naturally, that bandit of a
publisher." The grasping publisher had insisted that Uncle Rıfkı
put aside his stories of Turkish children playing cowboys and rob-

bers on behalf of American railways, and start drawing popular stuff on the order of *Karaoğlan*, or *Kaan*, or *Blade of Justice*. "I will not draw any illustrated adventure that does not include at least one frame sporting the picture of a train," maintained Uncle Rıfkı, and that's how his association with the faithless publisher had ended. For a while he had drawn the comics at home and looked for other publishers, but he had given up after a period of being rejected.

"So where are those unpublished adventures now?" I said, running my eyes over the room.

She did not answer me. She concentrated for a while on the difficult journey the long-suffering female black crab has to make crossing the entire island in order to lay the fertilized eggs in her belly at the most auspicious moment during high tide.

"I threw out the lot of them," she said. "Cupboards full of pictures, magazines, cowboy stories, books on America and the heroes of the West, movie magazines out of which he copied the costumes, oh, and all the stuff on Pertev and Peter, God knows what all . . . He loved them and not me."

"Uncle Rıfkı adored children."

"Yes, he did; he did, indeed," she said. "He was a good man, he loved everyone. Where do you find a man like that these days?"

She shed a few tears, perhaps prodded by the feeling of guilt about having said a couple of bitter things about her dead husband. While she watched the few crabs that were able to make it back to the beach without falling victim to the seagulls or the rough sea, she dried her eyes with a handkerchief she produced with an astonishing sleight of hand, and she wiped her nose.

"And so it seems," said the cautious detective at that particular moment, "that Uncle Rıfkı also wrote a book called *The New Life* for adults, and he apparently had it published under a pseudonym."

"Wherever did you hear that?" she interrupted me. "There's no truth to it."

She gave me such a look and assumed such an air of quiet rage, blowing roughly the smoke of the cigarette she lighted with indignation, that the crackerjack detective was forced to stifle it.

We did not talk for quite some time. Still I could not bring myself to take my leave, waiting for something to happen, hoping that life's hidden pattern might finally manifest itself.

The educational film on TV was over, and I was trying to console myself by imagining that a crab's life was far worse than a human's, when Aunt Ratibe rose from her seat with a severe and determined gesture, and grasping me by the arm pulled me toward the breakfront. "Look," she said. When she turned on a gooseneck lamp, it lighted a framed photograph on the wall.

Thirty-five or forty men who were wearing the same kind of jackets, the same tie, and similar trousers, and most of whom were sporting identical mustaches, had smiled into the camera where they stood on the steps leading to the Haydar-Pasha train station.

"Railroad inspectors, one and all," Aunt Ratibe said. "They were all so convinced that the development of this country depended on the railroads." Her finger pointed someone out: "Rıfkı."

He looked just like I remembered him from my childhood and just like I had imagined him all these years. He was taller than average. Slender. Somewhat handsome, somewhat pensive. Pleased to be with the group, pleased to look like the rest of them. Smiling slightly.

"I have no one in the world, you know," Aunt Ratibe said. "I couldn't come to your wedding, so here, at least take this." She stuck into my hand the silver candy dish she took out of the breakfront. "The other day I saw you with your wife and daughter at the station. What a good-looking woman. One hopes you give your wife her due."

I kept looking at the candy dish in my hand. If I claimed I was
stricken with feelings of guilt and inadequacy, the reader might
perhaps not believe me. Let me just say, I remembered something—without really being conscious of what it was that I remembered. The reflections of Aunt Ratibe, myself, and the room
became diminutive, rotund, and flattened in the mirror-like surface of the candy dish. How magical it is to see the world not
through the keyholes we call our eyes but for an instant through
the logic of another sort of lens. Smart children intuit this, and
it makes smart adults smile. Half of my mind was elsewhere,
Reader, and the other half was stuck on something else. I don't
know if it happens to you, but you are about to remember something, yet just before you figure out what you remember, for some
unknown reason you postpone remembering.

"Aunt Ratibe," I said, neglecting even to thank her for the
candy dish. I pointed at the books in the other half of the breakfront. "May I take these books home with me?"

"What for?"

"To read them," I said. I didn't mention I could not sleep
nights because I was a murderer. "I read at night," I said. "The
TV tires my eyes, I can't watch it too long."

"Oh, all right then," she said suspiciously. "But when you're
done reading, bring them back. So that part of the breakfront
won't have to stay empty. My late husband read them all the
time."

So, after Aunt Ratibe and I finished watching the film on the
late late show about some bad guys in the city of angels called
Los Angeles, unhappy aspiring actresses who didn't seem to mind
turning tricks, zealous cops, and pretty young people who at the
drop of a hat made love with the innocence of children in paradise
but then said some incredibly awful and shameful stuff about one
another behind each other's backs, I returned home at a very late
hour with two plastic bags full of books in my hands, the silver

candy dish on top of one bag reflecting the bag of books, the world, streetlights, the denuded poplar trees, the dark sky, the melancholy night, the wet pavement, and my hand carrying the bag, my arm, and my legs pumping up and down.

I lined up the books meticulously on the desk that used to be in the back room, my daughter's room, when my mother was alive but which was now in the living room, the same desk on which I did my school and university homework for years and read for the first time *The New Life*. The cover of the candy dish was stuck and could not be pried open, so I put it next to the books too; and lighting a cigarette, I viewed everything with pleasure. There were thirty-three books. Among them there were reference books such as *The Principles of Mysticism, Child Psychology, A Short History of the World, Great Philosophers and Great Martyrs, Illustrated and Annotated Dream Interpretations*, translated works of Dante, Ib'n Arabi, and Rilke from the world classics series published by the Ministry of Education and sometimes distributed free of charge to directorates and ministries, anthologies such as *Best Love Poems, Tales from the Homeland*, translations of Jules Verne, Sherlock Holmes, and Mark Twain in brightly colored covers, and some stuff like *Kon-Tiki, Geniuses Were Also Children, The Last Station, Domestic Birds, Tell Me a Secret, A Thousand and One Puzzles*.

I began reading the books that very night. And from then on, I kept observing that some of the scenes in *The New Life*, some expressions, and some fantasies were either inspired by things in these books or else had been lifted outright. Uncle Rıfkı had availed himself of these books while he was writing *The New Life* with the same ease and routine he had developed when he appropriated for his own illustrated children's stories illustrated and written material from comics like *Tom Mix, Pecos Bill*, or *The Lone Ranger*.

Let me give a few examples:

"The Angels were unable to divine the mystery in the creation of the viceroy called Man."

—Ib'n Arabi, *The Seals of Wisdom*

"We are soul mates and traveling companions; we were each other's unconditional allies."

—Neşati Akkalem, *Geniuses Were Also Children*

"So I returned to the loneliness of my room and began to think about this gracious person. As I thought of her I fell asleep and a marvelous vision appeared to me."

—Dante, *La Vita Nuova*, III

"Are we on this earth to say: House, Bridge, Fountain, Jug, Gate, Fruit Tree, Window—at best: Column, Tower . . . ? but to *say* these words you understand with an intensity the things themselves never dreamed they'd express."

—Rilke, *Duino Elegies*, The Ninth Elegy

"But there was no house in the vicinity, and nothing was visible other than some ruins. It appeared these ruins were not the work of time but the result of a series of disasters."

—Jules Verne, *Famille-Sans-Nom*

"I came across a book. If you were reading it, it appeared to be a bound volume, but if you were not, it turned into a bolt of cloth that was of green silk . . . Presently, I found myself examining the numbers and letters in the book, and I knew from the handwriting that the text had been written by the son of His Honor Abd-ur-Rahman, the Chief Magistrate of Aleppo. When I came back to my senses, I found myself writing the section you are presently reading. And suddenly I knew that the section written by His Honor's son, which I

had read in a trance, was identical to the section I am writing
in this book."

—Ib'n Arabi, The Meccan Openings

"Love's influence was such that my body, which was then
utterly given over to his governance, often moved like a
heavy, inanimate object."

—Dante, La Vita Nuova, XI

"I had set foot in that part of life beyond which one cannot
go with any hope of returning."

—Dante, La Vita Nuova, XIV

16 I ASSUME WE HAVE ARRIVED AT THE APOLOGIA SECtion of our book. For months on end I read over and over the thirty-three books lined up on my desk. I underlined words and sentences in the yellowed pages; I took notes in notebooks and on pieces of paper; I frequented libraries where janitors stare at readers with a look that says, "What the hell are you doing here?"

Like many a broken fellow who for a period of time has eagerly plunged himself in the thick of the commotion called Life, when I compared the various fantasies and expressions in my readings, I discerned encoded whisperings between texts from which I could detect their secrets; and putting these secrets in order, I constructed connections between them, and proud of the complexity of the network of connections I made, I worked away patiently like someone digging a well with a needle, in an effort to atone for my having shrugged off so much in life. Instead of being amazed that library shelves in Islamic countries are crammed full of handwritten interpretations and commentaries, all one has to do is take a look at the multitudes of broken men in the street to know the reason why.

All through my struggles, whenever I came across a new sen-

tence or image or idea that had seeped into Uncle Rıfkı's slim
volume from another source, I was initially disappointed, like the
young man who discovers the angel of his dreams is not the angel
she seems; but then, like the unmitigated slave of love that I was,
I wanted to believe that what did not look pure at first sight was
in fact the sign of a profoundly enchanting secret or a unique
significance.

I had been reading and rereading *The Duino Elegies*, as well as
the other books, when I made up my mind that all could be solved
through the intercession of the angel, perhaps for the reason that
I missed the nights I spent in Janan's company hearing her talk
about the angel, rather than that the angel in the elegies reminded me of the angel Uncle Rıfkı had mentioned in his book.
In the stillness of the night, long after the long freight trains went
past the neighborhood interminably clattering on the tracks on
their way East, I longed to hear the summons of a light, a stirring,
a life the memory of which I liked recollecting; I turned my back
on the silver candy dish which reflected the television that was
playing as well as me sitting and smoking at my desk which was
cluttered with papers and notebooks, and I walked to the window
where from in between the curtains I looked out into the dark
night. A faint light cast by a streetlamp or one of the apartments
across the street would momentarily be reflected in the water
droplets on the windowpane.

Who was this angel I wished would call out to me from the
heart of stillness? Like Uncle Rıfkı himself, I knew no other language besides Turkish, but I paid scant attention to the fact that
I was beset with poor and slipshod translations which were garbled
by fortuitous fleeting fads in an obscure language. I presented
myself at universities, asking questions of professors and transla-
tors who snapped at me for my amateurishness; I obtained addresses in Germany where I sent letters; and when some kind and

gentle persons responded to me, I tried convincing myself that I was making progress toward the locus of some enigma.

In his famous letter to his Polish translator, Rilke says the "angel" of the *Elegies* has less to do with the angel of the Christian heaven than with the angelic figure in Islam, which was a fact Uncle Rıfkı had gleaned from the translator's short foreword. Having learned, from a letter that he wrote to Lou Andreas-Salomé from Spain the very year he began writing the *Elegies*, that Rilke had read the Koran, which "astounded, astounded" him, I was engrossed for a time with the angels of Islam, but I did not find in the Koran any of the accounts I had heard from my mother, the elderly women in the neighborhood, nor from any of my know-it-all friends. Although Azrael's likeness was available to us from many sources, be it in cartoons in the newspapers or in traffic posters or in natural science class, he was not even named in the Koran; he was simply referred to as the Angel of Death. I couldn't find anything more than what I already knew about Archangel Michael nor about Israphel who was to play the trumpet on Judgment Day. A German correspondent closed the subject by sending me a pile of likenesses of Christian angels, which had been photocopied from books of art, in response to my question as to whether the distinction made in the beginning of the thirty-fifth surah in the Koran in terms of those angels possessing "two, three, or four wings" was peculiar to Islam. Aside from trivial differences such as the Koran referring to angels as a separate class of beings, or that the fiendish crew in Hell was also considered to be of angelic descent, or that the Biblical angels provided a stronger connection between God and His creatures, there was little else to prove Rilke right about his distinction concerning the angels of Islam versus those in the Christian heaven.

Even so, I thought it possible that even if Rilke were not alluding to Archangel Gabriel appearing to Mohammad "on the

clear horizon," witnessed by the stars "running their course and
setting" at the very moment between the darkness of night and
the light of day, as it is told in some of the verses in the surah
called Al Takwir, Uncle Rıfkı, when he was in the process of giving
his own book its final shape, could have been thinking of the
divinely revealed Book in which "everything is written." But that
was during the time I considered Uncle Rıfkı's slim volume as
having been brought into existence not only from the thirty-three
books under his hand but from all the books there are. The more
I reflected on those poor translations piled on my desk, the photocopies and the notes mentioning Rilke's angel, or the reasons
for the beauty of angels, the absolute beauty that excludes what
is causal and accidental, on Ib'n Arabi, on the superior qualities
of angels that exceed human limitations and sins, their ability to
be simultaneously here and there, on time, death, and life after
death, the more I remembered having read of these not only in
Uncle Rıfkı's slim volume but also in the adventures of Pertev
and Peter.

Toward spring one evening after supper, I was reading in one
of Rilke's letters for the nth time—only heaven knows how
many—where it said, "Even for our forefathers, a house, a well,
a familiar tower, their own clothes, their jackets: these were beyond reckoning, they were more personal than can be reckoned."

I remember looking around me for a moment and feeling pleasantly giddy. Hundreds of black-and-white shades of angels were
looking on me not only from among the books on my old desk,
but from places where my disruptive little daughter had carried
them, on the windowsills, the dusty radiator, the rug, the side
table with one short leg, which were then reflected on the silver
candy dish: they were the photocopies of the reproductions of the
actual oil paintings of angels done in Europe hundreds of years
ago. I thought I liked these better than the originals.

"Pick up the angels," I said to my three-year-old daughter. "Let's go to the station and watch the trains."

"Can we get some caramels too?"

I took her up in my arms and we went to see her mother in the kitchen, which smelled of detergent and grilled food, telling her we were on our way to see the trains. She looked up from the dishes she was doing and gave us a smile.

It pleased me to walk to our local station in the cool spring air, holding my daughter close. I thought cheerfully that when we got back home, I would watch the soccer game, then my wife and I would catch the Sunday Night Movie. The candy store called Life at the station square had dispensed with winter by lowering the store windows and installing up front their ice-cream counter sporting ice-cream cones. We had them weigh us a hundred grams of Mabelle caramels. I took the wrapper off one and placed it into my daughter's impatient mouth. We went up on the platform.

Exactly at nine-sixteen, the Southbound Express that came through without stopping announced itself first with the heavy roar of engines that came from somewhere deep down, as if from the very soul of the earth, and presently its searchlight was being reflected on the walls of the bridge and the steel pylons; then, as it drew into the station, it seemed to grow quieter, only to raise a ruckus with the full power of its jarring and inexorable engines as it went by us two puny mortals holding on to each other. Inside the brilliantly lit cars being pulled along clattering with a more humane noise, we saw the passengers who were leaning back in their seats, leaning up against the windows, hanging up their coats, lighting their cigarettes, all completely unaware of us watching them slide by in the blink of an eye. We stood in the faint breeze and stillness left behind by the train, staring for a long time at the red light at the back of the train.

"Do you know where this train goes?" I asked my daughter on an impulse.

"The train goes where?"

"First to Izmit, then Bilecik."

"Then?"

"Then Eskişehir. Then Ankara."

"Then?"

"Then to Kayseri, to Sivas, to Malatya."

"Then?" said my daughter with the light brown hair, happy to be repeating herself and still watching the barely visible red light on the caboose with a sense of play and mystery.

And her father recalled his own childhood calling out the names of the stations he remembered where the train stopped— and then, and then—as well as those he did not remember.

I must have been eleven or twelve. My father and I had gone to Uncle Rıfkı's one afternoon. While Uncle Rıfkı and my father played backgammon, I had the sugar cookie Aunt Ratibe had given me in my hand, and I was watching the canary in the cage, then tapping on the barometer I had yet to learn to read; I had just pulled out one of the old comics on the shelf and was getting absorbed in an old adventure of Pertev and Peter when Uncle Rıfkı called me, and, as he always did on our visits, he began quizzing me.

"Run through the stations between Yolçatı and Kurtalan."

I had begun with "Yolçatı, Uluova, Kürk, Sivrice, Gezin, Maden," and had named the rest without any omission.

"And those between Amasya and Sivas?"

I had reeled them off without a hitch because I had memorized the train schedules Uncle Rıfkı maintained every intelligent Turkish child must know by heart.

"Why does the train departing from Kütahya en route to Uşak have to go by way of Afyon?"

This was the question I knew the answer to by way of Uncle Rıfkı and not the train schedules. "Because the government has unfortunately abandoned its railroad policy."

"And here's the final question," Uncle Rıfkı had said, his eyes gleaming. "We're going from Çetinkaya to Malatya."

"Çetinkaya, Demiriz, Akgedik, Ulugüney, Hasançelebi, Hekimhan, Kesikköprü . . ." I had begun, but I drew a blank before I was through.

"Then?"

I was silent. My father had the dice in his hand, and he was studying the pieces on the board, looking for his way out of a tight spot.

"What comes after Kesikköprü?"

The canary in the cage went click, click.

I backtracked some and then started up with renewed hope, "Hekimhan, Kesikköprü," but I got stuck again on the next station.

"Then?"

There was a long pause. I thought I was about to cry when Uncle Rıfkı said, "Ratibe, go ahead and give him a caramel; he might just remember."

Aunt Ratibe offered me the caramels. As Uncle Rıfkı had suggested, I remembered the next station after Kesikköprü the moment I popped the caramel in my mouth.

Twenty-five years after the incident, there he was with his pretty daughter in his arms, watching the red light on the rear of the Southbound Express, and our stupid Osman once more couldn't remember the name of the same station. But I forced myself to remember for quite some time, trying to stroke and prod my associations into action, telling myself: What a coincidence! 1) The train that has just gone past us will pass tomorrow through the same station the name of which I cannot remember. 2) Aunt Ratibe had offered me the caramels in the same silver dish she had given me as a gift. 3) There is one caramel in my daughter's mouth, and in my pocket a little less than a hundred grams of caramels.

Dear Reader, I derived such pleasure from my memory getting stuck fast where my past and future intersected on this spring evening at a point that was so far removed from what's accidental that I was stuck where I was standing, trying to recall the name of the station.

After a long interval, my daughter in my arms said, "Dog."

The dirtiest and the most pathetic of stray dogs was sniffing the cuffs of my pants, and a light breeze was cooling the modest evening that had settled over the neighborhood. Soon we were back home, but I did not immediately rush to the silver candy dish. My daughter had to be tickled first, nuzzled, and put to bed; then my wife and I had to settle down to watch the kisses and murders on the Sunday Night Movie; and then I had to bring some order to the books, papers, and angels on my desk before I could begin to wait, my heart pounding, for my memories to thicken and reach the right consistency.

The heartsick man who had fallen victim to love as well as to a book summoned his associations: Speak, Memory. And I raised the silver candy dish in my hands. My gesture had something in it of a Municipal Playhouse actor raising pretentiously the skull of some poor peasant passing for Poor Yorick's, but if you consider the result, it was not a fake gesture. How docile the enigma called Memory was after all: I remembered instantly.

Those readers who believe in chance and accident, as well as those readers who believe Uncle Rıfkı would not leave things to chance and accident, probably have already guessed that the name of the station was Viran Bağ.

I remembered even more. When I looked at the silver candy

dish with the caramel in my mouth twenty-three years ago and
piped up, "Viran Bağ," Uncle Rıfkı had said, "Bravo!"

Then, then the dice he had thrown had come up five and six,
hitting two of my father's pieces with one throw, and he had said,
"Akif, this boy of yours is awfully smart. You know what I am
going to do one of these days?" But my father whose attention
was on his captured pieces was not even listening, so Uncle Rıfkı
had addressed me directly. "I am going to write a book someday,
and I will give the hero your name."

"A book like *Pertev and Peter?*" I had asked, my heart pounding.

"No, not an illustrated book, but one where I will tell your
story."

I had kept silent, unconvinced. I couldn't imagine what sort of
thing that book might be.

That was when Aunt Ratibe had called out, "There you go
again putting children on!"

Was this a real scene? Or was it a fiction that my well-
intentioned and good-natured memory had made up on the spot
to console a broken man like me? I just couldn't figure it out. But
I had no desire to rush out at once and question Aunt Ratibe,
either. I walked up to the window with the silver candy dish in
my hand, and I was lost in thought looking out on the street,
although I don't know if I could rightly call it thinking, or just
talking in my sleep. 1) Lights went on in three different homes
simultaneously. 2) The pathetic dog at the station went by looking high and mighty. 3) Whatever possessed my fingers through
all this mental confusion, they got into the act and removed—
oh, look!—the stuck lid from the candy dish without too much
trouble.

I admit to thinking for a moment that like in fairy tales the
candy dish might produce amulets, or magic rings, or poisoned
grapes. But what it contained were seven of the New Life brand
caramels I remembered from my childhood which no longer ap-

peared in groceries and candy stores even in the remotest of provincial towns. On the wrapper of each there was the trademark
angel, adding up to seven angels in all, sitting politely on the edge
of the letter L for Life, their beautiful legs slightly extended into
the space between New and Life, looking at me with gratitude
and smiling sweetly for having released them from the darkness
of the candy dish which they had endured for these past twenty
years.

I removed with extreme care and difficulty the wrappers on the
caramels which had turned into marble with age, making sure I
did not harm the angels. There was a doggerel rhyme inside each
wrapper, but it could not be said that they were of any help in
understanding either life or the book. For example:

> Behind the canteen
> The grass grows green;
> What I want from you
> Is a sewing machine.

What's more, I even began repeating this nonsensical stuff to
myself in the still of the night. Before I completely lost my mind,
I sneaked into my old room as a last resort, and quietly pulling
out the bottom drawer in the old dresser, I found by feel the
plastic multipurpose thingamajig from my childhood which was
a ruler on one side, on the other a letter opener, with the blunt
end a magnifying glass; and like some Treasury Department agent
examining counterfeit money under the light of the desk lamp, I
gave the angels on the caramel wrappers a thorough examination:
they bore no resemblance either to the Angel of Desire or the
four-winged angels standing statically in Persian miniatures; nor
were they anything like the angels which many years ago I anticipated seeing any minute in the bus window, or their photocopied
versions in black and white. My memory, in an effort to look busy,

reminded me uselessly that when I was little, vendors who were children themselves used to hawk these caramels on trains. I was about to conclude that the figure of the angel had been appropriated from some European publication, when I focused on the manufacturer who kept signaling to me from the corner of the wrapper.

Ingredients: glucose, sugar, vegetable oil,
butter, milk, and vanilla.

New Life™ Caramels are a product of
Angel Candy and Chewing Gum, Inc.
18 Bloomingdale Street
Eskişehir

Next evening I was on the bus to Eskişehir. I had told my superiors at City Hall that a distant and forlorn relative had fallen ill; and I had explained to my wife that my mentally ill bosses were sending me out to distant and forlorn towns. You do get me, don't you? If life is not a tale told by an idiot signifying nothing, if life is not just a haphazard bunch of scratches on a piece of paper made by a kid who's got hold of a pencil as my three-year-old daughter sometimes does, if life is not just a cruel chain of idiocies completely devoid of any sense, then there must be some sort of logic to all the fun and games that appeared coincidental but which Uncle Rıfkı had placed there when he was writing *The New Life*. If so, then the great planner would have had to have some purpose in putting the angel in my way, hither and yon, all these many years, in which case if an ordinary and broken hero such as myself succeeded in finding out from the horse's mouth, so to speak, by talking directly to the candyman who had decided why the picture of an angel was put on the wrapper of the caramel the hero loved in his childhood, then he might possibly be able to find consolation, on autumn evenings when sorrow descended on his being, in the meaning of what was left of his life, instead of carping about the cruelty of coincidences.

Speaking of coincidences, it was my pounding heart and not my eyes that had first registered that the driver of the late model Mercedes bus which took me to Eskişehir was the same one who fourteen years ago had driven Janan and me from a tiny steppe town with minarets to a city that rain floods had turned into a swamp. My eyes, as well as the rest of my body, were busy trying to adjust themselves to all the modern comforts available on buses lately, such as the drone of the air-conditioning, individual reading lights over the seats, bus attendants dressed in hotel valet's getups, the plastic taste of the food wrapped in gaily colored plastic pouches and served on trays, and napkins carrying the winged insignia of the tourism agency. At the touch of a button the seats could now be converted into beds that reclined over the laps of the unfortunates sitting in the seats behind them. Now that the "express" buses were scheduled to travel directly from one specific terminal to another and no stops were made at any fly-infested restaurants along the way, some buses had been fitted with toilet stalls reminiscent of electric chairs where one would hate to be stuck at the time of an accident. Half the time what appeared on the TV monitor were commercials featuring the tourism agency's vehicles which dragged us toward the asphalt-paved heart of the steppe, so that as one traveled on the bus napping or watching TV, one could watch umpteen times how pleasant it was to travel on this bus while napping or watching TV. The wild and desolate steppe Janan and I had once watched out of the bus window had now been rendered "people friendly" by virtue of having been riddled with billboards advertising cigarettes and tires, and the steppe took on various hues at the pleasure of the color the bus windows had been tinted to cut out the sun—sometimes a muddy brown, sometimes the green of Islam, sometimes the color of crude oil that reminded me of graveyards. But even so, drawing closer to the secrets of my life which had slipped away and to the desolate towns buried in oblivion as far as the rest of civilization was concerned, I felt that I was still alive, still breathing with rage, and still pursuing—let me put it this way, borrowing a word from the past—certain desires.

I suppose it has already been guessed that my journey did not end in the city of Eskişehir. On the site where the offices and production facility of the Angel Candy and Chewing Gum, Inc. were formerly situated at 18 Bloomingdale Street, there now stood a six-story building used as dormitories for students at the Imam-Preacher School. The elderly fellow in the archives of the Eskişehir Chamber of Commerce, who offered me linden tea laced with Health brand soda pop, informed me after spending hours rifling through the books that Angel Candy and Chewing Gum had closed down their operations in Eskişehir with the object of relocating their business, which was now registered with the Kütahya Chamber of Commerce.

In Kütahya it soon became apparent that the company had ceased their operations there after seven years of production. Had I not thought of going to the Public Registry Office in the Town Hall and followed it up in the quarter called Stage-House, I wouldn't have found out that the founder of Angel Candy and Chewing Gum, a gentleman by the name of Süreyya, had moved fifteen years ago halfway across the country to Malatya, which was the hometown of the man his only daughter had married. In Malatya, I learned that Angel Candy and Gum had thrived for a final couple of years some fourteen years ago, and I remembered that Janan and I had come across these last-ditch-effort caramels in bus terminals.

When New Life Caramels had once more found favor in Malatya and its vicinity, the Chamber of Commerce, in an effort much like stamping a final coin for a collapsing empire, had published an article in its newsletter concerning the history of the company that had made the caramels once consumed all over Turkey, reminiscing how New Life Caramels had once been used in lieu of small change at groceries and tobacconists; then a few advertisements featuring angels had appeared in the *Malatya Express*; and just as the caramels were about to resume their status as coins in people's pockets once more, everything had come to an end when the well-advertised fruit-flavored products produced by a big international company were seen on TV, being consumed very attractively by an American starlet with beautiful lips. It was in a local paper that I found out about the sale of the vats, the packaging apparatus, and the trademark. I tried piecing together from the information provided by the relatives of the son-in-law the whereabouts of the manufacturer of New Life Caramels, the gentleman by the name of Süreyya, after he left Malatya. My investigations took me even farther East, to distant obscure towns that don't even show up in secondary school atlases. Like people who used to flee the plague once upon a time, the gentleman called Süreyya and his family had fled far away to tenuous towns, as if they were trying to escape from the gaudy consumer products with foreign names which, thanks to the support of advertisements and TV, arrived from the West and infected the whole country like a deadly contagious disease.

I got on buses, got off buses, went around terminals, walked through shopping districts, I poked around registries, precinct offices, back alleys, neighborhood squares that sported fountains, trees, cats, coffeehouses. For a while, in every town where I set foot, on every sidewalk I walked, in every coffeehouse I stopped for a glass of tea, I thought I came across the traces of a relentless conspiracy that linked these places to the Crusaders, to Byzantium, and to the Ottomans. I smiled indulgently at streetwise kids who attempted to sell me newly stamped Byzantine coins, thinking I was some sort of tourist; I took it in my stride when the barber dumped down my neck a urine-colored cologne called New Urartu; and I was not surprised to observe that the magnificent gateway to one of those fairgrounds that have sprung up like mushrooms all over the place had been dismantled and brought over from a Hittite ruin. It was not necessary that my power of imagination soften like the asphalt pavement on which I walked in the heat of midday for me to suppose there was something of the dust raised by the Crusader horsemen settled on the man-size spectacles that served as the sign for Zeki's Scientific Optometry.

Yet, at other times I sensed that those historical and conservative conspiracies that rendered this land resistant to change were going bankrupt, realizing that the marketplaces and neighborhood groceries and streets hung with laundry, which fourteen years ago had seemed to Janan and me as sturdy and static as a Seljuk fort, were being blown away in the predominant wind that blew from the West. All those aquariums, as well as the fish inside them, the contemplative silence of which used to distinguish the place of honor in restaurants in the provincial capitals, had suddenly disappeared as if in response to a hidden command. Who had decided in the last fourteen years that not only the main streets but even the dusty back alleys were to burgeon with messages screaming on glossy plastic billboards? Who had the trees on town squares felled? Looking at the concrete apartment buildings that besiege the statues of Atatürk like prison walls, I wondered who had ordered that the iron railing on the balconies be made monotonously uniform. Who had instructed the children to pelt the buses with stones? Who was it that came up with the notion of using some poisonous antiseptic to stink up hotel rooms? Who distributed all over the country those calendars on which Anglo-Saxon beauties grasp truck tires between their long legs? And who had determined that it was obligatory for citizens to give each other hostile looks in order to feel safe in novel spaces such as elevators, currency exchange counters, waiting rooms?

I had become old before my time. I tired quickly, walked as little as possible, and I was unaware how my body was being dragged along by the incredible throngs of people and gradually disappearing among them; I did not look into the faces of those who elbowed me as I elbowed back on the narrow sidewalks, forgetting them the instant I saw them as I did the names on the plastic signs of countless lawyers, dentists, and financial advisors streaming by overhead. I could not understand how those innocent little towns and neighborhood streets that seemed to have come out of miniatures, where Janan and I walked around feeling playful and enchanted as if we had been allowed into a tender-hearted elderly lady's backyard garden, had now turned into scary stage sets that were carbon copies of each other, rife with danger signs and exclamation points.

I saw dark bars and beerhalls operating in the unlikeliest of places, around the corner from mosques and retirement homes. I witnessed a slant-eyed Russian model who went about from town to town with a suitcase of clothes in her hand and gave one-woman fashion shows on buses, in local movie theaters, or at marketplaces, and then sold the clothes she displayed to veiled and turbaned women. I observed that the Afghan immigrants who used to peddle Korans that were smaller than my little finger had been replaced on buses by families of Russians and Georgians who were peddling plastic chess sets, Bakelite binoculars, battle medals, and Caspian caviar. I ran across a man I imagined to be the father still looking for his daughter, the girl in blue jeans who had died holding hands with her dead sweetheart after the traffic accident Janan and I lived through on a rainy night. I saw ghostly Kurdish villages deserted on account of a war that remained undeclared, and I saw infantry regiments pounding the dark areas in distant craggy mountains. In a video arcade where truants, unemployed young men, and local geniuses gather to test their capabilities, their luck, and their rage, I witnessed a video game which required twenty-five thousand points before a pink videogame angel, which had been designed by a Japanese and realized by an Italian, would put in an appearance and smile sweetly as if promising good fortune to us unfortunates pushing buttons in the darkness of some musty and dusty game room. I saw a man who reeked of OP shaving soap, moving his lips, sounding out the columns of the deceased journalist Jelal Salik which had been posthumously discovered. I saw newly transferred Albanian and Bosnian soccer players sitting and drinking Coca-Cola with their pretty blond wives in coffeehouses on the square in newly rich towns where old wood-frame mansions had been torn down to put up concrete-and-steel apartment buildings. I also saw apprehensively shadows whom I took to be Seiko or Serkisof in hovellike taverns, in marketplaces where people teem thick as fleas, or reflected on the pharmacy window where the window of the store across the street was reflected and in which elastic bandages for sufferers of hernia were being displayed; and at night I was buried in my colorful dreams of happiness or else in my nightmares either in some hotel room or in my seat on a bus.

While we are on the subject, I must mention that before I ended up in Son Pazar, which was my final destination, I stopped briefly in the remote town of Çatık that Doctor Fine had wished to place in the heart of the country. But there I found the town so changed due to war, migration, some odd loss of memory, hordes of people, fear and smells—you must have guessed from my inability to put it into words, how my mind had lost its bearings among the aimless masses in the streets—that I became anxious, fearing that the memories of Janan, which were all that was left to me, might be damaged. The digital Japanese-made watches lined up in the pharmacy window attested, in fact and in image, that Doctor Fine's Great Counterconspiracy and the organization of watches in his service had long since collapsed; and to add insult to injury, dealers with concessions for soft drinks, cars, ice cream, and television sets had lined up in the shopping district, displaying in row after row their signs with foreign trade names.

Even so, unfortunate and foolish hero that I am, trying to discover the meaning of life in this land suffering from amnesia, I thought I might find a cool and quiet shady spot that would provide me with a happy refuge for my dreams, where I might rekindle what remained in my memory of Janan's visage, her smile, and the things she said; so I walked toward the mansion where Doctor Fine once lived with his lovely daughters, and the mulberry tree that was to be the site of my reminiscences. Power lines and electric poles had brought electricity to the valley, but there was no house in the vicinity, and nothing was visible other than some ruins. It appeared these ruins were not the work of time but the result of a series of disasters.

It was when I saw the letters advertising AK BANK placed prominently on one of the hills Doctor Fine and I had once climbed that I first began thinking, in bewilderment, that I had done a good deed in killing Janan's former lover, who had believed he could attain the peace of eternal time and the mystery of life—whatever you want to call it—through the act of writing and re-writing the same lines for years on end. I had saved his son, after all, from having to witness all these filthy sights, from drowning in a deluge of videos and billboards, from having to go blind in a world that lacked illumination and radiance. But then, who was to wrap me in light and rescue me from this land of circumscribed freakishness and diffident cruelty? That angel whose incredibly resplendent colors I could once dream on the screen of my imagination and whose words I could hear in my heart now gave me no sign.

The train scheduled to Viran Bağ had been suspended on account of Kurdish rebels. The murderer had no intention of returning to the scene of his crime, even after all these years, but since I had to go through Viran Bağ in order to reach Son Pazar which was the town where, according to my information, the gentleman called Süreyya, who had conceived of putting an angel on his caramels, lived with his grandchild, it was critical that I take the day bus across this region where Kurdish guerrillas were resurgent. Going on what I could see of Viran Bağ through the bus window, this place too had lost all that might be worthy of remembering; but just in case someone might see the murderer and remember something, I buried my head in the *Milliyet* newspaper while waiting for the bus to depart.

When the bus started going up north, the mountains became sharply pointed and dominant in the first light of morning, and I couldn't decide whether the silence inside the bus was due to fear, or whether we were all somewhat dizzy from going round and round these severe mountains. We stopped from time to time either on account of the military checkpoints where our identification cards were inspected, or to drop off some fellow who would have to walk with only the clouds for company all the way to his village which would be so out of the way that even birds did not stop there. I could not stop staring with awe at the mountains which were so self-possessed that they were inured to all the cruelty they had witnessed for centuries. Before the reader who has raised an eyebrow reading the previous sentence tosses aside in disgust this book which is almost at an end, let me just say that a murderer who has gotten away with murder is allowed to write this kind of vulgar sentence.

I assumed Son Pazar was beyond the influence of the Kurdish guerrillas. It could be said the town was also beyond the influence of modern civilization because the moment I stepped off the bus, I was met with an enchanted silence that came out of some obscure fairytale about felicitous sultans and peaceful cities. Not one thing to make me think, "Here I go round and round,"

arriving, as I always had before, seemingly at the same place where
I was overwhelmed with billboard greetings from all those banks,
and those dealers in ice cream, refrigerators, cigarettes, and television sets. Here I saw a cat. It was licking itself with a leisurely
rhythm and seemed exceedingly self-satisfied in the peaceful
shade of the trellis attached to the café overlooking the intersection that must be the town square. A happy butcher in front of
the butcher shop, a carefree grocer in front of the grocery, a sleepy
produce man and his sleepy flies in front of the produce stand,
they were all sitting in the mellow morning light, peacefully dis-
solving into the golden light in the street as if they were fully
cognizant that the most ordinary activity of simply being alive is
the greatest blessing. As to the stranger in their town whom they
took in out of the corner of their eyes, he was instantly caught
up in this fairytale scene, imagining that Janan with whom he had
been madly in love once would appear to him around the first
corner, carrying in her hands some timepieces that had belonged
to our forefathers, a roll of old comics, and a teasing smile on her
lips.

Walking along the first street I became aware of the stillness
in my mind; in the second street, a weeping willow caressed me;
and when I came across a long-lashed and angelically beautiful
child in the third street, I thought of pulling out of my pocket
the slip with the address and asking him the way. Was the al-
phabet of my filthy world foreign to him? Or could the child not
read? I didn't know. But when I looked at the slip of paper on
which I had managed to get a local functionary two hundred
kilometers south of here to write the address, I realized it was
hardly legible. I tried making out the syllables aloud, but before
I could say "Ray Hill Street," a crone stuck her head out of her
enclosed balcony. "There," she said, "there it is, over there, the
street that goes uphill."

17 THE END OF THE ROAD HAD TO BE UPHILL; THAT'S what I was thinking to myself when a horse cart carrying metal drums full to the brim with water beat me turning into the street. I assumed the water was for a building under construction somewhere up on the hill. Watching the water spill out of the drums as the cart went up, I wondered why the drums were made of galvanized iron and not plastic. Had plastic still not made an appearance in this place? It was not the busy driver with whom I exchanged glances but the horse, and I was ashamed of myself. His mane was drenched in sweat; he was angry and help-less; he was under such a strain pulling the heavy weight, what he was suffering could be called pure pain. For a moment I saw myself in his large sorrowful, grieving eyes, and it dawned on me that the horse's state was even worse than mine. We climbed up Ray Hill Street, accompanied by the sounds of the metal water drums clanging noisily, the wheels clattering on the stone pave-ment, and my humdrum existence huffing and puffing uphill. The horse cart turned into a small yard where mortar was being mixed, and I, just as the sun vanished behind a dark cloud, entered the garden and then the dark and mysterious abode that belonged to

the originator of New Life Caramels. I stayed six hours in that
stone house surrounded by a garden.

The gentleman called Süreyya, the manufacturer of New Life
Caramels, who might provide me with the key to the secrets of
my life, was one of those octogenarians who blissfully puff away
at two packs of Samsun cigarettes a day as if tobacco contained
an elixir that prolonged life. He greeted me as though I were a
longtime pal of his grandson, or a close friend of the family; and
as if continuing a story he had left at midpoint yesterday, he
proceeded to tell me about a Hungarian spy who had come to his
place of business in Kütahya on a winter's day. Then he ex-
pounded on some candy store in Budapest, on the identical hats
all the women had worn to a ball given in Istanbul in the 1930s,
on the mistakes Turkish women made in their efforts to look
beautiful, on the reasons why his grandson, who kept leaving the
room and who was about the same age as myself, had failed to
get married, going into detail about a couple of engagements that
had gone sour. He was pleased to hear I was married, making it
clear it was a true sign of patriotism in a young insurance man
like me to be willing to take long trips that deprived him of his
wife and daughter in order to organize the country, alerting citizens and marshaling them to protect themselves against catastro-
phes.

It was at the end of the second hour that I told him I did not
sell life insurance, but that I was curious about the New Life
Caramels. He stirred in his chair, his face turned to the gray light
that came in through the shady garden, and he asked me out of
the blue if I knew German. Without waiting for an answer, he
said, "Schachmatt." Then he explained that the word "check-
mate" was a European hybrid made of the Persian word for *king*,
"shah," and the Arabic word for *killed*, "mat." We were the ones
who had taught the West the game of chess. In the worldly arena

of war, the black and white armies fought out the good and evil in our souls. And what had they done? They had made a queen out of our vizier and a bishop out of our elephant; but this was not important in itself. What was important, they had presented chess back to us as a victory of their own brand of intellect and the notions of rationalism in their world. Today we were struggling to understand our own sensitivities through their rational methods, assuming this is what becoming civilized means.

Had I noticed—his grandson had—that storks coming up north at the end of spring and migrating south in August back to Africa flew at a higher altitude than they used to in happier times? This was because the cities, mountains, rivers they flew over were in such a sorry state that those birds no longer wanted to behold the misery of all these lands. Talking of storks with affection, he was reminded of a stork-legged female French trapeze artist who had performed in Istanbul fifty years ago, and then he reminisced about old-time circuses and fairs, describing in great detail the kind of candy sold at these places, which involved more local color than nostalgia.

I was invited to their table for lunch; and while we ate and drank cold Tuborg beers, the old gentleman told the story of a bunch of knights stuck in Anatolia during the Eighth Crusade who had gone underground by way of a cave in Cappadocia. Their influence had continued increasing over the centuries; their children and grandchildren had enlarged the caves, dug new passageways underground, discovered new caves, and founded underground cities. Sometimes covert agents from the sunless land of labyrinths where lived the Multitudes of Persons of Crusader Ancestry (the MPCA) would surface under a different guise, and infiltrating our towns and streets they would begin preaching to us about the glory of the Western civilization, so that the MPCAs who undermine us by digging under our territories could

complaisantly rise above ground by undermining our thoughts.
Had I known that these spies were known as OP? And that there
was a brand of shaving cream also called OP?

I don't know whether it was Süreyya who brought up the ad-
diction to roasted garbanzo beans which Atatürk considered a
great national catastrophe, or if I was merely imagining it at the
time. Did he lead the conversation to Doctor Fine, or was it me
who alluded to him through some association? I can't tell. Doctor
Fine's mistake, he said, was that of a materialist putting his trust
in things, assuming that he could prevent the dissipation of the
spirit inherent in objects by preserving them. If that were true,
then flea markets would be bathed in spiritual enlightenment.
Enlightenment. Light. Luminous. Brilliant. So many products
made use of such words, all fake—light bulbs, ink, what have you.
When Doctor Fine realized he could not save our lost souls by
preventing the loss of objects, he had resorted to terrorism. Naturally, that had suited the Americans just fine; the CIA was second to none in dirty tricks. Today winds howled where his
mansion once stood. His rosy daughters had fled one by one; his
son had already been killed. As to his organization, it had fallen
apart; and perhaps, as it happens when great empires collapse,
each assassin had declared himself the sovereign of his own autonomous fiefdom. That was the reason why the magnificent terrain which through a clever tactic of the colonialist genius had
been dubbed the "Middle East" was swarming with inept colonial
prince-assassins who had declared their independence. He aimed
his cigarette not at me but at the empty chair next to me, un-
derlining the colonialist paradox he pointed out: we were at the
end of the autonomous history that pertained to colonized lands.

Evening was descending on the shady garden as if on a graveyard, augmenting its stillness, when he suddenly opened the subject I had been waiting for hours to broach. He had been telling
me about some Japanese Catholic missionary he had encountered

in the vicinity of Kayseri who had attempted a brainwashing operation in a mosque courtyard, but suddenly he changed the subject: he could not remember where in the world he had come up with the trademark of New Life. But he thought the magical name was appropriate because caramels had associations for the people who had lived on this land for a considerable length of time, binding their own lost past to a new taste and a new awareness. Contrary to what is commonly surmised, neither the word caramel nor the candy itself was a French import or imitation. After all, the word *kara*—or *cara*, as it had become when it migrated into the Indo-European languages—was the most basic word in the language of the people who have lived here for ten thousand years, supplying the prefix for all the words that take up several pages in the dictionary, meaning things that are *dark*, both good and bad; so he had included the word for thirty-two years in each and every wrapper on his candy, which was good and dark.

"Yes, but what about the angel?" the unfortunate traveler, the patient insurance man, the hapless hero again inquired.

By way of answering, the old gentleman recited eight of the ten thousand doggerel rhymes he had included inside the wrappers. Guileless angels that were neither beguiling nor in keeping with the memories of my childhood signaled to me from the lines of doggerel verse, where they were compared to world-class beauties, likened to drowsy young women, drenched with fairytale magic, and increasingly endowed with a childishness that was repellent to me.

The old gentleman confessed that he himself had written the rhymes he had recited. He had penned almost six thousand of the ten thousand rhymes placed in New Life Caramels. During those golden years when the demand for the candy had reached incredible proportions, there were some days when he had come up with twenty such rhymes. Anastasius, who minted the first Byzantine piece of money, had his own portrait stamped on the head side of the coin, had he not? The old candy maker reminded me how his own creations once used to be kept in glass jars between the scales and the cash register, how the product that bore his stamp had been carried in millions of pockets, how they had once been used in lieu of change, telling me that he had tasted all the gracious things in life that might be enjoyed by some emperor who had once created his own coinage, such as wealth, power, good fortune, beautiful women, fame, success, happiness. It was for this reason that he had no need to take out a life insurance policy. But to make it up to his young insurance agent friend, he would explain why he had put the image of an angel on his caramels. In his youth when he frequented movie theaters, he had especially loved watching Marlene Dietrich. He absolutely adored the film called *Der Blaue Engel* which was shown here as *The Blue Angel*, based on the novel by the German writer Heinrich Mann. The old gentleman had read the novel in the original, the title of which was *Professor Unrat*. Professor Unrat, played by the actor Emil Jannings, is an unassuming high school teacher who falls in love with a woman of easy virtue. Although the woman appears angelic, in reality . . .

Was there a strong wind outside rustling in the trees? Or was it my mind listening to itself being swept away by the wind? For a while I was "not there," as good-natured teachers say about dreamy and innocent students who are confused enough to be indulged. The vision of my youth enveloped in the light that surged from *The New Life* when I first read it glided past in front of my eyes like the blazing lights on a wondrous ship disappearing inaccessibly into the darkness of the night. In the silence where I had descended, it wasn't as if I didn't know the old gentleman was telling the sad story in the movie and the novel he had loved in his youth, but it was as if I heard nothing, saw nothing.

Presently his grandson came in and turned on the lights; at that moment I realized simultaneously three things: 1) The chandelier that hung from the ceiling was identical to the one which the Angel of Desire at the tent theater in Viran Bağ presented nightly to the lucky winner along with peerless advice on the subject of life. 2) The room had become so dark that I hadn't been able to see the old candy maker for quite some time, whose name, Süreyya, meant the star cluster, the Pleiades. 3) He couldn't see me either because he was blind.

Before some belligerent and contemptuous reader scoffs at my intellect and attentiveness for not having realized for six hours the fact that a man is blind, may I inquire just as belligerently if that reader has expended enough attention and intellect at every turn of this book? Let's see you remember now the description of the scene, for example, when the angel was first mentioned? Or can you immediately say what kind of inspiration Uncle Rıfkı's list of companies in his work called *Railroad Heroes* provided for *The New Life*? Have you caught on to the clues through which I would eventually figure out that Mehmet was thinking of Janan when I shot him at the movie theater? In the life of those people like me whose lives have slipped off the track, sorrow presents itself in the form of rage that wants to pass itself off as cleverness. And it's the desire to be clever that finally spoils everything.

Looking up from my own sorrows, I realized the old man was blind when I observed the way he looked up at the chandelier that cast its light over us, regarding him for the first time with a kind of reverence, a kind of awe, or speaking honestly, a kind of envy. He was tall, slender, graceful and, considering his age, quite fit. He knew how to employ his hands and fingers dexterously, his mind still chugged away with vigor, and he was able to talk for six hours without losing the interest of the dreamy murderer who he stubbornly refused to believe was anything other than an insurance agent. He had been able to achieve some sort of success in his youth which had been replete with happiness and stimulation; and even though his success had melted away in the stomachs of millions of people, and even though the six thousand doggerel rhymes he penned had ended up in trash cans, they had provided him with a sound and optimistic assumption on the subject of his place in the world; and what's more, he had been able to smoke up two packs of cigarettes a day until he was eighty-some years old with a great deal of pleasure.

In the silence, he sensed my sorrow through the sort of perceptiveness that comes with blindness, and he attempted to expiate it: So that was life; there was accident, there was luck, there was love, there was loneliness; there was joy; there was sorrow; there was light, death, also happiness that was dimly there; it was necessary one didn't disregard all that. At eight o'clock there was a newscast on the radio which his grandson would turn on presently; and would I please stay and share with them their evening meal.

I made my apologies, claiming an awful lot of people were waiting to take out life insurance policies in the town of Viran Bağ. Soon enough, before anybody knew what was going on, I was out the door, down the garden path, and in the street. Once outside, seeing how chilly the air was on this spring evening, I guessed how rough the winters must be out here, and I found myself standing more solitary than the dark cypress trees out in the yard.

What was I to do henceforth? I had learned what was necessary—as well as what was unnecessary—and I had arrived at the end of all the adventures, voyages, and mysteries I could possibly invent for myself. The slice of life I might call my future was cloaked in darkness just like the town of Son Pazar below the hill which, aside from a few dim streetlights, was in oblivion, existing cut off from sparkling night life, effervescent crowds, and well-lit streets. But when some dog who meant business began growling in earnest, I took off down the hill.

Waiting for the bus that would take me back to the hustle and bustle of billboards for banks, cigarettes, soft drinks, and television sets, I wandered aimlessly through the streets in this tiny town at the end of the world. Now that I had no more hope and desire to attain the meaning and the unified reality of the world, the book, and my life, I found myself among fancy-free appearances that neither signified nor implied anything. I watched through an open window a family gathered around a table eating their supper. That's how they were, just the way you know them. I learned the hours for the Koran course being given from a poster tacked on the mosque wall. At the café with the trellis, I observed without too much concern that Branch soda pop still persisted here against all sorts of assaults from Coca-Cola, Pepsi, and Schweppes. I watched the repairman in front of the bicycle shop across the street tune up a bicycle wheel in the light coming from inside the shop, and his friend who hung around with him, smoking and gabbing away. Why did I think they were friends? They were perhaps embroiled in conflict and seething with enmity toward each other. In either case, they were neither excessively interesting nor excessively uninteresting. For those readers who think I am much too pessimistic, let me make it perfectly clear that sitting in a café with a nice trellis, I preferred watching them to not watching them.

The bus arrived and I left the town of Son Pazar with this feeling. We went round and round up craggy mountains, and then we listened anxiously to the grinding of the brakes going downhill. We were stopped several times at checkpoints where we pulled out our identifications for the benefit of the military patrol. It was when the mountains, the military zone, and identity checks were over that our bus began to speed up as it pleased, going like crazy and out of control across the dark and wide plains, and my ears began to pick out the sorrowful notes in the familiar old music made by the growl of the engine and the gaily twittering tires.

Perhaps because the bus was one of the last of the durable,

burly but noisy old Magirus buses that Janan and I used to take, perhaps because we were on rough asphalt pavement where the tires rotated eight times a second making that special moaning sound, perhaps because my past and my future appeared in the purple and leaden colors on the screen where the lovers who misunderstood each other wept in a movie made by Yeşilçam Studios—I don't know why, I didn't know why—perhaps because some instinct guided me to find the meaning I couldn't find in life in the hidden pattern of chance, I sat in seat No. 37—perhaps because leaning into the seat where she would have sat, I beheld the dark velvet night that had once appeared so mysterious and magnetic to us that it seemed as if it was as endless as time, dreams, life, and the book. When rain that seemed even more sorrowful than me began pattering on the windows, I leaned back into my seat completely and abandoned myself to the music of my memories.

It began raining increasingly harder, parallel to the sorrow that increased in my heart, then turned into a downpour sometime around midnight, accompanied by wind that hurled our bus around and lightning the same color purple as the flowers of sorrow blooming in my mind. The old bus which leaked around the windows into the seats went by a filling station blurred in the downpour and mud villages beset with phantoms of water, and slowed down to take the curve into a rest stop. When the neon sign that said MEMORY LANE RESTAURANT bathed us in its blue light, "Thirty minutes," the tired driver announced. "Compulsory rest stop."

I was intending not to move out of my seat but to watch alone the sorrowful movie I called my memories; yet the rain that pelted the roof of the old Magirus was thickening the heavy sadness in my heart so intensely, I was afraid I might not be able to endure it. I ducked out along with the other passengers hopping through the mud, newspapers and plastic bags shielding their heads.

I thought mixing with the crowd might do me good; I'd have some soup and a pudding, distracting myself with tangible pleasures of the world, so that instead of getting emotional surveying the past portion of my life that was left behind, I might pull myself together, turning the rational high beams of my mind on the portion that stretched out before me. I went up the two steps, dried my hair with my handkerchief, and entering the brightly lit room that smelled of grease and cigarettes, I heard some music that left me shaken.

Like an experienced invalid who can sense a heart attack coming, I remember floundering helplessly in my attempt to take precautions, to stave off the crisis. But what could I do? I couldn't very well demand—could I?—that they turn off the radio, just because when Janan and I first chanced upon each other following the accident, we had heard the same tune, holding hands. I could not cry out telling them to take down the photos of the movie stars, just because Janan and I had such a good time looking at the pictures, laughing and eating our meal here in this very restaurant called MEMORY LANE. Since I did not have in my pocket a nitrate tablet against my crisis of the heart, I picked up in my tray a bowl of lentil soup, a little bread, and a glass of double raki, and I retreated to a table in the corner. Salt tears began dripping into the soup I stirred with my spoon.

Don't let me carry on like those writers who imitate Chekhov, trying to draw out of my pain the dignity of being human which all readers can share; instead, like a writer from the East, let me take the opportunity to tell a cautionary tale. In short: I had desired to set myself apart from others, someone special who had a goal that was entirely different. Around here, this is considered a crime which can never be forgiven. I told myself I had received this impossible dream from Uncle Rıfkı's comics which I had read in my childhood. So I considered once again what the reader who likes extracting the moral of the story has been thinking all along;

it was because the reading material in my childhood had precon-
ditioned me that I had been so mightily affected by *The New Life*.
But like the great old tellers of exemplary tales, I did not believe
the moral of the story myself, so my life story remained merely
my own individual tale and failed to assuage my pain. This merciless conclusion that had slowly been dawning on my mind had
long been guessed by my heart. I was weeping uncontrollably to
the music on the radio.

I realized my state did not make a favorable impression on my
fellow passengers who were spooning up their soup and gobbling
up their pilaf, so I sneaked into the washroom. I splashed my face
with some warmish and murky water that came sputtering out of
the spigot, drenching my clothes; I wiped my nose, took my time.
Then I returned to my table.

Shortly, when I glanced at them out of the corner of my eye,
I saw that my fellow travelers watching me out of the corner of
their eyes seemed somewhat relieved. Presently, an old peddler
who had also been peering at me came up carrying a straw basket
and looking me straight in the eye.

"Take it easy!" he said. "This too shall pass. Here, take some
mint candy, it's good for whatever ails you."

He placed on my table a small pouch of mints that carried the
tradename BLISS.

"How much?"

"No, no, it's a present from me."

Something like being consoled by a good-intentioned "uncle"
handing some candy to a child crying in the street . . . I stared at
the avuncular candyman's face like that child, looking guilty. Calling him an uncle is a figure of speech, perhaps he was not even
that much older than me.

"Today we are altogether defeated," he said. "The West has
swallowed us up, trampled on us in passing. They have invaded
us down to our soup, our candy, our underpants; they have fin-

ished us off. But someday, someday perhaps a thousand years from now, we will avenge ourselves; we will bring an end to this conspiracy by taking them out of our soup, our chewing gum, our souls. Now go ahead and eat your mints, don't cry over spilt milk."

Was this the consolation I had been looking for? I don't know. But like the child crying in the street seriously listening to the story told by the nice man, for a while I reflected on the words of consolation. Then recalling a notion kicked around by early Renaissance writers as well as Ismail Hakkı of Erzurum, I came upon a thought to console myself. I considered that they might have been right in thinking that sorrow is a substance that spreads from the stomach to the brain, and I made a decision to pay more attention to what I ate and drank.

I broke up the bread into the soup and then spooned it up; I took careful sips of my raki and asked for another along with a slice of melon. Like some cautious old man concerned with what goes on in his stomach, I diverted myself with food and drink until it was time for the bus. I got on and sat any old where. I imagine it is obvious: I wanted to leave behind me the usual Number 37 where I preferred to sit, along with everything else connected to my past. It seems I dropped off to sleep.

After a long and uninterrupted snooze when I slept like a baby, I woke up when the bus stopped toward morning and went into one of those modern rest places which are an outpost of civilization. I was somewhat cheered seeing the pretty and congenial girls in the bank and Coca-Cola ads on the wall, the scenes on the calendars, the bright hodgepodge of colors in the words of advertisement that invited me loudly, the plump "hamburgers" spilling out of their buns in glass cases on one corner of which there was a sign pointing out shrewdly in English "SELF SERVICE," and the pictures of ice cream that came in colors like lipstick red, daisy yellow, dreamy blue.

I served myself some coffee and sat in a corner. In the bright light in the place, while three television sets were on, I watched a smartly dressed little girl who couldn't manage to pour on her french fries a new brand of "ketchup" that came in a plastic bottle and required the help of her mother. There was a plastic bottle of the same TASTEE brand of ketchup sitting on my table, and the golden yellow letters on the bottle promised me that if I collected within a span of three months thirty of those bottle caps, which were so difficult to open that they made a mess of little girls' dresses when they finally did, and sent them to the address below, I would be eligible to enter the contest that would take the winner for a week's excursion to Disney World in Florida. Presently, one of the soccer teams on the TV set in the middle scored a goal.

I watched the same goal being scored again in slow motion along with all the other males sitting at the tables or waiting in the "hamburger" line, feeling an optimism that was not at all on the surface but was quite as rational as it was appropriate to the life that awaited me. I liked watching soccer games on TV, lazing around home on Sundays, getting soused some evenings, going to the station with my daughter to watch the trains, trying out new brands of ketchup, reading, gossiping with my wife and making love, puffing on cigarettes, and sitting in peace and drinking coffee someplace or other, as I was doing just now, and a thousand other things besides. If I took care of myself and managed to live as long as, say, the old caramel maker who was named for the Pleiades, I had almost another half century before me to enjoy all these things . . . For a moment I felt an intense longing for my home, my wife, and my daughter. I dreamed how I would play with my daughter when I got home around noon Saturday, what I would get her at the candy store in the station, and while she played outside in the afternoon, how my wife and I would make love genuinely, ardently, and without being slipshod, then how we would all watch TV later, tickling my daughter and laughing together.

The coffee had really waked me up. In the deep silence that descends on a bus just before morning, the only other person awake aside from the driver was myself, sitting just behind him, a little to his right. A mint candy in my mouth, my eyes wide open, staring at the perfectly smooth asphalt road paved across the steppe that seemed infinite, concentrating on the dashes in the median line and the headlights of trucks that passed by now and then, I was impatiently waiting for daybreak.

It took no more than a half hour before I began distinguishing the first signs of morning in the window to my right, which meant we were traveling in a northerly direction. First the outline of the land against the sky seemed to become vaguely, indistinctly visible. Then the outline of the frontier between the earth and the sky took on a silken crimson color which invaded the dark sky in one corner yet without lighting the steppe; but the rosy-red demarcation line was so fine, so delicate and so extraordinary that both the tireless Magirus, which tore through the steppe like a wild horse speeding willy-nilly toward the darkness, and the passengers being carried along were plunged into a mechanical frenzy that was of no avail. No one was aware of this, not even the driver.

A few minutes later, due to the faint light emanating from the line of the horizon which had turned slightly more crimson, the dark clouds in the east seemed to be illuminated from below and along the edges. I realized something looking at the wondrous shapes assumed in the faint light by these ferocious clouds that had kept it raining without respite on the roof of the bus all night long: Since the steppe was still pitch dark, I could see in the faint light inside the bus my own face and body reflected on the windshield directly in front of me, and simultaneously I could see the magical crimson flush, the wondrous clouds, and the broken lines in the highway that tirelessly repeated themselves.

Looking at the broken median line in the high beams of the
bus, I was reminded of the refrain, that same refrain that rises
out of the very soul of the tired and dejected traveler riding on
the weary bus to the rhythm of the tires going around at the same
rate, the engine whining at the same tempo, and life reiterating
itself with the same measure, which is then repeated by the power
poles along the highway: What is life? A period of time. What is
time? An accident. What is accident? A life. A new life ... So
that was my refrain. At the same time, I was wondering when my
reflection would disappear off the windshield and when the first
ghost of a tree or the shadow of a sheep pen would be visible on
the steppe; it was at that magic moment of equilibrium between
the light inside the bus and the light outside that suddenly my
eyes were dazzled by a bright light.

In that new light on the right side of the windshield, I beheld
the angel.

The angel was so close to me and yet how far. Even so, I still
knew this: the profound, plain, and powerful light was there for
me. Even though the Magirus hurtled through the steppe with
all its might, the angel would neither draw close nor draw back.
The brilliant light kept me from seeing what the angel looked like
for sure, but I knew from the sense of playfulness, the sense of
lightness, the sense of freedom I felt inside me that I had recognized the angel.

The angel looked nothing like those in the Persian miniatures,
nor like the ones on the wrappers of the caramels, not anything
like the photocopied angels or even the presence in my dreams
all those years whose voice I longed to hear.

For a moment, I yearned to say something, to speak with the
angel ... perhaps because of the vague sense of playfulness and
surprise I still felt. But I made no sound; I became anxious. The
sense of camaraderie, affinity, and tenderness I had felt from the
first moment was still alive inside me; I hoped to find peace in

this, thinking it was the moment I had been anticipating all this time, but to allay the fear that grew inside me even faster than the speed of the bus, I wished the moment would provide me with the answers to time, accident, peace, writing, life, and the new life.

The angel was as pitiless as it was distant and wondrous. Not because it wished to be so, but because it was only a witness and could do nothing more. In the incredible light of daybreak, it saw me sitting bewildered and anxious in my seat in the front, riding on the tin can of a Magirus hurtling through the half-lit steppe; that was all. I felt the unbearable power of what was merciless and inevitable.

When I instinctively turned to the driver, I saw the entire windshield surging with an extraordinarily powerful light. Two trucks were passing each other about sixty or seventy yards from us, both had us in their high beams and were fast approaching on a collision course with our bus. I knew the accident was unavoidable.

I remembered the anticipation of peace following the accidents I had lived through years ago . . . the feeling of transition after an accident which seemed filmed in slow motion. I remembered the passengers who were neither here nor there stirring blissfully, as if sharing together time that had come out of paradise. Shortly all the sleepy travelers would be awake, and the stillness of the morning would be broken with happy screams and thoughtless cries; and on the threshold between the two worlds, as if discovering the eternal jokes existent in a space without gravity, we would collectively discover with confusion and excitement the presence of bloody internal organs, spilled fruits, sundered bodies, and all those combs, shoes, children's books that spilled out of torn suitcases.

No, not quite collectively. The fortunate ones who were to live through the unique moment that followed the incredible tumult of the accident would be among those passengers left alive sitting in the seats in the back. As to myself, ensconced in the first seat in the front, looking straight into the light of the approaching trucks, my eyes dazzled in amazement and fear, just as I had once looked into the incredible light that surged from the book, I would be instantly transported into a new world.

I knew it was the end of my life. And yet I had only wanted to return home; I absolutely had no wish for death, nor for crossing over into the new life.

Istanbul
1992–1994